THE HOUSE *of* BLUE MANGOES

THE HOUSE *of* BLUE MANGOES

DAVID DAVIDAR

HarperCollins books may be purchased for educational, business, or sales promotional use. For information, please write: Special Markets Department, HarperCollins Publishers Inc., 10 East 53rd Street, New York, NY 10022.

Published in Great Britain in 2002 by
Phoenix House/Weidenfeld & Nicolson.

FIRST EDITION

Printed on acid-free paper

Library of Congress Cataloging-in-Publication Data
is available upon request.

ISBN 0-06-621254-5

02 03 04 05 06 ❖/RRD 10 9 8 7 6 5 4 3 2 1

In loving memory of my mother
SUSHILA DAVIDAR

And for my wife
RACHNA SINGH

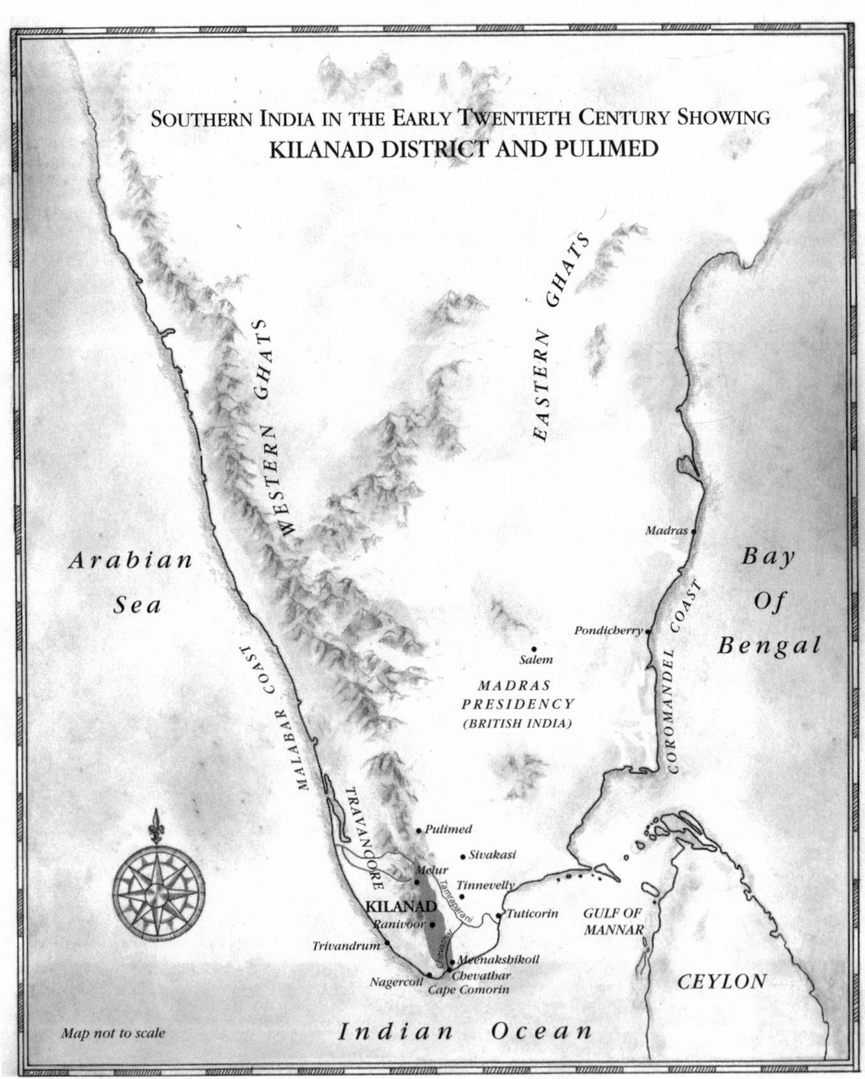

Kilanad District and Pulimed are fictitious

CONTENTS

FAMILY TREE

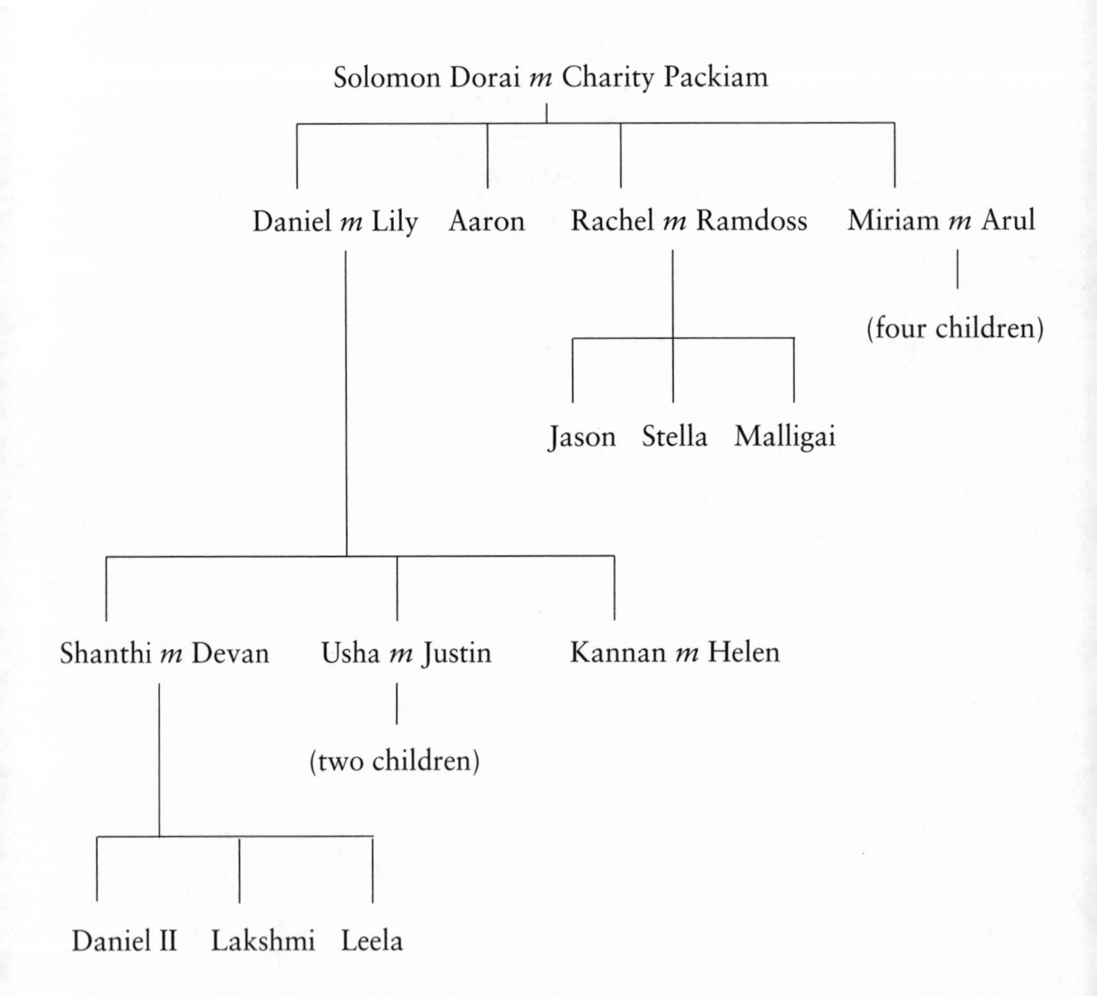

Solomon Dorai *m* Charity Packiam
Daniel *m* Lily
Aaron
Rachel *m* Ramdoss
Miriam *m* Arul
(four children)
Jason
Stella
Malligai
Shanthi *m* Devan
Usha *m* Justin
Kannan *m* Helen
(two children)
Daniel II
Lakshmi
Leela

A land of miracles and fire
– Marina Tsvetayeva

BOOK I

CHEVATHAR

I

SPRING 1899. As the ordinary violence of dawn sweeps across the lower Coromandel coast, a sprawling village comes into view. The turbulent sky excepted, everything about it is tranquil. Away to the west, a great headland, thickly maned with coconut palms, juts into the sea, partially enclosing a deserted beach on which long slow swells, clear and smooth as glass, break with scarcely a sound. Beyond the beach, the waters of an estuary reflect the rage of colour overhead. This is where the Chevathar, the country's southernmost river and the source of the village's name, prepares for its final run to the sea.

On a bluff overlooking the estuary, almost hidden by coconut palms, is a small church. From there, the village straggles upriver for about a mile and a half, ending at the bridge that connects it to the town of Meenakshikoil on the opposite bank.

Through the village runs a narrow tarred road that stands out like a fresh scar on the red soil. The road connects all Chevathar's major landmarks: the Vedhar quarter to the north, the ruins of an eighteenth-century mud fort, Vakeel Perumal's two-storey house with its bone-white walls, the Amman and the Murugan temples, and on a slight elevation, the house of the thalaivar, Solomon Dorai, barely visible behind a fringe of casuarina trees and coconut palms. Surrounding the walls of the Big House, as it is known, are several trees that aren't usually seen in the area – a tall umbrella-shaped rain tree, a breadfruit tree with leaves that explode in green star-shaped clusters and many jackfruit trees laden with heavy, spiky fruit that spring directly from the trunk. These are the result of the labours of Charity Dorai, who does not come from these parts. In an effort to allay her homesickness she began planting trees from her homeland. Twenty years later they have altered the treescape of Chevathar.

Down to the river from the Big House tumble groves of Chevathar Neelam, a rare hybrid of a mango native to the south. The trees are astonishingly beautiful, the fruit glinting blue against the dark green leaves. The locals will tell you that the Chevathar Neelam, which has made the Dorai name famous throughout the district, is so sweet that after you've eaten one you cannot taste sugar for at least three days. So the locals say.

The rest of the village is quickly described. More coconut palms, the paracheri to the southwest, a few shops by the bridge over the Chevathar river, the huts of the Andavar tenant farmers close to the road, and a dozen or so wells and tanks that raise blind glittering eyes to the morning light.

The villagers rise early, but as it's some way yet before the fields are to be prepared for the transplanting of rice, the men are not up and about. Most of the women have risen before dawn and are racing to finish their household chores. Today the village celebrates the Pangunni Uthiram festival and they're hoping to snatch a few minutes at the festive market that's being assembled, bright and tawdry, by the walls of the Murugan temple.

Movement on the tarred road. Two girls, one thirteen and soon to be married, the other a year younger, are on their way to the fair. They are dressed in their best clothes, the older girl in a violet half-sari, jasmine in her well-oiled and plaited hair, her cousin in a garish pink skirt. Their foreheads are adorned with sandalwood paste, vibhuti and kumkumam from the Amman temple where they worshipped before dayfall. They walk quickly, even though they're very early, their feet light on the deliciously cool road, eager to get to the market. The older girl has been given four annas to spend by her mother. It's a small sum but it's more money than Valli has ever had before and she can barely contain her excitement at what she might be able to buy with it. Bangles? Earrings? Silk for a blouse perhaps, or might that be too expensive? Parvathi hurries to keep up with her cousin.

The girls pass a grey outcrop of granite polished by wind and rain to a smooth rounded shape that resembles the knobbly forehead of an elephant. Anaikal, as it is called, is popular with children playing hide-and-seek but they barely register this most familiar of sights as they hurry onwards. They enter a short stretch lined with banyan trees beyond which is the path that leads to the fair.

And then the younger girl notices them. 'Akka,' she says, but the remark is unnecessary for Valli has also seen the four young men lounging under the big tamarind tree that shades Vakeel Perumal's house. The acute peripheral vision of the two girls, shared by every woman under the age of forty in the small towns and villages of the hinterland, is geared towards noticing just one thing: men. Sometimes it is exercised to give them pleasure as they flirt expertly even with eyes cast down. But more often than not it is used to spot danger. No young or even middle-aged woman is safe from the slyly outstretched male arm that seeks to brush and feel up, the crude insult, the lascivious eye, and so they learn early to take evasive action before things become unpleasant.

The two girls quickly assess the situation. The men are about fifty yards away and do not appear threatening. Still, there is no one about. Every instinct tells them to turn and retreat to the safety of their houses. But the promise of the new bangles is too strong. After all, just a few yards more and they'll be on the dirt path which will take them to the market grounds.

The men under the tamarind tree begin to move towards them and now the girls are truly alarmed. They turn to hurry back in the direction of their houses but it's already too late. The footsteps behind them gather speed and the girls begin to run. Terror sharpens their senses. They register with unnatural clarity everyday sights: the fire of shoeflowers against a limewashed wall, the waxy green leaves of a calotropis plant by the roadside, an orange butterfly on the road, and then everything begins to blur.

The younger girl keeps her head, or perhaps she just chooses right. She stays on the road and runs as fast as she can towards the huts of the tenant farmers barely half a furlong away. Valli veers off the path and begins running away from the river, through the acacia forest that clothes the uncultivated area by the Murugan temple. The horny soles of her bare feet negotiate the rough ground beneath her with ease but she is no match for her pursuers. Remorselessly they overtake her. She feels hands tearing at her clothes, hissed imprecations in her ears, she stumbles, goes down ...

2

About two furlongs from the spot where the girls had begun their desperate run, Chevathar Gnanaprakasam Solomon Dorai Andavar, the thalaivar of the village, sat on the veranda of his house, deeply absorbed in the antics of a woodpecker. Round and round the furrowed trunk of the neem tree it went, and not for the first time the headman thought that the way the bird rose up the tree was uncannily similar to the manner in which his tappers ascended the tall palmyras to harvest toddy.

Clad only in a colourful lungi, Solomon Dorai looked as if he might have been carved from teak. There wasn't an ounce of superfluous flesh on his forty-year-old frame, and his hair and moustache were luxurious and untrammelled by grey. For many years now, he had decreed that on Sundays and festival days he wasn't to be disturbed in the morning on any village or household matter unless it was an emergency. The order was respected, not least because of the trouble that could be unleashed if it was ignored. This morning as usual he had risen before dawn, washed his face at the well, and then wandered into the courtyard to pluck a neem twig to chew on. He loved the tall stillness of the night at this hour when even the stirrings of the world were muted. Soon red would tongue into black, followed by the rest of the sequence that was so dear to him: the emerging of trees, hayricks and other familiar objects from the dark, the grumbling of crows in the casuarina trees at the edge of the compound, the lowing of cows impatient to be milked, all the comforting noises of his world.

The rich smell of jaggery coffee told him that Charity had come and gone, soundlessly, leaving the coffee in its customary place on the veranda. He drank his coffee so hot that he could only hold the tumbler between the folds of his lungi. Carefully he raised it to his lips and sipped. Excellent, as always. Then suddenly, for no reason that he could pinpoint, Solomon was no longer relaxed.

There was still some time to go before his barber would arrive to shave him, so Solomon decided to investigate the cause of his unease. Perhaps he could go down to the river, where he anyway wanted to inspect some newly planted mango trees, and then stroll as far as the Murugan temple to check that all was well. The watchman was probably sleeping off a drunken jag and there would be nothing to prevent strangers from wandering into the village. Ever since the deputy tahsildar had insisted on building his accursed new road to connect Chevathar to the town, you could not be too vigilant, he thought. Finishing his coffee, he rose to his feet. The discordant bray of a donkey drifted in on the breeze and he smiled, for it portended good luck. Perhaps his fears were groundless. No matter, it would be good to stretch his legs. As he walked across the beaten earth of the courtyard, the woodpecker flew away in a streak of green and yellow. He paused to watch its rapid jerky flight for a moment, then went down to the river.

*

The strangers were gone long before Solomon reached the Chevathar. One of them carried three bloody furrows on his cheek where Valli's nails had scored him. They avoided the bridge and negotiated the shallows of the river instead. Once across, they melted into the countryside, as invisibly as they had come. Hidden in the recesses of the acacia forest was the only sign that they had ever been in the village: the barely conscious wreck of a young girl.

Standing at the river's edge, Solomon worriedly stroked and pulled at his moustache. His anxiety had nothing to do with Valli; it would be an hour or so before she was found and the news conveyed to the thalaivar. What disturbed him was what lay before him. Since the Great Famine of 1876–8, he had never seen the Chevathar so shrunken in its course. Rocks poked out of the water like tobacco-blackened teeth, and it was only in the very centre that the current flowed, slowly and sluggishly. They couldn't afford another drought. If the rains failed again, he and every villager in the area would suffer. For now the village looked green and fertile enough, but he knew from experience just how quickly everything could change. Only two days ago, a deputation had visited him, saying that their fields were showing traces of salinity. It was always a problem: as the river and the sweet water receded, the sea seeped in. If water became scarce, they could lose half their cropland. In perpetuity. And with drought and famine, there was the ever-present danger of epidemic.

His mind went back nearly twenty-one years to the time when eight thousand people, over a tenth of the district's population, had died. Smallpox had followed drought and famine had swept away another ten thousand, among them his parents, his older brother, two younger sisters, two uncles and their entire families. Seventeen of the people who had made up his world, all sacrificed to the ferocious goddess, Mariamman. The only survivors in his immediate family had been his wife Charity, his younger brother Abraham, his sister Kamalambal and his dearly loved cousin Joshua. Solomon had come into his inheritance when he was barely twenty, as had many of the young men in the region.

Fortunately for the community, they had been spared epidemics over the next decade and a half. Also, the rains had held up, and the process of recovery slowly began. But barely had things returned to normal when the rains had started playing truant again. For the past three years, both the monsoons – the southwest and the northeast – had been below average and the Government had initiated drought relief works once more. Not entirely trusting to Government, the people had redoubled their prayers in temples, mosques, churches, wayside shrines and family pooja rooms. In our land, religion is expected to do everything, including feed the people, Solomon thought grumpily.

He turned from the river and walked up the bank to the newly planted mango grove. The sight of his beloved trees was usually enough to lift his spirits, but this morning they failed to work their magic. He sensed that his anxiety sprang from more than just the prospect of an erratic monsoon.

Could there be caste trouble in the offing, he wondered, as he bent to examine the healthy jade-green leaves of a mango sapling. The two dominant castes in the district – the Andavars, to which he belonged, and the Vedhars – had a history of strife, and he had heard rumours that there might be unrest in the trouble-prone areas of the north near Melur. He hadn't noticed anything untoward here but he would go and meet Muthu Vedhar, the leader of the Vedhar villagers, later in the day, to see if there was anything troubling him. The Dorai family had kept caste violence out of the village for generations. Solomon wasn't about to see that change under his stewardship. The day was quite advanced by now, and he decided to cut short his stroll and head back.

When he reached the Big House he was annoyed to find that the barber had still not arrived. One of the few things his father had taught him was the importance of being neatly turned out as thalaivar of the village. This meant a daily shave, whereas the average villager would be content with one every few days. Solomon was yelling for a servant to go and find the errant barber when his keen ears picked up a sound and he frowned.

He turned to look in the direction from which it came and what he saw displeased him greatly: three bullock carts coming leisurely down the metalled road. Solomon could not believe that his order forbidding traffic from town on festival days was being so blatantly flouted. It was the deputy tahsildar, he thought, no one but that son of a prostitute would dare cross him! His rage grew. So what if Dipty Vedhar was the top government official in the region; it was he, Solomon Dorai, who ran the village. Who was the young donkey to disregard him? First, he had gone and built the new road through the village, and now with his hunger for profit he was ignoring the thalaivar's orders. Solomon stood irresolute for a moment, then walked swiftly into the house and into his room. On pegs driven into the wall rested a prized possession – his Webley & Scott twelve-bore shotgun. Solomon lifted it down, crossed over to a wooden chest, opened it with one hand, rummaged around in it and unearthed a box of cartridges. He put the gun down, took out two cartridges, loaded the weapon, and walked to the entrance of the house. The carts were less than a hundred yards away when he raised the gun to his shoulder and fired both barrels. A storm of barking erupted, with his own Rajapalaiyams leading the chorus. Still holding the gun, Solomon ran, lungi flapping, towards the carters. The sight of the enraged thalaivar clearly terrified them and, as one man, they leapt off their slow-moving vehicles and were preparing to run when they were stopped by Solomon's loud voice: 'Run and I'll cut you down like motherless dogs.'

The carters protested ignorance of the thalaivar's injunction. They were only following the orders of Kulasekharan, Meenakshikoil's biggest dealer in palm products. They had been instructed to go down to the beach to bring back three cartloads of pure white sand, lately popular among townspeople for flooring wedding and religious pandals. The news angered Solomon further. Kulasekharan! His own kinsman! Ignoring his orders!

He ordered the carters to turn around and told them to inform the trader that they were prohibited from entering the village for a week. Then he returned to the house, more irritable than ever. As soon as he had bathed, he would go into town and have it out with the deputy tahsildar. Even as the thought crossed his mind, it occurred to him that the barber had still not arrived. And he couldn't have a bath until he had been shaved. The polluting touch of the low-caste barber had to be washed away.

Fretfully, Solomon returned the gun to its rack and emerged into the courtyard. A few minutes of pacing up and down and he could bear it no longer; the day was advancing and he needed to bathe, shaved or not. What sins had he committed to be born in this ungodly time, where a kinsman could ignore his explicit ruling and where every ambattan thought he was a Pandyan king!

3

The morning had begun in the usual way for Charity Dorai. Up before first light, she had bathed, prayed, made the coffee and measured out the day's food for the twenty or so family members in the house. The number of people under Solomon's roof was never constant, but expanded or contracted depending on who needed his help or shelter, or both. Visitors would arrive for a week and still be there six months later. No one minded. Solomon was the patriarch of the clan, and it was expected of him, as it had been of the ruling Dorai since his great-great-grandfather's time, to take in any member of the family who needed hospitality or succour.

As Charity bustled about the great kitchen, tending to three of the five wood-burning stoves which had begun their daily contribution of ash to the layers that already blackened the walls, she was joined by her sister-in-law. Kamalambal, widowed these past two years, was a plump and even-tempered woman. Charity and she got on very well and between them they ran the household. Kamalambal went off to supervise the milking of the cows and Charity began issuing instructions to the two women who helped her in the kitchen. There was still no sign of her brother-in-law Abraham's wife, but this didn't surprise her for Kaveri was a frail and sickly woman who frequently took to her bed, especially when her husband beat her, a regular occurrence. Abraham was away visiting some of their properties so maybe she was just ill.

Charity was planning to make fish biryani, as she had done every festival day for twenty years. The grinding and mixing of the various masalas and spices had to begin early. But she could not ignore the morning meal either, puttu and stew; she had the puttu steamers, lengths of bamboo stem, cleaned and ensured that the huge iron vessel of stew was ready to be heated.

Charity Dorai was a beautiful woman. Fair in a land where the paleness of a woman's complexion outweighed every other attribute, it was expected that she would make a good marriage and she did. Rumours of her beauty travelled to the ears of the Dorai family, who had broken with Andavar tradition that cross-cousins marry and instead reached across the mountains to Nagercoil where her father was headmaster of a school. They had even foregone a dowry and paid all the marriage expenses.

The fish biryani, her signature dish, had been unknown in the Big

House when she had first arrived. Her husband and in-laws had taken to it. Indeed, they had come to like it so much that they had demanded it on every festive occasion. Only during the monsoon months, when the fishermen did not put out to sea, would they settle for the traditional biryani made with goat meat.

The great cast-iron vessels in which the biryani would cook had been cleaned and oiled by the servants and she began setting out the ingredients swiftly and surely. Thick seer fish cuts, fresh and glistening, a gleaming mound of rice that had been washed and drained, onions, green chillies, garlic, ginger, coriander, red chillies, turmeric, curd, mint leaves, cinnamon, cardamom, clove, nutmeg, aniseed, cumin seed, cake seed and mace (all to be ground to make the masala which gave the dish its unique taste), a pinch of saffron, ghee, thick and fragrant. She smiled to herself as she thought of the experimentation she had resorted to when she had first arrived, trying to come up with acceptable substitutes for some of the ingredients used by her father's neighbour, a friendly Mappilai lady, who had treated the motherless girl like her own daughter, teaching her, feeding her, and imparting to her the secrets of the tasty cooking of northern Malabar.

As she worked, she kept an eye on the servants who were preparing the morning meal. In a corner of the kitchen one of the girls was filling the puttu steamers with rice flour, alternating it with layers of feathery coconut. In about an hour, Solomon would need to be fed. He would, as he always did when his brother Abraham was away, eat alone. After that there would be a dozen children clamouring for food. Charity would need to make haste. She had been doing this every morning for twenty years, but she still expected some disaster to strike and disrupt the smooth routine of the household. By now the vast kitchen had filled with sound and smell: rice was being pounded in the great stone quern in the corner, the deep bass thumps reverberating through the kitchen in sharp counterpoint to the ratcheting noise from the grindstone where spices and herbs were being ground. A sleepy child, a cousin's son, wandered into the kitchen. Charity gave him a piece of cucumber to chew on and sent him off in search of his mother.

Ten minutes later, Charity and Kamalambal took their first break in nearly two hours. The cows had been milked, the servants instructed, the morning meal organized, and they had an hour to themselves, possibly a little longer, before the next rush. The sun was not yet hot, and the two women relaxed on a broad earthen platform at the back of the house. Charity's older daughter, Rachel, sat at her feet. Her mother's practised fingers probed and massaged the girl's scalp, preparatory to oiling her long, black hair.

The girl would need to get married soon, Charity thought – nearly thirteen years old, and still unmarried. She herself had been five months short of her fourteenth birthday when she was married and she had been considered old. The times were changing, she understood that, but girls had to be married at the right age. What a pity her only brother Stephen had no sons. He had daughters, three of them. It would be perfect if Daniel and Aaron could each be betrothed to a sister. They could be married off as soon as a boy was found for Rachel, and the Dorais would have a month of weddings so grand the whole district would talk about it!

From where the women sat, the ground sloped gently down to the mud wall that enclosed the courtyard of the house on three sides. The Big House was the largest in the village, and had been so ever since Solomon's great-grandfather built it over a hundred years ago. Little of the original mud-and-thatch house now survived. Successive generations had enlarged the house according to their own needs and whims, and now it had over a dozen rooms, some of which were never used. When Charity had first arrived she had been appalled to find that the larger livestock shared their living space. Now a cattle shed sprouted from the western side. Until Vakeel Perumal had built his house two years ago, this was the only house on two levels in the village. Charity smiled as she recalled her husband's grumbling about Vakeel Perumal's ambition. For all his distinction and wealth, he could sometimes display an almost childlike sense of outrage and disappointment.

The morning routine continued to unfurl at a measured pace in the backyard of the Big House. A servant girl was stripping a few glossy green leaves from the karuvapillai bush that grew next to a row of drumstick trees, their long green fruit swaying in the breeze like gypsy earrings. A rooster strutted along at the head of a small group of chickens, pausing every few moments to strop the earth and peer in its foolish squint-eyed way at any food it might have uncovered. The sound of the shotgun being fired carried back to them, but Charity was unperturbed. Solomon and Aaron, her younger son, were known to try and bag doves or other game birds when the fancy took them. She did feel a slight twinge of anxiety – the reports had sounded alarmingly close to the house. 'Wonder what we'll have to cook this evening,' she laughed. Over by the well, another servant girl was drawing water, the squeak-squeak of the windlass clear and strong in the morning calm. A black goat with white points, which had ambled up, lowered its head and charged the girl. With a shriek, she let go of the rope and took off, the goat at her heels.

'That shaniyan, I'll cut his throat and put him in a biryani if he doesn't learn how to behave,' Charity said. 'He's been impossible to control ever since he was a kid. Ratnam, where are you, Ratnam?' she yelled. A man with a pockmarked face looked out of the cowshed and Charity told him to find the goat and tie it up. A couple of the dogs woke up and their barking added to the confusion.

Just then Charity noticed an old woman with steel-grey hair squeezing through a gap in the back wall. 'Never seen Selvi here so early, she must be bursting with gossip,' Charity said idly, giving her daughter an affectionate little push to indicate that she was done with her. As Rachel disappeared into the house, Selvi came panting up and sank with great relief on to one of the lower steps. 'Aiyo amma, you will never believe what has just happened ... '

Twenty men had attacked the Andavar tenant farmers' houses (the old woman said forty and Charity prudently divided that figure in half), killed three of them and raped five girls. When pressed, the old woman had no further details; all she could do was further embroider whatever facts there had been.

4

When Solomon returned to the house after his bath, he was surprised to see his wife waiting for him on the veranda. Usually he did not set eyes on her until she served him his morning meal. Charity could see that Solomon was in a bad mood and she wondered whether the shots she'd heard had anything to do with it. She hesitated, not wanting to add to what was troubling him, then told him anyway, omitting much of the detail and scaling down the events.

'These girls, one of them was about to be married, you say?' Solomon asked, interrupting his wife's narrative.

'Yes, Valli.'

'Could it have been a dowry matter?'

'Selvi says it wasn't. She insists that the girls were attacked by strange men from outside the village!'

Could this be the source of the unease he'd felt all morning, Solomon wondered. But it was best not to jump to conclusions. Selvi was such an unreliable informant, he should probably wait for more news. Nevertheless, he interrogated his wife further.

'Where are the injured girls now?'

'I don't know,' Charity replied. 'Selvi wasn't very clear ...'

'It's best not to believe everything Selvi says. Do you know where that illegitimate son of a donkey is?'

Guessing that her husband was referring to his barber, Charity said she would send someone to fetch him immediately.

'Don't bother, I've already bathed,' Solomon said wearily and went to his room.

Later that morning a deputation of villagers arrived at the Big House and Solomon received a more coherent version of the day's events. Kuppan, Valli's father, was one of his most dependable tenants, farming five acres of double-crop rice and three acres of coconut. He paid his rent on time, and was one of the most hard-working men in the village. Now, as he watched tears mingle with sweat on the man's lean face, Solomon's own impassive face softened with concern. As thalaivar, he had to listen to a daily litany of complaint and plea but Kuppan's story moved him. He felt sympathy and concern, but also anger. He did not let it show but it scorched him from within.

Alerted by her distraught cousin, it seemed that a search party had gone looking for the girl and had found her deep in the acacia forest. Like a wounded animal, she had sought out the most inaccessible place to take refuge in. Her sari was torn and her blouse shredded and she had not been able to utter a single intelligible word.

'How is your girl now?' Solomon asked.

The anguished father seemed not to have heard the question and he repeated it.

'Your daughter – how is she?'

'Aiyah, what am I to say? She does not eat or speak, thrashes around like a goat whose head has been cut off, and her eyes, in her eyes there is something that I have never seen in all my life. After this, it would be better if she was dead, perhaps that way she will be able to cope with it ...'

'Come now, things will be taken care of ... Show me where it happened.'

Solomon was careful to keep his voice free of anger; it wouldn't do to further upset the near-hysterical man. He took Kuppan by the arm, his mind all the while flickering over the likely list of culprits. Muthu Vedhar was quite capable of it, but would he be so obvious? An outsider? But if there had been any strangers lurking around bent on mischief, he would have known. The village had no secrets.

Parvathi, the younger of the girls, was part of the deputation and Solomon interrogated her as they walked towards Anaikal.

'So you didn't recognize anyone?'

'No, aiyah,' she replied.

Outsiders, he thought. Scum who had floated into the village on the new road. What a pity that he hadn't followed up on the disquiet he had felt early that morning and investigated the area surrounding Anaikal instead of going down to the river! He might have been able to apprehend the culprits or at the very least have identified them. Solomon told the village watchman to inform the deputy tahsildar in town of the incident and said that he would be along shortly with a full report.

Near their destination, the road was tiger-striped with brightness and shade, the sunlight filtering through the branches of the giant banyan trees that lined it. Its beauty made no impression on Solomon. Plenty of hiding-places here, he mused, the men could have taken cover among the banyan trees. He looked up and was dismayed to see Vakeel Perumal standing in the courtyard of his house, which overlooked the spot where the girls had been attacked.

Solomon disliked Vakeel Perumal. The lawyer never failed to remind the headman of the success he had enjoyed as a lawyer in Salem before he had come to this dismal place three years ago. And never missed an opportunity to criticize the headman's decisions. In my great-grandfather's time, perhaps even in my father's, a nuisance like Vakeel Perumal would simply have been banished from the village, never to be seen again, he thought, as the lawyer descended on him.

'This is an outrage. A slur on all Andavars,' Vakeel Perumal began ponderously. 'A blemish on the fair face of the village, and a challenge to your leadership.' He was a thin man with a fat man's face. His peculiar looks made him even easier to dislike.

'I know. That is why I'm investigating the matter personally.'

'Do you know what they are trying to do?'

Solomon wasn't quite sure what the lawyer was getting at, so to be safe he said, 'Who?'

'Trying to make us ashamed of our birthright, that's what they are trying to do, don't you see?'

'No, I don't,' Solomon said shortly. 'Two girls were attacked near here. I don't see how that relates ... '

Vakeel Perumal did not let him complete his sentence. Loose flesh heaving like the dewlaps of a cow, he pointed dramatically to the smooth face of Anaikal and said, 'We should not be wilfully blind to what they are trying to do.'

Solomon looked to where the lawyer was pointing. On the granite outcrop someone had scrawled in lime:

REMEMBER THE 1859 BREAST WARS. IF LOW-CASTE DOGS DO NOT KNOW THEIR PLACE, THEIR WIVES AND SISTERS WILL SOON REMIND THEM OF IT.

Solomon was thunderstruck. When he had walked past the rock the previous day it had been bare. The lawyer was still talking but his words did not register. This was serious, far worse than anything he had had to cope with during the years of his leadership – epidemics, drought, quarrels and feuds. It was bad enough that outsiders had attacked his people. But if this marked the beginning of a full-scale caste war, they were in for a very bad time.

What Solomon really wanted to do was scream, rave, rant, throw up his arms in despair as he regarded the obscenity on the rock. For a fleeting moment, he wished he was the young boy he had once been – before responsibility had descended upon him, along with self-consciousness, restraint, and a sense of his own inadequacy. He composed himself.

5

Solomon had first heard about the infamous Breast Wars from his mother and later from his father and uncles. The conflict, which latter-day historians label more neutrally the breast-cloth controversy, marked the culmination of an especially vicious phase in the caste struggle in the deep south. It began in the small towns and villages of the kingdom of Travancore but inevitably spilled over into neighbouring Madras Presidency, which by the middle of the nineteenth century had grown into one of the largest and most populous provinces of British India. Tinnevelly and Kilanad, in which Chevathar was located, were the two worst affected districts in the Presidency.

The violence had been brewing for some time. Non-Brahmin caste groups like the Andavars and Nadars, who had acquired wealth and economic clout, demanded enhanced social and religious standing. Those above them in the caste hierarchy were determined to resist their aspirations.

Unlike in the rest of the country, the caste tree in the south had, broadly speaking, only three levels of branches – Brahmin, non-Brahmin and those beyond the pale. Initially, the skirmishing was principally between the powerful non-Brahmin castes like the Nadars, Andavars, Thevars, Maravars, Vedhars and Vellalas. The Brahmins were concentrated in the cities and the great temple towns, and would only be properly singed by the flames of war a little later on.

Exacerbating the dissent was Christian missionary activity from the seventeenth century onwards. Tens of thousands of non-Brahmins, especially those near the bottom, accepted the Word of Christ, principally in order to edge their way past those who opposed them by claiming, as their new religion urged, that all men were created equal in the eyes of God. One of the social customs to be challenged was dress: hitherto tradition had ordained that the various members of the caste tree should bare their breasts as a sign of deference and subservience to those perched higher in the branches. Accordingly, the untouchables went bare-breasted before the Pallans, the Pallans before the Nairs, and so on until the Nambudiri Brahmins, who deferred only to their deities. At the urging of the missionaries, Andavar and Nadar women began to cover their breasts. This, unsurprisingly, threw the upper castes, especially the men, into a frenzy of insecurity and frustration. Andavar and Nadar women who clothed themselves were abused in public, even beaten. Finally, unable to bear the torment, the middle-ranking castes went too far. 'We have a divine right to gaze upon your filthy breasts and you should be flattered that we do so. They are ours to enjoy. Whatever benefits your new faith bestows upon you, this is not one of them,' declared a landlord in Travancore in 1858, tears rolling down his cheeks, as he wrenched the blouse off a pretty Andavar woman who had recently converted to Christianity. Riots tore through the area following the outrage. Despite the royal government stepping in to ease the situation, tension continued to simmer in the kingdom and in the adjacent districts of Madras Presidency, which shared a long, porous border with Travancore.

It soon became apparent that if the authorities did not take swift and decisive action, there would be unrest on a massive scale. Despite this, neither the British authorities nor the Travancore Maharajah took any action for a while.

Slightly over a year earlier, some Indian regiments in the army had spearheaded the first major uprising against British rule. The 1857 conflict (variously called the War of Independence or the Mutiny or the Sepoy War, depending on whom you consulted) was sparked off by the rulers' ignoring of local caste and religious taboos. For some years afterwards the British showed a marked reluctance to interfere with Indian customs and traditions.

In the face of the authorities' lack of action, the people took matters into their own hands. In January 1859, violence exploded throughout Travancore. A local official, claiming the authority of the state, stripped some Nadar women of their upper garments. Rioting broke out and lasted for days. The next to be targeted were Andavar women in Melur, the capital of Kilanad district, who were similarly disrobed. Retribution was swift. A band of Andavar toughs went on the rampage, looting and burning houses in the Vedhar quarter. Prompt action by the authorities contained the violence, but elsewhere the situation was still extremely volatile.

Across the border, in the extreme south of Travancore, a mob, a couple of hundred strong, armed with silambus and aruvals, descended on a village near Nagercoil, barely five kilometres from where Charity Dorai would be born a couple of years later, and attacked the Christian Andavars there, burning and looting and stripping breast-cloths and bodices from the women. The Andavars began to retaliate. Instead of being assertive, the Travancore court made vague noises about respecting custom and tradition. But it was too late for that. When it became evident that the Travancore Maharajah wouldn't be able to sort out the problem, missionaries and other concerned citizens petitioned the supreme authority in the south, the British Governor in neighbouring Madras, Sir Charles Trevelyan. Aware of the riots in his own Presidency and mindful of the gender of his chief, Queen Victoria, Trevelyan ruled that Travancore should prohibit the stripping of Andavar women. The intervention of the British authorities broke the back of the situation. When the ugliness in Travancore subsided, it had a calming effect on the tense districts of Madras Presidency.

The memory of the 1859 Breast Wars was burned into the minds of all those castes who were affected. Now it seemed that someone was trying to revive those terrible days ...

Solomon began to register the words of Vakeel Perumal, who had never once stopped talking in all the time he had been thinking. 'And the fact that the message was written at all and that, too, in grammatical prose, proves that whoever was responsible for this outrage was an educated man, which rules out most of the villagers.' The man had a point, Solomon conceded.

From where he stood, Solomon could see the bustle and energy of the Pangunni Uthiram fair. Gypsies in bright clothes wandered among the soberly dressed villagers, little stalls offered tempting trinkets and foodstuffs, and the world seemed to go on much as before, largely unaware of the terrifying future that lay in store. 'I'll convene a meeting of the village panchayat this evening,' Solomon said, and he began to walk away. Vakeel Perumal muttered something too low for Solomon to hear, and then repeated it in a louder voice. 'I hope this will at least see better leadership from you.'

Solomon's self-control left him. He saw himself walk up to Vakeel Perumal, catch a fistful of the blinding white shirt the lawyer wore, and say slowly into the fat face: 'You will not speak to me like that ever again, in my presence or out of it. I hear of anything and I'll break you in half.'

He released the lawyer and took the path towards town. A few minutes later he heard racing feet behind him, and turned slowly. It was his younger son Aaron, his favourite child, unruly hair flying in the wind, his sleekly muscled legs propelling him effortlessly along the road. He caught up with his father, and said worriedly, 'Appa, I just heard ...'

'Yes, Aaron, things don't look so good.'

'My friends and I can go and find the men who did this. They'll wish they'd never emerged from their mother's ...'

'No, no violence. The village panchayat will meet this evening and decide what to do.'

'Oh, and appa, I thought you should hear this ... Someone said they had seen Joshua-chithappa in Meenakshikoil ...'

Solomon smiled. If true, this was the best news he had received all day. He was closer to his first cousin Joshua than to his own brother and he had missed his support and friendship in recent years. Could it be that Joshua, whom he had last seen a decade ago, was back in Chevathar?

'Who saw him?' he asked eagerly.

'Oh, Nambi said a friend of his had heard that someone had seen Joshua-chithappa ...'

Solomon's smile disappeared. So it was a silly bazaar rumour then!

6

Deputy tahsildar Shanmuga Vedhar, the ranking government functionary in this part of the district, thought rather highly of himself. His self-esteem rose even further when he was ensconced in his office in one of the busier parts of Meenakshikoil town. It wasn't much, six foot by six foot and sparsely furnished, but he liked the feeling of authority it gave him. It made him forget that he was stuck in the least important town in Kilanad, itself the smallest district in Madras Presidency.

Indeed, whenever he sat behind his table, he saw himself as part of a chain of command that stretched all the way to the office of the Collector, the head of the district, and beyond that to the most powerful figure in the Presidency, the Governor in Council, no less. And, if he was lucky and his lobbying of his superiors was successful, Meenakshikoil might become a fully fledged taluqa very soon and he would be promoted to tahsildar. That had a nice ring to it, Tahsildar S. Vedhar! This was what he had studied for; this was what he had passed exam after exam for; this was why he was the first man in his village to receive a college education; this was what made it all worthwhile: this table, this chair, the cupboard filled with innumerable land records and yellowing files that contained within them reams of verbiage relating to incomprehensible disputes ...

His musings were cut short when he saw, through the window, Solomon Dorai approaching the office. He immediately began making preparations to meet the thalaivar. He settled himself more firmly in his chair, stiffened his posture, smoothed down his thin sliver of moustache, and opened a file on his table in order to look busy. The door opened, and he saw, with not a little irritation, that his clerk had let the headman in without asking him to state his business. This wasn't entirely his subordinate's fault, for Shanmuga Vedhar himself wasn't sure how to deal with Solomon. As deputy tahsildar he outranked him. There was no dispute about that. But on the other hand, he was beholden to Solomon who, as the wealthiest mirasidar in the taluqa, made the single largest contribution of taxes and rents to his treasury. Why, only a year and a half ago, Solomon had acquired a cotton-growing village to the north of Chevathar, which meant he now owned three villages outright in addition to owning or renting much of the land in Chevathar. Why couldn't Solomon be like the other mirasidars, the powerful landlords of the deep south, and luxuriate in his wealth instead of meddling in administration? Surely being a mere thalaivar was beneath him. Why did he bother? When he had once summoned up the courage to ask the thalaivar, Solomon had been brusque. Four generations of Dorais had served as headmen of Chevathar village before him; he wasn't about to shirk his hereditary responsibility. None of this would have mattered in the ordinary course of events, for both of them had more than enough to keep them occupied. But lately they had clashed over the issue of the new road. The deputy tahsildar had had his way, but not without a battle.

As the thalaivar entered his office, Shanmuga Vedhar rose to greet him. He would have preferred to receive him sitting down but there was something about the thalaivar's presence that made him feel like an errant schoolboy.

'Vanakkam Dipty Vedhar,' Solomon said shortly, using the appellation the locals had bestowed on the official soon after he had arrived in Meenakshikoil.

The deputy tahsildar returned the greeting and the headman wasted no time in getting down to business. Swiftly he added to the facts Dipty Vedhar knew.

'I've called a meeting of the village panchayat this evening. If this is going to turn into a caste fight, we'll have to be ready. I hope you will be there ...'

'Yes, yes, I will be there.'

They chatted for a little while longer and then the headman left. To Dipty Vedhar's great relief he hadn't brought up the new road again, but his relief was tinged with dread as he contemplated the evening's meeting. He could already hear the headman's argument: without the new road, the thugs couldn't have entered the village unseen, the natural order wouldn't have been upset and so on and on and on. Dipty Vedhar feared caste violence as much as Solomon did. But it was absurd to argue that the village should remain exactly as it was a hundred years ago, sunk in ignorance and poverty. When would people like Solomon Dorai understand that progress was inevitable?

The new road had increased the revenue collections of the Government. The main earnings of the state, besides land tax and rent, came from the salt-works by the estuary. More land was requisitioned for salt-pans, but even as production increased, transport was still limited to coolies who had to wade across the river with sacks of salt on their heads. Dipty Vedhar had proposed an all-weather road connecting the village to the town by means of a stone culvert to be thrown across the river.

At first everyone in Chevathar had welcomed the idea of a pukka road, except Solomon, not that he knew quite why. Most of the villagers had seen the road that ran through town, rutted and pitted though it was, and wanted a similar one for themselves. But when the villagers learned that Dipty Vedhar proposed to run the new road in as straight a line as he could from the bridge to Solomon's house and then on to the salt-works, objections rose thick and fast. Muthu Vedhar, Vakeel Perumal and the priests of the Murugan temple felt that their stature in the village entitled them to a piece of the road at their doorstep. When they finally realized that the Government would not allow extra expenditure on the road simply in order to appease their egos, they immediately began to oppose the project. They argued that the traditional laws of pollution which forbade untouchables and the lowest castes from even venturing near the main village path would be broken not only by the inhabitants but by outsiders who would be able to wander at will into the village.

If he wanted his road, Dipty Vedhar had to somehow break down resistance. He had summoned representatives from the major caste groups – the tiny Brahmin community (there were only three Brahmin families in the village, hereditary keepers of the Murugan temple), the Andavars and the Vedhars – to a meeting. The Paraiyans, as always, were excluded. The first conclave ended in a shouting match and a second was convened. This too proved inconclusive. More meetings followed. Deliberations dragged on for eight months and still nobody could agree on how the road should be laid. For once, Solomon was completely stymied. He could not support Dipty Vedhar without offending his fellow villagers. But nor did he want to be seen to be obstructing the deputy tahsildar. In the end, hugely frustrated, Dipty Vedhar called the whole thing off. Six months later, he exhumed the proposal once more, on account of an event that had taken place decades earlier, half a world away.

The American Civil War had interrupted the flow of cotton to Lancashire because much of the strife was centred on the cotton plantations in the South. But it is one of the conditions of mass manufacture that machines can never be kept idle. If cotton from America could not be had, it had to come from somewhere else. About that time, a shipment of Indian cotton, from Tinnevelly, found its way to England. 'Tinnie' cotton, as it was known, was of exceptionally good quality. Suddenly the impoverished cotton-growing areas in the south

– Tinnevelly, Kilanad, Virudhunagar and the Andhra country – began generating vast amounts of revenue and fortunes were made. The ending of the Civil War and the resumption of the American cotton trade did not end the importance of tinnie cotton. It continued to be in demand in England and locally.

One of the principal cotton-growing areas in Kilanad district lay far north of the Chevathar river. The cotton was transported to Chevathar, where it was weighed, measured and sorted, and then taken across to Meenakshikoil, on the heads of coolies, to be sold. Just when Dipty Vedhar had finally decided to shelve the new road, the district authorities secured a large order for cotton. Along with other local officials, the deputy tahsildar was instructed to procure supplies of the crop speedily. He explained to Solomon that construction of the road and culvert would need to begin before the rainy season started. They both knew that this time there could be no backing down.

After days of consultation, Solomon visited Dipty Vedhar with a compromise. The road would pass through the Vedhar quarter, and also skirt Vakeel Perumal's house and the Murugan temple, thereby assuaging the egos of the higher castes. But as this was a government road, members of every caste would have the right to use it, and it was up to him as thalaivar to ensure that as far as possible caste rules were not broken. It wasn't the perfect solution but it was the best he could come up with. There was really no way around it.

Now, as he walked home from his meeting with the deputy tahsildar, Solomon mulled over the various problems created by the new road. All through the summer of its construction he had felt a sense of foreboding. Once it was laid, he'd thought, nothing would be the same again. And he had been right. Within a year of its inauguration, there were at least a couple of incidents directly linked to the road.

Soon after it was finished, during the Pongal festival, a group of young girls had been molested by drunken youths who had crossed the bridge and wandered into the village. The rowdies had been thrashed by the villagers but there had been no end to the recriminations showered upon Solomon and the deputy tahsildar. Four months later, a Paraiyan had been beaten almost to death by some Vedhar men for daring to stroll through their quarter, blithely smoking a beedi, with his turban firmly on his head rather than around his waist as was customary in the presence of the higher castes. The Paraiyans had come in a body to Solomon to plead for justice. They repeated his own words to him: the road was a government road and therefore had no caste restrictions placed on it. A man was free to walk on it as he pleased. They had, of course, no intention of causing trouble, they owed their lives and everything else to their masters, but this was unfair. Solomon had received the deputation with disfavour. He thought the Paraiyan had gone too far. But he knew he could take only one decision. He ruled that everyone could use the government road without hindrance, though the polluting classes would have to comply with the rules as far as possible – their shadows could not fall on the upper castes, they would continue to take off their turbans in the presence of their superior caste fellows, they should not approach villagers of the highest caste closer than thirty-two paces, and their lungis should always be folded above the knee. There was surprisingly little objection to Solomon's ruling and thereafter the road was freely used.

But although he had stood firm and the storm had passed, Solomon Dorai knew that the trouble wouldn't end there. He had lived on this land all his life, as his family had for generations before him, and he respected its customs and traditions. Although thirty-four of the eighty-seven families who made the village their home were, like him, Christian Andavars, he had never tried to impose the Christian way on the Hindu villagers, whether they were Brahmin, Andavar, Vedhar or lower caste. He donated generously to the Murugan temple but never tried to enter its precincts, in keeping with caste strictures, and when he gave food to the Brahmin priests during festivals he was careful to ensure that it was uncooked, for it was proscribed to give cooked food to superior castes. He was aware that not everyone shared his strong belief in tradition. But he had always kept Chevathar (and the other villages he owned) free of caste conflict. Until the coming of the road had unsettled the existing order.

Only eight days ago, on Ram Navami day, there had been a scuffle at the Murugan temple, when two Andavar men had been caught trying to enter. Solomon had ruled against the Andavars. He had argued long and hard in defence of his ruling and pointed out that the Andavars had their own temple, the Ammankoil, and that there was no profit in fighting with the Vedhars to gain entry to the Murugan temple. In the end, the Andavar elders had no option but to agree, especially as the majority of them were tenant farmers on his estate. Solomon's most vociferous opponent, Muthu Vedhar, the leader of the Vedhar group, had also been neutralized by his tough and forthright action.

A great flapping in the stand of tamarind trees he was passing interrupted Solomon's thoughts. He looked up to see a large handsome bird, its plumage rusty red on white, lifting clumsily up from the branch of the tree on which it was perched. Once it was in the air, its movements steadied, grew more graceful. He remembered what the padre of the local church, an amateur ornithologist, had called the bird when they'd encountered it on one of their walks. Father Ashworth had joked that even the birds were sucked into the caste structure with this, the most striking raptor, called the Brahminy kite, and the most dowdy, the Pariah kite. The priest was right, he thought, caste had permeated every aspect of their lives.

He watched the kite drifting along the thermals and wondered how the village looked from way up there. The great palm groves, Charity's unusual trees, the huts, the river, the bridge ... As it soared even higher, the immediate detail of the village would begin to soften and something else, not immediately apparent, would come into view: a fine mesh of lines incising the ancient earth of the village, several little paths that began and ended for no reason or wandered erratically across the place. Some of them had been worn into the soil by the boys who herded cows, goats, buffaloes and other livestock. But Solomon understood the significance of the other paths. These conformed to the rules of pollution and caste. For example, the path from the Paraiyans' quarter, the cheri, began at the southern most point of the village and ran in a great arc around it, before ending at the bridge. In practical terms, it simply meant that an inhabitant of the cheri would have to walk nearly twice the distance that a Brahmin would, in order to cross the village. Similar rules governed the siting of houses, areas earmarked for defecation and bathing, access to the river and cropland. The highest castes got the best, and the inhabitants of the cheri at the lowest point downstream, before the river turned to salt, got the worst. That's the way things were and for all its beauty and deceptive serenity, Chevathar, like any other village in the area, was rigidly ordered by caste strictures and traditions that hadn't changed for as long as anyone could remember. Until the road, the accursed road, had come along and upset the balance.

When he entered the courtyard of his house, a flock of doves, brown as the earth, whirred to the ground and began scratching for food. A Rajapalaiyam, its long face alight with anticipation, charged the birds and they flew up in alarm. The dog raced away. In time, Solomon thought, the road would be assimilated into the timeless rhythm of the village, as had every other new influence and idea over the centuries. But acceptance of it would not be easy. Everything that abraded the established order released anguish and pain before the healing process began. And it was up to people like him to manage the change in the best possible way. God give me the strength to do that, he muttered, as he irritably scratched the stubble on his chin.

7

St Paul's Church was a pentangular building, roofed with cherry-red country tiles, now dark and shadowed by age, its walls glowing with the brilliant white of limewash. Three other buildings stood within the mission compound: a school, a small dispensary and the parsonage, all hidden by ancient palms. Only the steeple of the church towered above the trees, in keeping with the biblical injunction that no house of God be lower than its surroundings or the dwellings of the faithful. The church had been rebuilt twice, once when it had been partially destroyed by fire in 1837 and again, after a sudden cyclonic storm, thirty years later. But its essential architecture had remained unchanged. On the outside, it looked no different to other missionary-built churches in the area, but its interior was unique.

Some months after the 1837 fire, while the church was being repaired, fifteen villagers from the Paraiyan caste had converted to Christianity. Solomon Dorai's grandfather, who was thalaivar at the time, had been adamant that the new converts could not be allowed to worship in the church. The pastor, a thrawn Scot, had insisted otherwise. Matters were coming to a head when the headman proposed a solution. In order that the priest did not even inadvertently favour his lower-caste flock, the headman proposed that a hollow wall be constructed from the doorway of the church to the altar rail. The priest would walk through the wall and emerge before his congregation (the worshippers of the Andavar caste sat on the more favoured right of the church) to conduct the service. Separate communion tables and chalices would ensure that Andavar and Paraiyan didn't drink from the same cup or eat of the same bread. Neither group had set eyes on the other in all the years that they had worshipped together, for the lower castes left the church immediately after the service through a door set into their side of the building.

Over the next sixty-two years, all the priests of the Chevathar mission had tried to dismantle the offending wall, without success. The present rector had often thought it a pity that Solomon, that most fair-minded of men, should refuse to take down the wall. Arguments that Christianity did not admit of caste were routinely ignored and after some years of trying, Father Ashworth gave up.

The Reverend Paul Ashworth was a short man, comfortably proportioned, with a few threads of greying hair straying across his otherwise bald head. His eyes seemed almost too blue for his face, which was burnt a dark red by the sun. Today his face was more flushed than usual for he had spent the morning wandering along the beach with Daniel, the thalaivar's older son.

Father Ashworth enjoyed the boy's company, and whenever they could find the time, Daniel and he would set off on some small adventure, either prospecting along the shore for rare shells and sea creatures or making forays into the coconut and acacia forests looking for herbs and exotic plants. They were both interested in the therapeutic properties of plants, and they would often take specimens to the vaidyan to find out what their healing properties were.

Usually, they ventured out quite early but this morning the sun was well up in the sky and the day was already hot by the time they got to the seashore. However, the allure of the tide pools was too strong and they had begun walking along the shore, the thunder of the sea filling their ears, stopping at every rocky indentation to probe and tease out the treasures that lay beneath the clear water. In an hour or so they had amassed quite a haul. Then Father Ashworth found a rare wentletrap, a large ribbed and whorled shell that they had never come across before. As if to compensate, Daniel made the next finds – a glittering red-and-gold marvel, shaped like a sultan's turban, and a pair of purple sea snails with carapaces of the palest lavender. Galvanized by these finds, they had begun searching the pools with renewed intensity, unearthing fantastically carved murex shells, periwinkles, speckled and ribbed in crazy undulating patterns, exquisite strawberry conches, sundials with complex spirals on their shells, and their favourites, the beautiful cowries that had been used as currency in the country about a thousand years before. Even by their standards, their haul was impressive: in addition to the common tiger cowrie, Father Ashworth found a rare Isabelle cowrie, glistening like a highly polished ear stud, and Daniel snagged a mole cowrie with cream and brown bands as well as an unusually coloured sieve cowrie with reddish instead of cream spots. A wave broke and receded, and Father Ashworth's eyes had widened.

'Money cowries. Dozens of them, we're rich,' he'd yelled.

'Now I can go to Melur and become a doctor. You can send me,' Daniel had yelled back, above the thudding of the sea.

'I wish I could, Daniel, I wish I could,' the priest had said to himself as they bent to gather up their trove.

Trudging home, Father Ashworth had covertly studied the boy. His fine, delicate features, matchstick-thin arms and large expressive eyes properly belonged in a more cloistered world. Studious and gentle, cosseted by his mother and his aunt, Daniel was a misfit in the very male world of the Dorais. None of the Dorais of Solomon's generation had ever studied beyond the fourth standard, which was all that the mission school offered. With Father Ashworth's support Daniel had managed to get his father to send him to the Government Secondary School in Meenakshikoil (Aaron had reluctantly followed in his older brother's footsteps but had dropped out after a while). Daniel had made it plain to everyone that he wanted to study further, to be a doctor or at the very least a botanist. However, every time he or the padre brought it up, his father refused permission. Only last week, Solomon had said to the priest in Daniel's presence, 'We are farmers and you do not learn to read the weather from books.'

But the boy refused to give up his dream. There's the Dorai steel in him somewhere, Father Ashworth thought. He might look and think differently to the other men in his family, but beneath the gentle exterior there was a stubbornness and determination that would not yield easily.

Thinking of the boy's plight, Father Ashworth's mood grew sombre. He looked pensively out of the window of the church at the Gulf of Mannar. The sea was flat and grey as a heron's eye, the sky overcast. As always, except when the fishermen put out to sea and returned in the evening with the day's catch, the beach was deserted. Just then the sacristan walked in and announced Solomon Dorai. This was wholly unexpected. The priest rose hurriedly, walked down the hollow wall and welcomed his visitor.

The thalaivar looked disturbed and when he had finished relating the day's events, Father Ashworth could see why. Over the years, he had come to admire how Solomon's iron will and clear-headed rule kept the village free of caste and religious conflict.

'Dipty Vedhar and I agree that we must take the strongest possible action. All the taluqas here and in Tinnevelly district have been told to be on their guard as there is talk that major caste disturbances are expected. But why should such things happen in Chevathar? We've always been free of this infection, even when the rest of the district was in turmoil,' Solomon said unhappily.

'It's the times, my friend,' Father Ashworth said. A thought struck him. 'Do you remember the episode from the *Bhagavatam* that those visiting villupaatu players enacted at the Pongal festivities?'

'Which one?' asked the headman distractedly.

'You know, the one where the Gods churn the ocean using the mountain Mandara as the churn and the serpent Vasuki as the churning rope?'

'Yes, yes. What of it?'

'Well, the Gods were looking for amrita, the elixir of eternal life, that lay in the depths of the ocean, to protect them in their war against the demons, and Lord Narayana told them that the only way to get it would be to churn ...'

'I know the story,' Solomon said.

'But do you remember what happened before Dhanwantari appeared from the bottom of the ocean with the golden vessel containing amrita?'

'Yes, I do, the divine cow Kamadhenu appeared, then Airavata, the four-headed tusked elephant, and then Parijata, the tree of life, and then, and then I forget ... But what does this have to do with the poison that's affecting Chevathar?'

'Poison, that's what,' the priest said, triumphantly if mysteriously. 'The first thing that appeared when the ocean was churned was the deadly poison Halahala. It tainted and killed everything it touched. That's what's happening today. As discontent, envy and unhappiness swirl through all the castes, communities and creeds in this land, it's inevitable that poison, hate and envy will be generated. But if we hold firm, do what is right in the eyes of God and man, then eventually virtue and goodness will prevail. Peace and prosperity ...'

Any further thoughts the priest may have had on the subject were cut short, for his visitor rose. 'I'm sorry, padre, I've got to be going. I've told Dipty Vedhar that I will have everyone who can throw light on the matter interrogated.' As he stooped to enter the hollow wall, he called out, 'There's a meeting of the panchayat this evening. It would be good if you could come.'

After Solomon had gone, the padre retreated to his position by the window. The sun had burned away the overcast and hammered the back of the sea into a mass of shimmering golden scales, but even this sight did not lift his spirits. Seeing Solomon Dorai so twitchy and nervous was depressing. But the headman was right to be anxious. And it upset the priest that he had been unable to offer him the reassurance that he had sought.

As he lingered by the window in the lengthening morning, the enchantment of the scene before him began to soothe and settle his mind. At the limits of his vision, the pale beige of the sky merged with the golden skin of the sea, with only the thinnest of lines showing where the earth's rim separated the two. Out of those depths they had come, foreign adventurers and travellers by the shipload, to marvel at and to be seduced by the astonishing riches of India. Megasthenes, Pliny, Strabo, Eusebius, Marco Polo, Ibn Battuta, Wassafi, Rashid-ud-din, Caesar Frederic, Vasco da Gama – the greatest voyagers and writers of their time – knew of the magnificence and wealth of the nations of the Coromandel coast long before Robert Clive and John Company began to dream of shaking the pagoda tree.

He thought of the village as his home now. He had not visited England for seven years. His only surviving relative, an aged aunt who lived in an old people's home in Buckinghamshire, had gone senile, and had not recognized him on his last visit. In addition, he found the dark drizzly weather a trial. It was with a sense of relief that he had boarded the steamer at Southampton for Madras. Seventeen of his fifty-two years had been spent in Chevathar. This was where he wanted to live and work and this was where, by God's grace, he hoped he would die.

His thoughts returned to the problem Solomon was facing. When he had arrived in India twenty-five years ago, he had been appalled above all else by the institution of caste. He had tried to understand the viewpoint of those who argued that caste was necessary to give the country's vast and diverse population a sense of identity and belonging, but surely that did not excuse the injustice and barbarity perpetrated in its name! How could any sane and compassionate human being abide the discrimination sanctioned by caste and religion upon his fellows, based entirely on self-serving interpolations in the great religious texts? The solution, he believed, wasn't to do away with the Scriptures but to refashion them. To preserve the extraordinary truths at their core and discard the rest. The *Manusmriti*, the Old Testament, and scores of other holy texts could do with judicious editing and interpretation. But would it ever happen? He knew that he had neither the scholarship nor the sagacity to attempt such a task. It could only be accomplished by a savant and visionary of the highest order.

In the meantime, in an attempt to further his own understanding, he had begun work on a book that sought to collate and compare the sublime truths of Hinduism and Christianity, shorn of the thickets of obfuscation that surrounded them. Work on it had progressed slowly because of his own failings as a writer and a thinker, but also because of the numerous other matters that fought for his attention. He glanced across at the communion table on which lay sheets of the manuscript of *Some Thoughts on the Hindu-Christian Encounter.* Perhaps he should start work on it now; it might help clarify his thoughts, give him some helpful insight that he could pass on to Solomon.

8

In Chevathar, the birth of a son was greeted with the kuruvai – a long-drawn-out call ululating from the throats of aunts and sisters. It sounded like a dirge but was in fact an expression of overwhelming joy. Blessed was the mother of a son. Blessed was the family into which a son was born. He would extend the family line, bring in dowry and good luck and attract the blessings of the Gods. A girl, on the other hand, was greeted with downcast faces. A girl meant nothing but sorrow. One more unproductive mouth to feed and heavy expense for the family – dowry, marriage costs, the endless demands of in-laws who had done her parents a favour by taking her off their hands. Many despondent mothers quickly extinguished the life of the luckless baby, especially if she had arrived at the tail end of a succession of daughters – by smothering her, feeding her the poisonous sap of the calotropis plant or the roots of the valli shrub, or encouraging her to ingest sharp-edged husks of rice grain which could fatally puncture the alimentary tract of an infant. If she was allowed to live, the girl was never allowed to forget that through her the family was paying for its sins in past births. All this in a land where the highest deity was Devi, the Mother Goddess, created by the commingling of the essence of the great Hindu trinity – Brahma, Narayana and Parameshwara – to rid the world of an evil they could not handle themselves.

Every woman in the village quickly learned her place in life, no matter how exalted her station. When Charity first arrived in the Big House as a young bride, she was shocked when Solomon hit her for not bringing him his coffee at exactly the right temperature. Tearfully she had returned to the kitchen. When she told her mother-in-law about the incident, Thangammal had wiped away her tears with her sari pallu, and told her something she had never forgotten: 'In these parts, my daughter, a woman must be prepared to be beaten by her husband. If he's a good man he won't beat you too much, and not without reason. We put up with it. It's the way things are. When you are newly married, you are beaten for not bringing enough dowry, when you give birth to your children, you are beaten for not producing a male heir, or if you have already given him a son, for not producing only sons. And then, when you have produced enough children, you are beaten for losing your looks and your youth.'

'But it was not so in my father's house.'

'You are not in your father's house.'

'But, mami, it's wrong.'

'There's no question of wrong or right. My son is a good boy. Here, take him the coffee again.'

The circumstances of their birth and the evolution of their separate lives gave the men and women of Chevathar village sharply differing perspectives on the rape of Valli. While the men grew robust in their hate and mistrust of each other, and obsessed about the larger consequences of the tragedy, the women identified with the girl's trauma and were reminded once more of the misfortune of being born a woman.

After the first shock of hearing the full details of the attack, a thick unease settled in Charity's mind. She grew snappish and irritable with her sisters-in-law Kamalambal and Kaveri, she yelled at the servants and was especially harsh on her older daughter Rachel. She was surprised at first, then realized that it was the particularity of the situation that was so upsetting: the violated girl was about the same age as her own beloved daughter, she was about to be married. It could have happened to Rachel. And her mother would have been powerless to protect her. Though she kept repeating to herself that nothing had happened to Rachel, that nothing would happen to Rachel, Charity was anxious all day. She took it out on her daughter, slapping her for forgetting to put the sliced onions for the pachidi in water and for gossiping with a servant girl. The second time she slapped her, Rachel burst into tears. Charity was quick to console her. She forced herself to calm down, to concentrate on the preparation of the refreshments and the dozens of other tasks that needed to be finished in time for the meeting of the panchayat that evening.

All through that interminable morning, news continued to filter into the Big House and Charity took it all in. The girl who had been attacked had a fatal flaw in her birth horoscope as well as in her menstrual horoscope, it was whispered, the dreaded mula natchattiram would explain her misfortune. After a while it was reported that it was not the mula natchattiram that had led to the girl's downfall, but the even more feared naga dosham. A few women claimed to have seen a large cobra-shaped discoloration near the girl's groin, the mark signifying that an invisible snake lurked in the girl's genitalia to cause the death of the first man to have sex with her. It was said that her parents had concealed the information for fear that the girl would never get married. Others said it had nothing to do with imperfect horoscopes at all, it was a jilted lover who had assaulted Valli.

Charity had barely met the girl's family but by noon she knew most of the details of their lives, some accurate, most invented. She was informed that Ponnammal, the girl's mother, had recently given birth to her ninth child, even though, in her late thirties, her childbearing years should have been almost over. She was told that misfortune had visited the family because of a curse directed at the girl's father by his brother-in-law who lived two villages away for defaulting on a loan. As the fragments and stories grew more fanciful and extreme, they began to distance Charity from the horror she had felt earlier in the day.

She started to get Solomon's lunch ready. As she worked, she hoped she would be able to discuss the attack with him, but long experience had taught her that she could only do so when the time was right. She had learned, over two decades ago, that her job was to keep the household running smoothly, that she had no part to play in the affairs of the village. If she'd had any doubts, an incident that had occurred when she first arrived in Chevathar had removed them. The wives of two sharecroppers had asked her to mediate in a land dispute and she had promised to talk to her husband. She had broached the subject when she was serving the evening meal and Solomon had hit her for only the second time in their marriage. Shocked and fearful, she had agreed never to interfere in matters that did not concern her.

Since then, she had discovered how to bide her time, to use elliptical ways to influence events – gentle nagging, charm, the insinuation of requests at opportune moments. It was clear, when she began to serve lunch, that this was not the right time. Solomon was brusque with her, and barely touched his food. Refusing a second helping, he washed his hands and left. His disquiet bothered Charity. She longed to help him, but what could she do? She sat silent and disturbed over her own meal, barely tasting what she ate.

Arriving at a decision, she waited for the house to quieten and retreat into its afternoon somnolence before slipping out into the heat of the day. Solomon would not be pleased with what she was planning to do, but then he need never know. Drawing her sari pallu over her head to protect it from the sun and also to disguise herself, she made her way to the Andavar quarter.

At the entrance to the lane of low-standing shacks of mud and thatch, she realized that she had no idea where Valli's house was. She couldn't remember when she had last been in the Andavar quarter, perhaps five years, maybe even a decade ago. There were very few people about. Flies, stunned and oppressed by the sun, crawled in the gutters and coated the dirt- and snot-stained faces of a small knot of children who sat, drained of all energy, in the meagre shade of a coconut palm. Upon seeing the headman's wife, they came to life. As they swarmed around her, she spotted a woman she knew quite well squatting in the doorway of her hut, languidly picking lice out of her daughter's hair. The woman jumped up when she saw Charity. She walked her over to Valli's hut, barely a couple of doors away. 'The girl is sleeping, the vaidyan gave her a potion. But it's no use, amma. When she wakes up she'll be just as damaged as before. It's useless ...' Charity thanked the woman, and stooped to enter the hut.

Inside the sweltering windowless space she could just make out the dim form of Valli lying on a mat, an old sari draping her. She slept heavily, her breath rasping. Near the doorway sat the girl's mother feeding her baby. Two other women, neighbours, gossiped quietly a little further into the room, bending over from time to time to brush away the flies that moiled around the girl's mouth.

When they saw Charity, the neighbours immediately grew animated, vying with each other to greet her and give her the latest news. Valli's mother said nothing, but continued to stare vacantly at Charity. Under that terrible gaze, drained of tears, emotion, hope, Charity grew anxious again. The full horror of what this mother, this family had gone through broke over her, and yet, and yet, could she really know what they had suffered? She felt guilty and ashamed that in her concern for her own, she had forgotten the trauma of those most affected by the attack. She was glad she had come, although she doubted that she could do much for this woman, who seemed to have gone beyond sorrow to some bleaker place where no one could reach her.

'I'm here on the thalaivar's behalf,' she said, slipping easily into the lie. 'He wondered if there was anything that could be done to help.'

The girl's mother made no response. Charity was about to try again when one of the other women spoke: 'There's nothing to be done. What has happened has happened, no one can alter her fate. We can only hope that her suffering is eased quickly.' Charity half-turned to look at her, and the woman inclined her head slightly and continued to speak. The girl was born under a bad star, she was paying for sins committed in a past life, things would be better for her in the next ... the words flowed without pause in the oppressive dark. The woman stopped after a while, and then there was only the harsh breathing of the sedated girl, drawn it seemed from some deep chamber by only the force of will, and the noisy snuffling of the infant at his mother's breast.

There's nothing I can do, Charity thought. These women have already begun to move on; they would be able to help the girl and her mother better than she could. There was no terrible spill of anger here, none of the fury that drove the mythical Kannagi to burn up her tormentors. This way was different, more practical, perhaps the only way left to the women of the village. There was good and evil, and both were necessary to keep the world in balance – you raged against Fate only when you didn't understand. It was best to accept and go on. Charity knew this too, of course, but she had forgotten it in her concern for Rachel. Quickly getting up, murmuring words of condolence, she fumbled in the knot of her sari for some coins, pressed them into the hands of the woman nearest to the girl and rose to go. As she stooped to leave the hut, the breeze of her passing disturbed the flies crawling over the baby. They stirred sluggishly, then settled once more.

9

Towards late evening, having completed the chapter he was working on and feeling calmer, Father Ashworth decided to take a walk on the beach. Chevathar's sunset was as dramatic as its dawn, and this evening the show was as good as it had ever been. As the sun subsided into the sea, a marvellous play of light and colour opened up. Shimmering bolts of orange, red, gold and a delicate lilac spread out in every direction. The fishing catamarans were coming in, further up the shore, slim black projectiles spearing through the bronzed surf. One of the fishermen would paddle and direct the nose of the craft, the other would stand and brace its passage through the waves, precise rhythmic movements as timeless and graceful as the world that lay about them. The return of the boats under the waning sun filled Father Ashworth with a deep melancholy, which had nothing to do with the recent events – it was something he often felt at this hour. Curiously enough, it was not a depressing feeling, more a sense of things closing down as night took over, putting an end to the day, its triumphs and its evils, its pain and its pleasure. This was the defining moment between light and dark. Its power and majesty came from its agelessness. It had been so when the spirit of God had moved upon the waters and it would be so a hundred years hence. Verses from Ecclesiastes came to him:

One generation passeth away, and another generation cometh:
but the earth abideth for ever.
The sun also ariseth, and the sun goeth down, and hasteth to his
place where he arose ...

He walked to where the Chevathar broke away from the estuary and cut through the tinted sands to merge with the quiet thunder of the Gulf of Mannar. More verses from his favourite book of the Bible rose in his mind:

All the rivers run into the sea; yet the sea is not full; unto the
place from whence the rivers come, thither they return
again ...

There was a verse he could never remember, and then the terrible beauty of the next:

The thing that hath been, it is that which shall be; and that
which is done is that which shall be done: and there is no new
thing under the sun.

The boats were almost all in now, the sun reddening the passage of the stragglers. The frail craft, the trim, work-hardened bodies of the fishermen, the great echoing power of the beach, none of this had been changed by time. This could be the Sea of Galilee; these the humble workers the master called to be fishers of men. Jesus would have been at home here, the priest thought. His followers were carpenters and peasants, not very different from the tenant farmers of Chevathar.

They lived and worked under the blazing sun, suffered under the colonial yoke, were tormented by devils and disputes, rape and murder ... As he watched the fishermen haul their catamarans up the beach he wondered what the message of Jesus would have been, had He lived and preached in India. Essentially the same, that was evident, but the parables would have changed. Instead of the vine and the fig tree there would have been rice and the mango tree, toddy would have replaced wine, and the Good Samaritan would probably have been the Good Marudar. But the basic truths that lay at the heart of the teaching would not have changed, could not have changed, for the Son of God had been fashioned by much the same circumstances as obtained in Chevathar.

A long way up the beach, he spotted a lone figure facing the westering sun. The speck of saffron that was wrapped around his indistinct body was all Father Ashworth needed to see to know who it was. It was the elderly poojari from the Murugan temple, and if it had been dawn and not dusk it was quite likely that he would be chanting rhythmically one of the most powerful mantrams the Gods had ever deigned to pass on to man, the Gayatri mantram, which the old man had taught the Christian priest before he had begun withdrawing from his duties and the world.

A disturbing image troubled Father Ashworth for an instant. He had heard it said that untouchables and the lowest of the low were forbidden from even hearing the holy chant and if they did, molten lead was poured into their ears. Will I ever come to terms with this country that is now my home, he thought. Will I ever understand it enough to be a truly effective vessel of Your will, Lord?

It was time to go to the headman's house. As he began making his way there, the question posed so exquisitely in Psalm 137 occurred to him: How shall we sing the Lord's song in a strange land?

The light was failing by the time he reached the house. There was no one about on the veranda. He slipped around to the back, hoping to meet Charity and Kamalambal. A frequent visitor to the house, his arrival didn't elicit more than a few half-hearted barks from the unsecured dogs in the backyard before they went back to more interesting pursuits. Only Daniel was outside. The boy was playing with something on the earthen stoop. As the priest approached, he looked up, frowned, then smiled.

'Look what I found this morning, Father, on my way home. From the big tank near the river.'

Father Ashworth looked down to see two little tortoises the size of his thumb, with a sunburst pattern on their black backs, moving creakily across the packed earth.

'Enchanting. We should try and find out what kind they are.'

'Will they grow any bigger?'

'I doubt it, they are not like turtles, though I have heard of land tortoises somewhere that grow to an enormous size.'

'Appa is in a terrible temper today,' Daniel said, changing the subject abruptly.

'I know, and with reason.'

'You're here for the meeting, then.'

'Yes, my son. Do you know where your mother is?'

'In the kitchen. Would you like me to tell her you're here?'

'No, no, I'll just walk around. The meeting is supposed to start soon.'

10

It was dark by the time the meeting began. Pinna-oil torches were lit, throwing a flickering light on the gathering. The courtyard in front of the house was covered with the colourful sedge mats indigenous to the region. There were more mats on the veranda. When Father Ashworth took his place at the back, he noticed the headman deep in conversation with Subramania Sastrigal, the poojari of the Murugan temple. He was sure Solomon was urging the priest to keep the peace among the Vedhars. Father Ashworth's joints creaked as he lowered himself to the ground. It had taken him months to get used to sitting on the ground when he had first arrived in Chevathar but then it had become more familiar to him than sitting on furniture. Of late, however, age had crept into his joints and sometimes he felt himself wishing for a comfortable chair. He looked around at the faces that rose out of the twilight. Vakeel Perumal, dressed as always in spotless white; Muthu Vedhar, the tall, imposing leader of the Vedhar community, whose wealth and prestige were next only to Solomon's; Swaminathan, the priest's son, who had virtually taken over the running of the Murugan temple; a scattering of village officials and tenant farmers, among them Kuppan, the father of the girl who was attacked; Chokkalingam, the grain merchant, who now lived across the bridge in town; a small deputation of Paraiyans; and four or five others.

There was a brief eruption of noise as the deputy tahsildar walked into the courtyard. Solomon stopped talking to the poojari and came forward to greet him with folded hands. The young official returned the thalaivar's greetings, acknowledged everyone else with a sweeping namaskaram and sat down facing the gathering, Solomon next to him.

Servants emerged from the house bearing palm-leaf plates holding coocoos, the famous honeycomb-shaped local sweet, black-wheat halwa, oompudi and banana chips, fat, yellow and crackly. Father Ashworth noted that the Brahmin priests were not served and that the chief of the Paraiyans, who sat some distance away from the main gathering, was served last. The buttermilk that was served in earthen cups to everyone else was served to him and his caste fellows in palm-leaf cups. Solomon, always the meticulous observer of caste rules!

After they had eaten and drunk, and the minimal courtesies and formalities were dispensed with, Solomon began to speak. 'Friends, brothers, people sprung from the earth of Chevathar,' he said, 'it is with great sadness on this holy Pangunni Uthiram day that I say that the disease of caste and religious violence has struck at the heart of our community. You all know some of the facts, but I would like to share with you everything I know, because together we must keep this demon from our village.'

Solomon's voice carried clear and crisp to his audience, who listened without sound or movement, the wavering light of the torches washing across their faces like gold. 'Last week on Ram Navami, two members of the Andavar community were caught by Swaminathan entering the inner precincts of the Murugan temple to offer prayers. They were beaten up by the other worshippers and although I condemn the beating I condemn too the actions of those who went against time-tested traditions and customs.'

'Tradition and custom are the handiwork of puny little men and perverted priests,' Vakeel Perumal roared. Solomon glared angrily at him. A voice behind the lawyer murmured, 'The polluting castes should know their place.' It was Swaminathan, the young Brahmin priest, who had spoken. Quickly twisting around, Vakeel Perumal said, 'And what would you know, you illiterate fool? Anyone who is acquainted with the shastras knows that the greatest seers were not Brahmins but belonged to other castes, who by their deeds proclaimed their superiority. Lord Krishna said this to Arjuna, every holy work says this: it is by your deeds that you are known, not by your birth.'

'And everyone knows you were misbegotten,' the young priest sneered. Vakeel Perumal scrambled to his feet and had taken a step towards the man, when he was arrested in his tracks by Solomon's incensed voice. 'If none of you can behave with the dignity of elders, is it any wonder that this village is being consumed by pisasus? Be quiet now, unless you would rather face my wrath.'

The gathering went completely silent. The palm trees rustled in the darkness. A couple of minutes passed and then Solomon began to speak again. 'As you all know, this morning the ultimate indignity was visited on the soon-to-be-married daughter of our brother Kuppan. It's a cruel irony that this tragedy took place on a day we celebrate the marriage of the Gods.' The father of the girl sat as if carved from granite, not a feature of his face moving. 'Valli was attacked near Anaikal. The girl who was with her didn't recognize the attackers but thought they were strangers. But the matter became even more serious when we discovered an obscene message written on Anaikal. Someone here is trying to destroy the peace and brotherhood of our village by besmirching the honour of our sisters, mothers and daughters.'

As Solomon said this he looked straight at Muthu Vedhar. The implication was not lost on anyone at the meeting. Muthu was quick to react. Getting to his feet with an agility that belied his vast size, he spat, 'Am I being accused of something?'

'I'm not accusing you of anything, Muthu, please sit down.'

'No, I will not sit down, nor will I be insulted by you.'

'I haven't insulted you.' Solomon's voice was cold.

'Am I imagining things then?' Muthu said dramatically. His gigantic frame and the anger that lit his eyes made him a terrifying figure to behold. 'You may not have accused me by name, but not everything needs to be said to be understood. Enough, I will not be part of these ridiculous proceedings.' Without looking at anyone, he walked off into the night. A couple of the Vedhar farmers who were present followed their leader.

After a long, long pause, Solomon spoke into the silence that had descended. 'This is truly Kaliyuga, the age of degeneration, when dharma limps along on one leg, and wickedness and evil walk the earth.' He paused, then spoke again with a new firmness in his voice. 'But let this be known. As one born on this soil, and as the representative of Government in this village, I pledge that whoever has committed this atrocity will not be spared. I have discussed the matter with the esteemed deputy tahsildar, and he has said that the culprit will be punished with the utmost severity.'

Having delivered himself of this, Solomon called on the deputy tahsildar to speak. Dipty Vedhar spoke briefly and gravely about the seriousness with which the Government viewed any outbreak of caste and communal violence. He said if there was any further escalation of violence, he would be forced to requisition a detachment of special riot police which the villagers would have to pay for. In addition, there would be a punitive tax on the whole area if the matter were allowed to get out of hand. The police were investigating the molestation of the girl, and when the culprits were apprehended they would be dealt with severely. For the sake of the villagers, he hoped it was outsiders who had perpetrated this outrage.

The proceedings dragged on as the other elders spoke and voiced their concern, but the outraged departure of Muthu Vedhar cast a shadow over the meeting. The suspicion would grow that he was the victim of gross injustice at the hands of the thalaivar. Where was it going to end, Father Ashworth thought with dismay. Where was trouble going to erupt next?

11

After the meeting concluded, a sombre Solomon Dorai once again ate his wife's delicious fish biryani without savouring it. Once again, he refused a second helping although his manner was not brusque. When Charity pressed him, he said, 'I have no appetite tonight.'

'Can I get you anything?'

When he shook his head, she made to go, but he asked her to stay. This was most unusual, for he rarely wanted her around when he ate. After she had disposed of the plantain leaf he had eaten from, and Solomon had washed his hands, she settled herself on a mat. For a moment, she wondered whether to mention her afternoon excursion, then dismissed the thought. They sat in silence for a while, then Solomon spoke. 'The meeting went badly. Muthu left in a rage. He thought I was accusing him of the crime.'

He looked tired and harassed. 'I can't allow this matter to get out of hand. It will be the end of Chevathar if I do.'

'Perhaps you should speak to Muthu-anna,' she said, and immediately wished she hadn't. Solomon glanced sharply at her, then, to her amazement, nodded slowly.

'Yes, I'll go and see him soon.'

They sat a while longer in silence, and then Solomon said unexpectedly, 'You don't wear jasmine in your hair any longer.'

Charity looked away, her eyes shining.

For the past two years, ever since he had built the new front room, he had slept alone, while she had shared a room with their daughters. She couldn't even remember the last time they had talked at night.

'Are you sure you have everything you need? I must go and serve food to the others.'

Solomon said nothing but as he watched her leave his worries seemed to lift away.

Later, when Charity had finished her work in the kitchen, she slipped out into the backyard. By the wall stood a few jasmine bushes, the fragrance of their flowers infiltrating the cool air. Deftly, she plucked the little white malligai orbs and began threading them into a garland for her hair.

12

Two days after the attack, Valli hanged herself from a tree at the edge of the Andavar quarter. The women in the village grieved. For a brief moment, each one of them experienced afresh the deep sadness of being born a woman. They were sorry that the girl had taken her life and they prayed that in her next birth she would be born with a luckier alignment of planets. But their sorrow was tempered by the hope that her passing would ease tensions a little, make all their lives a bit easier. In a land where everyday realities were harsh, what did the death of a tenant farmer's daughter signify anyhow? As it turned out, quite a lot, much to everyone's surprise.

Happening as it did, in an anxious time, in an idle time before the fields could be prepared, in a desperate time when the entire land simmered with frustration and hate, her death transformed her from an insignificant girl without affiliation (not quite married, on the point of leaving her natal home) into a weapon that would deepen the division and rancour within the village.

When news of the suicide reached him, Solomon abandoned any idea he might have had of going to see Muthu Vedhar. He went to see the deputy tahsildar instead, and persuaded him to post a couple of policemen in the village, armed with the long Snider carbines that were brought out only in emergencies. One was stationed in the Andavar quarter and the second near the Vedhar houses. This brought an immediate and furious response from Muthu Vedhar, still smarting under the insult he had received at the meeting. 'Either you control that man or I will,' he roared at his kinsman, the deputy tahsildar.

Dipty Vedhar did not flinch. 'I have my instructions, Muthu-aiyah,' he said courteously. 'Law and order is the top priority at the moment and I cannot allow any disturbance in the village.'

'So you believe I was responsible for the attack?'

'Not at all,' Dipty Vedhar replied smoothly. 'And to show my good faith I'm removing the policeman posted near your house. Why should I fear any trouble when I have a powerful leader such as you to keep the peace?' This piece of flattery, which fooled neither man, nevertheless had the effect of mollifying Muthu, and he returned to the village, bad-tempered as before, but not inclined to violence and destruction.

His temper did not improve that night when his wife passed on some gossip picked up during the day. Saraswati Vedhar had heard versions of the episode at the various points of her morning round – the tank where she and a couple of high-ranking Vedhar women bathed, the backyard where her servants and relatives gossiped and fought. Apparently, a close ally (as always unspecified) of the thalaivar had said that Solomon himself had hired the four loafers to molest the girl and to write the slogan on the rock in order to provoke Muthu to action so he would have cause to have him arrested, or maybe even banished from the village. Muthu, who would normally have rejected this fantastical scheme out of hand, spent some time mulling over it. Gradually, he dismissed it from his mind. He had known Solomon for a long time, and while he disliked him, he didn't think he was capable of such machinations. That slimy Salem lawyer, yes, but Solomon, no. This exoneration of his great enemy did not in any way lessen his antipathy towards him.

13

Muthu Vedhar and Solomon Dorai had been pitted against each other from the time they were young. Even though at eighteen Muthu was eight inches taller than Solomon at seventeen, he had never managed to beat him at silambu-attam, the art of stick-fighting, which was the skill by which all young men in the village were judged. Solomon made up for his lack of inches with speed and ferocity, and time and time again Muthu had to accept defeat at the hands of his younger rival.

They had married within a year of each other and to Muthu's chagrin, his wife had produced daughters to Solomon's sons. His third child was a son, but once again his rival had the advantage. Muthu had been delighted when Solomon's first son displayed none of his father's toughness but was soon disappointed when his second son, Aaron, had proved to be an even better athlete than his father.

This rivalry extended to land and village. Unlike Solomon Dorai's family, Muthu Vedhar's claim to the soil of the Chevathar was relatively new. His family had come from the upcountry town of Korkai. His great-grandfather, a second son, had left the ancestral property and wandered south in search of a place to raise his own family. He had eventually landed in the service of a big zamindar in neighbouring Tinnevelly district. Amassing enough wealth, he migrated to Kilanad, bought land and built a house in the small Vedhar settlement on the outskirts of Meenakshikoil.

The family had prospered and within the space of two generations owned forty-two acres of rice fields on both sides of the river, in addition to coconut and banana groves. By then the town of Meenakshikoil had grown and started encroaching upon Vedhar land. To the astonishment of his family, Muthu's father, Parameshwara Vedhar, announced that he was going to construct a new house for himself on a vacant patch of land across the river. This was regarded as a sure sign of crankiness, if not outright madness. How could he leave the safety of the Vedhar quarter and contend alone with devils, robbers and low castes who would attack a single dwelling without hesitation? But Parameshwara was undeterred. He managed to bribe a couple of his kinsmen to accompany him, with promises of land and a remission in tribute. And, to everyone's consternation, he invited the lower castes to build houses free of charge within sight of his own house. Within a generation, the lower castes were relocated and the bulk of the Vedhars had moved across the river, coming into direct conflict with the ruling Andavars. However, although Gnanaprakasam Andavar, Solomon's father, and Parameshwara Vedhar were not close friends, they were bound by ties of mutual respect. It was not until Muthu's time that the two families grew hostile. The antipathy between them was heightened when Solomon began farming seven acres of land by the river that Muthu claimed was his. Lately, the whiplash of caste wars between Andavars and Vedhars in the district had added to the tension between the two. But the peace had held. Until now.

Over the past days Muthu had brooded obsessively about ways in which he could get the better of Solomon. This morning, after his bath, he had even briefly considered seeking out Solomon and challenging him to battle, just the two of them, with the loser leaving the village for ever. The thought passed quickly; this was no longer the India of duels and heroic deeds by warriors and princes, the authorities frowned on that sort of thing. But Muthu knew that wasn't the only reason for backing away from a fight. Deep down, he wasn't sure he would be able to win. As he made his way to his house, his grim countenance ensuring that everyone gave him a wide berth, he continued to agonize over the situation. Like Solomon, Muthu didn't really need to be thalaivar of Chevathar. As the second biggest mirasidar in the taluqa (the one hundred and seventeen acres he owned or rented were dwarfed only by Solomon's two hundred and twenty-three), he had wealth and prestige to spare. He could easily have moved to one of the other villages he owned so that he didn't come into conflict with Solomon. But their long-standing rivalry ruled out that option.

As he stalked up the steps into his house, ignoring the usual supplicants who gathered daily for favours, money or advice, he wondered, for the umpteenth time since the latest clash with Solomon, whether he or his people would ever be able to come up with something to drive the wretched Dorais from Chevathar.

Perhaps it was simply that his kinsmen were not destined to flourish on this soil as the Andavars were. Every villager knew that a man who didn't find soil that suited his nature would not prosper. Brahmins thrived on sweet soil, like that found in the delta at the mouth of a river, which is why Subramania Sastrigal and his ambitious young son would never thrive on the astringent soil of Chevathar. They might squeak and flail away at the Dorais but one roar from Solomon would send them scurrying for cover. But surely the kunam of the Vedhars matched the soil of Chevathar, which was neither sweet nor sour, salty nor pungent but was fairly bitter – the soil of people of the earth, farmers and artisans. That is what the young priest of the Murugan temple said, but what the fool forgot was that Solomon was as much farmer and artisan as Muthu himself. He and his family had flourished on this land for generations, and what better proof that the nature of the soil was eminently compatible with the nature of his caste than this fact? No, the red earth of Chevathar was not going to be of much help in his attempt to dislodge Solomon. He would need to act boldly and decisively if ever he were to succeed.

14

Vakeel Perumal's cleverness as a lawyer was often neutralized by his impatience. Time and time again, on the verge of victory in an important case, he would either lose interest in the proceedings or insult his opponent, or simply forget a crucial argument, thus landing his unfortunate client in jail or worse. His father had left him a modest fortune, thus increasing his irresponsibility. What had finally done him in was his casual handling of a case of armed robbery against a Marudar client. Vakeel Perumal's defence was so brilliant that he had almost got the man off, until in his arrogance he had quite openly tried to turn a witness for the prosecution with a bribe. The English District Sessions judge was not amused and would have disbarred him, but with some brilliant legal legerdemain Vakeel Perumal had squirmed out from under. His client wasn't as fortunate. He received the maximum possible sentence for his crime. As he was led away, the man had hissed – 'When I have finished with the vakeel, not even the pigs of Salem will be able to make a meal of him.' Vakeel Perumal left town with his wife and two daughters before the thug could put his threat into action. Chevathar, where his wife had a distant cousin, seemed the perfect place to wait out the storm.

When he arrived in the village, he had immediately tried to make his presence felt. After the excitement of Salem, he was impatient with the slowness and rusticity of Chevathar. He felt the only way to make his period of exile bearable was to stir things up. He had no doubt that he would succeed in making an impact on the affairs of the village. He had the money, he had the brains, and he had his town-bred sophistication – what could be easier? But he hadn't reckoned with himself. With his impatience and vanity, he swiftly succeeded in offending everyone of consequence. Muthu Vedhar had beaten him up in the presence of his wife and children, after the lawyer had been overheard referring to Muthu as a stupid buffalo. And he had annoyed Solomon on more than one occasion with his meddling ways. The ordinary villagers were impressed with Vakeel Perumal's wealth, his two-storey house, and the outdoor lavatory he had had built to his specifications, but Solomon seemed impervious. In Vakeel Perumal's scheme of things, it was important to get the headman on his side if he wanted to get his own back on Muthu, which he was determined to do. And, if the headman managed to subdue or drive out Muthu, Vakeel Perumal assumed he would automatically become the secondmost important person in the village. His would be the voice Solomon would be forced to listen to, until he, Vakeel Perumal, was ready to move against the headman himself. Although nominally an Andavar, Vakeel Perumal felt no especial loyalty towards members of his own caste. The only thing that mattered to him was his own welfare, so he had no qualms about plotting against a kinsman.

It was immensely frustrating for Vakeel Perumal, then, that nothing was going as planned. Even his latest initiative had ended in disaster. Vakeel Perumal had never meant to have Valli molested. It was a Vedhar woman the thugs had been hired to terrorize in retribution for the attack on the Andavars at the temple. Once the deed was done, the lawyer was sure the tension between the two groups would run so high that it would be easy for a man of his genius to turn it to his advantage. But it hadn't worked. He might still have salvaged the situation but things had continued to go wrong. Nothing had come of his idea of painting the incendiary message on Anaikal. Who would have expected those two idiots Solomon and Muthu to exercise such restraint? For a few days it looked as though a confrontation might actually take place, in which case there would have been opportunities that he could certainly have used. Now it appeared that there would be no fighting after all, despite the lawyer seeding the village with the rumour that Solomon had hired the thugs in order to discredit Muthu. Vakeel Perumal had half-expected Muthu to charge at the headman in a fury and get poleaxed in the process. It hadn't happened, and he had been very disappointed. But he wasn't the sort of person to dwell on his defeats for too long, and he had already started planning other schemes.

Vakeel Perumal had considered befriending Father Ashworth soon after he had established himself in Chevathar. But when he noticed his deep interest in India, he had decided the priest was unworthy of his attention. He had none of the contempt for natives that other Englishmen had in abundance, and this in the lawyer's view was an important disqualification. But now the Englishman was the only person left whom Vakeel Perumal might utilize, so he decided to be nice to him.

He was thinking of Father Ashworth as he read an article in the newspaper about Easter being celebrated the following day. By the time he was halfway through the piece, an idea came to him. He yelled for his wife. When she appeared in the room, he said excitedly, 'We're going to become Christians.'

Kamala, a rather stolid woman, was used to her husband's sudden enthusiasms and said incuriously, 'Why? I thought we were quite happy being Hindus.'

'Yes, yes, but Easter is tomorrow.'

'What about it?'

'Oh, you stupid woman, that's when Jesus Christ, the Christian God, is born again.'

'You mean like one of Narayana's avatars?'

'No, no, you madwoman. Anyway, from today you are Mary and I am Jesus Christ.' These were the only Christian names Vakeel Perumal could find in the rather sketchy account. Just then his younger daughter, Vasanthi, wandered into the room.

'And what will she be?' his wife asked, getting into the spirit of things.

Vakeel Perumal was nonplussed for a moment, then he said airily, 'No harm in her being Mary as well!'

'And Nirmala, will she be Mary too?'

'No, she will not be Mary. I'll find her a name. Get me my shirt and trousers, I'm going to visit the Christian priest.'

Father Ashworth received Vakeel Perumal in the front room of the parsonage.

'Good morning, aiyah. I'm Jesus Christ,' Vakeel Perumal began.

The priest wasn't sure he had heard right and asked with exquisite courtesy, 'Can I offer you some tea?'

It took a few moments of puzzled conversation before Father Ashworth worked out the purpose of the lawyer's visit. It had been so long since anyone had come to him asking to be baptized into the faith that it took him a while to come to terms with Vakeel Perumal's request. Then he grew suspicious. In all the time that he had known the lawyer, he hadn't detected the slightest interest in Christianity in him. He began quizzing him, and his suspicions deepened. Vakeel Perumal seemed to know very little about the religion. Sensing the priest's hostility, Vakeel Perumal quickly said that he was prepared to install an idol of Jesus Christ in his prayer room that very day, to which his family and he would do pooja.

'Christianity does not encourage that form of worship,' the priest observed.

'Yes, yes,' Vakeel Perumal replied flustered, 'we won't do pooja.'

Father Ashworth was about to rise and show his visitor out when Christ's injunction to His apostles in the Sermon on the Mount came to mind: 'Judge not that ye be not judged ...' Father Ashworth looked at the man before him, and despite his misgivings heard himself say, 'To be baptized into the one true faith is the greatest gift that any human being can receive.' As he said this to the lawyer, another image rose in the priest's mind: of Saul on the road to Damascus. No light illuminated the figure of the lawyer but the glory of Christ's love had transformed worse men. If the Lord had commanded the man before him to cast off his old raiment and put on the garments of Christ, who was he, Paul Ashworth, ineffectual fisher of men, to object? And his bishop was certain to be pleased. After years of drought this flood of converts (for the lawyer claimed, untruthfully, that in addition to his own family, there were ten others who wanted to become Christians) would be very welcome.

Before the lawyer left, the padre invited him with his family to Easter service the next day and provided him with two editions of the New Testament. He also gave him a choice of Christian names, gently dissuading him from Jesus Christ. They finally settled on Peter Jesu for Vakeel Perumal, Mary for Kamala, and Martha and Hannah for Vasanthi and Nirmala respectively.

Back in his own house, Vakeel Perumal was well pleased with the morning's activities. He was glad he hadn't given in to a stray impulse to confess that he'd been behind the attack on the Andavar girl. He had vaguely heard that Christians confessed to priests, but what if the priest told Solomon? He had been disappointed that the priest couldn't baptize him immediately, but cheered up when Father Ashworth said he would be received into the faith in a fortnight.

Vakeel Perumal put aside the preoccupation of the morning and focused on work that had been interrupted by his reading of the article on Easter. It was a letter to the *Hindu*, the fifty-fourth in a series that he had sent to the newspaper at the rate of one a fortnight. The fact that only one letter had been published didn't faze him at all. This was something he did in between his other schemes, and he intended to keep it up until the editor gave in and began publishing him regularly.

Today's letter was little different in substance from the fifty-three letters that had preceded it.

> Respected Sir, [Vakeel Perumal wrote]
>
> I would like to draw the attention of the esteemed readers of your great newspaper to the monstrous indignity visited upon the whole clan of persons known as the Andavars. As every member of the Tamil race knows, the Andavars trace their origins to the chief of the Vedic Gods, Indra. These divine origins made the Andavars rulers; indeed, as every Andavar knows, some centuries back, Andavar kings ruled mighty kingdoms that now lie buried under the burning red sands of the teri wastes. Not a day passes when further ruins do not come to light, justifying this belief. When, through dastardly tricks and stratagems, the ancestors of our great race were defeated by the foreigners from the north, the Telugu Nayaks, they were forced into exile. Divested of their lands and privileges, branded as lower castes by the insecure invaders, the Andavars had to learn how to practise a variety of trades for which their refinement had not prepared them. Meanwhile, their enemies were busy fabricating records to show that they were high and the Andavars low, while simultaneously destroying the actual historical records that proved the Andavars were rightfully Dravidian kshatriyas, emperors of the first rank. Woe betides us. But the enemies of the Andavars should beware because we will come again to rule the Tamil lands ...

Vakeel Perumal rambled on in this manner for a further two sheets, his arguments growing increasingly disjointed and shrill.

Neatly finishing, 'Your correspondent from Chevathar Village, Meenakshikoil P.O., Kilanad District', he signed the letter with a flourish: Peter Jesu Perumal. Perhaps they would publish this letter, Vakeel Perumal thought, given that it was signed with a Christian name.

15

Father Ashworth had found sleep elusive as he fretted over the thalaivar's reaction to Vakeel Perumal's conversion. Somehow he knew Solomon wouldn't receive the news gladly. He had decided to delay telling him and now, as he waited by the church door for the Easter service to begin, his nervousness grew. The strains of the opening hymn came to him, sung tunelessly but lustily, and he began the walk that he hated through the narrow, ill-lit wall to the pulpit.

Up from the grave He arose
With a mighty triumph over his foes.
He arose a visitor from the dark domain
And He lives forever with
His saints to reign.
He arose! Hallelujah! Christ arose!

As the last 'arose' died away, Father Ashworth stepped out of the wall and read the Collect of the day. The service settled into the familiar pattern, with the appropriate modifications that Easter called for, and he began to relax.

A fleeting memory passed through his mind of an especially ungracious pastor who would deliberately choose obscure hymns that nobody knew and secretly enjoy (of this the young Ashworth was convinced) the discomfiture of his flock. He was beginning to smile when he caught the eye of Solomon, who was glowering at him from the first line of mats, and immediately composed himself. The reason for Solomon's annoyance was clear: Peter Jesu Perumal, until recently known as Vakeel Perumal, sat two places behind him, with his wife and daughters. They sat stiffly, holding their new Bibles and dressed in their best saris and skirts. Vakeel Perumal was, as usual, resplendent in white trousers and shirt.

The service rolled on, against the deep rumble of the sea in the background. Abruptly a breeze arose, setting the fronds of the palm trees rustling and giving the congregation some small respite from the gathering heat. An incongruous thought popped into Father Ashworth's head as the sweat began to dry on his cassock: three hundred million years ago, Asia and Africa had been ice-bound at the Pole, while Europe and North America had sweltered at the

equator. Wouldn't it be wonderful if the world rearranged itself again in the not-so-distant future? It would set the seal on Chevathar's perfection if it could be chilly at Easter. The thought passed, and he wondered what he would say to Solomon at the end of the service.

As the Nicene Creed finished, the Reverend Ashworth, carefully avoiding the eye of Solomon, made the day's announcements. After detailing church activities and births and marriages, he said, 'And I would now like to welcome into our midst Peter Jesu Perumal, Mary Perumal, Martha Perumal and Hannah Perumal.'

As he read out the last name, the Reverend Ashworth finally looked in Solomon's direction but the headman was scowling down at the floor. Father Ashworth hoped the spirit of Easter would help sweeten the other's disposition a bit.

But for now he couldn't afford to dwell too much on Solomon or Vakeel Perumal; he had a sermon to deliver. He closed his eyes for a moment, lost in the beauty of the one Eternal Truth, and thus dissociated from the confusion of the immediate, launched into his sermon. It was one of the best he had ever given. Without naming Andavar, Vedhar, Brahmin or Marudar, the priest attacked the divisions that rose among men on account of their losing sight of the peace and love of God. 'Put on the new man,' the Reverend Ashworth cried, echoing the words of Paul the Apostle, 'which is renewed in knowledge after the image of him that created him. Where there is neither Greek nor Jew, circumcision nor uncircumcision, barbarian, Scythian, bond nor free: but Christ is all, and in all.'

No longer shrinking from the eye of Solomon, he lashed at the petty conceits of men. He dwelled on the fact that the paths to God were many and he called for the spirit of Easter to walk abroad in the land. Even his newest recruits seemed to realize that this was a special moment.

'Forbearing one another, and forgiving one another, if any man have a quarrel against any: even as Christ forgave you, so also do ye.'

The words flowed over them, welling up from depths that Father Ashworth didn't know existed within him. He had forgotten his prepared sermon and though he didn't quite have a vision of the Creator speaking through him, it was almost as though that was indeed the case.

By the time the service was over, the breeze had steadied and become constant; the fronds of the palms fringing the mission compound rustled back and forth like elephant ears. In the shade of two massive puvarasu trees the women of the congregation, supervised

by Charity, were organizing lunch. Three long rows of mats were laid out; as the guests sat down, plantain leaves were placed in front of them. When the first serving boys appeared, each guest automatically picked up his leaf and expertly rinsed it with water from his tumbler. In years of plenty, St Paul's always served a great feast at Easter – avial, two kinds of poriyal, pachidi, raw mango kootu, mutton curry and rice, curd rice and payasam – but this year there was only one main course: mutton biryani followed by paal payasam. However, the biryani was cooked to perfection, each mouthful of rice spiced with nutmeg, clove and cashew-nut, and full of tender meat. As its fragrance filled the air, the members of the flock, seemingly impervious to the heat, glare and flies that swarmed over the food, began to stoop to the serious business of eating.

Solomon stood by the wall of the mission compound, looking out to sea. He was dressed formally: gold-embroidered turban, dusty black coat buttoned at the collar, a new white veshti. He even wore shoes. When Father Ashworth walked up to him, he returned the priest's Easter greeting mechanically and continued to look out to where the sea lay shimmering, a rich confection of gold and green.

'Why did you accept them into the Church?' Solomon asked finally.

'It is not for us to judge those who hunger for God's Word.'

'Vakeel Perumal does not hunger for anything but his own importance.'

'Didn't our Lord Jesus Christ take the humblest, most ill-suited vessel to carry out His work?'

'I doubt whether our Lord would have been able to use Vakeel Perumal. I wouldn't be surprised to see him using the Lord for his own purpose. He is a lying, crooked, mischief-making rascal and I don't think you and I can even begin to imagine the consequences of this conversion.'

The object of their conversation was looking a bit lost. He looked around not a little anxiously. The Reverend Ashworth smiled at him, which was enough for Vakeel Perumal to break away from his group and make his way over to them. The priest greeted the lawyer cordially, and stiffly Solomon followed suit.

'I'm very pleased that I can now call Solomon-aiyah a true elder brother,' the lawyer said unctuously. Fleetingly, the thought of what the headman might do to him if he discovered that he was responsible for the Pangunni Uthiram troubles shook Vakeel Perumal's composure, then his elastic conscience came to his rescue. How could he be held responsible if the incompetent thugs had attacked the wrong girl! Without giving the matter another thought, he said to Father Ashworth, 'This is the most wonderful religion, padre, and the stress it lays on forgiveness means Solomon-aiyah and I can put the past behind us and become part of the universal brotherhood of the one true Lord. In fact, there's something I've been meaning to discuss with you, Solomon-anna ...'

Solomon managed to suppress the retort that rose to his lips, but only just. He didn't bother to conceal the disgust Vakeel Perumal's presence roused in him. Glaring at the priest, who pretended not to notice, Solomon abruptly turned on his heel and went to join his family. The lawyer's face fell, then grew furious.

Adding to Father Ashworth's discomfiture was the fact that the Dorais left without pausing to sample the Easter lunch.

16

Before genetics, electricity and modern irrigation techniques confused the seasons, the farming communities of the deep south ordered their lives by the monsoon. Through most of the region there was but a single harvest, which meant that for six months of the year the villagers were furiously busy, and then for the next six months time lay heavy on their hands. The first monsoon clouds streamed out of the Indian Ocean in June, crashed into the Western Ghats, and shed rain on the parched land. The princely state of Travancore and other points north and west got the lion's share of the southeast monsoon, but even the scanty showers they received meant the difference between full bellies and the spectre of starvation for the farming communities of Kilanad district. Besides, the heavy downpour in the mountains brought rain-fed rivers such as the Chevathar to life.

As the first showers fell, the rice fields were ploughed and readied for sowing. Rich landowners, like Solomon Dorai, had their own ploughing animals but the tenant farmers had no option but to rent bullocks, thus increasing their indebtedness. The rains increased in intensity and frequency, and the rice was transplanted from seedbeds into flooded paddies by the village women, a thankless, backbreaking task, somewhat alleviated by song and neighbourly chatter. When the monsoon was bountiful, the paddies were soon thick with young rice, green and bright as an emerald dove.

The grain ripened on the stalk and then the northwest monsoon swept in. This time the farmers prayed that the rains wouldn't damage the standing harvest. Finally, green having turned to gold, the rice was ready to be reaped. The villages filled with activity – the busy days of the harvest, followed by a myriad other tasks: stone or wood grindstones threshing the last vestiges of grain from rice stalks, heavily laden bullock carts trundling single file along dusty paths shadowed by great banyan trees, vast hayricks being built in the yards and fields ... If the crop was bountiful, January was a time to celebrate. During that most auspicious and lively of festivals, Pongal, the villagers rejoiced with new clothes, gifts, song, dance and worship and, most traditional of all, the boiling of new rice from the first harvest, fragrant and sweet as a baby's breath. After the exhilarating days of Pongal, the short spring would commence, and in years of good harvests when money and goodwill were not in short supply, everyone looked forward to the great festivals of March and April – Ram Navami, Pangunni Uthiram, the beginning of the Tamil New Year, Easter, Madurai Shri Meenakshi's wedding, Mohurram, and wrapping up the first half of the year, the dramatic Chitra Pournami festival that took place on full moon day in late April or early May. In good years, the villages exploded with joy, warmth and religious fervour. In bad years, when the granaries were empty, they exploded because anger, hunger and frustration brought out the worst in the villagers. At such times, the festivals became occasions of strife, abuse and bloodletting.

It was Solomon's custom to visit all the villages he owned in the dry months of April and May to check their preparations for the coming monsoon. This year he had sent his brother Abraham to visit their land in the southeast. He himself would travel to the north and the west.

From the beginning of the month, drums had sounded in various temples. The drumming increased in intensity as Chitra Pournami approached. Normally, the first pre-monsoon showers should have hit the dry, parched fields and river beds, the cue for the farmers to begin their frenzied preparation of rice fields. But this year, although the sky grew rough and scaly with clouds, no rain fell. As the last week of April arrived without a whisper of rain, Solomon grew worried. One more drought and he would need to petition the Government for help in digging wells and he knew how slim his chances were. He himself was fortunate. He had mixed crops and at least some of them would continue to provide revenue. But his mango groves, paddy and cotton would suffer if the rains failed. And how would he provide for the tenant farmers who rented land? And the other villagers in his care?

Thankfully, Muthu had held his peace and even Vakeel Perumal, or Peter Jesu Perumal as Solomon should now remember to call him, had not caused any difficulty. When his brother Abraham returned from his visit, his report was less than encouraging. On the spur of the moment, Solomon decided to set out on his own inspection tour the next day. He promised Father Ashworth that he would be back in time for Vakeel Perumal's baptism, set for later that week.

There would be no time to alert the headmen and overseers of the various villages but perhaps that was just as well: he would be able to see for himself just how bad the situation was. He ordered three covered carts to be ready to leave before daybreak.

A brain fever bird piped them out of the village before dawn. The carts creaked and rattled through a closed and sleeping world. They made good time on the metalled road and were soon at the bridge across the Chevathar. In Meenakshikoil a few pariah dogs barked desultorily at the little convoy, but soon gave up. They took the main road out of town, heading north. Huddled in a blanket, Solomon could smell the sharp acrid tang of his magnificent Nellores, their horns shaped like an embrace. He whispered a command in the ear of the cartman, who gently twisted the tails of the bullocks. That was all the encouragement they needed; their trot became a canter, then a dead run. Solomon was exhilarated. The nippy morning air, the smell and rhythm of his bullocks at a gallop, this was what he lived for.

The moon was almost full and it hung low in the sky. They had probably an hour and a half until daybreak. A couple of miles on, they turned off the main road on to a dirt track. During the rains this path would be a treacherous morass, but now the dust lay soft and fine as rice flour, the cart's passage leaving a long brown streamer hanging in the still air. Their progress slowed but not by a lot; the bullocks knew the way, and needed little urging to keep up the pace. They flew past isolated little huts of palm-thatch and mud, rushed through villages that slept and still they kept on under the pale light of the moon.

Sometimes their path would run along the Chevathar and it saddened Solomon to see the cracked and dry bed of the river. He remembered the time, nearly twenty-five years ago now, when Joshua and he had decided to follow the river all the way to its source. It had been the monsoon season and about ten miles upriver the Chevathar had become a monstrous swollen beast, full of turbulence and violence, as it sought to free itself from its course. Their journey had been interrupted at a place where the river had breached its banks, rendering the road impassable, and they'd had to turn back. Although they'd promised themselves that they would try again the coming year, they had never done so.

As the carts rattled on beside the shrunken river, Solomon tried to follow it in his mind's eye to its beginnings as a tributary of the mighty Tamraparani. Their boyhood ambition had been to get to the headwaters of the Tamraparani itself, where it rose on the slopes of Agastya Malai, the mountain to which the great northern sage Agasthiar had retired after giving the Tamil country its language, grammar and enough myth and legend to support several generations of priests, scholars and scribes, not to mention releasing the Kaveri from the confines of his water-pitcher, vanquishing hosts of demons and asuras, drinking up the water of the ocean to enable the Devas to exterminate their enemies who had taken refuge beneath the waves and, most famously, commanding the Vindhyas to stop growing until he returned from his sojourn in the south, which of course he never did. From its source Joshua and Solomon had planned to wander along the course of the river – down the Southern Ghats, across the vast Tinnevelly plain and all the way to the Gulf of Mannar. River of pearls, rajahs and rishis, the Tamraparani was only seventy miles long but it had been celebrated from the most ancient times and had firmly lodged in their imagination. As, of course, had the Chevathar. A mere stream at twenty-eight miles in length, it had certainly not been exalted in poetry, myth and travelogue, but still it was their river and it had always been a regret that they had never been able to complete the journey. Perhaps he would still make it, especially if Joshua were to return.

The convoy turned right at a tumbled mass of boulders. The road began to rise but the Nellores made light work of the climb and they had soon topped the incline and were in a rougher, less cultivated world, where the dead fields with their blond stubble of hay and rice stalks gave way to flat-topped acacia and gnarled outcrops of gneiss and granite. The young Sub-Collector from Ranivoor had once told Solomon that the rocks in this area were among the oldest in the world. What stories these stern silent witnesses could tell, he thought. There was need for caution now, as the cart-track had almost petered out and knobs of stone rose abruptly out of the ground. A cart could lose a wheel, or worse, an axle. They slowed to a trot. A village assumed shape and solidity as light began to trickle into the world. There had been a short, sharp caste riot here a few years ago in which four people had died, but now it looked peaceful enough. They rattled through it, a cacophony of sound – cocks crowing, dogs barking – marking their passage. The few villagers who emerged from their huts silently watched the three carts pass. And then they were through.

Ahead rose the great palmyra forest, the cockaded palms tall and erect. Eighty-seven acres and the bedrock of the Dorai fortune. All around them the land glowed a deep red as though the intense heat of summer had plunged deep within the earth and taken up permanent residence there.

A polished sky of crimson and rose hung low over the palmyra forest; any lower, Solomon Dorai thought, and the spiky tops of the trees would score its smooth surface. The toddy tappers were already at work, for they couldn't leave their trees unattended, even briefly, when the sap was flowing during the hot summer and monsoon months. He got off his cart and watched a climber begin to ascend a palm. The man, short, wiry and almost as black as the trunk of the tree, slipped a short loop of rope around his feet, then took a little jump and gripped the rough, serrated bark with the instep and soles of his feet and his powerful arms on which the muscles rippled like silk. Clasping the tree tightly, he surged upward with a series of smooth jumps, moving as fast as a man walking on level ground. At the top he reached for the fleshy spathe of flowers and made a delicate incision with a small curved knife he carried. From the folded lungi which was the only garment he wore, he took out a small earthen pot. He secured this to the spathe and descended. Every day when the sap was running, the tree would yield three to four litres of sweet toddy. This precious 'nectar of the Gods' would either be allowed to ferment to produce the strong country liquor that was the staple of most of the villagers or it would be boiled down in cauldrons by women to make delicious jaggery.

A few of the toddy tappers recognized Solomon and came forward, snatching off their turbans, tying them around their waists and bowing deeply. One of them shouted something and a cup, deftly fashioned out of a palmyra leaf, was deferentially handed to the thalaivar. Another man brought up a pot of freshly milked toddy, unfermented and sweet, and poured it into the cup. Solomon lifted it and drank deeply. The taste exploded on his tongue. He accepted another cup as he talked to the tappers. The sap was flowing strongly this year, they said, but if the rains were poor they couldn't be so sure about the next harvest. The palmyra was a tough palm (a prerequisite for anything that wished to thrive in the inhospitable wastes of the red teri plain), sinking its roots up to forty feet below the ground to find water, but even it needed rain.

At irregular intervals among the palms, fires winked red; those would be the women boiling the sap to get jaggery. All across his acres, this would be the scene that met the observer's eye: ill-clad men ascending trees and women assisting them on the ground. Climbing the giant palmyra palm was hard and dangerous work, and falls that resulted in severe injuries were common. Sometimes the climbers were killed outright. Indeed, these were the most wretched of Solomon's constituents, living far from their villages in little makeshift shacks of mud and thatch during the harvest season, but now it appeared that they were the ones who would see him through what promised to be another lean season.

Solomon spent a couple of hours in the palmyra forest; then he set off for the northernmost of his properties that lay more than half a day away. At noon, the convoy's route again ran along the river. At this point the Chevathar pooled under tall rocks that soared out of the stony ground. A rough country dam that Solomon had had constructed about ten years ago created an elongated pool in which there was at least six feet of water. A group of laburnum trees leaned over the water, their pendent blooms a blaze of golden yellow.

A herd of skinny cattle had settled down in the shade of the trees, placidly chewing their cud. The boys in charge of them were swimming in the pool like big brown tadpoles. Without pausing to think, Solomon ordered his carts to stop, stripped off his shirt and lungi and ran down to the water's edge, where he jumped with a huge splash into the deepest part of the pool. The boys showed some alarm at the arrival of this large stranger in their midst; then, all unknowing of his exalted stature, they splashed water in his face, giggled and swam away. Solomon paddled around the pool, feeling his worries evaporate under the strong sun and the cool touch of water. Memories of his childhood flooded him – of swimming in the wells and ponds with the other village boys, trying to catch the little quicksilver fish with his bare hands, wrestling and stick-fighting in the months after the harvest. All it needed, he thought with a deep sense of contentment, was the right set of circumstances for this middle-aged body to dance to the tune of a young child. He got out of the water after a little while, and let the sun dry him. His carters had spread a mat for him under the trees, a little away from the cattle. Solomon was about to begin eating when a thought struck him and he yelled to the chief carter, who had been with him for twenty years, to bring him some of their food in exchange for his. He handed over the mutton curry, rice and thoran that Charity had packed in exchange for their day-old rice and mango pickle. It was the food he had enjoyed in his youth, when caste, class and position hadn't distanced him from this earth from which he had sprung.

The great magic of the afternoon enveloped him as they continued their journey northward. The bullocks were rested and they kept up a decent pace. A couple of hours across a rough boulder- and scree-strewn wilderness and they were within sight of civilization again, heralded as always by the challenge of fierce village dogs. Doves flitted across their path, the dun of their feathers scarcely distinguishable from the surrounding landscape. Reaching back into the cart for the shotgun he always carried with him on these journeys, Solomon loosed off a couple of barrels. The three doves he potted would make a nice accompaniment to the evening meal.

In the late evening, they hit black-soil country. Another half-hour or so and they would be at their destination. The cartmen clicked their tongues and twisted the tails of the bullocks and the animals increased their speed. The countryside around them was flat and cotton fields spread out in every direction. A flight of crows flew past, rough black tracks on the burnished shield of the sky. A few minutes later they were driving through the village: sixteen mud-and-palm-thatch huts on either side of a deeply rutted cart-track. The headman's house was slightly larger than the others and brick-built but not even as grand as the small house Solomon owned in the village, a three-roomed structure of brick and mortar. The prosperity that the cotton boom had left in its wake had not yet changed the face of the village, for its harvests had continued to be poor due to lack of rain. Their arrival was clearly unexpected and a comet's tail of runny-nosed children, dogs and idlers formed behind their convoy. Solomon drove straight to the headman's house. Appa Andavar was clearly not expecting his landlord and was dressed casually in a dirty lungi. He leapt up from the mat on which he was sitting, simultaneously discarding his beedi, when he saw Solomon.

The headman was full of concern about another rainless year – how would he provide for his villagers and for himself if the crop was meagre? Solomon tried to reassure him as best as he could. It was an

Andavar village and the headman had heard about the attack on the Andavar girl, except in his version seventeen women had been attacked by a gang of Vedhars and Marudars. Solomon said that he was taking a personal interest in the matter and that there was no cause for worry. A goat was slaughtered before Solomon could even protest – the villagers had to provide the requisite hospitality to an honoured guest. After a while he sat down with the headman and the other elders to a meal of rice and a thin goat curry that was too heavily spiced with turmeric. The doves he'd bagged had been roasted but were inedible, and his estimation of the culinary ability of Appa Andavar's household dropped even further. He politely refused an offer of toddy, despite knowing that that would mean the others couldn't drink too, because he was suddenly very tired and wanted to wake up with a clear head.

He went to bed quite early. The inside of the house was hot and stifling, so he dragged his mat out on to the brick stoop and lay down. The moon, almost perfectly round, was pinned to a velvety sky; he turned over on his side and looked beyond its glare to the high reaches of the night where the stars frothed like glittering surf; every so often a slash of silver would scar the faintly glowing onyx backdrop, soundless and swift. He had not felt as relaxed as this for a long, long time. He fell asleep dreaming of rows of laburnum flowers lighting up the church by the sea. The padre had Vakeel Perumal's face and was trying to tell him something urgently but he was too tired to pay attention. He slept.

17

His work done, Father Ashworth would usually try to get down to the beach at sunset to watch the sand crabs at play. They would scuttle ahead of the incoming swells, frail and disembodied as wraiths, then pause as the sea ebbed away, waiting for the next surge of water. The waves paid no heed to the dance of the sand crabs. Gathering themselves up, they would advance upon the beach, cover the dull white gleam of the sand for a brief while, and then retreat, fast or slow, depending on time, tide and weather.

This evening as he watched the crabs flirting with the waves, the priest grew reflective. His eyes followed the movement of the tide as it flowed over the beach and ebbed away. Invaders were like that, he thought. Just as the waves altered the shoreline, so too did conquerors. They might remain for a short while or overstay their welcome, but long after they had disappeared traces of their presence remained. He had no idea how much longer his own kind were likely to remain in this country; he didn't think they would stay for ever, but they had certainly made an impact. One of the things they had had an effect on was the concept of time.

He had been fascinated when he had first arrived to learn about the Hindu way of ordering time – the belief that the universe went through an unending cycle of creation and destruction. Each cycle was equal to a hundred years in the life of Brahma, the Creator, and at the end of each cycle the entire universe was destroyed, along with Brahma, in a cataclysm. A hundred years of chaos ensued, then a new Brahma arose and the cycle began again. Within this main cycle were many subdivisions. One of these related to a day in the life of Brahma, which was equal to 4,320 million years on earth. As soon as he awoke, the world was created; when he lay down to sleep, it was destroyed. Each day of Brahma was further divided into a thousand Mahayugas or Great Ages, which were in turn further divided into Yugas – the Krita, Treta, Dwapara and Kali. Kaliyuga had begun on 18 February 3102 BC and would last 432,000 years. The concept had given him a real insight into the capacious nature of time in his adoptive country.

But things were changing. The cyclical nature of time now had to contend with the linear and the solar. And sometimes it seemed to him that the old way of regarding time was losing out. How else would you explain the fact that 1899 was being greeted with as much foreboding and hysteria in many parts of this country as it was elsewhere on the planet?

Father Ashworth's ruminations had substance to them. In the subcontinent, where irritable Gods and rogue planets were a fact of daily life, it didn't take too long for alien superstitions to take root. The end of the nineteenth century, as measured by the Gregorian calendar, began to weigh unbearably on the conscious and subconscious minds of large numbers of people. What malefic influences were about to be unloaded in the twentieth century?

Rituals and festivals were carried out with extra punctiliousness and fervour as the new century approached. Though priests and astrologers profited, few others did. The spirit of the land turned dry and brittle. All it needed was a match. In the end there was more than one. Riots raced across the south, flaring up in black-soil country, up around the great granaries of the Cauvery and the Vaigai, and in the lee of the blue mountains that hemmed in the Presidency. Kilanad and the neighbouring district of Tinnevelly were the two worst-hit areas. There had already been a riot between Andavars and Thevars in a village close to Melur, the capital of Kilanad. As the summer heat intensified, reports came in that one of the biggest conflagrations the region had ever seen would take place in Sivakasi where the Nadars and the Maravars, who had been skirmishing for decades, were preparing for a final showdown.

Collector Hall in Kilanad and his counterpart in Tinnevelly were worried men, as were their colleagues elsewhere in the province who feared the virus would spread to their own districts. Their concern was communicated to the Governor of the Presidency who called for a meeting of his Council. After sitting in deliberation for two days and nights in Madras, the Council issued proclamations, messages and urgent orders to representatives of Her Majesty the Queen. By telegraph, dispatch rider and post, these spread throughout the districts.

As the tension escalated the leader writer of the *Hindu* wrote: 'It is incumbent on Her Majesty's representative to immediately secure the situation before it gets out of hand.' That issue of the paper reached St Paul's mission in Chevathar a week later, where Father Ashworth read the editorial and sighed. What in heaven were things coming to? But he didn't have much time to ponder the ills of the world for, after many delays, Peter Jesu Perumal was to be baptized the day after tomorrow, along with his family. There was something else on the priest's mind. His newest convert had made a request, after an especially long Bible session. Over coffee and murukku, he had said that while he was mindful of the fact that Christianity prohibited idolatry, it would make him very happy if he could have a family deity to worship like most of the others in the village. However, unlike the others, who invariably worshipped the founding ancestor or some distinguished member of the family or a local deity who had been good to them, he wanted to erect a small shrine to Jesus Christ, the founding father of the universe. This was most irregular, he knew, but he was so passionately in thrall to his new faith that he wanted to proclaim it to the whole world.

The sincerity and devotion of the lawyer had gradually won the priest over. Surely there was nothing wrong with a Chevathar

Christian having his own little place of worship? It was common in Europe and other Christian nations. He had given Vakeel Perumal a lithograph of Christ, and the lawyer said he would arrange to have a cross carved and placed in the shrine. He humbly asked Father Ashworth to consecrate the shrine, which he hoped would be ready in time for the baptism. The priest had agreed, thinking as he did so that Solomon would be astonished by the new convert's fervour. If this didn't serve to allay his reservations about the newest members of St Paul's congregation, nothing would.

Besides the Perumal family, only the headman was present at the baptism ceremony in the church. After it was over, they set off for the lawyer's shrine. A few people awaited them there. A small hollowed-out mud-and-stone construction, about four feet high, it stood under the shade of a towering banyan tree directly opposite the lawyer's house. The lithograph of Jesus was carefully stuck inside and small lamps were ready to be lit in the niches. Father Ashworth realized that the edifice was little different from the hundreds of village shrines that dotted the countryside and smiled in appreciation. How beautifully the Lord had been assimilated into the soil of this ancient and devout land. He began the consecration ritual. A short while later, he brought the ceremony to an end with a brief prayer. As their bowed heads rose, the noises of the village in the morning surrounded them: squirrels and doves screeching and cooing overhead as they fought for the ripening ruby-coloured banyan fruit, a flock of crows cawing and wheeling through the air a short distance away. Father Ashworth made the sign of the cross and blessed all those present. P. J. Perumal now had his very own family shrine.

18

On the evening of the Chitra Pournami festival, the very tip of the Indian peninsula, abode of the virgin goddess, Kanya Kumari, is witness to a remarkable spectacle. Before the eyes of tens of thousands of devotees thronging the striated red, white and black sands of the beach, the sun plunges into the confluence of three seas, staining the water the colour of blood. At that precise moment, the full moon rises, cool and lambent. Fire and frost, the two sides of God. The locals say the phenomenon is unique. But in a dozen villages up the

Coromandel coast, Chevathar among them, the claim is scoffed at. Villagers in these areas do not go to Cape Comorin to celebrate Chitra Pournami. They throng to their own beaches, each village boasting that theirs is the one where the sands are the cleanest and the view the best.

This would be the last time Subramania Sastrigal, the poojari of the Murugan temple, was officiating at the festival. At seventy-seven, all he now wanted to do was meditate upon the Merciful Countenance of God without pause: Subrahmanyom! Subrahmanyom! Subrahmanyom! His son, Swaminathan, had assisted with all the ceremonies for eleven years now and from next year would do it alone.

For two days and three nights, with only the smallest of pauses, the udakkai drum had sounded along with the chants of worshippers and priests and the ringing of the temple bell. The devotions in praise of Lord Murugan at Chevathar were famous and attracted visitors from all over the district. Today was the day when the God-possessed would lead the procession of the Lord from the river to the temple. Their route would pass through the village, thereby ensuring blessings for every devotee who was witness to the Lord taking human form.

The first time Father Ashworth had seen the God-possessed, their bodies pierced by spears and metal hooks called alaku, he had felt faint. Then fascinated. It was the most visible demonstration of faith in action that he had seen, and he never failed to be impressed. He knew that not everyone saw it that way and was careful to keep his brethren away during the Murugan festival. But the terrible majesty of the God-possessed continued to mesmerize him still, seventeen years after he had first seen it.

At the edge of the century, those who needed the reassurance of the Merciful Lord had increased dramatically, so fourteen men would wear alaku this year. They had spent two weeks in a state of ritual purity, abstaining from sex and indeed from the company of others, spending all their time concentrating absolutely on the Lord. Now the fourteen were the centre of attention on the banks of the Chevathar. Virtually every man in the village was present, and a few old women (younger women being considered ritually impure). There was an unusually large number of visitors, perhaps thirty or forty.

Subramania Sastrigal stood directly in front of the fourteen men, chanting hymns in praise of Muruga, while by his side his son beat rhythmically on the uddakai. The professional alaku-piercer who visited at this time of year stood by. The sun was well up by now and the chanting of the sacred invocations and the thudding of the uddakai twined in the heat-soaked air to create a glassy cathedral of sound within which the fourteen men stood rigid, slowly falling into a trance. The legs of a man towards the middle of the group started trembling and shortly afterwards waves of ecstasy travelled upward through his body. Subramania Sastrigal signalled to the piercer and his assistants to start work. Without wasting any time, the piercer, a middle-aged man from Melur, took hold of a seven-foot-long spear and approached the devotee. His assistants each took hold of an arm, holding the devotee erect and immobile. The piercer compressed the man's cheeks, causing his mouth to open and shut like a goldfish's. Then, holding the point of the spear to the devotee's cheek, he pierced it swiftly and precisely. He thrust the leaf-shaped tip of the spear through, then pierced the other cheek, and pulled the spear all the way over, so that its length was balanced nicely. The devotee had his eyes open throughout the procedure and showed no signs of discomfort, nor was there any bleeding. By now six of the men were shuddering, as they grew entranced. Four more would be pierced with spears and one would draw the Lord's cart through the processional streets to the temple. The other eight would be pierced with hooks adorned with flowers, limes and packets of sacred ash.

The piercer and his assistants worked swiftly. One of those who had wanted to be pierced by a spear had failed to achieve a trance-like state, attributed to the fact that he hadn't been sufficiently pious or had perhaps been the victim of someone's envious eye. Six of the hook wearers (two were adjudged unsuitable) were festooned with gleaming metal fangs. One man had hooks inserted though the skin of his back and attached to the little wooden cart on which a clay representation of the Lord reposed. The procession was now ready to move forward. The crowd was ecstatic. Eleven men had been visited by divinity, the most for as long as anyone could remember. It was proof enough that Vel Murugan looked upon his devotees favourably.

The entranced devotees, heavily garlanded and besmeared with vibhuti, bare-chested and clothed only in clean white veshtis, led the procession. They went first to the Vedhar quarter where they stopped in front of Muthu Vedhar's house. Here, Muthu's wife Saraswati bathed their feet, then knelt and pressed her forehead to the miry earth. The priests were given trays containing agarbattis, bananas, coconuts and other traditional objects of worship. With a swift motion of a chopper provided to him, Swaminathan cleaved a coconut, which he returned to the family; the tray was waved in front of one of the devotees and then returned to Muthu Vedhar's family, transformed now into holy prasadam. A woman anxiously whispered into the ear of Kathiresa Marudar, the devotee pulling the cart, that her young son was very ill. 'Do not worry, the Lord is with you and your family. He will take care of your son.' He dropped vibhuti on her palm and she smeared it in a wide swathe across her forehead. Slowly, the procession moved down the narrow street, the women of each house worshipping the God-possessed as Saraswati Vedhar had done.

Father Ashworth hadn't gone to the river bank for over a decade, preferring to stroll down to Anaikal and watch the processionists as they made the final approach to the temple. Solomon had joined him at this vantage point for some years now. The priest decided to walk over to the headman's house so that they could go together to watch the procession.

Solomon was waiting for him on the veranda and they strolled leisurely down the road. As they emerged from the curve where the road swerved around Anaikal, they stopped. Both saw the obstruction blocking the road at the same time. Transfixed for a moment, they slowly took in the sight before them, and then began to run as one. Fear and anxiety drove Father Ashworth over the fifty or so yards more quickly than he would have believed possible. The structure hadn't existed the day before. Thrown up during the night, the makeshift pandal, constructed from thatch and bamboo poles, and enclosed on three sides, stretched from Vakeel Perumal's little shrine on one side of the road to his house on the other, and barred the passage of anyone who wanted to use the road. With dawning horror, Father Ashworth was beginning to understand why the newest members of his flock had been so eager to convert. Ahead of him Solomon had reached the pandal. It appeared they were too late. Angry voices already twisted through the air. They dashed around the pandal just in time to see the huge figure of Muthu Vedhar strike Vakeel Perumal down. A couple of the lawyer's supporters tried to come to his aid but Muthu brushed them off and was reaching down for the prone figure at his feet, when he was brought up short by an urgently shouted command from Solomon.

Behind the little knot of people, the great Chitra Pournami procession had ground to a halt. It was imperative that Solomon act immediately.

'Don't bother with that scum, I'll handle him,' Solomon called out.

Instead of accepting the thalaivar's offer to mediate, which would have had the best chance of defusing the situation, Muthu lost control.

'You low-caste pariah cur, I will make sure I grind you and your degenerate peoples into the dirt or my name isn't Muthu Vedhar,' the giant mirasidar said balefully. He spat at the thalaivar. Time ticked by in stone. The spit was slowly absorbed by Solomon's shirt. Nobody moved, until Muthu, possessed now by forces that had been a long time building, launched himself at Solomon with an awful roar.

Muthu had almost a foot on him and was in excellent shape, but Solomon hadn't gone to seed either, and as his adversary bore down on him, he moved quickly out of the way, and seemed only to cuff him as he went past. Carried forward and down by his own momentum and Solomon's assistance, Muthu crashed face first into the road. Instantly, Solomon was upon him, pinning him to the ground with a wrestler's grip. He spoke quietly into the other's ear: 'You big black buffalo, for all these years I have tolerated you and the other jackals that work for you because I have tried to keep the peace. You have insulted me before the village and for that you will pay. I will give you and all those who owe you allegiance a month to leave. If you haven't gone by then I will personally make sure that you'll wish you had never emerged from your prostitute mother's womb.'

Muthu snarled back, his mouth full of the sour and gritty taste of dirt and humiliation, 'I said I would reduce you to dust and I will reduce you to dust. I'm not leaving this village, it's you and your stinking family who will leave or be destroyed.'

'We'll see who leaves and who provides a feast for the crows and the jackals.'

Everything happened so fast that there was not the slightest chance to intervene, even if anyone had dared to. Solomon released his adversary, got up and without a backward look walked over to where a sullen Vakeel Perumal stood beside the pandal. Without a word, the thalaivar slapped the lawyer hard. 'You are a disgrace to our caste, and to our village. You and your family will leave with your possessions by sundown or I will have you thrown out.' Solomon signalled to some of the crowd following the God-possessed devotees to come and tear down the pandal. When it lay in tatters, he respectfully urged the priests and processionists to continue with the festival. The drums began to beat again, and the spear- and hook-stuck devotees and the rest of the procession, a surly Muthu Vedhar amongst them, edged past the shrine and continued on their way to the Murugan temple.

That evening, for the first time since he had come to Chevathar, Father Ashworth did not go down to the beach to watch the epic rising of the Chitra Pournami moon, choosing instead to watch from the safety of the mission compound. The morning's scuffle had alarmed others as well, for the worshippers on the beach were sparse. Only the spectacle didn't disappoint. As the sun plunged down the wide throat of the ocean, the moon rose, huge and handmade, a giant's plaything suspended from the rusty sky.

19

Summer came early to Chevathar that year. From very early in the morning, the dead white eye of the sun would enamel the sky and the plain with heat and glare until they burned. And then a searing wind that was locally known as the Fire Wind would start blowing in from the teri wasteland, carrying with it dust and heat until you could hardly breathe. By mid-morning every tree, rock and building would take on a life of its own, shimmering and writhing in the heat-bent air, the only things that moved as far as the eye could see. Even the little goatherds took refuge where they could, lying three-quarters submerged in the noxious little pools on the shrunken river bed or skulking in the shade of trees. About the only things that stirred in the sun-bludgeoned landscape were tiny tar-black scorpions and long red and black ants whose bite could reduce a grown man to tears.

The short nights offered little respite as the laterite soil and rocky outcrops of gneiss and sandstone released the heat absorbed during the day into the still, hot air. And then, by six in the morning, the sun would glare into view again.

Dipty Vedhar spent much of May shuttling between Muthu and Solomon, trying to get the two men to make the peace. To his great relief, the deadline set by Solomon, the end of the month, came and went. It helped that Vakeel Perumal had disappeared from Chevathar soon after Chitra Pournami and hadn't been seen since. Father Ashworth had done his bit to persuade the headman not to act upon his threat and he was as pleased as the deputy tahsildar that the expected clash did not take place.

Then, on 6 June 1899, the most devastating riots the Presidency had ever seen ravaged the town of Sivakasi in the neighbouring district. Tensions escalated once more in Chevathar.

Muthu Vedhar sent Solomon Dorai an ultimatum. He should leave the village by sundown on 15 June or he would feel the wrath of the Vedhars. Solomon's response was to thrash the messenger until he could barely stand. He was then told to repeat the ultimatum to his master in slightly altered form – if Muthu was in Chevathar after 15 June, he would regret it.

This was the response Muthu had expected and he began to make preparations. Emissaries were sent to the various caste groups who supported him in the neighbouring villages – the Marudars, Pallans, Thevars – to come and join him. He promised them land and loot. Muthu also had a stormy meeting with his kinsman, Dipty Vedhar. If the deputy tahsildar did not do as he was told, he would meet the same fate as the headman of Chevathar!

In the district capital Melur, Collector Hall had just returned from a trip to a fractious village when he received an urgent message from the Bishop, saying he had heard from the head of the Chevathar mission that there was going to be a riot in the village that threatened to be as disastrous as the Sivakasi one, if the authorities didn't act at once. Accompanied by the Superintendent of Police of the district, Hall left immediately with a couple of policemen and servants. A third of the way to Chevathar his party was held up by an immense train of bullock carts which had for some reason grown becalmed on the narrow road.

Nathaniel Hall, a tall, attenuated man with a blotchy complexion, fumed and fretted on his horse. Fanged outcrops of gneiss rose on either side of the road, effectively preventing them from riding around the obstruction. The Superintendent of Police sent a couple of men ahead to try and move things along. The heat was immense. Sweat trickled down Hall's neck into his collar; sweat blossomed in great unsightly patches across the back of his khaki shirt and under his armpits and beaded his face. God, how he hated this country! And to think he had lasted seven years, hating almost every minute of it. He hated the heat, the flies, the dark ugly people, his work and his colleagues. A large fly hovered around his face and then delicately settled on it. Hall brushed it away furiously. Just then, the cow in front lifted its tail and relieved itself of a rapid succession of greenish-brown lumps of dung. The odour rose to his nostrils and whatever little self-control he had left deserted him. He turned around to the two Indian policemen who rode behind him and snapped, 'I want this thing moving immediately. Shoot a cow or two, that should teach them.'

'You don't shoot cows in India,' Franklin, the Superintendent of Police, said quietly. He was a slight, sandy-haired man who had spent a quarter of a century in India and seemed to have absorbed the rhythm of the country; he was slow to argue and had never been known to raise his voice. But it was rumoured that beneath the calm exterior lay a giant temper. Hall was careful around him. He quickly amended his order.

The bullock carts suddenly began to move, and Hall nudged his horse forward. Chevathar was two days of hard riding away and Hall cursed his luck. Why on earth should the natives choose the remotest corner of his district to cause trouble? And why should that fat toad of a governor care if a few hundred natives died? They died all the time anyway! Floods, droughts, famines, plagues, riots constantly decimated them. And death was, when you thought of it, a better alternative to the miserable lives they led.

20

They stopped in a grove of towering tamarind trees to escape the fiercest heat of the day. The servants with the group took out a folding table and chairs for the Englishmen and laid out lunch. Franklin was taciturn by nature and Hall wasn't up to conversation so it was a quiet meal. After they had finished, the policeman wandered off with a shotgun to see if he could find something for dinner and Hall was left alone with his thoughts. Not a leaf stirred and the heat pressed down on the land. The Collector grimaced to himself. So this was what he had spent thirty years of his life working towards. All the rage, frustration and unhappiness that had fuelled his progress had led to this!

When he had finally received his promotion to Collector of Kilanad, Hall had been overjoyed. He would be lord and master of over one hundred thousand people in a district that was a quarter the size of England. Disillusionment hadn't taken long to set in. Melur, the district headquarters, was a dump, Kilanad didn't figure very high in the Government's priorities and he had little or nothing in common with his English colleagues stationed there. He had stuck it out now for just over a year but it had been torture. The only thing that had prevented him from throwing it all up and crawling back to England was the thought of finally accepting defeat.

At the age of twenty-three, just after he had finished his probationary period for the Indian Civil Service at Oxford, Hall had written a letter to his father, a clergyman in a little parish in Kent where it drizzled eight months of the year. It had been a short letter. In it he had bidden farewell to his family. 'You will never see me again for I do not intend to return to England, the land of your defeat. I do not intend it to be mine. Farewell, and may you have the joy of our accursed homeland.'

It had been an ugly letter but Hall had believed it was the right thing to do. In the time he had been away he had never once gone back to England on furlough or even on a short visit; he had no desire to visit the country that had in his view humiliated and almost destroyed him.

Nathaniel blamed his birth into the wretchedly poor family of the Reverend Austin Hall as the beginning of his misfortunes. It had been uniformly bad from then on: a miserable childhood, two siblings he had hated, an elementary school he had disliked. He hadn't made a single friend at school and his teachers didn't like him. But he had studied with a ferocity and determination that had kept him at the top of his class and won him a scholarship to Christ's Hospital where he had gratefully assumed the blue gown and yellow stockings. School was where he had first encountered India. But the stories of bravery during the Mutiny and on the Frontier had left only a fleeting impression. Within weeks of arriving at Christ's Hospital, the English class system had him on the defensive once more. Scholarship boys weren't considered quite pukka, and if you weren't any good at cricket or footer, you were immediately the target of the sort of exquisitely refined torture that only schoolboys could devise. Reminded almost daily of his inadequacies, Hall assaulted his books again with a vengeance. He stood near the top of his class throughout school, king of the swots, and at eighteen won a scholarship in Classics to Jesus College, Cambridge. He wished his miserable family could see him now, but of course he would not let them.

Unfortunately, Cambridge didn't think much of him either. Here the class system was worse than ever. That was when the idea of India hit him with the force of near-divine revelation. The ICS still had an enormous degree of prestige, it was the highest-paid bureaucracy in the world and it could offer him a passage out of England. And the best thing about it would be that he would be able to lord it over the natives, servile creatures who worshipped the white man. Nathaniel did very well in his final term but he was taking no chances. The civil services had been thrown open to deserving candidates from the middle classes some years previously and a host of crammers had sprung up to cater to those who desperately wanted to pass the competitive exam. Hall had some money saved from summer jobs and he travelled up to London to enlist in Wren's, a crammer with a high rate of success in getting candidates through the written exam. He scored high marks but nearly came a cropper in the viva. To the standard question, 'Why do you want to join the civil services?' he almost gave an honest answer: 'To make money, to leave England, to ride roughshod over the natives,' but a lifetime of manoeuvring to make the best of his chances came to his rescue. He duly obliged the examiners by telling them what they wanted to hear: that there was much work to be done in India and that he wanted to do his mite in the glorious tradition of the ICS. He was through.

The probationary year at Oxford ensued, during which Nathaniel struggled valiantly to master phonetics, codes and laws, and the history of ancient India, but strangely little on the administrative system in force in India. The unfamiliar subjects did not bother him – he had achieved his objective. When he encountered snide remarks like 'Cambridge was established by those who were sent down from Oxford' or 'The Cambridge man walks as though the world belongs to him, while the Oxford man walks as though he doesn't give a fig about to whom the world belongs', he didn't react. He would leave these pallid fools behind soon enough, and there would be little chance that he would seek them out in India where a thousand men administered a few hundred million people. The only thing he found onerous were the riding lessons he had to take. He disliked the hard bony spine of the horse he rode. And every time the horse was set at a certain five-bar gate it would brake or crash into it, with disastrous consequences for the rider. It was instantly dubbed the ICS Gate but thankfully for Hall it wasn't a condition of his posting to India that he jump the obstacle. He never became more than an indifferent rider, which was another reason why he hated his job.

The inadequacy of his equestrian skills made the end of every ride a relief and Hall was glad to see the cluster of fly-blown shacks that marked the outskirts of Ranivoor. They had made good time after lunch, though the heat had thoroughly enervated them. Everyone in the party looked forward to a wash, some food, rest. They nudged their horses quickly through the crowded streets. Finally free of the clutter and grime, they cantered past a sprawl of stuccoed brick buildings which contained the offices of the Sub-Collector as well as those of his immediate subordinate, the Sub-divisional Officer. The Sub-jail, white as a tombstone in the dwindling light, stood a few hundred metres from the offices.

Chris Cooke, the Sub-Collector, met them at his bungalow. He had decided to make sure that everything was in order at home for Hall was known to be particular about such things. Cooke lived in a large bungalow that he found much too big for a bachelor, although its spacious sitting room, dining room and four bedrooms came in useful on occasions like this. It was rare for a relatively junior man to have such quarters but Cooke was the only European district officer in the sub-division and was therefore entitled to the bungalow. It was probably his only real perquisite, compared to the life which English district officials enjoyed in other more lively stations. But Cooke wasn't unhappy. He was deeply interested in the historical and archaeological aspects of his division and was genuinely keen to get to know the Indians he worked with and administered. He tried to do his job fairly and impartially, and unlike many of his countrymen he liked and respected Indians. Visits home on furlough and at Christmas to Madras or Bombay for a week of roistering with his batch-mates and other young Britons gave him all the European company he needed. India's multifarious attractions, that were so unlike anything to be found anywhere else in the world, mesmerized him. He wanted to imbibe as much of them as he could.

The visit of his Collector was an important event. Even though he was only to stay overnight in Ranivoor, Cooke wondered how he should entertain him. If he knew Hall, the little officers' club was out of the question for it wasn't racially segregated. No, he would need to play host to the visitors at home. The pastor of the famous Ranivoor church had begged off as his wife was indisposed, and his subordinate district officer was touring. His Anglo-Indian Inspector of Police, Kidd, was away too, called to a village some twenty kilometres away to investigate a double killing. Which effectively meant he would have to entertain the visitors on his own for he doubted that Hall would enjoy meeting any of the Indians he spent time with.

They dressed for dinner, something Cooke found faintly ludicrous in the searing heat of Ranivoor, but that was the way Collector Hall liked it. And if Cooke wanted his Fortnightly Confidential Reports to pass muster, he would do well not to push his luck on these matters. At seven-thirty precisely, while it was still light outside (the heavy curtains of the dining room were drawn), they sat down to dinner at a fine carved teak table that Cooke had commissioned from the prisoners at the Sub-jail. They perspired gently in dinner jacket and black tie, as the first course was served. Cooke had inherited a cook who made European food brilliantly and the mulligatawny soup was perfect. As the plates were being cleared away, Cooke tried to break the profound morbidity of the evening by telling shikar stories, which always went down well at male gatherings. He began by narrating an incident he'd heard just the previous month about a tiger in the Cuddapah division, which had seized and shaken a villager so violently that the man flew up in the air and broke his front teeth against a branch.

'Saved his life, though, because he managed to cling on.'

'Good shooting in Cuddapah,' Franklin remarked. The taciturn policeman, who was a keen shikari, grew positively loquacious, and they began swapping stories about various shoots they'd been on. After some minutes of this Cooke realized that Hall was growing irritated with the turn the conversation had taken. He tried a little humour, recounting the eccentricities of a sub-divisional magistrate in a neighbouring district who went in such fear of snakes that even during the day he had a peon precede him with a lighted lantern.

'As if this wasn't enough, he was careful to put his feet exactly in the footprints of the peon!' Cooke said with a smile.

'Reminds me of a story I heard about a Collector who had a problem with rats in his district headquarters,' Franklin said. 'He decided to import a large number of cats, until he found they had little interest in the rats but preferred poultry and, of all things, coconuts. Did he learn from the experience? Not a bit of it. The last I heard he was trying to find out where he could obtain suitably large owls that would sort out both the cats and the rats ...'

Cooke chuckled and was about to launch into a tale about the nocturnal habits of a judge he'd once shared a travellers' bungalow with when he was dismayed to see Hall's mouth tighten. They passed some time in silence, until Cooke could bear it no longer. Archaeology had been one of his subjects at Oxford, and it seemed safe.

'Have you visited Adichallanur in Tinnevelly, sir?'

'No,' Hall said shortly.

'I have and it's fascinating, all those burial urns with their coins and artefacts and jewellery. It's curious how people are remembered centuries after they walked the earth. Archaeologists and anthropologists talk of the Grey Stoneware Civilization and the Red and Black Pottery Era and, and ... it's funny, isn't it, that these everyday things we pay scarcely any attention to seem to be the things that survive us.'

Cooke prattled on. 'Wonder how they'll remember us a century from now. Perhaps,' he looked down at the cutlery he held, 'the Sheffield Steel Culture.' He laughed, much too loudly, at his own witticism, and when he looked up he was dismayed to see that Hall was eyeing him with distinct disfavour.

Nathaniel Hall had always disliked his young subordinate. He represented everything he had cringed before: Winchester, Oxford, a third-generation ICS man, carelessly brilliant, goodlooking, deeply engaged with India, good at his job, an excellent horseman, popular with his subordinates and in good standing with his superiors. He himself, no matter how hard he tried, could find no fault with Cooke in the time he had been his boss. His confidential reports were precise and well written, he administered his sub-division well, and he was suitably deferential. But that didn't mean he liked him any better, especially at times like this: Sheffield Steel Culture indeed!

'Mr Cooke, perhaps you could tell us how you assess the situation in Chevathar?'

'Yes, of course, sir. As you know, our fear was that the troubles in Chevathar could explode into the sort of nonsense that went on in Travancore in the fifties. You know, where the sudras went around tearing the blouses of women of another sudra sub-caste, saying they were controverting custom. And, of course, Sivakasi!'

'Yes, yes, we know all that,' Hall said testily.

Cooke wondered whether his Collector was always such a pleasant dinner companion.

'To cut to the chase, sir, my own view is that there's an ancient rivalry between the leading family in the area and one that's challenging it for supremacy. I believe there's a matter of disputed land to add to the troubles. All this caste nonsense is merely a smokescreen to mask the real issue. The deputy tahsildar believes it will blow over very quickly, especially as the headman is the sort of man who will not put up with any nonsense. The deputy tahsildar was telling me that it was because of the Dorai family that Chevathar was free of caste violence. I have met the headman, Solomon, on a few occasions and must say I've been very impressed by him. Our presence there is intended to be a show of strength, and an investigation into the recent incidents, of course.'

'I doubt we'll discover the truth. All natives are barefaced liars,' Hall snapped. 'Anyway, I hope our man over there knows what he's doing because after Sivakasi the Governor is seriously worried. The

Tinnevelly Collector has resigned, the district is on the verge of going up in flames, the army has been called out. He doesn't want the same thing to happen here.'

The three men absorbed this information gloomily. After a while, during which time the only sound was the squeak and rattle of cutlery on crockery, Hall said: 'Do you trust our man in Chevathar, the deputy tahsildar?'

'Yes, I do,' Cooke said. 'Smart, ambitious, and I think not given to sectarian and caste bias.'

'Well, I should think not. Nobody who works for HM's Government should have caste sympathies. What's it all about anyway? One miserable set of natives trying to keep another miserable set of natives down by cooking up all sorts of fantastic rules which are then conveniently attributed to one of their millions of Gods. I haven't come across such a lot of twaddle in my life.'

Cooke was on the verge of saying something, but decided he had already annoyed the Collector enough for one evening.

Hall had a small smile on his face. Looking around the table he said, 'Did you have to read Thurston's *Castes and Tribes of Southern India* while training? Nine volumes of it. Fascinating stuff. Most of these natives should be in a circus. Some of their customs are positively filthy, yet amazingly one lot considers itself superior to the rest!' Having delivered himself of this, Hall addressed the caramel custard. What an obnoxious racist bigot, thought Cooke. No wonder we had the Mutiny.

There was a short silence, then Hall spoke again. 'And the extraordinary thing is I've been told that these high-caste fellows with their absurd tufts and caste marks even have the nerve to think of us Englishmen as polluting! This country astonishes me.'

For all the wrong reasons, Cooke thought angrily. He held his tongue with difficulty. Thankfully Hall appeared to have vented his spleen and hardly spoke again until it was time to turn in.

21

By eleven in the morning, Collector Hall was settled behind the table in the deputy tahsildar's office at Meenakshikoil. The journey had not improved his temper. Franklin, Cooke and he had interrogated the deputy tahsildar at some length and were reassured to hear that everything was under control in Chevathar. The inquiry could now be quickly concluded, Hall thought, and he could leave this abominable place to moulder in its heat, dirt and flies.

Father Ashworth was summoned first and arrived dressed in a white cassock that was slightly the worse for wear, although it was his best. When he stepped into the room, Cooke smiled and greeted him. He liked the priest and whenever he was in the area he made sure that he spent time with him. He found Ashworth very knowledgeable. Hall's reaction was in sharp contrast. He had met the priest once before when he had toured the district and his innate dislike of the clergy hadn't been helped by the other's obvious sympathy for Indians. Besides, in common with many bureaucrats, the Collector felt that priests like Father Ashworth made the job of administration more difficult by meddling in local affairs, converting Indians to Christianity and God knows what else. The heathen was meant to live and die mired in superstition. What good could the Word of the Lord do? Make him refined? Make him white? He noticed that the priest's cassock was torn and he could almost smell the curry on him. A curry priest! A chair was found for Father Ashworth and without any ceremony the proceedings began. The priest recounted the sequence of events as he knew them: the attempt by the two Andavar men to enter the Murugan temple, retribution in the form of the rape of the Andavar girl, her subsequent suicide, the Chitra Pournami confrontation, and the impending battle, scheduled for 15 June. Hall scoffed at the priest's concern but Father Ashworth stuck to his story with increasing vehemence. In the end, the officials said they would speak to him again when they had finished with the others.

Solomon Dorai, who was called next, arrived with seven people. There wasn't an inch of space to move in the tiny room and the Collector threw everyone out but his colleagues and the man they were questioning. After those who remained had settled down, Cooke asked after the headman's family; he remembered being impressed by the older boy's sharp mind. Noticing his Collector's impatience, Cooke cut short the small talk and the interrogation began. Solomon corroborated the priest's account, except in one important way. He was confident there would be no further trouble in Chevathar. No amount of prodding would make him change his statement, and as he had the support of the deputy tahsildar, no serious effort was made to challenge him.

Muthu Vedhar's head almost touched the low ceiling of the office.

He looked impressive in his neatly washed jibba and veshti. Like the headman, he arrived with a retinue, but there were now standing instructions that only those who were to be questioned were to be allowed into the office. Muthu's grave demeanour and striking presence made a favourable impression on his inquisitors.

It was almost noon by the time they had finished with Muthu, and the Englishmen adjourned proceedings until the late afternoon when it would be less hot. They rode back to the tents that had been put up in a coconut grove on the outskirts of town. Their horses were led away, and they had a wash and settled down to lunch: roast chicken, gravy and potatoes and the ubiquitous caramel custard.

'So, who do you think is lying?' Hall asked his young colleague as they ploughed through dessert.

'The padre's suspicions didn't seem unfounded,' Cooke said cautiously.

'Yes, but he's a fool. Living too long in the tropics has addled his brain. In my view, neither side is telling the whole truth, but I think it doesn't really matter. They've lived together for generations, grumbling away like an old married couple, and occasionally there'll be a little scuffle that allows both sides to let off steam.'

'But Father Ashworth was convinced that a large-scale riot was in the offing,' Franklin said.

'I doubt it. Tell you what, Franklin, get that Sub-Inspector of yours to keep an eye out for trouble. That should do it. This disgusting little place isn't going to erupt.'

'Maybe I should stay for a day or two more, sir, poke around a bit.'

'I don't think that will be necessary. I don't know why, but the priest is making too much of a couple of stray incidents. I think it's interesting that neither the thalaivar nor the other mirasidar supported him. So, what do we have for this afternoon?'

Cooke consulted a notebook. 'A lawyer who claims to have proof that he is about to be murdered by the thalaivar.'

'Can't you deal with that on your next tour to these parts? Don't you have a jamabandi coming up soon?'

'I do indeed, but the complainant maintains that what he has to say is connected with these riots that are anticipated.'

'Very well then.'

At four it was still hot. When Vakeel Perumal's name was called, the lawyer presented himself before the investigating officials. Shabbily dressed and unshaven, he wore an unevenly coloured turban. Closer inspection proved it to be a dirty bandage that had been wrapped around his head. Blood had discoloured considerable portions of it.

'Honourable sirs, I have lived in fear of my life for the last month. The thalaivar said in front of hundreds of witnesses that he would erase me from this soil. And even though we fled the village he almost succeeded in doing so, but for the grace of God. We beg you to protect us.' So saying, the lawyer marched across to the door and flung it open. Beyond it stood five people with alarming injuries. A youngish man had his arm in a sling, and a blood-soaked bandage around his head. An elderly woman, who looked as if she might crumple to the ground, was supported by a plump middle-aged woman dressed in a dull blue sari; both the women sported bandages as did Vakeel Perumal's two extremely pretty young daughters.

'Revered sirs, these are close members of my family who were brutally attacked by Solomon Dorai's men. They did not spare my young daughters nor my aged mother nor my nephew who was only visiting us. I beg of you distinguished gentlemen to please help us with the might of Her Blessed Majesty. And our Lord Jesus Christ.' Hall was nonplussed by the lawyer's performance but Cooke had leaned forward and was staring at Vakeel Perumal, a frown wrinkling his forehead. What was that story Soames had told him when they were sitting around swapping tall tales at the Boat Club in Madras last Christmas break? Vakeel Perumal had begun speaking again but Cooke was concentrating so hard on his thoughts that he didn't hear him. Everything suddenly became clear. 'Take off his bandage ... Take off all their bandages,' he said to one of the constables. His companions looked at him, astonished. As stunned as the officials, the lawyer offered little resistance to the policeman who walked up to him and yanked the bandage from his head. Before the wondering eyes of his inquisitors, Vakeel Perumal stood whole and unmarked.

'Goat's blood,' Cooke said triumphantly. 'A colleague told me something similar had happened in his district.'

All at once, the Collector had had enough. The noise, the heat, these people, the deceit ... he couldn't bear it any longer. He stood up and said to the lawyer and his family, 'I wish I could hang every one of you, but unfortunately the law does not permit me to do that. You're rascals and blackguards, one and all, and you deserve everything that's coming to you. Mr Cooke, I would like you to take over proceedings immediately. Give these people the maximum sentence, but make sure it also includes everyone being fed enough castor oil to ensure their shit submerges them completely.' Hall's outburst silenced the noise that had swept the room as soon as Vakeel Perumal's deception was uncovered. The Collector strode from the room, his peon and the village watchman preceding him.

Cooke and Franklin quickly wrapped up the proceedings. Vakeel Perumal and all the members of his family were sentenced to prison terms varying from two weeks to three months, the maximum Cooke was empowered to award. Every one of the tricksters was to be administered castor oil.

The officials called no one else and shut down the inquiry. They debated whether or not to detain Muthu and Solomon, at least until the supposed crisis blew over, but on the advice of the deputy tahsildar, they abandoned that notion.

As Cooke's clerk began to gather their papers, Father Ashworth rushed into the room, his habit flapping wildly about him. 'You're making a terrible mistake if you think there isn't a real danger of a confrontation. If you're basing your decision on Vakeel Perumal, you're wrong. He has never been very important, he's just an irritant, but you're letting the dangerous men go free. Can't you detain Muthu Vedhar? Even Solomon Dorai?'

'On what grounds?' Cooke asked patiently. 'They haven't committed any crime.'

'What about the rape of the girl?'

'Her companion wasn't available for questioning. She has been sent to a relative in another village. Without witnesses and no suspects, we don't have anything to proceed on.'

'What about the disturbance at the Chitra Pournami festival?'

'A small matter, quickly settled due to the prompt action of the headman. Surely you don't want to put a man away for doing good? You shouldn't worry, the deputy tahsildar has agreed to keep a weather eye open for any trouble. He doesn't think there will be a problem.'

'Then he must be part of the conspiracy. I was a witness to the threats both men made. And I know Muthu delivered an ultimatum to Solomon. I've already given you the date. Please ... Question them in front of me ... Please ... I think I know what's going on ... You must stop it.'

Cooke's affability and patience vanished. 'Reverend Ashworth, I've been patient with you but don't get carried away. Otherwise ...'

But Father Ashworth had already turned away. At the door he paused. 'A couple of days from now I wonder how easily you'll sleep with the blood of innocent people on your hands.'

When Franklin and Cooke arrived at their camp, they were surprised to learn that Hall had already gone, taking only his personal bearer with him. He had left word that he would spend the night in Ranivoor and set out early the next morning for Melur.

When Hall reached Melur, he had a long slow bath, then packed a single steamer trunk. The following morning, he went to his office and wrote out his letter of resignation and sent it to the Governor. Another note was dispatched to the District and Sessions judge, asking him to hold the fort for a couple of days. He took the first train to Madras and booked a passage to Singapore. Nathaniel Hall was finished with India.

22

In the second half of the nineteenth century, the Madras Presidency was visited by famine seven times: in 1853–4, 1865–6, 1876–8, 1888–9, 1891–2, 1896–7 and 1899–1900. The worst of these was the Great Famine of 1876–8 which lasted twenty-two months, affected fifteen of the twenty-two districts of the Presidency (including Kilanad), and caused the death of thirty-five lakh people. It cost the state six hundred and forty lakhs of rupees in famine relief. A substantial portion of government spending was devoted to the building and digging of new tanks and wells and the strengthening of existing ones in the affected areas.

The farmers and thalaivars of Kilanad district constructed nearly two hundred and eighty-seven wells and tanks over a ten-year period, a substantial number of them with government assistance. The new wells were made of mortar and stone for the most part, and masonry replaced the mud walls of earlier times. Some of the wells, especially those which served several houses in the driest areas, were very large and deep.

Solomon Dorai, determined never to let the horror of 1876–8 be repeated in his villages, commissioned and funded the construction of wells and tanks wherever possible. These ranged in size from mere indentations in the ground to a monstrous well at the entrance to the Andavar tenant farmers' quarter.

One of the unexpected consequences of the profusion of wells in Kilanad was the growth of the sport called well-jumping. It was known nowhere else in the Presidency, or for that matter in the country. For a time there were even organized well-jumping competitions during Pongal and Deepavali, but the best jumpers spurned these tamashas as being much too tame, unless of course the prize was mouth-watering.

It required a great deal of ability and immense courage to attempt any well more than twelve feet wide, especially those with masonry retaining walls over two feet high. Often you had only one attempt at the big wells, for if you failed you were lucky to have a clear fall into the murky waters below. Sometimes a jumper broke a leg or an arm or suffered a concussion. Or he could knock himself unconscious on the far side of the well and drop like a stone into the deep shaft, and his companions might not be swift enough to rescue him.

The year 1896 had been a bad one for well-jumpers. Eleven had died in the district, and a couple of dozen had injured themselves badly. At the urging of several panchayats and thalaivars, Hall's predecessor had banned well-jumping. But it grew and thrived in secret, now that the headiness of breaking the law was added to its thrills. In 1897, sixteen young men were killed. In 1898, this figure inexplicably fell to a mere three, and in 1899, two young men had died so far. All the authorities and their representatives could do was watch and attempt to be as vigilant as possible.

Solomon Dorai's younger son Aaron was one of the best well-jumpers ever. He had cleared most of the major wells in Chevathar and the surrounding villages, including a fifteen-footer in Panakadu village, which he had jumped about a year ago, easily the most thrilling and satisfying event of his life. By clearing the monster, he had surpassed virtually every existing record. Only the man he admired most, his uncle Joshua Dorai, had done better, clearing a sixteen-footer in his prime.

For a long time now, the well that served the Andavar quarter in Chevathar had been a challenge to well-jumpers, but no one could quite bring themselves to tackle its seventeen-foot span and three-foot retaining walls. Every so often a brash young man would declare that he was attempting the well, in order to crown himself the best well-jumper in Kilanad, in the world, but his nerves would always let him down.

The well was perfectly situated. It stood in the open and there was nothing to prevent the jumper getting a good run at it. The ground around it was hard, offering purchase and boost, especially during the all-important run-up and take-off. Scarcely a week passed but dirt lines scratched in the ground near the well testified that someone had intended to try but had lost their nerve in the run-up.

Aaron decided that he would have to attempt the Andavar well immediately. He might break a leg or an arm in the hostilities they all knew were coming and never be able to jump a big well again.

On the morning chosen for the jump, he was at the well early, along with three friends. He had practised for weeks now, and knew every inch of the terrain. He decided that he would make two practice jumps and one dummy run. He perched on the parapet wall, feeling the deliciously cool stone and mortar under his thighs, relaxing, letting his body go slack, then gradually focusing, until he had the concentration he was looking for. As dawn came crowding through the night, he slid off the parapet and, digging his toes into the gritty red laterite, paced out his run-up in great, hopping long-jumper's strides, from the strip of white chunam that marked the take-off line to the point at which he would begin his run. He crouched for a moment at the mark, then moved sideways to begin the practice jumps. The ground for these had been prepared by his friends, taking into allowance the extra distance he would have to cover to clear the parapet on both sides. For a moment he thought about Joshua-chithappa. He was nervous, more nervous than he felt he could ever be, although he had done many difficult jumps and understood how to take advantage of the feeling, part excitement, part fear, that overcame him at such moments. What a boost his hero's presence would give him. He put Joshua out of his mind, did a few cursory knee bends, then began his run-up, going slowly at first, and then racing towards his take-off point with the stiff, steel-springed, bounding steps that were particular to well-jumpers. Well short of the take-off line, he soared into the air, legs tucked tightly under him, body hunched forward. As his momentum slowed, he splayed his feet and landed. Perfectly, except that his feet were squarely athwart the far line. If he had jumped the well, he'd have fractured both legs on the parapet. He remained where he crouched, eyes shut, and suddenly began to shake uncontrollably.

A hand on his shoulder, strong fingers pressing down painfully on his bare upper body. He looked up and thought at first that he was dreaming.

'Joshua-chithappa! When did you arrive?'

'Yesterday. One of your friends told me about this morning, but I told him not to tell you, didn't want to spoil your concentration.'

'Appa ...'

'He doesn't know I'm here, I want it to be a surprise. And don't worry, I won't tell him ...'

'You might as well, I don't think I can do it. Did you see my practice jump? I would have crashed into the wall.'

'Yes, very painful I can tell you,' Joshua said calmly. He walked with a limp, the result of the fracture that had ended his own well-jumping career.

'It's too huge, chithappa, I can't do it,' Aaron said, shaking his head and rising to his feet. The boy was almost as tall as his uncle. Though they didn't look alike, they were built the same way – tall, with strong features, and the lean, high-hipped bodies of long-jumpers.

'Aaron,' his uncle said slowly, 'you can clear the well. You took off three feet before the take-off line, and yet you almost did it.'

'I know, but this one's too big for me. It scares me ...'

'If you walk away from here, Aaron, you'll spend the rest of your life wondering about what might have been. We have a very, very short time in which to make the best use of the gifts we've got. You could be the greatest well-jumper this place has ever seen, and I've seen the best. Now, you can walk away ...'

'Will you watch ...'

'Only if it doesn't spoil your concentration.'

'No, chithappa, I want you to, it'll help me.'

'Fine, I'll be here. Remember, there is just one thing you need to hold in your mind. Empty it of everything else. Me, the practice jump, the well, your friends. The only thing that you need to focus on is the take-off line. You'll need to hit it perfectly, you'll already know by the time you get to it if your stride is right, and then you'll just need to relax and enjoy the perfection of your jump.'

'And if I don't get it right?'

'You will,' Joshua said imperturbably. 'Remember, the take-off point, then you're lifting into the air, you're a bird, you're Hanuman crossing the oceans in one mighty bound.'

His second practice jump was perfect. Timing his take-off precisely, he made the best jump of his life, clearing the far line by about a foot and a half. Joshua nodded his appreciation. When Aaron came up to him, he suggested casually that he dispense with the dummy run-up to the well and take the actual jump immediately.

Aaron agreed and walked to the beginning of his run-up. He could feel the breeze on his back, his shoulders. He focused on the white band of chunam in the middle distance until his eyes strained with the effort, then relaxed, jogging in place for a few seconds, letting his body go slack, his mind go blank. Then, gradually, he began to focus again on the line of white chunam. Its faraway presence in the mud of Chevathar grew defined and strong, crossing over, as his concentration deepened, from its reality on the ground into his consciousness. He began moving then, arms swinging in time to his pumping legs, his body perfectly poised. The line grew in magnitude, a broad white band of crumbling little particles of calcified stone, growing wider with each passing stride. It was a sea now, a bright white sea, drawing him closer and closer, so enormous he could vanish into it if he overbalanced. At its very lip, at the point the white would have engulfed him if he had gone any further, he took off smoothly, not checking his stride, soaring up, up, up into the sword-bright band of sky above. His passage was very quiet. Into the enormous silence and milky light, a whirr of glittering blue. Automatically a hand closed over the object, and then he had landed, no longer some fabulous creature of the empyrean, but a strong, handsome sixteen-year-old boy coming to earth effortlessly, without fear, the very best well-jumper in the world.

Joshua hastened up with his awkward stumbling gait, the boys following him, strangely quiet. Aaron, still bent in his landing position, looked up at his uncle. They did not speak. Slowly, the boy brought up his clenched left hand. A bright splatter of blue leaked out of his locked fingers. With great deliberation he opened his fist. In the palm of his hand, a tiny kingfisher lay blinded in the light, dazed by the crashing open of its prison. A moment, two, then its feathers flicked into place, its knobbly feet found purchase on the soft flesh of the boy's palm, and it launched itself into space, blue on blue, conferring as it dwindled into the distance the perfect burnish to a morning that would pass into legend.

23

Despite his disability, Joshua Dorai was one of those men who walked lightly upon the earth, seemingly without care. Indeed, his limp seemed the only thing that kept him rooted to the earth. Without it, he would have become one of those dark, weightless shadows that race along the earth every time clouds slide across the sun. He was still in good shape, and middle age had left few marks on him: a slight slackening of the skin around his eyes and mouth, the faintest trimming of grey around the edges of his thick black hair.

Joshua and Solomon had been inseparable as children, and the day his cousin left Chevathar Solomon had felt more alone than he would have thought possible. Joshua was the only one he would listen to or confide in, the only boy who could occasionally beat him at stick-fighting, the only one who could mock his natural solemnity without fear of retribution ... He had been so much a part of Solomon's youth that his departure had abruptly signalled the end of the boy within him. Joshua had returned to Chevathar only once before, a dozen years after he had left, and had seemed much as before, neither rich nor poor, neither exultant nor unhappy in the life he had made for himself in the humid rubber plantations of Malaya. He showed no interest in settling down, although Solomon had urged him to stay. A few months and the familiar restlessness had taken hold of him again, and he was gone. That was a decade ago, and now he was back. There were gifts for the children, exquisite wooden toys carved from the hardwoods of the rain forest, lengths of shimmering silk, green as the sea at noontime, for Charity and the girls, and an ornate batik shirt for his cousin.

Solomon monopolized him for most of the day. The two of them sat out on the veranda, revisiting their youth. Joshua asked about Father Ashworth. The two had liked each other well enough, though Joshua's lack of interest in the Church had often frustrated and irritated the priest. 'How's the old man's Tamil? He used to sound so funny, as though he had pebbles in his mouth!'

'Oh, his Tamil is excellent now. He's quite an authority on local customs and traditions. Knows more than most of us here.'

'Yes, he was very diligent.' Joshua paused, then said with a laugh, 'I still remember Aaron telling me that he thought the padre's face looked like a monkey's bottom. He asked me if his eyes were made of blue glass and wondered if he took them out when he slept. In fact, he was planning to steal them.'

Solomon laughed. Inside the house Charity heard the laughter and was glad. It was the first time in many days that her husband had sounded at ease.

After a while Solomon said, 'The padre is not very happy with me these days.'

'Why?'

'Because he thinks I should make peace.'

'Do you want to?'

'I don't know, I keep thinking of the pain and destruction that a battle would bring. Perhaps I should go and talk to Muthu.'

'He won't listen to you. He won't rest until he has driven you from Chevathar.'

'I know.'

They sat without speaking for a while, their mood suddenly sombre. Then Solomon asked his cousin, 'What do you think I should do?'

Joshua didn't reply immediately. Then he said quietly: 'I think you must fight this battle. You must cut off Muthu's head or your grandchildren will suffer.'

'Rather a drastic solution. But that's always been your way,' Solomon said drily.

'As it should be yours. I'm sure you've tried everything to keep the peace, but that's no longer an option, anna, you know that just as much as I do!'

'Tell me, Joshua, why do you think Muthu hates us? His sole purpose in life seems to be to erase us from the face of the earth.'

'I can't think of any other reason except what we just spoke about. He must rule Chevathar or die trying. Whatever his faults, he's as proud and stubborn as us, anna ...'

He paused for a moment, then went on: 'You know, there is something I promised not to reveal to you, but I'm going to say it anyway and hope you will forget I said it. This morning Aaron jumped that big well in front of the Andavar quarter.'

'The big well,' Solomon said wonderingly. Then, a little angrily, he added, 'And you didn't stop him! You know it's illegal.'

'Oh, who cares about that, anna. But your son, he was glorious. The greatest well-jumper in the world, but it wasn't that that was important. At the moment of his triumph, he had escaped the world, the hundreds of little things we say and do to ourselves to bind us down, make us helpless little worms, who on their deathbeds only remember and lament what they always wanted to do, but never had the courage for. Think about it, anna. What a waste of a life, no matter how pitiful or earnest or triumphant it has been. Do you honestly want to die, and in your last moment go into the dark thinking only of what might have been? You will fight, anna, you must fight, for if you die without fighting, if you capitulate to Muthu, you will repent it all your next life. We do not bow to anyone, Solomon-anna, you and I, we do not cave in quietly.'

'True enough,' Solomon said, 'but I wish there was some way of resolving this matter without bloodshed. You know, Joshua, sometimes I wish appa hadn't died so young, I feel I would have been so much more prepared if he'd been able to give me just a little more of his strength, a little more wisdom.'

Joshua nodded. 'Anna, you already possess the sort of strength and wisdom that is granted to few.' He laughed. 'And besides, you have me, don't you think you are fortunate?'

'Of course, of course,' Solomon said with a smile, 'but I'm curious. Why have you come back just at this time?'

'To see you all,' Joshua said lightly. Then he added, 'Actually, a kinsman I met in the west told me about the troubles in Melur and Sivakasi and I wondered whether they were being echoed here. It gave me an excuse to return ...'

'Things are different here now,' Solomon said sombrely. 'Muthu is not the only problem. A general sorrow has come over the land. Drought, taxes, unrest. It seems as though the evening of the world is upon us, Joshua.'

Joshua said, 'Everywhere I've been, I've seen suffering and tension. The world is tired, anna, it's been around for so long that its cares press heavy on it.'

'They press heavy on me. There are fools and enemies everywhere I look. I've told you about Vakeel Perumal. Thank the Lord that he's in jail where he can't cause too much trouble. And Muthu, well, you know him ...'

'This is a violent land, anna. Muthu is more representative of it than you will ever be.'

'Isn't that sad? If discord and bullies are the norm.'

'Yes,' Joshua said, 'but that is the way things are. Everything seems to have fallen apart, the white man is losing his grip, and in the absence of any real authority even the smallest of men becomes a tyrant.'

'Do you really think the white man is losing control?'

'It's not so much about losing control, as a general indifference to the problems of the country. The British came here not to rule but to take what they could get. All they're doing is revealing their true colours.'

'But there are good men among them ...'

'There will always be exceptions but sadly such men are rare,' Joshua said, 'and that is why we will need to find our own answers.'

After lunch, they sprawled out on the veranda again. The serious mood of the morning had passed and Joshua, loquacious as ever, regaled Solomon with the many wondrous things he had seen and heard during his relentless travelling. He described the crowded streets of Madras, the grand British officials and merchants, so different from Father Ashworth, and unparalleled wonders such as the mysterious round objects of glass that sprang into radiance brighter than anything he had seen. 'Rooms would fill with the sun at night,' he said to Solomon, who laughed indulgently. When he was telling his stories, Joshua was known to be fanciful. He had even taken a train to Bombay. But he had soon tired of the press and crush of urban living and set off southwards again.

He had met with adventures everywhere. He told the incredulous Solomon about a village of high-caste women so fair that when they sneezed, their faces stained red with the onrush of blood. 'They're incredibly beautiful, anna, but they're deadlier than kraits. In fulfilment of an ancient vow to Devi, the mothers-in-law are expected to kill their daughters' husbands. They catch and kill a gecko and hang it over a small pot. Over the days, the poisonous fluids in the dead lizard slowly drip into the receptacle. When they have enough, they dry the liquid and mix it with the food of their victim in small quantities. Until he dies. Slowly. The locals call it the village of widow-makers, but the women are so beautiful that there is no dearth of men willing to defy the odds.' Joshua's stories grew wilder as the day stretched into evening. After they had dined off appams and a rich mutton stew simmered in coconut milk and spices, they wandered into the compound, and stood around for a while, listening to the sounds of the night.

They didn't speak for a space, then Joshua said, 'In the course of my wanderings I met a baba at one of those crude roadside shrines; there was no one about. It must have been somewhere in Dharwad. The old man seemed bored and glad to have some company. We talked for a long time. Most of what he said was the usual religious stuff but one thing stayed with me. He asked me why I was so restless, why I wandered so far from home, and I said my village held nothing for me, it was something I had always longed to escape. He said, no matter how far you run from Chevathar or for how long, it will never let you go because you have been fashioned by Chevathar, it is in you, you are Chevathar. Maybe that's why I came back; maybe this is where I'm destined to be. And if Muthu's people kill me, I'll be here for ever.' He gave a short laugh to dilute the weight of the moment, and added: 'Besides, nobody can escape what the stylus of the Creator has carved on our foreheads.'

They walked back to the veranda then, and sat quietly for a while, lost in their thoughts. Night deepened, and still they lingered on the veranda, talking little. Above them a storm of stars stretched across the unwrinkled sky, their brilliance unmarred by the diminished moon.

24

High above the altar in St Paul's was an exquisite example of local craftsmanship: an image of Christ carved out of deep brown, almost purple, rosewood, the eyes sorrowful, the features contorted in pain. When Father Ashworth had first set eyes on it, he was shaken. It was the very picture of the Lord he had carried within him since he was a schoolboy.

His public school sat on the edge of the Sussex downs. He had loved to tramp the ancient paths that criss-crossed the region. One morning, he had been out walking when the harebells in the grass in front of him had suddenly disappeared. A man stood before him, dressed in long flowing robes of white. He had seemed very familiar to the young boy's eyes. He was of medium height but possessed of such great beauty and presence that Paul fell to his knees. But it was as if he had not moved at all, for he saw himself walking with the man, who while not saying a word was yet speaking to him. 'Ye are not of the world, even as I am not of the world' were the only words Paul could later recall.

When he got back to school, he realized why the man had seemed so familiar. In the chapel, to which they had lately become regular visitors as Easter approached, there was a stained-glass window with an especially skilful rendering of Jesus. There was a perfect resemblance, except in one crucial respect. The man Paul saw was brown-skinned and his hair and eyes were black. This appeared so remarkable to him that he had summoned up the courage to ask his history teacher about it. 'Did Jesus really have blue eyes and blond hair?'

'Of course not,' Mr Barnes had replied. 'Come, let me show you what I mean.'

On a globe, Mr Barnes showed him the harsh desert lands of West Asia. 'If Jesus was to appear in England today, he would shock most of the people who worship him. For this was where he was born, lived and preached – in Asia. He was brown-skinned, black-eyed. He didn't speak English but Aramaic, a tongue of the people of the desert. He was really a very minor peasant leader from Galilee. He would have barely warranted a footnote in the history books – if he hadn't been the Messiah, of course. In fact we know there was a historical Jesus who lived during the Augustan period. I can look it up for you.' Mr Barnes scrambled around among the books on his cluttered table until he found what he was looking for. 'Ah, here we are. According to the Jewish historian Flavius Josephus, whose account dates back to the first century, there was a wise man called Jesus who lived and taught in the approximate period of time in which he was historically located, who was put to death by Pontius Pilate ...' Barnes was off, like a greyhound after a hare, and there had been no stopping him after that.

Father Ashworth had risen as usual before dawn to pray. Under the gaze of the rosewood Christ, he creaked to his feet, blessed himself and walked over to the communion table. A gust of wind had scattered the pages of his manuscript, and he slowly began picking them up. The events of the past week had, in addition to everything else, brought work on the book to a halt.

He had visited Solomon daily but was unable to make much headway with him. He had tried talking to Joshua but that had come to nothing. Muthu Vedhar had refused to see him. And, incredibly, the deputy tahsildar had chosen this time to go on a tour of the other villages under his purview. Father Ashworth had tried contacting Chris Cooke, but he was touring as well. He had spent some time with the poojari of the Murugan temple, but it was clear that the old man's concerns were no longer of this world. When Father Ashworth pleaded with Subramania Sastrigal to use his immense power to stop the madness that was about to ravage Chevathar, the saint had replied: 'What you grieve about is unworthy', and had quoted scripture in support of his view.

He could expect nothing, he knew, from the poojari's son, Swaminathan. He was sure the scheming young man was encouraging Muthu Vedhar to fight. If Muthu became headman, Swaminathan's own importance would increase immeasurably.

As Father Ashworth put the pages in order, he read what he had written.

At the heart of every religion in the world is the divine mystery. The problem that the teachers who have contributed to the evolution of each faith have always been confronted with can be simply stated: How to plumb the divine mystery, describe it, explain it to themselves and the followers of the faith? It is a problem almost without solution, for how do you describe God? There are no facts that can adequately explain the Supreme Reality; none but the greatest seers are granted the intuition to experience the Divine. As a result, each religion has evolved a host of symbols and myths and convention and dogma, to make its central mystery better understood. Over the centuries, these have often obscured the central mystery to the impoverishment of the faith. And the priestly class has only itself to blame for obscuring and misinterpreting the Truth, perverting religion for its own selfish ends, setting brother against brother, saint against saint, dogma against dogma. Is Krishna's memorable message to Arjuna on the battlefield of Kurukshetra any less important than Christ's Sermon on the Mount or the Buddha's explication of the Eightfold Path? No, a thousand times no! Men of vision of all faiths need to explain to their followers that the goal of every religion is the same – to achieve the transcendent state, experience the one true Reality, understand fully the eternal Truth ...

He liked the opening paragraph, but he would need to work on the rest of it. He longed to get back to his book. But even when everything was normal he found the act of writing so taxing that he had often been tempted to give up; the only thing that had kept him going was the thought that if he ever finished the book and had it published, it might be of some use in countering the evil men who tried to set man against man in the name of religion. Lord, please let me finish the book, he prayed, shutting his eyes briefly. Then a thought struck him so forcefully that he forgot all about his writing. I have appealed to the good sense and sanity of virtually everyone in Chevathar, Father Ashworth thought, but not the women. Perhaps they could divert the tragedy.

That evening he paid a visit to the Big House and was very pleased to find Charity alone on the stoop. He accepted her offer of coffee, and then without wasting much time on preliminaries, asked for her support. 'I can't help, padre,' she said simply. He was about to try to persuade her when she spoke again: 'When Valli was attacked, I was terrified. Not so much for myself but for my daughter Rachel.

It could so easily have been her ...' She broke off the narrative as the coffee arrived. When the servant had finished serving them, she said, 'On the day it happened I went to Valli's home to see whether there was anything I could do to help. That's when the full horror of it hit me. There was nothing I could do. And none of the women there expected me to be of any use. They knew how powerless I was, even though I was the thalaivar's wife. For the first time I truly understood how defenceless we are. Not a day passes when I don't wake up frightened, but I'm powerless to do anything. We can pray, of course, that our men will protect us. My husband is a good man. He'll do his best. And if he's defeated, all I can pray for is that my daughters and I will be given enough time to prepare ourselves.'

For a moment Father Ashworth was incapable of speech, then he said, 'You mustn't speak like that, daughter. Our Lord Jesus Christ will keep you out of harm's way.'

'We pray that he will, but nevertheless we must be prepared.'

'Isn't there some way you can encourage your husband to resolve the issue peacefully with Muthu Vedhar?'

'I cannot influence his decision, padre.'

There was little more to be said. They chatted for a while, then he finished his coffee and prepared to leave. As he got up, Charity said, 'We are being tested, aren't we?'

He nodded, and she remarked, 'I hope we aren't found wanting.'

He walked home in the perfection of the evening. Dusk had sheared the tops off the trees, but the ground beneath them was still lit by the sun and it looked as though the great banyans were rooted in pale gold dust. Such beauty invests this place, he thought, such beauty, such despair!

25

The hardy acacia is native to Sindh but over the years it has spread to the rest of the subcontinent. In the north it's called kikar, in the west, east and centre it's known as babul. To the Tamils it's karuveli. But no matter what name it goes under, it is one of the most common trees in India, its dull green mop often spotted in terrain which supports no other foliage. In Chevathar, the acacia forest spread for a couple of furlongs along the wasteland beyond the Murugan temple. The trees grew so closely together that they formed an impenetrable canopy, keeping the ground cool on the hottest days. The forest had other benefits. Little grew in its shade, so the field of vision of the women who frequented it was unrestricted. Its greatest advantage, however, was the sharp white thorns that lay thickly on the ground, making it difficult for anyone to sneak up quickly or unobserved.

For these reasons, the most inaccessible part of the acacia forest was the natural choice of the women of Chevathar when it came to choosing a spot to relieve themselves. Safe from predatory men and prying eyes, in the early hours of the morning and in the late evening, the women, each armed with a little chembu, would gather to defecate. They would sit in small groups chatting about their children and husbands. Now and again a choice bit of gossip would galvanize the place with excitement, and within minutes every woman present would know about the married Marudar woman who had been caught with her Paraiyan lover or the venereal disease the deputy tahsildar's brother had contracted from a prostitute in Ranivoor.

Ever since the troubles had begun, however, the acacia forest had been filled with tension. The women huddled together among their own kin, barely speaking to one another as they considered what lay ahead. After defecating, they would go down to the river for a bath. Then they would make their way home.

At a fork in the road, equidistant between the Murugan temple and the river, Father Ashworth waited for the women on the morning after his conversation with Charity. He had not yet given up hope of persuading them to help.

He heard someone approaching him from behind. It was Saraswati Vedhar, walking home alone after her morning pooja. This was a stroke of luck. If he could convince her, the rest would fall in line. She looked irritated when he stopped her but let him finish before she said there was nothing she could do. She moved slowly away, deep in thought. Every woman he spoke to, whether Andavar, Vedhar or Marudar, said the same. Some of them even asked him to do everything he could to stop the impending conflict, but gave him to understand that they could or would do nothing to help him.

The next day, Father Ashworth woke up feeling defeated. He had fought long and hard, with every ounce of conviction and strength he possessed, but even as he'd struggled, he had understood that what was about to happen was as inevitable as the dawn outside his window. Was that what this country had taught him? That no matter how much you tried to change it, man was a creature of his destiny? He thought of Arjuna's mighty effort to halt his onward rush to war; he thought of the great ascetic, Ravana, who, unable to control actions that were crafted to fulfil the destiny of another, met his doom at the hand of the chosen one, Sri Rama; and he thought of the Lord's disciples, especially Peter, who watched the Son of Man go to His death. Filled with a deep despondency, he asked himself: Who am I, a miserable instrument of the Lord, to reverse the course set by divine will?

As the days passed, he was visited by dreams that grew steadily more frightening. Two days before Solomon's ultimatum was due to expire, the priest woke from a restless sleep, gripped as always now by despair. He washed and listlessly walked across to the church. He tried to occupy himself with the morning's tasks but soon gave up, consumed by the despair that had been his constant companion these past days. Does no one feel my desperation, O Lord, he thought as he looked at the physical evidence of his life's work before him: the scattered leaves of his manuscript, the St Paul's register of births, deaths and baptisms, an open hymnal.

All this for nothing! All these years of work, all these years spent among people he loved beyond life itself. All about to be destroyed. He turned his eyes to the purple-hued Jesus nailed to the wall, and prayed as he had done so often, 'Enter me, O Lord Most High, and show me in Your wisdom what I must do to stop this madness.' And, as always, the rosewood figure remained mute and beautiful and wooden on the rough stuccoed wall of the church.

26

In a house on the outskirts of Meenakshikoil, Muthu Vedhar sat in a room packed with men recruited by the chief of a nearby Marudar village. Seventy-nine had already arrived from the towns and villages surrounding Chevathar, and more were expected. They camped in and around town and made a nuisance of themselves in the tea shops with money their chief had given them. Their free-spending ways ensured they were tolerated; besides, the townspeople were afraid of the Marudars who were known to react violently at the slightest provocation.

Muthu was impressed by what he saw. They were dirty, malnourished and dressed in tattered lungis, banians and turbans but they were just what he needed: fighters hungry for loot. The Marudars didn't fight for principle. All that fuelled them was greed. It was a good thing they were on his side, not Solomon's. He expected to have at least a hundred of his own kinsmen join him over the next days, and two hundred, perhaps two hundred and fifty men for the confrontation. Solomon was going to get the whipping of his life. 'We are the best fighters around, and we will strike terror into the heart of our enemies,' he said to enthusiastic applause. 'I promise you enough loot and plunder to keep every man and his family prosperous for three generations.' Another cheer. 'All that stands between you and these riches is a pitiful force of old men and children. You must promise to be merciless, that's the only way you can assure yourself of a fortune.' The applause was somewhat muted this time as an altercation had broken out at the back of the crowd. They have been drinking, Muthu thought.

'No arrack, no toddy,' he said urgently to the Marudar leader. The man's face fell and Muthu grew furious. 'You lunatic, can't you see that if your men continue to be as undisciplined as this, they will either be arrested or beaten up? They will be useless to me.'

'I will discipline them but don't you ever call me a lunatic,' the man said testily.

27

Solomon's first blow drove the man to the ground. It wasn't so much a punch as a push, but Muniyandi had perfected the art of milking opportunities. He was a drunk with no family, his wife and children long gone. On his way to the beach, Solomon had found him sleeping off a night of heroic imbibing, and had prodded him awake with his foot. The old man had tottered up, muttering imprecations. Irritated, Solomon had cuffed him and the tamasha began. Muniyandi fell and blood dripped from his nostrils, spotting the ground. The first time this had happened, Solomon had been alarmed but now he knew that this was a trick. It merely ignited his wrath. Suddenly very angry, he raised his foot and kicked the old man as he lay on the ground. Muniyandi screamed with pain and

Solomon stopped, shocked. He believed in controlling servants, slackers and wastrels and was quick to raise his hand to those who crossed him. But he didn't kick people. It didn't seem right. The impending battle was getting to him; he would need to exercise more control. He stooped, lifted the weeping old man to his feet and gruffly muttered, 'Come and see me later in the day. I owe you some money.' There was no payment owed, of course, but it was the best he could do.

He walked away rapidly in the direction of the beach, disturbed and anxious. On the lip of a dune he stopped and his face settled. The sight that greeted him would have gladdened any eye. Framed against the sunlit plane of the sea, around forty men had paired off and were practising with the whippy five-foot bamboo staff that was a deadly weapon in the hands of a skilled stick-fighter. Stick-dancing, silambu-attam they called it in Tamil, and that's what it was, a fluid, flowing dance that could kill a man so beautifully it was an art. The fighters had been practising for two days now under the watchful eye of Joshua. Most of the younger men had required no training for this was something they played at every day. But it was astonishing how quickly the older men had shed their rustiness. Solomon watched the whirling staffs, now milling hectically like windmills, now thrusting forward, now settling gently like dragon-fly wings. He felt the anger drawing out of him. And then abruptly the tension returned. Near the back of the group, a young man was fighting clumsily. Just then, he dropped his staff and wearily bent to pick it up. Even at this distance, it was clear who it was: his older son Daniel. Solomon trotted down the dune towards the fighters. Joshua spotted him and waved, Solomon returned the greeting with a grim nod, then skirted the main group and headed straight for his son. His opponent was toying with him, it was obvious, and Solomon's anger flared up. He ordered them to stop fighting and plucked the staff from the hand of the tenant farmer who was sparring with Daniel. 'Now, I'll show you how to fight,' he snapped at his son.

He led him to a spot some distance away from the others. Joshua came up to them.

'Anna, what are you doing?' he asked.

'Teaching my son to fight.'

'That's my job, isn't it?'

'If I'd taught him better in the first place, he wouldn't disgrace me as he is doing now.'

'Anna,' Joshua said, a note of warning in his voice.

'Joshua, you have your work to do, I have mine. Now leave me.'

Solomon's firm tone left Joshua with no option but to go. What a pity that there's no rule book to help fathers and sons establish successful relationships, he thought, as he moved away.

'I don't want to fight, appa,' Daniel said quietly.

'What do you mean, you don't want to fight? No son of mine will disgrace me by saying such a thing.'

He raised his arm as if to strike Daniel but noticing Joshua, who was watching them from a short distance away, he stopped. Deliberately, he drew up his lungi, tucked it firmly so it didn't flap and assumed the classic stick-fighter's stance. As he glared at the youth standing before him, his eyes reflected his disappointment: those thin wrists, that narrow hairless chest, the stooped bearing, the large expressive eyes that wouldn't have looked out of place in a woman. Was this really his son?

Without a word, he aimed a blow at Daniel. It wasn't a hard blow, nor was it delivered with especial guile, but Daniel made no move to parry it or to duck. Solomon's staff thudded into his chest, and he staggered back several paces. Then he began to cry. 'Appa, I don't want to fight. Why can't you just stop this foolishness?'

'Don't you ever talk to your father like that,' Solomon roared, and raised the staff again. 'You will fight or my name isn't Solomon Dorai!'

Daniel was trying hard to get his tears under control when Solomon abruptly changed tack. 'Go home and wait for me there. And wipe away those tears. Now.'

Daniel walked off slowly, dragging his stick. Solomon followed him with his eyes until he reached the top of the dune and was lost to view among the giant sea agaves, then turned back to watch the fighters. His eyes sought out his younger son, and came alive with pride as Aaron executed a particularly difficult manoeuvre, leaping up in the air while his opponent's staff passed harmlessly below, then whipping around and, still airborne, attacking from a different angle. He watched for a while longer then began walking home.

Joshua walked a short distance with him. 'Don't be so hard on Daniel. He's different, but he has qualities of his own. Don't confuse him with Aaron, that's the worst thing you can do to both of them.' Solomon didn't respond. Joshua shrugged and went back to his men, and Solomon headed towards the house. The iron rage he felt towards Daniel had abated only a little and he could still feel the taste of it in his mouth.

He found Daniel with Charity. 'Do you know what your son has done?'

When she didn't reply, he shouted, 'You should be ashamed that you ever gave birth to him. He will bring disgrace to the Dorais.'

Charity said quietly, 'Daniel is a good boy.'

'What did you say?' Solomon asked furiously.

'I said he is a good boy,' she said, a little louder.

'He is not a boy. He is a grown man and I'm sorry he has turned out this way.' Solomon saw with disgust that Daniel was weeping again. Charity put a protective arm around him and this further stoked Solomon's anger.

'You should have been born a girl, Daniel. Very well, if that's the way it is, that's the way it shall be. Tonight, I want all the women and children of this household to be packed and ready to leave. Charity, you will go to your father's house and Daniel will be the friend and protector of the women.' He added sarcastically, 'To be on the safe side, I will have half a dozen men ride with you.'

'Appa, please don't send me away,' Daniel said tearfully. 'I will do my best.'

Solomon was brutal in his reply: 'Your best is of no use to me. And to think when you were born I was so proud of you, my first-born son who would carry this family into the next century. Do you know what the astrologer said to me when he came to see you? He said you would be the mightiest in our line. Your mother was right to disapprove of astrologers, for you are living proof of how stupid their prophecies are.' He strode out.

Charity tried in vain to console Daniel. After a short while he left his mother and walked out of the house. As he left, he saw Aaron in the doorway, and realized that his younger brother had heard everything. They had never been close. Still, Aaron had paid him the minimum of courtesy that tradition demanded. Today, for the first time, Daniel saw contempt in his eyes.

That evening Solomon reviewed his fighting men. He had received word that they could expect about a dozen more fighters from the neighbouring villages and he had also been promised some shotguns and muskets.

He wondered if he had left it too late to send the women and children of his own family to safety. In the last weeks the road north had been filled with fleeing families, many turned back by Muthu's sentries. But there was nothing Solomon could do but trust to luck and the fighting abilities of the men who would escort his family up to Ranivoor. There were no tearful farewells. Solomon had not got over the way his eldest son had let him down. He stayed away as the closed bullock carts left that night.

Despite Muthu's best efforts, the Marudars were an undisciplined lot and the toddy flowed freely. The lookouts he had posted at the bridge and on the road leading out of Meenakshikoil were drunk and the Dorais' armed escort easily overpowered them. As the file of bullock carts clattered onward, they overtook other carts as well as women and children on foot, pushing handmade vehicles or carrying large palmwork panniers on their shoulders or on their heads in which their worldly goods were stored. Nobody who could help it wanted to face the hostilities.

Muthu Vedhar was furious when he heard of the escape but there was nothing he could do. He redoubled his vigilance.

28

A child was the first casualty of the battle of Chevathar. He died the day before the actual fighting began. Most of the children had already fled the area. Those who were left behind began emulating the adults in their own playful way. The Vedhar children challenged the Andavar children to a game of goodu-goodu. In its classical version, each team would try and eliminate the opposition by one of two methods – either by attempting to tag as many members of the opposite team as possible while continuously chanting goodu-goodu or by capturing an attacker who entered their territory. But in this new version of the game, inspired by the tension around them, both teams armed themselves with staves and gave each other no quarter. The children who played ranged in age from seven to twelve but the fury with which they fought would have done justice to their fathers. And for the first time, the teams were selected according to caste.

The Andavar team had lost the first two games. At the start of the next game, as the strongest Vedhar boy launched himself into the attack, a single Andavar boy faced him head on. The rest of his team drew themselves up behind. Keeping a wary eye on the circling Andavars, the burly Vedhar boy swatted the boy in front of him to the ground with contemptuous ease. As the child fell, he grabbed hold of his attacker's staff and clung on. The bigger boy grunted, and tried to recover his weapon. He aimed a kick at his adversary, to no avail.

The only way out for him was to abandon his staff and accept defeat but he wasn't about to be bested by the annoying creature in front of him. Just then three well-aimed blows delivered with all the anger the opposing side could muster crashed into the nape of his neck, his head and his legs. He fell to the ground and lay still. The elated cries of the Andavars were cut short by the unnatural stillness of their victim. Both sides took to their heels.

When news of the tragedy spread, the first to arrive on the scene was Muthu Vedhar. He refused to allow the wounded boy to be taken to Father Ashworth's nearby dispensary. Instead, he was heaved into a rough litter and taken to the vaidyan's house a couple of furlongs away. He died on the way. That day, his father and the rest of the Vedhars solemnly vowed at the Murugan temple to avenge the death of the child with the blood of every Andavar male in Chevathar and Meenakshikoil.

Early the next morning, while the moon still hung in the sky, the Vedhars once again assembled at the Murugan temple. Bells rang out to focus the attention of the Gods, following which Subramania Sastrigal, who had been reluctantly pressed into service by his son, mumbled Sanskrit shlokas and gave every man vibhuti and prasadham. He exhorted them to emulate the fearless warrior Arjuna who had fought with no thought of friend, kinsman or neighbour. 'Yours is a just fight, these evil men do not even spare the lives of children. And, above all, remember what Lord Krishna said on the battlefield:

'There is nothing more welcome for a warrior
Than a righteous war ...

Die and you will enter heaven
Conquer, and you will enjoy the sovereignty of earth ...'

29

Barely a kilometre away, Father Ashworth and Solomon Dorai knelt in prayer before the rosewood Christ. As soon as he had learned of the death of the boy, Solomon had instructed his men to expect an attack at any moment. Just before dawn broke, he had walked over to the church.

The priest had spent the night in prayer and meditation. He had remonstrated and argued with the Lord, sought guidance, pleaded for answers. 'Tell me, Lord,' he had shouted at one point, 'what good can come of this unholy battle? If this is your will, how can you justify it? The Hindus see it as a part of the great wheel of life turning, turning, turning, every act of destruction mirroring or giving rise to an act of creation. The almighty Shiva performs his terrible dance that creates even as it destroys. But what answer do you have, Lord?'

When the headman was announced, he ran out of the church to meet him, but his brief moment of hope died when he saw Solomon's face.

'There is still time to call it off, Solomon.'

'I'd like to pray, Father,' the headman said. 'And some of my men would like to receive the Lord's blessing. My Hindu fighters have already visited the temple, and the Christians would like to be able to worship as well.'

'This is not right, Solomon. This fight will not add to your glory, your greatness.'

'Father,' the headman said formally, 'I would like to pray and listen to the Lord. If you are unable to assist ...'

'Let me help you stop this, Solomon. I'll be your emissary. You know you can prevent it. All you need to do is tell me what will be acceptable to you.'

'I've told you what I've come here for.'

'Solomon, I'm begging you to listen. How will men remember you? As someone who sanctioned the killing of other men just because they belonged to another caste. Think, Solomon, these men till their fields just as you do, they have families like yours. Do you think killing them, driving them away from this land, will end all your troubles? Do you think that if this becomes a purely Andavar village, all your problems will be over? Do you think there will be no more rape, no more fights? You can put an end to this ...'

'I did not start it, Father, but it must be ended one way or the other. I want to spend time with my Lord but if you cannot help me, I will go.'

Slowly, like an old, old man, the priest began looking through the Bible, and finally found what he was searching for. He read out the words of the warrior Joshua: 'One man of you shall chase a thousand: for the Lord your God, he it is that fighteth for you, as he hath promised you.'

Then they bowed their heads in silent prayer. Some time later Solomon rose, thanked the priest and left.

30

Under the setting moon, the sea lay thick and viscous, its thunder dimmed, the surf a thin white scar. It was hot and clouds blanketed the sky, threatening rain.

The men began assembling on the beach at dawn. Solomon's fighters were the first to arrive. They formed a semicircle under the shadow of a dune, tense and expectant, repeatedly checking their weapons, bamboo silambus for the most part. Joshua and Solomon carried shotguns, the headman of the cotton village fingered an ancient flintlock, the barrel of which was held together by wire, and two other tenant farmers had guns that were little more than barrels with faulty foresights. Most of the fighters were armed with fearsome-looking aruvals with broad flat blades that could slice a coconut in two with the merest flick of a wrist.

As colour welled up in the sky, the catamarans of the fishing fleet set out for their distant fishing grounds, skimming across the sullen surface of the sea. The delayed monsoon had given them a few more days of fishing. About half a dozen catamarans bobbed in the still water beyond the surf. Solomon wondered why they hadn't already left.

A thin blade of sound announced Muthu Vedhar's arrival. His men broke from under the giant fronds of the palms lining the shore, preceded by the young Brahmin priest, a nadeswaram player and a drummer. Before the astonished eyes of their adversaries, Muthu's forces advanced as though they were part of a religious procession. Vibhuti flashed on bare bodies, and the fighters held their arms with stately grace: staffs, aruvals, some crudely fashioned tridents, a dozen or so firearms, as motley in their assortment as Solomon's own weaponry.

Solomon's group was outnumbered almost two to one despite the fact that Muthu had managed to round up barely a hundred men for the fight, less than half the number he had hoped for. The Andavars fingered their weapons nervously, tense and exhausted from the constant vigil of the past week. Joshua sensed their mood and whispered to Solomon, 'We should do something. Let's get a couple of them as soon as they get within shotgun range.'

'No,' Solomon whispered back. 'They have the poojari and musicians with them.'

'But we're playing into Muthu's hands. He's obviously got a plan.'

'As we do,' Solomon said. 'We shall fight honourably or not at all.'

Just outside shotgun range, Muthu stopped. The music died down, and the musicians and the poojari trudged off. At a signal from the Vedhar chief, firearms began popping, their sounds rendered insignificant by the vastness of sea and sand. The firing was wild and the distance between the forces was too great. A lucky shot brought down one of the Andavars, who fell clutching his leg. He began to wail, a shrill, agonized sound that galvanized Muthu's men into action. They began running towards the Andavars, stumbling across the soft sand. To Joshua's dismay his men were beginning to shift about, as their enemies drew closer. A couple of them cut and ran, and he turned on the rest in a fury.

'You cowards, I will shoot the next man who moves. Hold firm and you will succeed. Remember Valli, remember you are the only ones who stand between your women and children being butchered. Now fight like men!'

Solomon heard his cousin's exhortations dimly, for it was as though an enormous space had opened between his physical body and his other senses. As if from a great height, he saw himself calmly sight down the barrel of his shotgun at the bulk of Muthu now fifty yards from him. A young man, speedier than the Vedhar leader, took the charge full in the chest and went down, his limbs softened and askew in death. Solomon shot again and another man staggered and fell. But Muthu charged on. Joshua got off a couple of rounds, as did the others, and three more Vedhars fell.

The impact of the charging Vedhar force broke through the defensive line. Their firearms now useless, the men went for each other with a ferocity born of the need to survive. With the exception of a couple of the Marudars, none of the men had fought professionally or for gain and certainly not to the death. There were veterans of drunken brawls, of course, and those who had kicked and abused neighbours and rivals over land or women. But peace had prevailed in Chevathar for over two decades and most of the men were not prepared for war. Their brief training melted away and with an undisciplined desperation the men slashed at each other with aruvals and silambus, determined only to live at whatever cost.

Some died immediately, their skulls cloven in two or frantically battered in. The rest heaved and struggled, trying to maintain their balance on the shifting sand. Joshua fought the stocky Marudar chief, their bamboo staffs swirling and slicing through the air like leaping fish, thrust countered by parry, followed by counter-thrust. His opponent was as unsteady on the sand as Joshua with his limp. And then Joshua began to tire. The years began to take their toll. Back, back, the Marudar chief harried him, and then neatly side-stepping a wild lunge by his opponent he brought his staff smashing into the bridge of Joshua's nose, driving splinters of bone into his adversary's brain. Without a murmur, Joshua fell face down on the beach.

Fortunately for his men, the whirling intensity of the battle meant that most of them were too preoccupied to notice their leader fall. Aaron, who had been fighting by Joshua's side, saw however. He turned savagely on the Marudar chief. When he saw who his adversary was, the man smiled. 'First I'll kill you and then I'll deal with the rest of your misbegotten family,' he shouted.

After the first furious assault, Aaron began to slow down. He knew he would lose in full-frontal combat so he put into plan a strategy he had devised for precisely such a situation. He began retreating to an empty part of the beach, as the Marudar chief pressed home the attack. Half a dozen of his men rallied to his side, rolling back the brave efforts of the Andavar youths who surrounded Aaron. Then, as one, the Andavar boys scattered and to the consternation of the Marudar attackers, the ground beneath their feet began to move. The fishing nets that Aaron's fishermen friends had buried beneath the sand slid forward now as the catamarans began to head out to sea. Aaron and his band attacked the Marudar men as they fell, clubbing them to the ground and then clubbing them some more. Flipping the nets securely about the injured and dying men, Aaron and his band raised their arms in a prearranged signal. Trapped like porpoises, seven men, including the Marudar chief, slid into the Gulf of Mannar.

31

After the headman had left him, Father Ashworth knelt for a long time before the altar, praying for a miracle. Then he wandered outside. Solomon had warned him not to come to the scene of battle. When Father Ashworth had protested, the headman had said firmly that he would post some of his men at the mission compound to ensure he did not leave. The priest did not argue but merely said that there was no need to send anyone to guard him; Solomon would need every fighter he had.

The sun shone fitfully through a sky packed with tiny grey curls of cloud. It was hot and oppressive and he began to sweat under his cassock. Leaving the mission compound, he climbed a small knoll that gave him a clear view of the beach.

Men, like insignificant stick figures, moved around languidly on the gleaming sand. Occasionally one would fall; he couldn't say with any certainty if it got up again. Horror rose within him, renewed and huge. There were men dying on the sands, Vedhar, Andavar, Marudar, people he had lived with, laughed with, worshipped with. Father Ashworth knelt under the woolly sky and prayed but he had no words left to beseech the Lord; all he could do was remain on his knees, sinking deep into misery. Then, suddenly, he felt a great light flood him. As he watched, the rosewood Jesus, clad only in a loin-cloth, walked up to him and took him, by the hand and led him down the slope to where farmers and thieves died in God's name.

From a distance, a battlefield before the advent of modern artillery and warplanes was a quiet, self-absorbed place. The oaths and screams of dying men and enraged adversaries, the popping of firearms and the clash of sticks and knives and other implements of battle rose up and were sucked down again into the vortex, much as the scum at the centre of a whirlpool rises before being pulled under. To the dozens of spectators under the palms, the battle of Chevathar made little more noise than the subdued murmuring of the sea, making the grim struggle unfolding before their eyes seem like a puppet show.

But in the heart of the battle, the noise was furiously loud. With a roar, Muthu brushed aside the two Andavar men who were fighting him, and hurled himself at Aaron and the other boys. He had watched them lure the Marudar chief to his death, and knew he would need to exact immediate and crushing revenge if he hoped to rally his forces. He had almost got to the boy when Solomon brought him up short.

'You will have to get past me to fight my boy,' he said, his breath heaving out of him in great gasps. He was bruised and battered, and for a moment, Muthu felt compassion for him. He saw before him a middle-aged man, all the lightness and dash of youth gone, forced into a situation that he had no real control over. Then anger erased the moment and he attacked with all the strength, and guile, he had left.

Solomon had fared worse than Muthu so far but the moment he saw the big man's staff cut through the hot air towards him, he found a new energy. He parried the blow and counter-attacked. Around them the battle swirled and ebbed, following its own momentum, but from the moment their staves crossed, the two men were totally absorbed in each other.

Within a very short time, it became apparent to both of them that Muthu had the advantage. He was bigger and stronger than Solomon and still relatively unscathed. Age and peace had dulled Solomon's fighting edge. Muthu's blows got through with increasing regularity and the adrenalin rush that had energized him was beginning to wane. A blow to the ribs knocked him sideways, and another that he just managed to avoid grazed his face. His mouth filled with the mineral taste of blood. The blows of Muthu's staff fell upon him without pause. Then, he remembered a lesson his old instructor had taught him – the one stratagem that was kept for the best student. He began to sink to the ground, waiting for Muthu Vedhar's concentrated ferocity to waver to give him the opening he needed. As if in answer to a prayer, Muthu's attack ceased all at once. Astonished, he looked up and saw what had caused Muthu to pause. Father Ashworth stood before them, his face transfigured and calm. The priest spoke firmly. 'Stop now, Muthu Vedhar, Solomon Dorai. In the name of our Lord I command you to stop this senseless killing.'

Father Ashworth was a small man but the new spirit that welled within him gave his words an unnatural clarity and power. As if a switch had been thrown, all fighting stopped at that instant. A moment only, before Muthu, apparently immune to the spell Father Ashworth had cast, muttered, 'Interfering Christian priest', and snatching up a rusty trident from one of his fallen fighters thrust it deep into the cleric's belly.

Father Ashworth was driven backwards by the immensity of the blow. He sat down heavily, his hands clasped prayerfully around the shaft of the weapon, and then slumped to his side. The sand was warm on his face and his rapidly dimming sight took in the vast green eye of the sea, the rumpled sky above, the white teeth of the surf, as he died. Thunder heaved and rumbled on the eastern horizon, lightning whitened the sky and hot hard needles of rain stitched earth and sky into an enormous grey shroud. Already shocked and bemused by the death of the priest, the villagers took the cataclysmic downpour as a sign of divine wrath. A few began to scatter and run, others bowed low to the earth and the rest stood around indecisively.

Summoning up his last reserves of strength, Solomon raised himself on one knee and, arcing his staff, struck the one blow that every master sought to land. The silambu smashed into Muthu's collarbone. Before he could react, Solomon swung his staff again, at the giant's knees. Both kneecaps shattered, his fighting hand swinging uselessly, Muthu Vedhar tottered and began to fall. Solomon was waiting for him, his staff braced and rigid as steel. As his adversary fell forward, the silambu's blunt end smashed through his chin, bone, gristle and blood ferris-wheeling through the air with the force of the impact. Muthu was dead before he hit the ground. Iron control faltering, Solomon fell by the side of his great enemy. The storm abated, thinned to a light drizzle, then grew into a steady downpour. The monsoon had arrived in Chevathar, a fortnight late.

BOOK II

DORAIPURAM

ed him and said he didn't deserve to call himself a siddha vaidyan. Dr Pillai was unfazed, for he cared neither for honorifics nor acceptance by the traditional vaidyans. He was obsessed with siddha but he was even more passionate about curing people, and he needed medicine that worked. As hundreds of patients were healed by his somewhat unorthodox methods, his fame and workload grew. Charity's father and Dr Pillai had played chess every Thursday evening for twenty years, so when Jacob Packiam asked whether his grandson could join the clinic, Dr Pillai had had no objection.

Having announced Daniel, Chandran left to take up his usual station by the door. The doctor's room opened into a large hall. Patients waited here on mats that lined the wall. As Dr Pillai finished with a patient he would mutter a prescription that Chandran would relay to another assistant, who would take it across to the room where Daniel and his colleagues worked to make up dozens of prescriptions every day.

For a while Dr Pillai took no notice of him, and Daniel's anxiety increased. He tried to calm himself down by looking around the room. The doctor sat cross-legged on a mat, taking the pulse of a woman so bent and polished by age, she seemed to be a branch growing from the wood of the low stool she occupied. An enamel bowl on a stand and a wooden cupboard constituted the rest of the furniture in the room. The unornamented walls were cracked and peeling. Dr Pillai, who had never married, cared nothing for such fripperies as freshly whitewashed walls and curtained windows. But the consulting room was spotlessly clean. Dr Pillai finished examining the old woman, then beckoned Daniel over. He asked him to hold out his hands. He grasped Daniel's right hand in his own, looked at it for a long moment, then said abruptly, 'How long have you been working here?'

'Four years, aiyah.'

'Good. Take this paati's pulse and tell me what you feel. Here, like this.' He showed Daniel how to place the index, ring and middle fingers on the radial artery of the patient's emaciated wrist, then sat back and waited. Daniel was terrified. He had no idea why Dr Pillai was asking him to do this. He had never diagnosed a patient's ailment before and he knew nothing about the taking of a pulse. All he could do was make up siddha formulations that had been taught to him by Chandran and the other assistants. He felt the old woman's pulse all right, a thin surge beneath the skin and flesh, but he had no idea what the doctor expected him to say. The silence increased his nervousness. Dr Pillai said, 'Tell me what the pulse sounds like. You're an observant young man ... Does it sound like the wind through the leaves, the flapping of a crow's wings ...'

A flash in his mind. An earnest youth displaying a prized possession to a friend. 'Aiyah, it sounds like a tortoise walking ...' The minute the words were out he felt foolish, he wanted to fling the patient's hand down, run from the room. To his astonishment, Dr Pillai's stern countenance relaxed, almost into a smile. Gently detaching the patient's hand from Daniel's grip, he said simply, 'As I thought, you have the gift. From today you start assisting me with patients.'

Daniel raced home that night and went straight to his grandfather's room. Jacob Packiam was seated at his table reading the Bible. Forgetting his usual diffidence in the presence of his grandfather, Daniel blurted out, 'Thatha, did you ask Doctor-aiyah to give me more responsibilities?'

Jacob deliberately took off his spectacles, placed a bookmark in his Bible and only then permitted himself a smile. 'Daniel, nobody can tell Pillai to do anything. But some weeks ago he did say he was reaching a stage in his life when he wanted someone to take some of the load off him. He thought you might be the one ... Now go on, tell your amma, she'll be very happy.'

'Thank you, thatha.' He walked off in a daze.

In the months that followed, Dr Pillai began to open up the mysteries of siddha medicine to his young pupil. He taught him that man was but a microcosm of the universe built from the same five elements, the panchamahabhutas, that constituted it: earth, water, fire, wind and ether. The bhutas combined to form, in each cell of the body, three kuttrams – vatham, pitham and kapham. When these were balanced harmoniously, people enjoyed good health. When they grew disproportionate, they fell ill. Siddha medicine, Dr Pillai explained, always tried to restore the balance.

As their relationship strengthened, Dr Pillai initiated Daniel into the lore contained in the ancient volumes on siddha medicine in his possession. He explained the similarities between siddha, the medicine of the Tamils, and ayurveda, the other traditional method of healing that had originated in the north, and he educated Daniel about the eighteen celebrated siddhars to whom all knowledge about siddha was attributed. He would talk to his pupil late into the night about the religious and mystical traditions of the science: how Lord Shiva had imparted the principles of siddha to his consort Parvati, who had passed it on to Nandideva, who in turn had revealed it to the greatest sage of the Tamil country, Agasthiar.

The months passed. Daniel spent most of his time at the vaidyasalai, arriving early and returning home late. He was exhilarated by what he was learning and experiencing. In Dr Pillai's view, the finest physicians were those who could make the best diagnoses and he patiently guided Daniel through the eight diagnostic methods in siddha medicine: the reading of the pulse, the examination of the eyes and the tongue, the interpretation of voice, touch and colour, the analysis of urine and faeces. Daniel watched, listened and learned.

By the time his first year as Dr Pillai's apprentice came to an end, he was beginning to come to grips with the fundamentals of siddha. It would be a while yet before Dr Pillai would allow him to examine patients on his own but Daniel grew more confident by the day. He learned to use his fingers on a patient's pulse like a musician playing a stringed instrument and he could tell the disease in a patient through the divination of the pattern made by a drop of urine in a bowl of oil. If the drop spread in the shape of an arrow, a bull, a spear or an elephant, the kuttrams were not balanced. If it arranged itself like an umbrella, flower, ring or wheel, all was well. He could diagnose a disease through touch and interpret a patient's tongue. The intimate secrets of the body yielded to him while his mentor looked on approvingly.

As he was leaving the clinic one evening Dr Pillai called him in and announced, without preamble, that he was sending Daniel to the Government Medical College in Melur to earn a diploma in Western medicine. 'In my experience, knowledge of siddha medicine alone will not make you a good physician, although you could spend several lifetimes studying it. It's important to be able to contrast it with other systems. It will teach you to appreciate the greatness of siddha. An LMP diploma will come in useful. You leave in a month.' Daniel could hardly believe his ears. He remembered Father Ashworth's futile attempts to get his father to allow him to study medicine. How proud the old priest would be if he could see him now, he thought.

33

Long before the grey husk of day filled with light, Charity was up and about. Normally, she would have completed much of the cleaning and cooking by the time the rest of the household awoke, but today she felt strangely listless and enervated. Daniel was to leave for Melur, the next day.

She sank into the comfortable cane-backed planter's chair on the tiny veranda of the cottage, Daniel's favourite spot until his life had been taken over by the clinic, and looked out into the little garden. In the breaking day, the contours of the plants and trees sharpened. A blue mango dominated the garden. It grew tall and beautiful beside the path that led from the gate to the front door. Tiger-striped crotons surrounded it with an explosion of colour. Charity had brought the mango seedling from Chevathar on her first visit home after her marriage and it had taken well. But it hadn't fruited even once. Every season, tiny mangoes, pale and shiny like lapis lazuli, would form, but would drop off the stalk before they ripened – living proof of the saying that the Chevathar Neelam would only fruit by the red river. For a while she had been afraid that Daniel too would be permanently affected by exile. He had taken a long time to recover, and she had suffered with him, his pain overwhelming and banishing her own. When he had begun to enjoy his work, she had rejoiced. And now he could hardly contain his excitement at the prospect of studying Western medicine! She had tried to be happy for him, and hoped that the sadness she felt deep down did not show.

The household was stirring as Charity made her way to the minuscule kitchen at the back of the house. She had promised to make Daniel paal kolukattai, his favourite sweet. As the milk began to warm, she mixed and kneaded the sweetened dough, and began to pinch off and shape the dumplings. The fire wasn't catching, and she turned her attention to the stove. Smoke billowed into her face as she blew into it, and her eyes grew teary. She thought: It's the tragedy of a mother to lose her sons. First Aaron, consumed by his father's passion that had spat him out, broken and bitter and full of hate for his surviving family, and now her favourite, Daniel, who was poised to disappear into a world where she could not follow. Charity wept, as the sadness of the present and the past fused and swept over her.

Solomon had died of his injuries a few days after the great battle, and she hadn't been able to reach the village in time for the funeral. When she did get to Chevathar with Daniel (her father had insisted she leave the girls behind in Nagercoil until things were more settled), she found it changed beyond recognition in the short time she had been away. A detachment of policemen was stationed in one of the houses. Three Vedhar families, Muthu Vedhar's among them, had been permanently banished, leading to a minor exodus of Vedhar villagers. The church by the sea, which had been set on fire while the battle was raging, was a smoke-blackened ruin. The Christian villagers now had to trek all the way to town to worship.

Abraham Dorai, who had lived in his older brother's shadow all his life, had become thalaivar and his wife Kaveri ran the Big House. At first, Abraham and his wife tried to be conciliatory, but as the weeks went by Kaveri began to take over the household, elbowing Charity aside. Most of the servants were dismissed, and those who remained were told that Kaveri was now mistress of the house. Drained and depleted, Charity watched her powers being eroded. However, her brother-in-law and his wife were not unkind to them, partly because they were terrified of Aaron. The death of his father and uncle had affected her younger son badly. Charity's heart went out to him, but there was little she could do, for he blamed her and Daniel as much as he did the rest of the world for having taken Solomon and Joshua from him. He loathed his uncle and aunt as well. Abraham and Kaveri were careful around the scowling boy with the limp (the only external scar he bore of the battle); there was no telling when he would do something unpredictable.

A few months later, Aaron got into a fight with Abraham. Everyone knew he spent his days and most of his nights in Meenakshikoil playing cards, picking fights and loafing around but nobody dared question him. Abraham usually gave him money whenever Aaron demanded it but on this occasion he refused to pay the ten rupees his nephew wanted. Aaron exploded, and when Abraham held out he abused him and rushed out of the house.

Five days later he hadn't returned. Charity persuaded her brother-in-law to look for him but it was clear that Aaron had left the area. Charity was devastated and even Abraham was concerned. The only one who was delighted was Kaveri, for she had feared the angry boy more than anyone else. When it was clear that he was not coming back, she was quick to consolidate her control over the Big House.

Matters came to a head less than a week later. One afternoon Kaveri slapped Kamalambal for not scrubbing the floors to her satisfaction.

Charity was quick to remonstrate, and Kaveri turned on her in a fury.

That evening Abraham told Charity and Daniel that it would be best if they left Chevathar. He was willing to settle a small sum of money on them, all that he was able to scrape together, for times were hard – the punitive taxes imposed on the villagers on account of the riot, and yet another crop failure had left very little to go round. If they gave no trouble, he was willing to pay them an annual rent in kind – mangoes and rice. Before the year was out, Charity and Daniel took a bullock cart across the border and headed back to Charity's home town of Nagercoil.

She heard footsteps outside the kitchen. Charity brushed away her tears and greeted Rachel, her older daughter, now a pretty seventeen-year-old with huge grave eyes like her own. 'Ma, Miriam is refusing to get up.' Charity could picture the scene all too well. Miriam, her youngest, spoiled and cosseted, refusing to do anything unless coaxed into it. Fortunately, Rachel was patient and slow to irritation. 'Never mind, kannu, we'll wake her up later,' she said, smiling at Rachel. She would need to get her married soon; a couple of years more and she would be deemed too old to find a good match. But she would make a beautiful bride. How Solomon would have enjoyed giving her away. Charity could feel the tears coming on again, and hastily began to get the morning meal ready.

Later that morning, she hovered around her son as he sat in his customary place on the veranda eating the paal kolukattai. The sun had not yet acquired the punishing heat of day and the garden pulsed with colour and sound. In the dry leaves under the mango tree, sparrows and babblers rustled and chattered. On the low stone wall that enclosed the grounds, a garden lizard made its slow and trembling way, while two squirrels chased each other up and down the mango tree. In the lee of the wall, Jacob had planted a row of hibiscus bushes and their flashy flowers had attracted a pair of exotic visitors.

'Look, amma, sunbirds, I haven't seen them in a long time,' Daniel said. Why is the world so full of enchantment, and yet so sad, Charity thought, as they watched the birds that morning, iridescent drops of gold and emerald motionless under the great bank of flowers that had drawn them to this magic garden.

34

Anniversaries of failed revolutions are nerve-racking occasions for rulers and the state. The embered ashes of defeat begin to glow, preparatory to bursting into flame, the unquiet spirits of martyrs walk the land, instilling the fire of revolution in those who would rise up again, and everywhere the tension heightens. As the fiftieth anniversary of the 1857 War of Independence drew near, the rulers in unified India watched its approach with trepidation.

The war had served to emphasize several things: the differences between ruler and ruled, the latent hostility and mistrust that existed between both sides, and the vulnerability of Empire in the subcontinent. The Crown had always been aware that should there be a mass uprising it might well mean the loss of its most prized possession. It simply did not have the numbers or the resources to control India's millions if they decided to sink their differences and unite against their masters. The 1857 revolt, ill-managed and short-lived though it was, could never be repeated.

Consequently, in the summer of 1907, as the anniversary approached, the British grew more vigilant. From the Sub-divisional Magistrate in his lonely posting on the banks of the shining Irrawaddy in Burma to the tea-planter in remote Assam, from the Governors in their mansions in the great Presidencies of Bombay, Bengal and Madras to the enlisted men in the cantonments, every one of the hundred thousand or so white subjects of His Majesty the King Emperor wondered how three hundred million Indians would react to the memory of the uprising.

Chris Cooke was among those who watched the gathering storm with deep foreboding. He had seen at first hand how quickly the seemingly submissive people of this land could explode out of control, and he often worried about the new horrors the anniversary could unleash.

But he wasn't fretting about the Mutiny now. For the past hour Cooke had been stuck in the main concourse of the Madras Central Station with practically every Briton in the city. In one of the pointless displays of sycophancy which the capital of the Presidency was prone to, pretty much everyone who counted was expected to be present at the station to dance attendance on the Governor whenever he left or returned to the city. Cooke looked grumpily at the people milling around dressed in their best suits or uniforms. What a complete waste of time, he thought; you would think all these important people had no work to do, and that their life depended on getting to shake Governor Lawley's hand. And all this in the hope of promotion or a couple more letters after their names.

This was one of the things he disliked most about Madras but there were others that ran it close – the politics at the office, the gossip at the club, the rule-bound social whirl – although he did enjoy his cricket at Chepauk and the music and amateur theatricals. But what really bothered him was the fact that he was stuck behind a desk when what he had liked about his career was the opportunity to serve in the field. In the capital, you were completely isolated from the people and their problems, and this was not what he had joined the civil service for. As a third-generation ICS man, he had been weaned on stories of the duty which members of the service owed to this land and its people. To be a part of the steel frame meant doing your best for the millions in your charge, not spending half the day waiting for one man to get on a train. He would put in for a transfer back to Kilanad as soon as was politic, or when he could take life in the capital no more, whichever happened sooner. It might not be the best career move he had made, the district he had served in was the least important in the Presidency, but Cooke didn't care. He had just turned thirty-three and was still unencumbered by family or other commitments. He would think about serving a sentence in the capital a decade or so from now. His neighbour accidentally stepped on his foot, the soaring heat made his stiff collar and suit unendurable, and Cooke was suddenly desperate for some fresh air. He began pushing his way to the edge of the throng.

Further up the platform, which had been cleared of regular travellers and its usual chaos, were some benches, most occupied by people like him who'd grown tired of waiting. Cooke headed for an empty bench in the distance, but before he got there a prematurely balding man with an open, cheerful face hailed him. An assistant editor with the *Mail,* Nicholas was one of the first people he had met in the city. They got on well and Cooke gratefully took a seat beside him. A red-faced man with scanty eyebrows shared the bench and the journalist made the introductions. When they shook hands, Cooke noticed with distaste that the man, who was the managing agent of one of the big trading firms, had a sweaty grip. Surreptitiously he wiped his hands on his handkerchief.

'What a dreadful waste of time this is, don't you think?' Nicholas said. 'All the Governor is doing is leaving on a two-day trip to Coimbatore. Surely that doesn't require the presence of virtually every Englishman in Madras?'

'Protocol,' said Cooke cautiously.

'Protocol be damned, old boy,' the journalist said cheerfully. 'Shouldn't you chaps be on your guard with all these rumblings in the city?'

'We're taking steps,' Cooke said.

'Spoken like a true bureaucrat,' Nicholas said gleefully. 'Taking steps, that's rich. Did you read the report in my paper about the furore that Bengali chap Bipin Chandra Pal caused last week? Practically urged our Tamil friends to burn every Englishman alive!'

'Surely not.' Cooke adopted his friend's bantering tone. 'Just got a little excitable. Isn't that supposed to be a Bengali trait?'

Nicholas laughed. 'It certainly is, if you go by the commotion they've been causing. But I suppose they have something to shout about, the division of Bengal and all that!'

'That's a problem, isn't it?' Cooke said thoughtfully. 'It's often hard to damn the protesters without feeling you're being a bit unfair.'

'Unfair!' the businessman sputtered. 'What on earth are you talking about, Mr Cooke? Do you know that the natives are talking of boycotting all English products? They're urging their countrymen to buy indigenous products. What's the word they use?'

'Swadeshi,' Cooke said.

Nicholas chimed in, 'And, my friend, you'd better print the other native word that begins with an S on your brain. Swaraj. Freedom. You're going to be hearing it a lot in the months to come.'

'What's the country coming to?' the businessman said irritably. 'You fellows should arrest the lot. Deport them. Show no mercy if you don't want a repeat of 1857.'

'I don't think there'll be a repeat of 1857. I think we can rely on the natives ...' Cooke wasn't allowed to finish.

'Rely on the natives,' the businessman said shrilly. 'I beg your pardon, sir, but you can't mean that.'

'Oh come now, without relying on them, the vast majority of them at any rate, we wouldn't be here. Do you really think we could control India if all of them got together and decided to give us the heave-ho?' Nicholas said, coming to Cooke's rescue.

'Well, I suppose not,' the businessman said grudgingly. He mopped his face with his handkerchief and looked hopefully down the platform. But there was no sign of the Governor. An engine exhaled somewhere. It was exhausting to talk in the heat, but the silence didn't last long for the businessman, who had evidently been brooding over what had been said, abruptly burst into speech again.

'I suppose the real problem is the educated native. Macaulay, a sterling fellow in most respects, made a mistake when he advocated that we develop a race that was Indian in blood and colour but European in opinion, morals and intellect. Gave the natives ideas above their station. That's why we had the Mutiny, and that's why we have these problems today. Keep the heathen illiterate and unchristian and control him with a whip, that's the only way.'

Cooke was dangerously close to anger. 'You don't happen to believe that, do you?'

'Yes, I do,' the businessman said bluntly. 'You can't trust the native. Not now, not ever. Unless you want to preside over the dissolution of Empire. It was because we trusted them that the Mutiny took place. God, women and children cut down in cold blood, dismembered, thrown into a well. Cawnpore and Lucknow will be remembered a thousand years from now, all because we weren't vigilant enough and trusted the brown man. Whenever I hear one of these Indians whining about injustice, all I need to do is recollect 1857 and I could cheerfully pistol-whip them.'

'We were no better,' Cooke said. 'Do you know that we made all the Indians who were captured at Cawnpore lick the blood from the floor of the building where the slaughter took place before hanging them? And that we erased whole villages, killing and maiming and torturing? The Devil Wind, they called it.'

'But they deserved it, the bastards, we had to stand firm to ensure it was never, ever repeated. And we have to be ruthless with these mischief-makers today,' the businessman said, refusing to back down.

'Enough,' Nicholas said, stepping into the breach, his voice soothing. 'There's no reason to get excited. Most of these so-called nationalist leaders have no real support and we have no cause to worry, unless they join forces. But that won't happen, especially now – there's an internal power struggle going on among the Extremists and Moderates in the Congress and some other organizations. So while there might be some fireworks, everything will die down quickly. The Tamil is a timid creature not given to sustained anger.'

With reason, thought Cooke. The inhabitants of Britain's first acquisition had had the stuffing knocked out of them in various campaigns: the Poligar Wars, the defeat of Tipu across the border, the suppression of the Vellore riots a hundred years ago. No, the Tamil had suffered and tended to behave himself. But you couldn't be too careful.

'Do you really think these protests will come to naught?' he asked the journalist.

'I expect so,' Nicholas said. 'Nothing we've heard seems to indicate anything to the contrary. A few children throwing stones at policemen, protest meetings, the usual stuff.'

'Natives cannot be dealt with too severely,' the businessman said darkly. 'Any misdemeanour and you should hang them. Do they still blow them from the barrels of guns?'

'Afraid we can't oblige you there, Mr ...'

'Damn, where's Lawley?' Nicholas exclaimed suddenly. 'He's never been this late. Anything we should know, Cooke?'

'Nothing that I would know about,' Cooke said.

'Think I'll just go and see what's happening,' the businessman said, getting to his feet. Without shaking hands with either of them, he walked off in the direction of the crowd.

'Who was that excrescence?' Cooke demanded when he was out of earshot.

'Oh, he's quite popular, my dear fellow. You should get out more, get to know your city's charming social set.'

'Damned if I will,' Cooke said. 'Not a day passes when I don't wish I was back in the district. Madras is beginning to get to me.'

'That's the problem with you district-wallahs,' Nicholas said. 'All you can think about is striding around the countryside being noble and worthy. You should learn to relax. Drink, after Lawley's gone?'

'No, thank you, I think I'll go for a long walk, clear my head.'

It was late evening by the time Chris got to the Adyar river, one of his favourite haunts in the city. The sun was low on the horizon, turning the water the colour of molasses. A young moon had scraped a sliver of yellow in the sky. The calm of the river and the scrub that massed on its banks, shot through with bird-calls and the unseen rustling of small creatures of the night, acted as a much-needed restorative. But his respite was brief, as his argument with the businessman returned to bother him. Was repression the only way to control this land? Would they be able to keep Indians from having a say in their own country for ever? Hardly likely, he thought, sooner or later something would have to give. Didn't that disgruntled boor see that unless the British worked with the people they ruled, they would, at some point, be faced with something far worse than the Mutiny? A phrase from one of the nationalist leaders, who had compared the

Swadeshi movement to a raging fire, occurred to him. It had been reported widely, often approvingly, by sections of the Indian-owned media. Would they all be incinerated in the blaze? He hated himself for feeling so panicky. That was another thing he disliked about the city. Detached from the immediate reality of the country, you spent your time obsessed with rumour, inaccurate newspaper reports and gossip. God, what wouldn't I give to be back in Kilanad, he thought. With real problems that I could actually have a hand in solving!

It had grown darker and he could hardly see the path, so he decided to turn back. About halfway to the car something about the river, the scrub, and the position of the moon in the sky awakened in him a memory of Chevathar. That time had been the most calamitous of his career. He'd worked without pause for weeks, especially as his acting superior had no knowledge of the district, and it had been a miracle that the troubles had been brought under control. He hoped his transfer orders would come soon. He would journey back to Chevathar, revisit the village that his friend the priest had fought so valiantly to save. If only they had listened to him. He hadn't heard any news of his former Collector, Nathaniel Hall. Nobody knew anything about him. But he had come to know a couple of years ago, from a colleague in Burma, that the crooked lawyer Vakeel Perumal had resurfaced in Rangoon. How unjust, he thought, that people like him continued to prosper while the good were buried, and in time forgotten.

35

Sunk in its own concerns, Chevathar was untouched by the rumblings of nationalist politics in 1907. The new year opened in the village with grey, headachy weather. The prospect of yet another weak monsoon, the fourth in a row, was awful to contemplate – crop failure, possible famine, which would in turn lead to an inability to pay taxes and government levies on land and farms.

By the bridge leading to Meenakshikoil, three young men were idly skimming flat stones across one of the pools that the river had shrunk to, the projectiles hiccoughing across the still rust-red surface. Aaron Dorai, the oldest of the three, abruptly left off what he was doing and stretched out on the rocky bank, staring into the closed face of the sky. He had inherited his mother's good looks, but was saved from appearing too feminine by a strong jaw and luxuriant moustache. He had lived his young life hard and looked old for his years. When he had run away from home he had ended up in Ranivoor where he had gone to work in a grain merchant's store. He had lasted a little over six months before the dark dingy store, the choking dust of rice, wheat and pulses that filled the air and the loud bullying voice of the proprietor, who sat behind the counter like a recumbent elephant, began to get to him. He moved on to Tinnevelly, Puthulum and Mannankoil, working for a while in each place, indulging in petty thievery and hanging out with the unemployed loafers, before moving on. He had been beaten up, he had gone hungry, he had faced unexpected kindness and equally unexpected blows, but he had lived intensely. A little over five years after walking out, he had decided to return to Chevathar.

He was surprised to find neither his mother nor his brother nor his aunt Kamalambal at the Big House. Abraham and Kaveri had a well-rehearsed story to tell: Kamalambal, poor thing, had died of cholera; they missed her greatly, but they weren't sure if they should tell him the truth about Charity and Daniel. With well-feigned reluctance, the concocted details had tumbled out: his mother and his brother, they said, had declared that they could no longer live in such reduced circumstances and were returning to Nagercoil. Nothing could make them change their mind, not even (Kaveri said) his chithappa reminding them of Solomon-anna's ultimate sacrifice in defence of their family home. Aaron was quick to grasp the unstated message. 'I always knew that my brother was unworthy of the name he bore. But my mother!' He had raved and ranted in a fury while his aunt and uncle tried to look aggrieved and sorrowful and empathetic all at once. As a result of these revelations Aaron was irrevocably confirmed in his hatred of his brother and his mother.

Abraham and Kaveri had succeeded in their purpose. What they hadn't counted on was that Aaron would decide to stay on in Chevathar. But, to their relief, it soon became apparent that he had no interest in farming nor did he want to be thalaivar. Life went on for Abraham and Kaveri much as it had before. All they needed to do was keep Aaron fed and clothed and stay out of his way when he was in a rage. As before, he spent most of his days hanging out with three or four other disaffected young men in Meenakshikoil, drinking endless cups of tea and smoking beedis in the tea stalls in town, teasing young girls or old men when the fancy took him – frittering away the days and nights and coming home only to sleep. A year passed, then another. He was filled with disquiet and a deep frustration, but he had no idea of what to do with himself.

This past week, the attention of Aaron and his friends had been temporarily diverted by the impending visit of the Abel Circus, a European-owned show that had never played in Kilanad before. Fearing trouble in the major towns of the Presidency, the proprietor had decided that Kilanad, and specifically its southernmost town, Meenakshikoil, would be more suitable for the circus's 'winter' tour, which usually began soon after New Year's Day.

As soon as the crude handbills were pasted on the walls of huts and the few public buildings in town, the inhabitants, especially the adult male population, were gripped by a feverish excitement. Abel was a smart businessman, and years of experience had given him acute insight into the minds of paying customers. His handbills, printed in one colour on cheap white paper, were not subtle. In the foreground, a European woman (it was easy to deduce that the boldly drawn figure with exaggerated breasts, hips and thighs was European because she wore her hair loose and bobbed, had oversize lips, and was costumed in undersized briefs and a scanty bra) smiled invitingly, while assorted lions, tigers, clowns and dwarfs formed a poorly drawn, barely discernible backdrop. In the mofussil, Abel's audiences were mainly male, entranced by the sagging thighs and tits of the poorly paid, fair-skinned Anglo-Indian women he employed, whose act consisted mainly of parading around the ring in sequins, tights and skimpy costumes. Only one of them had the skills and figure to do a simple trapeze act, the rest strutted and simpered, though for most of them even this was an act of torture, their weight and their bunions making the straightforward act of walking the boards in high-heels difficult and painful. The audience didn't care about the shortcomings of the artistes. They flocked to the circus to bury their collective face, or at the very least their eyes, in the fleshy white (or an approximation thereof) thighs of its star turns.

But a week was a long time to rely on the imagination: Aaron and his friends had discussed the buxom ladies of the circus until their conversation was tired and worn.

'Stranger in town,' Nambi, who was facing the road, said abruptly. Aaron and Selvan swivelled in that direction. The man approaching them was of medium height, with an aquiline nose and a high forehead. He was a couple of years older than them, and was dressed in a travel-stained jibba and veshti. He asked the trio directions to the Dorai house.

'Why do you want to know?' Aaron asked curiously.

'I need the thalaivar's help,' the stranger said simply.

'I'll take you there, I'm his nephew,' Aaron said, and he clambered to his feet. Waving goodbye to his friends, he climbed the slope to the road, and they set off in the direction of the Big House.

As they walked, the stranger introduced himself as S. V. Iyer, a lawyer from the capital.

'Melur?'

'No, Madras,' Iyer said, and Aaron's estimation of him soared. There was something about the man that had already prevented Aaron and his gang from harassing him, but now his feeling of respect deepened. The stranger was curious about Meenakshikoil, Chevathar and Aaron's own family. Flattered, Aaron told Iyer about the battle of 1899, about which the other had heard, the heroism of his father and his Joshua-chithappa.

'A tragic business,' Iyer said. 'We could have used men like them.'

They were quite near the house by now. Aaron asked the stranger why he was visiting Meenakshikoil.

'I'll tell you soon, especially as I think I'll need your assistance.'

'In what way?' Aaron asked.

'You'll find out, but the main reason I'm here is because of something every one of us needs to be involved in.'

The young lawyer's eyes grew animated, but before he could expand on what he was saying, they were home. Abraham came forward to greet them. After the preliminary courtesies, Iyer explained why he was visiting Meenakshikoil and Chevathar.

'Revolution, aiyah, revolution. It is up to every one of us to throw the white man into the sea. He has oppressed India and enslaved us for too long. And now he has gone and partitioned Bengal.'

'Be careful about what you say. You know that, as thalaivar, I'm responsible to the authorities for this place. Don't talk incautiously.'

Iyer took no notice of Abraham's warning.

'Aiyah, I'm not preaching sedition or treason. Or maybe I am. But what we're saying is that India is for us Indians. We need to support Indian enterprises, wear Indian fabrics, have Indians making decisions on our behalf, not have a few white men rule this land with little concern for us.'

'The English have ruled us, true, but they have ruled us wisely. Before they came it was village against village, rajah against rajah ...'

'Respectfully, aiyah, I must interrupt and disagree. Look at your own village, your own district. Year after year the rains have failed, the crops wither, there is threat of famine. And all the white man does is raise taxes and turn a deaf ear to our cries. So what do we do? We chant mantrams and perform ineffectual rituals to the Gods asking for rains, money, grain for crops and to feed our families, while never forgetting to bow to the white man, our latest God, for fear that we will incur his wrath. Imagine if we had our own people responsible for us. If they failed us we could challenge them, not genuflect before them ...'

'Enough of this city talk. We are peaceful people, and I am a responsible official. I will have nothing to do with this sort of thing.'

Iyer restrained himself with an effort. 'I'm sorry if I offended you, aiyah, but will you at least come to our meeting?'

'No, no, I'm sorry, I can't do that.'

'I'll come, I'll come,' Aaron said.

Abraham said nothing; he had long ago given up trying to control his nephew.

As they walked back to town, Iyer told his young friend stories of revolution and martyrs, firebrands from the east and the north who were rousing the cowed soul of the south. He told him of the split in the Congress Party between the Moderates who believed in appeasement and the Extremists. Names like Bipin Chandra Pal and Lala Lajpat Rai fell from his lips like incantations and they ignited the imagination of the listener.

They strolled across the bridge towards Meenakshikoil. The town now boasted a boarding house (where Iyer was staying), a high school, three hotels – a military hotel, an idli-sambhar place, and one which served quick-fried snacks and speshul tea-kaapi all day long – and an impressive compound of government buildings, all this a result of the authorities deciding to make the place a full-fledged taluqa headquarters, with a tahsildar instead of a deputy tahsildar in charge. Shanmuga Vedhar had been transferred to Ranivoor soon after the riots, and the new man, a Brahmin, had been thoroughly vetted with regard to his caste affiliations; the authorities were determined, to the extent possible, to prevent a recurrence of the tragedy.

They stopped at the tea shop and ordered two speshul kaapis. As Iyer talked, his stories filled Aaron's mind. Before they parted, Aaron promised the older man that he would help with his meeting in Meenakshikoil, to be held the following day on the outskirts of town, well clear of the police station and the tahsildar's office.

All the next day Iyer, and Aaron and his friends, met people, inviting them to come to the meeting, where the lawyer promised they would hear about how to get what they wanted from the Government. Nervous that the authorities would break up the meeting, Iyer enjoined secrecy on all those who were invited; the presence of Aaron and his gang ensured compliance.

By six-thirty that evening, while there was still enough light in the sky, about a hundred people had gathered in a large open piece of ground where the Abel Circus was due to pitch its tents in a few days' time. Aaron and his friends, seven of them, positioned themselves behind Iyer.

'Breathes there a man amongst you who would rather not do his duty, as Krishna reminded Arjuna on the battlefield?' With that opener, Iyer rapidly began expanding his thesis that the white man was a blemish on the brown face of the motherland. He presented a fine figure as he stood in front of the townspeople, but it was soon evident that he was not a practised public speaker, and he quickly lost his listeners. Aaron was beginning to get worried, but his anxiety lessened when Iyer took off on a new tack: the sacrifices made by patriots in the cause of the nation. This promised to be good meaty stuff, but again Iyer's inexperience showed. Instead of dramatizing his stories, he related the exploits of the martyrs in a dry, bloodless way. He rambled on about how the white man's seeming invulnerability had been exposed by the Japanese; he ranted about the differences between the old men of the Congress and the Madras Mahajana Sabha and young Extremists like himself.

'Rise up, brothers and sisters of Meenakshikoil and Chevathar, as our great patriotic poet Subramania Bharati has said,' Iyer roared, pumping his fist for emphasis. In the thickening twilight, Aaron could see many of the listeners glancing about or chatting among themselves. Some had even begun to drift away. He stepped up to Iyer and said urgently, 'Anna, talk about local issues. Otherwise you will have no support here.' Iyer looked annoyed at the interruption but, to Aaron's relief, took his advice. The heroes of the Russian revolution were skated over, and he began to talk of water shortages and famine, taxes and the law of land.

The effect was immediate and electrifying. Iyer spoke with conviction of the ills besetting the region, and then said at the top of his voice, 'And what must every one of us do? We must fight this injustice. We must strike directly at the heart of the evil empire by denying them our money, the fruits of our labour, and by brushing aside the white man's goods, his businesses, and supporting our own. And brothers and sisters of Meenakshikoil and Chevathar, by the will of God, the opportunity will present itself next week. When the Abel Circus comes to town, not a single one of you must go to it. Aaron and his friends will lead you in this action. Vande Mataram.'

Aaron's eyes snapped towards Iyer. The half-smile with which he had been watching the crowd as it absorbed his new friend's speech vanished, to be replaced by a look of incredulity. Boycott the Abel Circus! The show that they had been thinking of for weeks! The women's marbled white thighs flashing in front of their greedy eyes, engorging their imagination, their fantasies! Abruptly, he was afforded a pitiless insight: revolution always demands of its standard-bearers sacrifices greater than they can afford or comprehend, offering in return only the promise of an imperfectly understood, endlessly receding ideal. But, despite the crushing disappointment he felt, he thrilled to the idea of fighting for a cause, no matter that he didn't understand it. Besides, Iyer had caught his imagination. He reminded him of his Joshua-chithappa, with his passion and idealism.

With these thoughts running through his head, he stepped up beside Iyer and said firmly, 'My friends and I will ensure that Abel Circus does not have a single customer here.'

36

'Yesu Christuveh, Rachel is Your daughter, please do not let a single slip, a single mistake damage her prospects. Lord, in Your infinite wisdom, mercy and benevolence, bless Your daughter bountifully.' Daily, having placed the responsibility squarely in the Lord's hands, Charity tried to do everything humanly possible to ensure that Rachel's wedding passed off without a hitch. She would wake up even earlier than usual, double the amount of time she spent in prayer, and spend every other waking moment cooking, stitching and generally bustling about organizing the dozens of little things that needed to be done. A traditional marriage was an exhausting, complicated, expensive business, and she wouldn't know a moment's peace until the vows were exchanged. Bridegrooms knew their value, as did their families, and showed their displeasure at the smallest provocation.

Why, barely three weeks ago, the marriage of Savitri's daughter had been called off because the payasam at the engagement ceremony hadn't been sweet enough. Her friend had been devastated. 'My daughter's value in the marriage market has plummeted. Maybe she is destined to be unmarried for the rest of her days. What sin have I committed to suffer such a fate?' she had wailed. Even as she'd comforted her friend, Charity's mind had gone into overdrive – not only would she need to oversee the preparation of the payasam at Rachel's engagement ceremony personally, she would need to have back-up plans ready if for some reason the dessert didn't pass muster. Perhaps she could offer a gold chain of extra thickness to the bridegroom, maybe more dowry, although she would have little to fall back on once the marriage expenses were met.

She had begun preparing for Rachel's marriage the moment Daniel had returned to Nagercoil, an LMP diploma to practise medicine stowed in his trunk. One morning, she had asked him hopefully whether he was ready to be married and had received his standard reply: 'No marriage, not until I'm worthy of the name I bear!' She had, Yesu forgive her, felt irritated by the remark. When would he shake off the past, take up his responsibilities, take care of his family? Forgive me, Lord, she'd thought, I'm so tired. It was at such moments that she missed Solomon the most. Daniel would have surely been married by now, and Aaron, who could tell about Aaron? And how much easier it would have been to attract suitors if it had been Solomon Dorai, mirasidar and thalaivar, whose children were to be married, rather than the daughter of a widow, herself the daughter of a retired headmaster.

She could have got carried away, but Charity had spent her life stowing her fancies away behind an enormous pragmatism, so she'd composed herself and said to her son: 'If neither of you boys want to be settled, it'll have to be Rachel. If we leave it too long, we'll never find a good match.' Her tone must have been acerbic, for Daniel had looked at her, startled, then said, 'Yes, amma, let's look for a boy immediately.' The marriage network began to hum and within a fortnight they had received a proposal they liked. Ramdoss was a clerk in the Collector's office in Madura, and was distantly related to Jacob's sister's husband. The dowry was proposed, negotiated and agreed upon. It would stretch Charity's slender finances but there could be no compromise. Soon after, Ramdoss's mother, sisters and a brace of aunts announced their intention to visit. Charity cut down even further on her sleep as the visit approached and on the last night she didn't sleep at all. It was the first big hurdle to be negotiated if the marriage was to take place.

Ramdoss's mother and sisters resembled each other to a great degree – exceedingly short, but as if in compensation slim, fair and pretty. As they came up the path to the front door Charity thought to herself that they looked for all the world as if they were swarming along the ground rather than walking on it. She smiled and welcomed the ladies, offered them refreshments and gifts, and then Rachel was led in, beautiful and grave, dressed in her third-best sari, a shimmering peacock-blue Conjeevaram. Charity thought she looked exquisite, but the thought was immediately knocked off its perch by others:

1) Was she a shade too dark?
2) She was twenty. Would she be considered too old?
3) Had she greeted her sisters-in-law-to-be (if the marriage was to happen) with enough obsequiousness?
4) Had the dowry been enough? It had been fixed but you never knew.

Ramdoss's mother was asking Rachel the usual questions. Did she sing? Did she dance? Could she cook? Rachel could do all these with a fair degree of proficiency but was there a Tamil bride who couldn't? Charity's nervousness increased. Everything depended on what Ramdoss's mother would do next. To everyone's surprise she beckoned Rachel closer, made room beside her on the newly bought cane sofa and asked quietly: 'Will you be able to make my son happy, daughter?'

Consternation among the various relatives of the bride's family. Where was this woman from? Happiness? What sort of question was that? Of course, everyone wanted to be happy but the only things that really mattered were: Was she fair? Was she too tall? Was she of the right age? Did the caste and sub-caste match? Could she bear sons? Was the dowry handsome? Did her family have the right status? A muted buzz rose in the small room. Charity alone smiled as Rachel raised her head and said, 'Yes, mami, I'll make him happy. There will be no other aim in my life.' That was all, but it was enough. Ramdoss's mother leaned forward, broke off a bit of coocoos, and nibbled at it, signifying that the girl had been accepted.

The date for the engagement was fixed for January. Although the first hurdle had been cleared, the next months would be tense, for there was no telling what could upset the frail connection that bound the two families. Charity welcomed hordes of relatives to the little cottage, fed them, and put them up in various houses around town. Some of them would have an active part to play in the wedding; the rest would form the necessary backdrop to a successful alliance.

By the time the day of the engagement arrived, the cottage had been completely taken over by relatives. It was too small to hold the anticipated number of guests, so a pandal had been erected under the enormous cashew-nut tree in the backyard.

There were seventy people in the bridegroom's party, and they arrived in the midst of much gaiety and confusion. They were ceremoniously welcomed and duly installed under the pandal where they sweated gently in the mild heat of a Nagercoil winter. The shouts of cooks and other servants, the screams of small children as they raced about among the adults, the cawing of crows, the chattering of squirrels and mynahs, all the commotion and bustle narrowed and flowed towards the still centre of the afternoon – the moment when the bride would see her prospective husband for the first time. Charity escorted Rachel, clad in a dark red sari, out of the house. Her head bowed, the bride-to-be concentrated hard on the ground. She had spent months now dreading and anticipating this moment. Would he be handsome? Would his eyes be kind? His mouth shapely? Would he be fair and brave? And would he make her heart race? All through the morning as she'd been bathed, dressed, powdered and decorated, Rachel had been dreaming of the moment when she would raise her eyes to his. Then she looked into Ramdoss's strong-jawed, open countenance and exploded out of her trance with joy. But she permitted herself nothing more than a small smile, then immediately lowered her head. Charity, who stood directly behind her, saw the young man's eyes widen in appreciation and for just a moment felt wistful as she remembered her own first meeting with her husband. She had been a mere child, and it had all been so confusing at first.

A few words between bride and groom, banal, unmemorable, and then ceremony took over – Bibles and gold chains were exchanged, saris and flowers presented to Rachel, reciprocated in cash and flowers for Ramdoss. Then lunch was announced, with the seven dishes prescribed by tradition. Charity had personally supervised the making of the two kinds of vegetables, chicken, sambhar and rasam, appalam and payasam. The bridegroom's party was fed first. Charity waited anxiously for the first belch of appreciation and only then did she relax a little. There would be more feasts and ceremonies to be conducted before Rachel was truly wed to Ramdoss but the engagement had gone off successfully and she was content. The wedding was fixed for the most auspicious day available.

At last the morning of the wedding arrived and the noise of a marching band resounded down the narrow lane outside Jacob's house. The NAGERCOIL CHRISTIAN WEDDING BAND, as a rather forlorn banner announced, was a strange hybrid: eleven men on a variety of unmatched instruments – nadeswarams and cymbals, a big bass drum, a trumpet and a brace of bugles – combining in a discordant way to produce a bizarre medley of hymns and well-known Tamil songs, 'Rule Britannia' and rousing marching airs. Its founder was a retired band major weaned on martial music and popular melodies, so the band tended to fall back on these once it had exhausted its slim repertoire of hymns. But no one really minded for it made plenty of noise. The groom's party had soon attracted a fair crowd of hangers-on. By the time they reached the cottage they were nearly two hundred strong. Ramdoss and his eldest sister, both looking awkward and hot in Western clothes, opened the gate and walked up to the house. Banana stems on either side of the front door, flowers and other traditional ornamentation ensured that the groom's party had nothing inauspicious to fear. Daniel welcomed them with garlands and young Miriam enthusiastically sprinkled them with scented water. Sandalwood paste was smeared on their brows, and then Ramdoss's sister presented Charity with Rachel's wedding sari – a gorgeous white-and-gold Conjeevaram silk. The women went into the house, and the men, Daniel, Jacob, Ramdoss and his close male relatives, adjourned to Jacob's room to wait while the bride was dressed.

Nobody said much. The racket the band was making outside would have made talking difficult even if they had been so inclined. An hour, an hour and a half, and finally there was word that Rachel was ready. When she entered the room she could hardly be seen for powder, jewellery and flowers. The bride and the groom glanced at each other nervously, then took refuge among their own kin.

Charity's brother hadn't been able to make the journey from Ceylon so he wasn't going to perform the traditional ceremony of giving away the bride. Jacob stood in for him. Rachel received gold bangles from her grandfather, a short prayer was murmured over the couple and they were then led to hired carriages to make their separate ways to the great Home Church in town where the wedding was to be solemnized.

The ceremony passed off without a hitch. The packed church held its collective breath when Ramdoss fumbled while tying the thali around the bride's neck, but Daniel was there to steady him. And then it was over and the tension that had built up before the wedding disappeared in a grand feast in the pandal under the cashew tree.

Charity knew no rest. She supervised the preparation of every one of the eleven dishes to be served. Steaming mountains of white rice, aromatic vessels of chicken curry and platters of fried mutton, buckets of sambhar and avial richly seasoned with coconut, deliquescent mounds of curd rice, large containers of sweet paruppu payasam and wobbly cliffs of halwa shiny with ghee. By early evening, the last of the revellers had left or wandered away to sleep off the great feast.

But Charity's labours were not yet done. There were gifts to be given to the family barber and the dhobi for their part in the proceedings, the hired cooks needed to be paid and the arrangements for Rachel's journey to her husband's home needed looking after. She sent her father off to get some rest and supervised the loading of the seven boxes of murukku, athirasam, halwa, appalams, coconuts, bananas and uncooked rice that would form the next set of gifts with which the bride would endow her husband's house. She gave her daughter a quick hug and watched as Rachel clambered into the cart. There would be time enough for elaborate leave-taking when the ceremonies were over. Later that night Charity made her first visit to the house where Ramdoss and his family were staying. In the cart she travelled in were pots and pans, two almirahs (one with a mirror, one without), three cane chairs and a cane table, everything the couple would need to set up house. A feast was held at Ramdoss's house to welcome his mother-in-law, although it was the bride's family who paid for it, and Jacob presented the groom and his sister with gold rings.

The next day, Rachel returned to her own house with Ramdoss, and veshtis and other clothes were given to the groom's close male relatives.

Not once did Charity flinch at the expense, although only she knew that her finances were almost exhausted. That Sunday, before going to church, she counted and recounted the money for the last of the marriage ceremonies – the seventh-day feast when all the groom's relatives were fed. Six silver rupees, that's all there was, and she knew it wouldn't be enough. She went to church with her family, sipped coffee with her friends and relatives after the service and went about the rest of her day as usual. The next day she went to the street of goldsmiths and pawned her gold wedding thali, the only item of any value she had left. Ever since she had taken it off her own neck when Solomon died she had been saving it for Daniel's wedding, but the Lord would provide if and when that took place, she thought wearily.

The seventh-day feast was exceedingly well attended, and the guests had never been fed so sumptuously before. Charity even daringly departed from the tradition of preparing several dishes and served only her fish biryani. Ramdoss's family loved it and it came perilously close to being exhausted before everyone was fed. In the early hours of the morning the celebrations finally began to wind down. Charity saw Rachel slip into the house and followed her. Her daughter went to her old room and began rummaging through the battered wooden almirah. Charity touched her on the shoulder, and she turned, tears streaming down her cheeks.

'Were you looking for something?'

'Yes, no, amma, I was just looking, looking for something to take with me when I go away.'

Oh, my beautiful, beautiful Rachel, Charity thought, and the emotion that she had wound tightly within came undone and overwhelmed her. She held her daughter close and cried as she had seldom cried before. She wept to release the tension and the pain of the past days, she wept at the prospect of losing her daughter, she wept at the absence of Solomon and Aaron, she wept for herself. She thought about her pawned thali and how beautiful it would have looked around the neck of Daniel's bride and she wept all the more. Her grief grew to include mothers and daughters everywhere but most especially in her part of the world, where a girl child was a necessary evil, suitable only for producing sons. She felt the pain of the village women who fed their infant daughters poison or drowned them, she agonized with young brides rejected or raped or tortured ... She held her daughter and prayed that she would bear a dozen sons so that she would be spared some of the pain of being born a woman. The force of Charity's sorrow fed into Rachel's own and their grief grew immense. It blew out of that small room and wrapped itself around the remaining guests. Every woman present felt its power. They tried to hold back their tears, some not so successfully, while the men shuffled about uneasily, dimly sensing an enormous passion that, if unleashed, would consume them all.

Gradually, Charity got her weeping under control. Cradling her daughter's tear-streaked face between her palms, she said, 'No marriage is truly complete, kannu, until we've all had a good cry. Now I know you'll be happy.'

37

A little over a decade earlier, on the occasion of the Diamond Jubilee of her reign, Queen Victoria, wearing a dress of black moiré embroidered with silver flowers, had presided over the greatest show on earth. Fifty thousand troops, led by two of the most imposing soldiers of the British Army (Captain Ames, who was literally the tallest man in the armed forces at six foot eight inches, and the legendary Field Marshal Lord Roberts of Kandahar), marched through the streets of London. Behind them came Australian cavalrymen and Canadian Hussars, camel-riding soldiers from Rajasthan and head-hunting Dyaks from Borneo, Chinese policemen from Hong Kong and princes from India, Cypriots and Maoris, Jamaicans and Ceylonese.

Now the competition was catching up. Russia and Germany were arming at a frenetic pace and the patriotic Briton was alarmed. The anxiety of the world's greatest power was not misplaced, for the running sore of the Balkans threatened to infect Europe once again as Turks, Serbians, Montenegrins and Austrians broke alliances and massacred civilians and itched to resume barely restrained vendettas. In the capitals of the Great Powers, the chanceries stayed open late into the night as talk of war intensified.

In the Empire, the cracks were beginning to show. In India, the Extremists stepped up their activities against the rulers. A couple of months after the Abel Circus action, Aaron and his closest friend Nambi received a message from Iyer to go to Tuticorin where the revolutionaries were planning a major demonstration to protest against the arrest and detention of three top nationalist leaders.

Aaron and Nambi, whose knowledge of the twists and turns of the revolutionary movement was sketchy at best, knew little of the reasons for the protest meeting but they were delighted to be in the thick of the action again. When they reached Tuticorin, they found a number of agitated young men roaming around the narrow streets of the port town. As their superiors were not expected to arrive until much later, the pair set out to explore Tuticorin. It proved to be a dirty, unplanned maze of streets and shops. They found little to interest them and were glad to join the growing crowds near the Mosque Pettai. The leaders of the agitation arrived and began working the protesters into a frenzy. Aaron and Nambi were near the front of the crowd and they began to chant slogans vigorously.

Horses' hoofs sounded on stone and metal. A posse of policemen rode up with the new Joint Magistrate of the district, Robert William d'Escourt Ashe, at its head. The crowd was ordered to disperse. The announcement was greeted with stones. Aaron was overjoyed to see a red-faced policeman to the left of the magistrate wince as his missile struck his upper arm. He was bending down again to scrabble for stones when he heard the crowd sigh. Straightening up, Aaron was riveted by what he saw. Some of the policemen on horses had dismounted. They were joined by others on foot. Bayonets fixed, they prepared to charge. Nervously, Aaron looked around for his friend. Even as he watched, Nambi, his eyes dilated with excitement, prised a large chunk of stone from the road and flung it at a policeman. It was too big to carry the fifty feet or so that separated the two groups. Instantly, Nambi began looking around for another missile. Galvanized into activity by the sight, Aaron hunted around for more missiles of his own. The clamour and thrill of another battle long ago filled his head. He found a stone and hurled it towards the police force. He could almost feel Joshua-chithappa at his elbow urging him on. Aaron suddenly roared, 'Down with the English dogs and their faithful slaves.' He flung another stone that was wide of the mark.

By now the policemen were in formation and Ashe gave the order to charge. Bayonets held at the ready, the men trotted forward only to be stopped by a blanket of stones and abuse. A second volley of missiles and oaths followed and the line began to turn ragged. Several of the policemen were cut and bleeding. The gap between the crowd and the policemen had lessened to about thirty feet and from that distance Aaron could see the expression in the eyes of the foe: anger, fear and confusion. More shouted commands and the crowd cheered as the attackers fell back. The cavalry officers got back on their horses and then, to the horror of the crowd, the order was given to put rifles to shoulders. Aaron sought out the magistrate from this distance, focused on his eyes. He saw the terror there but also the fury. 'F-i-i-y-aah.' The command stretched out, guns snapped spitefully, and the protesters began to go down. Shouts of 'Run, run' mingled with 'Aiyo, they've killed me' and shrieks of pain and anguish. Aaron took off at a dead run, Nambi close behind him. The streets of Tuticorin were unfamiliar to them, but they were young and, despite Aaron's slightly awkward gait, speedy. They soon left all pursuit behind.

When night dropped, they'd been wandering around for what

seemed like hours. They had spent the little money they had brought with them, and the invigoration of battle had long worn off. To their added dismay, they realized they had no idea where they were. Walking through a poor, rundown part of town, oil lamps flickering palely in the humid dark, Nambi spotted a woman on the stoop of a largish house. Her sari looked incongruously expensive. She contemplated the two young men with interest.

'Don't look at her, walk with your eyes down, she's either a prostitute or a ghost. If she's a prostitute we don't have any money, and if she's a ghost she'll eat us alive,' Nambi said in a hoarse whisper.

Aaron was amused by his friend's reaction. Was this the hero of only a couple of hours ago who had fearlessly hurled stones at armed policemen? But Nambi appeared genuinely scared. Aaron followed his friend's lead and walked past the woman with his eyes on the ground, his step quick. He thought he heard her say as they sped past, 'Are you lost?' His gaze turned in her direction and met beautiful anthracite eyes but Nambi tugged urgently at his sleeve and he stumbled on.

Hours later they found the railway station. They managed to climb on to a slow goods train that was headed in the right direction and dozed off. Towards dawn Aaron awoke and couldn't go back to sleep. He sat in an open doorway, looking out at the night being peeled off the countryside. Dark smoky eyes floated in his mind for a time.

Two days after they had returned to Meenakshikoil they found Iyer waiting for them in the tea shop. He ordered three speshul teas and then grilled them about the Tuticorin action. His eyes grew ferocious when they told him about Ashe giving the order to fire. 'These English dogs will have to pay a heavy price,' he muttered. 'Who are they to come to our country and fire on our people? What sins have we committed in our past lives that we have to suffer the curse of the white man?'

They waited for Iyer to calm down, before proceeding. Once their tale was done, Iyer said they would soon be assigned new jobs. Meanwhile, they should spend their time educating themselves about the evils perpetuated upon the land by the imperialists.

'Are you aware how badly they've crippled us?'

'Only what you've told us, anna,' Aaron said.

A furrow, like a bird in flight, appeared between Iyer's eyebrows. 'Don't you read the papers?'

'No.'

'*India*?'

'No.'

'*Swadeshimitran*?'

'No.'

'The *Hindu*?'

'No.'

'The *Indian Patriot*?'

'No.'

'*Vijaya*?'

'No.'

'No, no, no! Is that all you can say?'

'Yes. I mean, no,' Aaron said. He felt foolish, and was starting to lose his temper just as it was clear that Iyer was beginning to lose his. Perhaps realizing that this was getting them nowhere, the older man said, 'To be effective revolutionaries, you need to read our newspapers and magazines, keep abreast of events; it's the only way to raise the consciousness of the brothers and sisters you'll be working with ...' A thought struck him: 'You can read, can't you?'

'Yes, anna,' Aaron said with some pride, 'I'm a fourth-form pass and even Nambi has studied up to the third form.'

'Very well then, put your education to some use. You'll hear from me soon.'

For some weeks after that Aaron and Nambi scoured the newspapers that came to Meenakshikoil, laboriously working their way through rhetoric, reportage, theory and fact. But as the days passed and there was no word from Iyer, they soon tired of reading and cogitation. The familiar feelings of frustration and ill temper took hold. Aaron had received several postcards from his mother at the time of Rachel's marriage, none of which he had bothered to acknowledge. He had been glad for his sister. He remembered her with affection and hoped she would be happy, but his anger towards his mother and brother had corkscrewed too deep within for him to even consider replying. His mother's latest letter, which had arrived a couple of days after Iyer's visit, had infuriated him, for she had asked whether she could look for a bride for him. This time he was tempted to reply. Why, he wanted to write, this sudden solicitude, this show of concern? When my father and I really needed you, where were you? And my precious brother Daniel, the big Nagercoil doctor! Why can't you get that treacherous little coward married off? That's what you really want to do, isn't it? Why isn't he married yet? Is there something terribly wrong with him? He didn't write the letter, of course, but that evening he rounded up a few friends and they drank so much cheap toddy that he was sick for the next three days.

Soon afterwards, his friends and he went back to the old ways – terrorizing women on their way to market, thieving from shopkeepers, getting into fights. Most of the money they pilfered went on poisonous arrack and home-brewed toddy. The money soon ran out, and the gang went in search of more. One morning Aaron and Nambi headed for Swami's grocery store. He was always good for a rupee or two. As they neared the open-fronted shop, Nambi said, 'The old fool has got himself some protection.' Six men who had been lounging around in the shade of the shop's awning got to their feet and arranged themselves across the shop's frontage.

'Come on, Aaron, let's go.'

'Are you afraid of these fellows? They'll soon learn not to interfere with me.'

'We can't fight six of them. They'll kill us.'

'I'm not afraid, Nambi, and neither should you be. When you could face armed policemen, what are these sons of prostitutes to you?'

'That was different, I got carried away by the excitement and the crowd's anger.'

'Well, here you're going to be carried away by my anger. How dare that eunuch Swami do this? I remember him bowing before my father.'

They were at the shop now but the men barred their way. Aaron vaguely recognized a couple of them. Fishermen from the next village, bound to be savage fighters. He felt a twinge of apprehension. He was about to push past them when he heard Swami's voice from within the shop. 'I don't want any trouble, Aaron-thambi, I'm a man of peace, and I have nothing but respect for the Dorais. Your father Solomon was a great man.'

'And you're nothing but dung, Swami.'

A crowd had begun gathering, sensing a fight. A crow cawed, a dusty sound on that hot day. Aaron looked around. Nambi had started backing away.

'Thambi, don't do this, we should live in peace ...'

'No, we won't ...' Aaron screamed, driving at the man nearest to him. The man sidestepped adroitly and the rest were upon him, ferociously punching and swinging. He went down, and kicks and blows began thudding into his body.

Aaron lay in bed for eight days. The moment he was able to hobble, he left the house. The first day, his aching body could carry him only as far as the veranda, but soon he was taking short walks into the coconut topes. He never went in the direction of town.

About a month after he had been beaten up, Aaron went down to the beach. The air wobbled in the white heat of day, and the distant fishing boats could scarcely be distinguished in the hard light that streamed off the sea. How easy it would be to end it all, Aaron thought, all he needed to do was walk into the warm ocean, keep going until he could no longer feel solid ground under him. It would all be over so quickly. No one would miss him. His uncle and aunt would simply think he had run away from home, and they wouldn't even bother to inform his mother and Daniel. And his mother's letters, those neat postcards that she had written to him every week for nearly eight years now, how long would it be before they stopped? Probably not until her own death, for although he hadn't replied to a single one, she had kept them coming. Anger flared within him once more as he remembered her latest. Kaveri had read it out to him with something approaching glee, for in it Charity had reiterated her wish to see him settled. When his aunt had asked with feigned concern whether she should reply to the postcard, he had glared and turned his back on her. But he couldn't hold on to his anger for too long. The heat and the unhappiness within him rose up, blotting out everything. He thought again of how easy it would be to finish it, put an end to the twenty-four depressing years that he had lived.

Further up the beach, mirages moved in the shimmering heat haze, stirred dormant memories of battle. Joshua-chithappa, his father Solomon, how often had he replayed in his mind the way they had fought! He remembered the day he had jumped the well, the strength of his uncle freeing him from his own limitations. Neither his father nor his uncle would approve, he decided, were he to kill himself. He saw himself battling the Marudar chief, avenging his uncle's death, and something occurred to him: How long had it been since he'd handled a silambu? If he'd had one in his hands, he would have thrashed those rowdies so badly that Swami would have given him free run of his shop for the rest of his days. He picked up a fallen coconut frond and stripped away the dried leaves. It was an awkward staff, with neither the weight nor the symmetry to give it any sort of balance, but he twirled it around experimentally, and then with greater concentration, trying hard to keep it under control. He was so absorbed in the endeavour that it was a while before he heard the sound of clapping, a feeble sound against the great expanse of sea and sky.

Iyer walked out of the fringe of palms that led down to the beach.

'Nambi told me about your little problem in town,' he said, after the initial pleasantries were over.

'I don't see Nambi any more,' Aaron said stiffly.

'Yes, I know that ...' A pause, and then Iyer said, 'What you did was wrong. The revolution does not prey on poor shopkeepers.'

'You do not tell me what I should or shouldn't do,' Aaron said furiously.

'The revolution is bigger than any of us, Aaron,' Iyer said quietly.

'I do not care about your stupid revolution,' Aaron said, still angry.

'I can see that. I'm wasting my time here,' Iyer said. He was making to go when Aaron stopped him, his mind racing. Minutes ago, he'd been thinking of killing himself ... his brief entanglement with Iyer's organization had been the only time in his life he had ever felt he was doing something worth while, and now he was throwing it all away. Trying to keep the desperation out of his voice, he said, 'Wait, wait, anna, I'd like to try again ... What would you like me to do?'

Iyer told him that volunteers were needed to participate in a risky game – the smuggling of banned or proscribed revolutionary literature printed in the French territory of Pondicherry into British India. Aaron didn't hesitate – he would be glad to take part.

On his second assignment (each 'mule' was used only twice for fear that their faces might get too familiar to the frustrated authorities), Aaron entered the second-class compartment at Pondicherry to find a young woman in a blue cotton sari already occupying a seat. It was virtually unknown for a woman to travel alone, but he was even more surprised when she spoke to him. 'Shekhar, I'm your cousin, Jayanthi. I arrived early as my classes finished sooner than I expected.' How resourceful the Extremist leaders were, he thought admiringly. Finding a pretty young woman to take on this assignment was a master-stroke. Who would ever think her capable? But wasn't her suitcase supposed to be checked for proscribed literature on the platform?

As if reading his mind, she said, 'The authorities have changed their routine. Now the luggage is to be checked on the train.' As she was saying this, he spotted two beefy European sergeants strolling up the corridor inspecting the baggage. They rummaged through their suitcases, found nothing incriminating (the incendiary literature was cleverly concealed) and moved on.

As the train picked up speed, Aaron covertly examined his travelling companion. He had never been alone with a woman outside his family, and he found the experience unsettling. She had immersed herself in a novel she had taken from her handbag as the train left the station and she hadn't looked up from it once. He strained to read the title. *Sense and Sensibility*. He had never heard of the author. So was she the bored daughter of some rich man from the city, with a fancy English education, doing this for the thrill of it? Then he remembered that he too had joined the Extremists out of boredom. Strangely, this thought made him annoyed. He glared out of the window for a while, then his eyes slid across to where she sat. A pair of coal-black eyes was studying him coolly, and he looked away in panic. When he next dared look in her direction, she was absorbed in the book. What could he say to her, he thought, to get a conversation started, make her pay him some attention? He wished miserably that he was sophisticated and wise, that he could discuss the great movements of history with her, perhaps even the finer points of the revolution. But the revolution was never to be discussed in public.

They parted wordlessly at the station. Aaron never saw Jayanthi again. But for a while, whenever he thought of her, and he often did, he would be filled with a delicious happiness. It was unnerving and annoying but he couldn't help himself. He would sometimes say the name, Jayanthi, out loud, before feeling foolish at uttering a false name reverentially. He would look at every young woman who resembled her as if by some alchemy she could become Jayanthi. He imagined her by his side. He thought about how his lips would feel on hers, how they would move over those smoky eyes, gently kissing them shut ... But even the most intense fantasies need fuel. As the weeks passed, her memory grew fainter and after a while he didn't think of her at all.

38

Dr Pillai disappeared from the vaidyasalai a few days before the onset of the monsoon. He told Daniel the day before that he would be gone for a short while, and that he would be in charge during his absence. Once he had overcome his initial apprehension, Daniel found that the first day went off rather well.

For over a week he hadn't run into too much trouble, but the young farmer he had just spent half an hour examining mystified him. He suffered from violent headaches that no amount of medication could relieve. Daniel had tried everything he knew. He had taken the patient's pulse, examined his tongue and eyes and found nothing abnormal. The young man's urine smelled a bit like wild rain, which hinted at a slight kapham disorder, but that couldn't be causing the headache. He knew he was doing all right, and the patients he'd treated seemed happy enough, but all it needed was one wrong diagnosis, one admission of ignorance, for his slender reputation to disappear. The prospect of failure didn't bear thinking about. He examined the patient once more. The young man seemed perfectly healthy except for the way he tilted his head awkwardly to one side. Daniel helped him across to the window, held his head up to the light and smiled at what he saw.

'Do you take snuff?' he asked the villager.

'Yes, aiyah,' the patient replied, 'but not for a few days, the pain is terrible ...'

Daniel looked thoughtful. 'Are you carrying any snuff with you?'

When the man nodded, Daniel asked him to take a generous pinch. He watched the patient take out the snuff, push it painfully into his nostrils. There was an explosive sneeze. Daniel called to Chandran to bring him a slim probing tool. He grasped the villager's head firmly and carefully removed a long leech from the nostril. 'Try not to bathe in the same tank as your cows and buffaloes,' he said as he sent the farmer off. He was about to call for the next patient, when he realized there was someone else in the room. How long had Dr Pillai been there?

'Excellently done, thambi. No physician ever learned his skills from books alone. A good doctor needs instinct, experience and common sense.' With that he was gone. Daniel realized he was still holding the leech in his fingers and hastily disposed of it.

In the months that followed, Dr Pillai taught Daniel how to use metals like mercury and cinnabar to avert the corruption of cells; he showed him how poisons like arsenic and datura could be used to cure and not to kill; and he even allowed him a glimpse into the dangerous therapy called varma where the physician manipulated the life centres of afflicted patients directly, a proscribed procedure for all but the most skilled, for it could lead to death or permanent disability.

Dr Pillai began to disappear more frequently from the clinic now.

Some of these trips, he told Daniel, were to prospect for rare herbs in the ancient Palani hills where he had received his own training as a physician. With every absence, Daniel grew more confident about managing on his own, but he was totally unprepared for Dr Pillai's announcement that he was turning the clinic over to him.

It had rained heavily all day. After the last patient had left, Daniel had sat for a while listening to the rain dripping outside his window, trying to summon up the energy to go home, when Dr Pillai had walked into his room. He said without ceremony, 'It is the duty of every practitioner of siddha to devote himself, when the time is right, to the single-minded quest for perfection – in siddha, in our lives, in our quest for the Lord, in our pursuit of kaya kalpa. It is time I freed myself from distraction ... It is time for me to go.'

'But what about your practice, aiyah, everything you've built up?' Daniel interrupted in alarm.

'The ancient physicians were wandering ascetics. They owned nothing and they wanted for nothing. Not all of us are called, but when we receive the call ... My time has come. My patients will not suffer at your hands, thambi. You were always an excellent pharmacist, but I'm really impressed by how good your diagnostic skills have become.'

Weeks passed, and Dr Pillai remained at the vaidyasalai. Daniel's initial panic relaxed. But he knew that when his mentor decided to go he would leave as suddenly as he had made his announcement. There was little Daniel could do but prepare himself as best he could.

Without telling Charity that the clinic would soon be in his charge, he said that he was ready to be married. Charity wasted no time in writing to her brother Stephen in Nuwara Eliya in Ceylon. They had agreed, when his second daughter Lily was born, that she would be Daniel's bride but it had been touch and go as to whether the marriage would take place. When Lily turned eighteen, Stephen had agreed to wait for just one more year.

Charity's brother arrived with his family a fortnight before the wedding, bearing all manner of gifts and gold to pay for the festivities. Charity cried when she welcomed Lily, a tall, slim girl with a delightfully tip-tilted nose. But this time they were tears of joy. At the church, as Daniel tied the thali around his bride's neck, Charity sniffled into her handkerchief in the approved manner.

Rachel was unable to attend the wedding as she was by then pregnant. Charity's first grandchild was born three days after Christmas. He was a large, unlovely baby, but in the eyes of his mother and grandmother he was the most beautiful creature in the world. On the forty-first day after his birth, Jason was blessed in the family church at Tinnevelly. Charity travelled to her son-in-law's house bearing gifts for the child: a silver belt, a gold chain and a gold ring. Just after the church ceremony she quietly put a large spot of kohl on the baby's cheek to absorb the effects of the evil eye.

39

'Which is the most dangerous caste among us, more dangerous than the cobra, more destructive than a cyclone?' Neelakantha Brahmachari asked the fifty or so villagers who gathered under a pipal tree.

There was no response, so the speaker began to work the audience. 'Could it be the Brahmin? I'm a Brahmin and you know how deadly we can be!' The crowd laughed at this and Aaron thought it was marvellous that a member of a community that had been accused of oppression and discrimination for centuries could poke fun at his own. Truly this revolution was a wonderful thing! The speaker, a compactly built young man in his mid-twenties, smiled fiercely. 'I'm waiting for an answer! I've heard about the great wisdom that is supposed to repose in this village!'

'Andavars,' someone shouted.

'No, no, Vedhars,' objected another.

'Tamasiks,' a voice yelled.

The speaker called for silence. 'No, my friends. The deadliest among us is the white man who has come from over the seas in the name of a distant king to take away our wealth, our well-being, our very essence. To them, we are less than the pariah dog that you kick out of the way.'

The young man was warming to his theme now. 'This is what every white man believes: that you and you and you, all of us, are inferior to him from birth.' He paused dramatically. 'And it gets worse. There was once an exalted white man called Macaulay who, after spending exactly three and a half years in India, had this to say about our medicine, literature and language which were flourishing when Europe was still a place of savages – that we had "medical doctrines which would disgrace an English farrier, astronomy which would move laughter in the girls at an English boarding school, history abounding with kings thirty feet tall and reigns thirty thousand years long, and geography made up of seas of treacle and seas of butter". 'Aaron had heard dozens of speakers, and he had often wondered why they persisted in using references that made little sense to a rural audience. But this speaker was quick to recover.

'If this is their opinion of us, what are they here for? The answer is simple, brothers and sisters: To take the rice from our mouths, to take the gold thalis from our daughters' necks, to eat our cows and bullocks, so that their children may fatten at the expense of ours. They are a blight on our lives, brothers and sisters, and it is the duty of every one of you to join the great battle.'

Later that night, Aaron, Iyer and Neelakantha Brahmachari ate together at a supporter's house. They had all congregated at this anonymous village to discuss future strategies for the region, far from the prying eyes of the authorities, who were now seriously worried by the upsurge of nationalist activity in the hitherto placid Presidency. After they had finished a simple meal of sambhar and rice with a single raw onion and two green chillies apiece, Iyer drew Aaron aside.

'The time has come for a parting of the ways, Aaron,' he said without preamble. 'You are ready for the next step. You will work with Neelakantha from now on.' Aaron hadn't been prepared for this. Iyer had been his one support during every moment of crisis over the past year and a half. As if sensing his thoughts, Iyer reached across and gripped him by the shoulder. 'The revolution does not encourage the forging of attachments, Aaron. It's greater than we are. We must be prepared for every sacrifice it demands.' Then, to mitigate the blow, he added, 'But you'll like Neelakantha. I've chosen carefully.'

Iyer had indeed picked his replacement with care. As they made their way to the railway station in the next town, Aaron traded notes with Neelakantha Brahmachari. His initial admiration deepened. He discovered that he was a journalist from Madras who had been sucked into the movement by a Bengali revolutionary. He belonged to a group called the Satya Vrata Sangam, but was thinking of starting his own organization, to which Iyer had recommended he recruit Aaron.

'I'll get in touch with you soon,' his new friend said as they parted.

*

All through 1909 Aaron criss-crossed the Presidency, along with dozens of other young idealists like himself, raising the nationalist consciousness of the people. A small stipend of twenty-five rupees a month paid by the organization took care of all his physical needs, and frequent meetings with a host of inspiring leaders kept his revolutionary instincts well primed.

He was exhilarated by the travelling, especially at night – the great black locomotives hissing and snorting out of dimly lit stations, expelling steam from every joint, their fiery hearts driving them through the endless dark. He loved arriving at dusty country stations – Maniyachi, Kovilpatti, Tenkasi, Rajapalaiyam, Sirivilliputtur, Shencottah – and towns that he might never see again but that nevertheless left their mark on him. He devised a mnemonic device to remember each of them, usually a local landmark or event that lodged itself in his memory – an avenue of enormous tamarind trees in Tenkasi, an ornate temple in Palani, a brilliantly coloured fair in Kumbakonam. He often thought of Joshua-chithappa and his travelling ways – what had driven him? Aaron could now understand at least a part of it: the excitement of new places opening up his mind, the sense of freedom that anonymity provided …

Aaron spoke at every town and village he visited, either to small groups at tea stalls or to larger audiences, especially if he proposed to spend a couple of days in a place. He was not a natural orator, but he spoke from the heart, and this usually masked any deficiencies in his delivery. He was glad Iyer had given him another chance to prove that he could handle reading, writing and speaking. He read slowly and laboriously and found much of what he ploughed through tedious but he kept at it. He would do anything for the revolution. He loved the sense of purpose it gave him but the sense of brotherhood it fostered was equally important. He thought less and less of his own family now; when he did so, they didn't fill him with rage any more. He would even wonder what it would be like to meet them. On the rare occasions that he visited Chevathar, the news contained in Charity's postcards that Kaveri had bothered to save for him was already old. Even hearing of Daniel's marriage and professional success did not enrage him, as it would once have done. Fulfilment isn't the best way to nurture hate and Aaron was more content than he had been in a long time. Solomon and Joshua were always present, far back in his mind, but he didn't mourn them as fiercely as he'd once done.

Towards the end of 1909 he arrived again in Tuticorin, where he had participated in his first action. He remembered the fear and excitement of that time. And then a memory rose within him of the mysterious woman in the rundown quarter. Anthracite eyes. Jayanthi's eyes. Suddenly he felt very alone. As the loneliness deepened, Aaron decided he would track down the mysterious woman.

That evening, his work done, he took off on his own. He wandered for hours and was finally so wretchedly tired that he decided to call off the search. He entered a dingy, near-empty tea shop and ordered tea and a vadai, then sat with his back against the wall and shut his eyes. With no surprise at all, he found that he was walking through a familiar quarter. He recognized the poor hovels lining the road and, looming out of their midst, the grand mansion. As he came up to it he saw that it must have been an imposing house in its prime, the residence of some fabulously rich Dutch merchant or English factor. It had gone to seed, its walls discoloured by monsoons and dirt, the wide stone steps leading up to the pillared veranda chipped. Some of the windows hung askew. He felt a bit apprehensive as he mounted the steps and walked across the veranda, his feet stirring the dust. The house seemed to be abandoned. He went on. Just by the front door a small bronze plaque gleamed brightly. Inscribed on it was a single word: VIDUTHALAI. Freedom. Release. He pulled the tasselled bell rope. Chimes sounded distantly within the house but nothing happened. He was on the point of pulling the rope again when the door opened suddenly. He was disappointed to see that it wasn't the mysterious woman he remembered so well, but an elderly servant.

He was about to make his apologies and leave when the servant said, 'Vanakkam aiyah, you are expected.' He had a sense of large and luminous mysteries waiting just out of reach, and then he was following the servant down a long tiled passage. He was ushered into a magnificent drawing room. Maroon drapes shut out the view and enormous fringed punkahs kept the temperature even. At least a dozen sofas radiated like the petals of a giant flower from a highly polished granite centre table placed directly under a many-branched chandelier. There were two or three people already sitting on the sofas when Aaron walked in. The servant led him to an unoccupied sofa. Then, as if on cue, music sprang up from behind a beautifully carved wooden screen, and servants appeared carrying silver trays of sherbets, raisins and nuts. When all of them were served the servants vanished and a tiny old lady came down the marble staircase. She was dressed in a sapphire-coloured sari and her complexion was only a shade darker than her white hair.

She came up to them and said delightedly, 'I never know what visitors each day will bring but I'm never disappointed by the rare diamonds who visit this house. Every one of you has been shaped by forces that most people would have succumbed to and you are all the more precious to me for that.' Aaron glanced at the three other men in the room. On the adjacent sofa was an enormously corpulent man, his eyes, chin and nose pouched in fat, his vast stomach spreading the cloth of his jibba. Further down was an older man, prosperous-looking but with a birthmark that disfigured half his face so that from some angles it looked as though he had been neatly sliced in half. Across the room was an impossibly handsome man, about his own age, sharp-featured, with angry eyes. The wounded of the world! Scarcely had the thought struck him than a healing fog invaded his mind, obliterating the idea even as he fought vainly to develop it.

'All of you have spent a lifetime searching for me, making your way to me, and I will promise you that once you have passed through my hands you will never lack for that thing that everyone looks for, but few truly find. What is this thing called love? Let my girls and I show you. For only when you learn how to love do you learn how to live, and it's only when you have loved that you know how to die.' Taking a small crystal bell off a side table, she shook it, and four extraordinarily attractive girls appeared beside her. Light, dark, slim, voluptuous, the only things they possessed in common were large sensuous coal-black eyes.

'Here they are, honoured guests, my beloved girls, whom you have created in the image of your deepest longings. They are yours for as long as you want. There is no charge for them and I implore you to treat them well, for the minute you mistreat them they will withdraw and you will be debarred from VIDUTHALAI for ever.'

Aaron and the other men couldn't take their eyes off the young beauties. The old lady gave them a few minutes, then sent her charges upstairs.

'There are a few simple rules this house observes. The girls have no names, and you cannot choose any of them in advance. Each of them is equally precious to me, and as you will discover, equally precious to you as well. Whether you are here for one night or many, you may choose only one name by which to address your partners. Every one of them will answer to that name, and the choice is entirely up to you. For the time they bear the name you have given them, that name will adorn them and they will be the people you want them to be. The only true reality, honoured guests, is that which is not real.'

By now Aaron had stopped fighting the fog that had crept into every crevice of his mind and everything the old lady said made eminent sense. He had no hesitation when he was asked to choose a name: Jayanthi. He found himself following the servant up the marble staircase in a state of pleasurable excitement. At the top of the stairs, a plushly carpeted corridor extended in both directions. White-painted doors opened off it. He noticed that each of them had a name carved on it in ornate script. The last door bore the name Jayanthi. The servant knocked, then withdrew.

She sat on the bed dressed in a blue cotton sari, just as she had been the time he saw her. But this girl was dark and voluptuous, her breasts straining against the thin cotton of her blouse. The other Jayanthi had been slim, almost sexless. Yet this was Jayanthi, he was sure of it. He let the contradiction float away, and sat down beside her.

She told him how handsome he was, how she was filled with joy at the prospect of pleasing him, harmless clichés that filled him with a tremendous warmth and happiness. He felt her hands on him, stroking his face, his hair, and then, so naturally that it seemed he had practised for this moment all his life, he made love to her in the vast four-poster bed – running his hungry tongue and eyes and hands over her full breasts with their honey-coloured centres, the convexity of her waist, her great curving thighs, and then entering her ...

Night after night, Aaron was a regular visitor to VIDUTHALAI. Every night he went upstairs with a different Jayanthi and every night he learned a different truth. *You have to love to live. And die.* And then, one evening, Aaron was unsurprised to find no trace of VIDUTHALAI when he arrived at the slum ...

Someone was shaking him. He opened his eyes and the proprietor of the tea shop asked him whether he had finished. Aaron looked at the untouched tumbler of tea and vadai before him and smiled, thanked the man, and left. The route back to the rest-house he was staying in passed though a very poor quarter. As he walked past a depressing collection of hovels, a young woman suckling her baby looked at him hopefully. 'Looking for love, aiyah? It's cheap here, eight annas an hour.'

The stranger gave her a silver rupee. Then he smiled at her and walked away, limping slightly as he went.

At the next town he stopped at, Tenkasi, he ran into Neelakantha Brahmachari at the railway station. He was surprised. He hadn't been expecting to see him for at least a month. The journalist told Aaron that he had started his own organization ahead of schedule. In fact, he had been about to get in touch with him. Neelakantha's organization was called the Bharatha Matha Association and its objective was violent revolution.

'We must do our bit to support our comrades,' Neelakantha said. 'They have offered themselves in the ultimate sacrifice and Madras must do its share. We have tried to negotiate with the authorities, we have tried to talk to them as our Moderate friends in the Congress suggested but where has that got us? Nowhere. The way ahead is clear. It's not an easy road but it has to be taken. Every day the Government grows more brutal and we have to fight back. Are you still willing to join us?'

Aaron did not hesitate. 'Yes, I would like to join you.'

'Excellent. Meet me this evening,' Neelakantha said and disappeared into the crowd.

Aaron didn't have a great deal to do in Tenkasi. He spent some time wandering through the crowded streets and bazaars and then returned to the temple guest-house where he was staying. In the evening he made his way to the address Neelakantha had given him. He found the place without much difficulty. A silent youth led him through the small front room into a larger room that was full of serious young men with enormous tilaks on their foreheads. In one corner was a representation of the Goddess Kali in her horrific aspect, with offerings before it. Glowing vilakus gave the image a brooding intensity.

Neelakantha introduced Aaron to the gathering. Aaron was given vibhuthi and flowers to offer to the Goddess. A pile of kumkumam, gleaming redly in the muted light, was mixed with water in a chembu and he was asked to drink it.

'Drink of this, brother, as you will drink the blood of the oppressor. From this day onwards, your life is dedicated to the goal of total swaraj by every means at your disposal. Now repeat this after me ...'

As he raised the container to his lips a clear memory appeared in his mind of the day he had jumped the big well. Sometimes the only way to move forward, despite having little idea of what awaited you, was to take firm, unwavering steps ... He drank deeply of the bitter liquid and tried not to gag on it.

Aaron repeated a simple oath, affirming that his own life was a small price to pay to free Mother India. A sheet of paper on which the oath was written was produced, and a needle was handed to

Aaron. He was instructed to prick his thumb and affix a bloody thumbprint to the oath. With that, the ceremony was over. Now all Aaron needed was instructions from his leader.

40

It took Daniel the better part of two years to grow confident of managing the clinic on his own. As he had feared, Dr Pillai left one day without warning and the number of patients immediately dipped. Not only had Daniel to try to win them back, he also had to learn to overcome the panic that struck him every time he realized that Dr Pillai wasn't around. But slowly things began to improve. He grew confident and transferred his confidence to the patients and the staff. His renown as a pharmacist and physician who could accurately diagnose and cure the most obscure ailment spread throughout the district. Soon there were more patients than he could cope with.

During this time, his own family scarcely saw him. His wife Lily had complained to Charity about his absences within a few months of the marriage. Charity's first impulse was irritation. What more did the girl want? She had snared a responsible, handsome young man, wasn't that enough? Then she remembered her own experience as a young bride, far from home, terrified and bored. Don't worry, she told Lily, things would get better as the newness of the marriage rubbed off and she grew used to her surroundings.

Lily managed with Charity's help and, over time, things did improve. As Daniel grew more sure of himself, he became less anxious about his work. He and Lily had a daughter, Shanthi, and soon Lily was expecting their second child. Daniel saw very little of his daughter during the week, but on Sundays he would spend hours watching Lily and his mother fussing over the little girl, grooming her, telling her stories, playing with her. He limited himself to holding her for short spells, and his daughter seemed to sense his awkwardness. She would wriggle and cry when he held her, until he handed her back to her mother.

One Sunday, when Shanthi was nearly two, the family was preparing to go to the Home Church for the morning service. Daniel, as always, was ready first and sat in the planter's chair on the veranda waiting for the others. Shanthi was proving unusually difficult. Her hair was done, jasmine and ribbons entwined in it, and she looked very pretty in her smart English frock and shoes, but every time Charity tried to powder her face she would twist out of her grasp. Daniel's smile never left his face as he watched his small daughter use all her ingenuity to thwart her grandmother. What a difference she's made to my life, he thought. Indeed, it was only since the birth of his daughter that he had begun to feel a sense of identification with Nagercoil, although he had lived here for several years now. Shanthi belonged here, and in a curious way that had made him feel as if he belonged as well.

Now, as he watched his daughter squirm in her grandmother's grasp, he recalled his own childhood, investigating the tide pools with the English priest for shells and fish, watching his brother jumping wells and swimming in the river, joining his father on shoots for flying foxes and water birds. He smiled to himself as he remembered his first day at the village school, dressed in new clothes, a nadeswaram player and a drummer in attendance, the sacristan of the church singing hymns in a cracked off-key voice – all for the first-born son of the most important man in the village.

These acts of remembering provoked an immense nostalgia in him for the place of his birth. All said and done, he mused, he was of the soil of Chevathar. He felt this most keenly in the early hours of the morning and as night approached. For the dawn was unique to each place and would ever be so: in Chevathar, the way the birds spoke from the branches and the light caught the casuarina trees, the lowing of the cattle and the chatter of the fowl, was different from this place or any other place. It was the same with dusk – the old light of day being dusted away by approaching night, the sounds of the village preparing to rest, all this was so unlike anything in the town. I miss Chevathar, he thought. I can never be truly myself anywhere else ... It was true that things had started working out for him after he had left Chevathar, but the yearning for it would never leave him.

He wondered about Aaron, as he often did. He had never thought that his brother's rejection of him would grieve him so much or linger so long, but it did, deep within him, rising up from time to time. At such times, he would stop whatever he was doing and immerse himself completely in his sense of loss. Long experience had taught him that this was the best way to treat wounds of the past. Experience them fully, and then set them aside to resume the daily business of living. This was what he did now. Charity's regular letters to Aaron never received replies but occasionally something would flutter back from the deep well of impenetrability that Chevathar had become. A missive of complaint from Abraham usually, whining about something or other which had prevented his sending the meagre annuity that had been promised, or full of complaints about Aaron. The last one, received some months ago, had painted a dire picture. Aaron had been missing for some time. Word was that he had joined the nationalists, no-good troublemakers who would bring disrepute to the family. Charity had urged Daniel to do something, but what? They had no idea where Aaron was. They didn't know which group he belonged to. Daniel murmured a short prayer under his breath for his brother. A moment or two more and he had pulled himself out of his depression. He told himself: Aaron is not my responsibility, he is a grown man, fully capable of looking after himself and making his own decisions. I have my own responsibilities, my own family now. If and when Aaron needs me, I'll be ready to pick up the threads again.

He looked at the little tableau before him: his wife, his mother, his daughter and his sister Miriam, who had just wandered in. Forget the past, he told himself. You belong here. This is your mother's home town, you are now of this place. Learn to see it through the eyes of Shanthi: she might never suck at the sweetness of a Chevathar Neelam but she knows the unmatched taste of the tiny honey banana; she hasn't prospected for shells in the Gulf of Mannar, but until you came here you had never seen a sunbird flash emerald in the sun! He shifted in his chair, impatient to get moving. But Shanthi and her grandmother were still deadlocked. He barked at Shanthi, 'If you don't let your paati put powder on your face, we'll leave you behind, do you understand?'

Shanthi began to wail.

'Oh let the little pisasu be. Don't put powder on her face,' Daniel said irritably.

'And let everyone see how dark she is? Who will marry her?'

'Amma, she's not even two.'

'Yes, but you know how people are.'

Daniel grew thoughtful. Everyone in the room, with the exception of Shanthi, was well powdered for the day out. He knew how important it was to let the pores of the skin breathe in the hot, humid climate of the town, but he, like everyone else, had taken to powdering his face with the new English talcum powders that had become all the rage. Only the poorest did without. The rest of the townspeople went around looking like the terrifying tantric sadhus who haunted cremation grounds, their faces sheet-white masks.

Daniel got up from the chair, went to the muttham and washed the powder off his face. He returned to the room, where the little girl's will had grown strong as iron, matched only by her grandmother's.

'Shanthi will go to church without powder,' he said.

Charity, Lily and Miriam looked at him as if he'd gone mad.

'Without powder? But everyone will laugh at her.'

'Do you see any powder on my face?' he asked sharply.

That shut the women up but only for a moment. They began arguing and only desisted when Daniel promised that if they let Shanthi go to church unpowdered, he would make a herbal cream for her that would lighten the skin without harming it.

The next morning, Daniel could hardly wait for a lull in the rush of patients to go off to the room where he made his mixtures and potions. He had been a physician for long enough now to know that his skill as a pharmacist outweighed his other medical abilities; he was exhilarated by the opportunity to push his talent to the limit. First, he reviewed everything he knew about the pigmentation of the skin. Could he in some way retard the activity of the melanocytes or would it be more effective to abrade the dead cells in the epidermis so that the skin would literally look brighter? All this without damaging the skin! He hadn't felt so excited in a long time. He began laying out ingredients – wild turmeric, cinnabar, sandalwood, medicated neem oil, the milk of tender coconuts, ghee, cassia flowers, aloe root, cow's milk, honey ... Soon he had before him over fifty herbs and spices and kuzhambus plucked from various shelves and cupboards. He began mixing and weighing, grinding and roasting, precipitating and melding. Hours passed. His assistant Chandran came in a couple of times to remind him that there were patients waiting, but for the first time since he had come to work at Dr Pillai's vaidyasalai, Daniel waved him away impatiently, telling him to ask the patients to wait a while longer. When Chandran came in a third time, he reluctantly tore himself away from his alchemy.

He hurried through the rest of his patients, impatient to be back in the laboratory. He worked through the evening, and when it got late, he sent one of his assistants home with the message that he would spend the night at the vaidyasalai. He didn't return to the cottage for five days and nights. At the end of that time, sixty-four metals, herbs, oils, unguents and other ingredients had been mixed, tested, retained or discarded. On the morning of the sixth day, Daniel looked down, exhausted, at a brown jelly that lay at the bottom of a retort. It looked like thickened gingelly oil. He smeared it liberally on his left arm. Every day for the next month he applied the lotion to his arm, taking care that water did not touch the treated portion. To prevent anyone from seeing the results of his experiment he began wearing long-sleeved jibbas. His arm began to smell decidedly odd but Daniel was undeterred. When Lily asked Charity to intervene, she shrugged helplessly and said, 'When the Dorai men are in the grip of an obsession, even an elephant in musth cannot move them.'

At the end of five weeks, he exclaimed in delight: that portion of his left arm where he had applied the lotion was discernibly lighter in colour than the rest of his skin. He made more of the formulation and coated his entire arm with it, rubbing it in briskly until it had vanished without trace. Nine weeks after he started rubbing the potion into his arm, there was a noticeable bleaching effect, but not too much to be alarming. Daniel added a colouring agent to make the mixture a pleasing shade of white and filled a small glass jar that was normally used for dispensing thylams. All the time he had been experimenting he had been dreaming up names, but there was only one he truly liked. He wrote it out on a piece of paper, in English and in Tamil – DR DORAI'S MOONWHITE THYLAM – and sat looking at it for a long time. Then he walked home in the dark.

Daniel postponed his departure to the clinic the next morning. Lily, vastly pregnant now, was beginning to get Shanthi ready. Triumphantly, Daniel pulled out his whitening cream and asked her to use it on the child. When his wife hesitated, he showed her his left arm, the colour of slightly overdone wheat. Within days, his family were converted to the cause.

Over the next weeks, stories about the miraculous new cream spread through the town. The vaidyasalai could scarcely keep up with the demand, and to Daniel's astonishment, the bulk of the patients at his door, fully half of them poor villagers, now demanded a half-anna bottle of MOONWHITE THYLAM (it was also available in a bigger bottle for six annas) along with their other medication.

41

The new century was scarcely a decade old when it seemed that the nascent Indian nationalism was about to wither and die. Moderates and Extremists had gone their separate ways, vulnerable in their disunity to the oppressor's blandishments. The British, it appeared, had won the battle before it had even begun. As a frustrated patriot of the time, Aurobindo Ghosh, announced dejectedly upon his release from prison, 'When I went to jail, the whole country was alive with the cry of Bande Mataram, alive with the hope of a nation, the hope of millions of men who had newly risen from degradation. When I came out of jail, I listened for that cry, but there was instead a silence. A hush had fallen on the country.' Small groups of young men and women in India and abroad decided that the only way forward was to try and force the pace. In Bengal, in Maharashtra, in London, in Madras, they plotted and planned. Aware that any mass movement would need years of preparation, the young revolutionaries decided that the quickest way to put the Raj on the defensive was to wreak excessive violence on its officials.

A month after he joined the Bharatha Matha association, Aaron received a summons to attend a meeting in Trivandrum. The venue was a low-roofed cottage on the outskirts of town. The house looked quite ordinary, beaten earth courtyard, the leaves of banana trees flapping in the breeze, chickens scratching around in the dirt, a woman in a mundu and blouse sunning herself on the front steps. For a moment Aaron thought he had come to the wrong place, then Neelakantha stood framed in the doorway. He beckoned him in.

The house had rooms opening off a muttham open to the sky. It was here that the meeting took place. Aaron recognized several from Neelakantha's group among the twenty or so present. They were told that they had been selected for a special mission and that they would spend the next weeks training for it. They were to assemble at four the following morning, ready to leave for an unknown destination.

Travelling by bullock cart and on foot, deeper and deeper into Travancore, Aaron and twelve others reached Thengatope, a small village on the Malabar coast, late that evening. The towering coconut palms which gave the village its name were so thickly clustered that they could only dimly glimpse the Lakshadweep Sea. The headman of the village was sympathetic to the cause, and the village itself was so remote that there was no risk of sudden discovery. They were divided into two groups, each allotted a hut. Neelakantha led Aaron's group. The thirteen men, of whom three were instructors, had two pistols and a bolt-action rifle between them. The recruits began to practise assembling and dismantling the firearms. As ammunition was scarce, they pointed the weapons and clicked the triggers on empty at coconuts lined up on the beach.

The days soon fell into a regular pattern: up at dawn, they would set off for a run, weaving between the palms and acacia trees, keeping a lookout for the long white acacia thorns that littered the ground for much of the route. The last part of the run, the hardest, was on the shifting sands of the beach. Aaron, who had thought his slight limp would be a disadvantage, discovered that his natural athleticism gave him an advantage over most of the others in the group, especially the city boys. The run was followed by breakfast, a thin kanji that tasted awful, then came weapons training, followed by a session of exhortation and discourse. The polemics and wisdom of Marx, Alfieri, Annie Besant, Aurobindo Ghosh, Subramania Iyer, V. O. Chidambara Pillai and Bal Gangadhar Tilak formed the foundation of the indoctrination. Aaron found the instructor hard to follow, and unimpressive, and after the first couple of days he switched off. He noticed that most of the others were as bored as he was. At the end of the first week, the instructors as well as five of the recruits returned to Trivandrum. The next day the five that remained, Neelakantha and Aaron among them, were joined by a top leader of the organization who would complete their training. Aaron had admired and respected men like Iyer and some others he had met, leaders with courage, dash and a fierce commitment, but next to M. S. Madhavan, they seemed like callow youths. Their new mentor was a slightly built man with a fine-boned face and a deliberate way of speaking. It was his gaze that betrayed his essential nature: flat and unblinking as a viper's, his eyes hinted at the hard man beneath the ordinary exterior.

His arrival galvanized the camp into frenetic activity. Madhavan was urbane, sophisticated and had travelled the world to sit at the feet of masters of the art of violent revolution and terror. Aaron respected the man's prowess with small arms, and he listened with something approaching awe to the tales of his time with Berbers and Russian revolutionaries in exile. The group clung to Madhavan's every word but their undisguised hero worship seemed not to have any positive effect on him. No matter how much he tried to conceal it, it was clear that he thought them a bunch of bumblers.

After a couple of days, Madhavan unveiled a marvellous new rifle that he had brought with him, a rapid-fire, bolt-action .303 with a six-bullet magazine. He had with him a plentiful supply of ammunition as well, and for the next days, the roaring waves of the Lakshadweep Sea provided a backdrop to the spiteful flat crack of the Lee Enfield.

A month passed. Then, one morning, Madhavan announced that their training was over and that they would leave on their first mission the following day. He wouldn't give them further details, saying only that they would be thoroughly briefed before they set out. That night, Aaron left the camp and walked for a time among the coconut palms, his mind seething with thoughts that were jumbled and confused like the choppy surf that broke on the shore. This was it, he thought. Now there was no withdrawing. He thought about his father, his Joshua-chithappa, his friends back in Chevathar. If I die, my only regret will be that I died among strangers, he said to himself. And then he dismissed the thought as cowardly. It was the sort of thing Daniel would think. He hadn't thought of his brother and his mother in a while and he wondered how they would feel if they could see him now. They would probably beg him not to go through with whatever lay ahead. Weak, weak, always weak, he was glad he was rid of them.

As he was returning to camp he heard Madhavan's voice and paused, unseen, behind a coconut palm to listen. Madhavan was telling Neelakantha how substandard they all were – as human beings, as nationalists, as fighters in the cause of the country and freedom. 'The devas will need to come down to help our motherland if this is the army that is going to kick the white man out.'

Aaron heard nothing more as Madhavan and Neelakantha walked out of earshot. He would show them just what he was made of tomorrow, Aaron thought savagely. He would make that cold-hearted viper beg his forgiveness for misjudging him.

They were up at five. Dressing by the aluminium gleam of the early morning sky, they moved out. Madhavan had briefed them about their objective: a police station across the border in British India. They would attack it and destroy it, decamping with whatever weapons and ammunition they could find.

Travelling by bullock cart, and on foot, they finally reached their destination two days later: a few huts rising out of the dun-coloured earth, on either side of a dirt track. The track led to a limewashed building that glowed white in the harsh light of day. This was the new police station that had been built to house a unit of riot police who would keep the peace in the area, which was known for its unrest. The unit hadn't arrived yet and the building was under the command of a head constable. For a day and a night, Madhavan and the group observed the activities of the head constable and the two men in his charge. The next morning, one of the policemen was called away to another village to investigate a theft. That left the head constable, a middle-aged man with a pronounced belly, large sad eyes, thinning hair and a slight stoop, and his subordinate, a callow village boy, with big ears and the beginning of stubble. The head constable spent most of his time in his house, a hut slightly bigger than the others, a couple of hundred yards from the station. His subordinate lounged about on the veranda of the new building, gazing out at nothing.

On the evening of the second day, Madhavan told them their mission. They were here to assassinate the head constable. The group was aghast. They had spent over thirty hours observing the man. It was plain to see that he was nothing more than a harmless village policeman – father to the seven children they had counted in the hut, husband to the poor woman who worked from morning to night. They had watched the man during his hours of duty, dressed in his threadbare uniform, and they had observed him at rest, gossiping outside the hut, dressed only in a lungi, his belly bulging like a landslide. They couldn't kill him.

'Your target is a decent man,' Madhavan remarked after a short silence. 'He takes only enough bribes to fill his belly, he tries not to be oppressive, he has lived here all his life, he has seven growing children (he lost two to smallpox), he does not have a mistress, he beats his wife only when absolutely necessary and then only sparingly, he's a good father and provides for the family, wasting only a little of his money on toddy. He's a good man, much like your own fathers and uncles and brothers. But he's also a representative of the white man, and for that you will kill him. Slowly and painfully, in the presence of his wife and children, so that your act will be accurately transmitted to the authorities. Your murder of him will leave his wife and children bereft, the baby will probably die, and the girls will not marry well. You will kill him, knowing all this, because he is a symbol of the oppression that grips this land. And by killing him, you will free yourself of any inhibitions that might constrain you from acting in the interests of our noble and just cause.'

Madhavan could have been speaking to stone statuettes. Even Neelakantha looked shocked. The policeman yawned and lit a beedi, his discoloured teeth visible to the watchers concealed less than twenty yards away behind a rocky hillock.

How do you kill a man? In cold blood? If you're a man like any other, a thinking, feeling, insecure man trying to lead a reasonable life, a man who is not in the grip of a great rage, a normal man, how do you kill a man who has done you no harm? Do you think of him as a disgusting envelope of shit and piss and dirty thoughts, whom it would be a blessing to erase from the pitiful piece of earth he occupies? Or do you paint him as a monster so that you can eliminate him with ease? The realization dawned on them that no amount of prevarication could conceal the awful truth – that their target was a man not very different from themselves, who lived and breathed, who could be so wearied by living that on occasion he could think how blissful it would be to live no more, but yet went on, day after day, getting on with the business of living, trying to make sense of life, to do his job, to escape the wrath of his superiors, trying to keep his wife and children fed. Was it possible, through some extraordinary sleight of mind, to see this poor ineffectual functionary of the state as the ENEMY? Could they? Could they?

As if reading their thoughts, Madhavan's voice sliced through their confusion. 'Clear your minds of all this emotional nonsense,' he said icily. 'Treat him like you would an animal. Track him as he moves, the foresight firmly aligned with the notch of the V on the rear sight, cheek steady against the stock of the firearm, safety off, finger crooked around the trigger. Don't pull, but squeeze as you would the breast of your beloved, adjusting for his speed. Squeeze all the way through. Aim, track, squeeze ... Practise the sequence over and over in your head, it will soon obliterate any misgivings you might have!'

That evening, just before night fell, the policeman strolled towards the station, a lit kerosene lantern in his hand. He conferred briefly with his younger colleague and retraced his steps home. He never got there. Madhavan aimed and fired.

The bullet whipped into the victim's right knee and he fell forward, the lantern dropping by his side, the glass miraculously intact. He began screaming, a high-pitched unearthly sound that permeated the deepening twilight. Madhavan then shot the younger policeman on the veranda, a sleeve of blood magically appearing on the boy's chest. He seemed to accept the bullet without pain, for he made no sound. Quietly, as if wishing to cause his murderer no more trouble than was absolutely necessary, he crabbed over and fell out of sight behind the balustrade. Calmly, Madhavan told the novices, 'I am now refilling the magazine. Six shots, one for each of you, and one for me. If one of you hesitates, that bullet is for you. You will place your bullet exactly where I indicate. Each shot you fire will give the dying man maximum pain.'

With torn lungi strips masking their faces, the killers followed Madhavan to where the constable lay screaming. As they surrounded him, his pain-crazed eyes stared wildly at them. He made as if to grab at the man nearest to him, Madhavan, who side-stepped casually and dug his foot into the gory mess of the policeman's knee. He screamed once, a full-throated sound, and then seemed to pass out. Before Madhavan could attempt to revive him, his eyes opened again. Madhavan walked across to Aaron and gave him the rifle. 'Shoot him in the stomach.' Was that contempt he saw in the other's eyes, Aaron wondered for a moment, the gun heavy in his hands. Revulsion swept through him; he made no attempt to point the weapon at the man who was writhing on the ground.

Madhavan's voice came to him. 'The stomach. Fill your mind with your frustrated contempt for me, you spineless fool, fill it with your desperate desire to make some sense of your wasted life and put a bullet in this good man's stomach.'

Aaron raised his eyes, met the other's level gaze, then looked away. The policeman at his feet was now muttering, a half-intelligible, pain-darkened chant. To his horror, Aaron realized he was begging for mercy. Commotion in the darkness, footsteps, the man's wife racing in their direction. Casually, Madhavan knocked her to the ground.

'The stomach. Otherwise all we'd have done is leave him a cripple. Like you.'

Aaron's head emptied. The rifle was pointing at Madhavan, then it wavered a fraction and the bullet thumped into the policeman's stomach. The blood was black in the diffused light of the lantern, and the screams though louder were strangely muffled, they seemed to be happening in a dream. He dropped the rifle and walked away. Three more shots, one more, and the screaming was shut off, an abrupt cessation of all sound.

42

Zephaniah Pick had established a small pharmacy on the Poonamallee Road in Madras in 1811. A hundred years later his great-grandson ran *Z. Pick, Chemist*. Zachariah Pick had made few changes to the store, which had become a local landmark, besides having the lettering on the frontage repainted in a rather florid, curling script. A wooden counter ran the length of the shop, ending in a glassed-in cubby-hole in which Zachariah sat, receiving the cash and keeping an eye on the three young men he employed.

For some years now he had stocked a shelf with native remedies and ointments. Some of his Indian customers seemed to prefer those vile-looking potions to the regular English medicines he sold. It had proved to be a wise move, for when the nationalist ruffians had started to boycott foreign goods, Zachariah's shop had escaped unscathed when he had shown the two polite young men who visited the pharmacy his stock of siddha and ayurvedic medicines. As the agitation intensified, Zachariah increased his stock of native formulations and, moreover, displayed them prominently.

His regular supplier had recently brought him a rather elegant eleven-sided jar with a garish pink label that proclaimed itself DR DORAI'S MOONWHITE THYLAM. Zachariah agreed to stock a dozen bottles of the cream on a strict consignment basis. The same week his eye caught a small advertisement on the front page of the *Hindu*:

DR DORAI'S MOONWHITE THYLAM
MAKES YOUR FACE SHINE LIKE THE PONGAL MOON!

There was even an amateurishly rhymed ditty:

On the darkest night your face will gleam
With Dr Dorai's MOONWHITE CREAM
A thylam which will make you glow
Whiter than the whitest snow.

Strewth, these damned natives, Zachariah thought irritably. Didn't they understand that white is white and black is black and brown is brown and no matter what you do ... But he had to admit it was a fine idea, given that every mother on the subcontinent prayed that her daughter would be fair. Otherwise, she had no option but to reach for talcum powder. This Dr Dorai could well end up making a fortune, Zachariah thought. He was right. His stock of Dr Dorai's MOONWHITE THYLAM sold out in two days and he fretted and fumed when he couldn't replenish it for four months.

Daniel was completely unprepared for the demand. In a desperate attempt to meet it, he converted a disused portion of Dr Pillai's vast home into a small factory and equipped it with vats, stills and a primitive bottling plant. As demand continued to outstrip supply, he bought more sophisticated manufacturing equipment and hired a workforce, including two young pharmacists, to control quality. He blessed the foresight that had led him to contact a family of traditional glass-blowers in distant Sivakasi to manufacture the distinctive jar that held the cream. Soon virtually every pharmacy in Madras Presidency and Travancore stocked Dr Dorai's MOONWHITE THYLAM.

Daniel Dorai was on his way to becoming a very wealthy man.

43

Charity woke up one morning feeling extraordinarily happy. For no reason at all, and for more reasons than she could think of. They kindled in her mind now, one by one, like lit candles, their glow coalescing into a great roaring blaze that flushed her entire being with warmth and rapture. Her daughter-in-law Lily had recently given birth to another adorable little girl. They had named her Usha. Rachel was pregnant for the third time. Charity thought she could never have enough of welcoming grandchildren into the world. She could barely wait for her daughter to give birth again. Daniel's business was thriving and she was delighted for him – he seemed to have finally overcome the crushing weight of his father's and brother's rejection. Her own father seemed healthy and content. But there was more than all that, just beyond the ready grasp of her mind. She did not try to capture what was out of reach; all that mattered at the present moment was that her happiness seemed invincible. She rose from her mat, looked for a long minute at the sleeping bodies in the room, and thought how blessed she was to have this family around her.

The feeling of well-being persisted all through that morning. Rachel, who was sleeping poorly as her pregnancy advanced, was the first to join her in the kitchen.

'How is our darling one?' Charity whispered to her daughter.

'Keeping me awake at night, the little rascal,' Rachel said as she put the milk on to boil.

'Go and rest now, I can manage here,' Charity said.

'But I can't sleep, amma,' Rachel said plaintively.

Charity was having none of it. 'You must rest,' she said firmly. 'Wake up Lily, she'll help me.'

'Let me at least make the coffee, you shouldn't be doing it.'

'Go, kannu,' Charity said simply.

Reluctantly, Rachel left the kitchen. At the door she turned.

'Amma, I have a great craving for idiyappam. With plenty of coconut milk and sugar.'

Charity smiled happily. She loved the way babies began to control the world months before they were born.

'You'll have your idiyappam, kannu. Go and rest. And don't forget to talk to the baby, she needs her daily dose of love!'

The previous evening, when she had been working in the kitchen, she had overheard Rachel and Lily talking outside the window. Without really meaning to, she had paused to listen. Lily was telling Rachel about a new development in her household. One day she had lavished her older daughter with more than her usual dose of endearments before rocking her to sleep. The next night, when she had put her to bed, Shanthi had grumpily refused to let her go. After being fussed over, she had finally told her mother the cause of her unhappiness – Lily had missed out two of the endearments of the previous night – Precious Diamond-Eyed Gift from the Sun, and Little Goddess Who Is Sweeter than a Chevathar Neelam. From then on, Lily had had to memorize the fifty-two names of love she had used for her daughter. Rachel had exclaimed delightedly and said she was going to start compiling a list for her daughter (she was sure Stella was going to have a sister) and whisper the unborn baby's names to her in the womb. The two women had laughed, and in the kitchen Charity had closed her eyes – this was what made a big family such a wonderful thing, it could always surprise and enchant you. Who would have imagined it – the fifty-two names of love!

Lily joined her in the kitchen just then and the two women made all the preparations for the morning meal. Then they carried their coffee through the sleeping house and out on to the front steps. They sat quietly, content to watch the crystal air of the morning. Charity thought about the forthcoming arrival. If it was a girl, there was only one name that would fit – Malligai! She'd been pleased that Rachel had taken to the name. Solomon had loved the smell of malligai blossoms in her hair. She blushed furiously. How shameless of her to be thinking such thoughts at her age. A grandmother of four and a fifth on the way. To cover up the confusion she felt, she began talking. 'How is your father, Lily? Is he coming over any time soon?'

Lily looked perplexed. She'd heard from her father a few days ago, but she was sure she had shown Charity the letter.

'Not until Christmas, mami. Didn't I show you the letter?'

'Yes, you did, how forgetful of me,' Charity said with a small laugh. As they chatted, she recovered her composure. It occurred to her how much she liked her daughter-in-law. How much good fortune has been showered upon me, she thought.

When Lily had first entered the Dorai household, they all had to make adjustments. Her life in her father's house in the Ceylonese tea district had been far from traditional. Her parents had tried to keep up their own customs as much as they could, but it had been impossible to prevent the infiltration of European and Sinhala influences drawn from the local community. As a result, Lily was unprepared for some of the things she had to contend with in Nagercoil. One day she had wandered into the front room where Daniel and Jacob were taking tea with some visiting male relatives. Spotting an empty space next to Daniel, she had sat down. The conversation had grown strained and had shortly ceased altogether. Daniel had glared at her, and instinctively she realized she'd committed some terrible faux pas. Then she had seen Charity beckoning to her and gratefully left the room. To her dismay, as soon as they were in the kitchen, Charity had been stern and admonitory. She had told her that no married woman should disgrace her husband and her family by doing what she had just done – casually consorting with men, even if they were relatives. In vain, Lily had protested that in her father's house she'd been able to mingle freely with everyone who had visited. Charity's response was blunt: 'You are not in your father's house now.' Daniel had been furious with his wife but Charity had intervened, saying it wouldn't happen again.

Lily had never repeated that error, but there had been other problems. A spirited young woman, she had clashed variously with her husband and with Miriam, her sister-in-law, and even on one memorable occasion with Jacob Packiam, when she had wanted to replace the woven blinds in his room with chintz curtains. But Charity had always been around to ease her through the difficult times, even if her daughter-in-law had sometimes found her unbending. Lily had wept and lain awake at night during her first months in Nagercoil, but under Charity's patient tutelage she had learned to fit in. 'Do not try to change things around you, that's almost impossible,' Charity had advised the young bride, remembering her own mother-in-law's wisdom. 'Change yourself as much as you can. That's easier. And as you change, good things will follow.'

Lily got on very well with Rachel whenever she visited. The two young women would spend long hours together, chatting and laughing and exchanging notes on their young children. From time to time

Lily and Miriam would still clash, but then Charity's youngest child fought with everyone. Spoilt from birth, Miriam had grown up to be a difficult girl. Her good looks had grown coarse in adolescence, and Charity had wondered if this had something to do with her tantrums. Whatever the reason, Miriam was quick to quarrel. Thinking of her now, Charity's happiness dimmed a little. The previous week there had been another battle: Miriam against the rest. Her daughter's latest demand was to be married off immediately. She had only one condition – that her husband should have a spanking new car. Daniel had flatly refused permission, and his grandfather had supported him. In these modern times, it was good for a young woman to have a college education. Marriage could come later. Charity would have been happy to see Miriam settled, but she couldn't find fault with the reasoning of the men. She was well aware of the great store her father and her son set by education. They hadn't been able to do anything about Rachel – she'd been out of school for too many years by the time she got to Nagercoil – but Jacob had obtained special permission for Miriam to be educated in his school as soon as she was old enough. And neither her father nor her son was prepared to interrupt her studies. To Miriam's rage and frustration, Charity weighed in with the men.

Miriam had broken her sullen silence the day before yesterday, with a complaint: 'You're Shanthi's paati, you're Usha's paati, you're Jason's ammama, you're Stella's ammama, you lavish all your love upon them, and you've forgotten all about me.' Having said this, she'd burst into tears, and Charity had seen the forlorn little girl lurking behind the prickly young woman. Wordlessly, she had gathered Miriam into her arms as she sobbed and sobbed, dampening her sari and her blouse. Miriam will be all right, Charity thought now. With luck she'll marry into the right family, her rough edges will be planed down and she'll grow into a fine young woman. After I've made Rachel's idiyappam, I'll cook a great feast for my family. It's a day to give thanks for being blessed. From within the house she heard Usha begin to wail. Lily raced into the house to be with her youngest and the crying ceased. With a smile, Charity headed for the kitchen.

Late that afternoon, the women of the house gathered in the backyard of the cottage. It was tiny, and mostly occupied by the towering cashew-nut tree. A small papaya grew by the wall, and next to the outdoor privy, a hibiscus bush spread its glossy green foliage. Rachel's husband Ramdoss had had to return to Tinnevelly that day and Daniel had gone to see him off. Jacob was taking a nap in his room. So the women had this time all to themselves. Miriam, who had joined them briefly – making peace, Charity thought – wandered back into the house. Just then Jason was nipped by a tiny red ant that he'd taken too close an interest in. Gathering the three older children around her, Charity began to educate them about the ants that swarmed around the backyard: the harmless quick black ones with raised bottoms could tickle you to distraction, but not so the tiny red ones that oozed along the ground in formation – their bite could sting. She showed them large ponderous black ants, shiny as papaya seeds, wandering slowly along the fissured bark of the cashew tree, and warned them never to go near them: their formidable pincers could make their little bodies swell with poison. And then, hoisting a granddaughter on each hip, with Jason trailing behind clutching her sari, she quartered the yard for the most dangerous of them all, the black-and-red kaduthuva ants. When she found one she killed it with her foot and showed it to the children. 'Remember the pisasus I told you about, who would take you into their awful world deep within the sea and eat you up, bones and all? This ant is worse than the pisasus. If you see one, keep as far from it as you can, do you hear me?' The children nodded, wide-eyed with wonder and terror. Well pleased with herself, Charity deposited them with Rachel and Lily, then took herself off to the kitchen.

As she prepared the meal that evening, a memory of Aaron insinuated itself into Charity's sense of well-being. Instantly her mood grew less buoyant. Where was her beautiful boy, she wondered. What was he doing now? She shook off her gloomy foreboding. Aaron will be all right; God is watching over him, and one day he will return. As she bent to light the fire she gave thanks for her perfect day. Even the shadow cast by Aaron had its place in it: too much happiness wasn't good for you; it was bound to be followed by great sorrow, as the world tried to keep the balance.

44

As the assassins trained in their remote rural camp, the top leaders of the various revolutionary organizations met to choose the next target. Several names were proposed – High Court judges, District Magistrates, Collectors, members of the Governor's Executive

Council, the Governor Arthur Lawley himself. And discarded – not prominent enough, too well protected, too obscure, too well liked. Gradually the list of names was whittled down to three: L. M. Wynch, the Tinnevelly District Collector who had harassed and arrested the great Swadeshi leader V. O. Chidambara Pillai; A. F. Pinhey, the Additional Sessions judge who had sentenced him; and R. W. D. Ashe who had fired on unarmed protesters in Tuticorin and was now District Magistrate of Tinnevelly. Ashe chose himself in the end.

The group received the news of their next assignment fatalistically. Vanchi Iyer was selected for the job. Sankara Iyer and Aaron Dorai would back him up.

The trio tracked Ashe for a week. They made an attempt to assassinate him at his house, but alert sentries deterred them from entering. Vanchi decided to try again in a public place in broad daylight when their quarry's guard was down. On 17 June 1911, Ashe and his wife left town on holiday. They drove to Tinnevelly Bridge Junction and were escorted to their compartment in the waiting train. It wasn't due to leave for a few minutes and they settled into their seats. The whistle blew. Just then the District Magistrate was surprised to see a skeletally thin man who looked ill, dressed in a green coat and a white dhoti, his forehead liberally plastered with vibhuthi, enter their compartment.

'Reserved, reserved. Not allowed,' Ashe said, waving his hands. Too late he realized that the Brahmin was no unwitting interloper. As the pistol materialized in the stranger's hand, Ashe took off his sola topi and flung it at him. It was pitifully inadequate as an act of defence. From their vantage point in the station, Sankara and Aaron heard the pistol pop, watched Ashe slump, saw Vanchi flee the scene. The assassin ran into a lavatory on the platform and the pistol popped again. Aaron and Sankara melted away into the crowd.

The police acted with remarkable dispatch. Of the nineteen conspirators whom they were looking for in connection with the Ashe murder, one escaped to Pondicherry, one cut his throat and another swallowed poison. M. S. Madhavan was shot in Virudhunagar when he tried to kill the policemen tracking him. Fifteen men stood trial, Neelakantha Brahmachari and Aaron Dorai among them. Nine of the accused were convicted under Section 121A of the Indian Penal Code and received prison sentences. Aaron was sentenced to six years' rigorous imprisonment.

45

Early one morning when Charity entered her father's room with his coffee, his posture suggested that something was wrong. When she checked, her worst fears were confirmed. Charity was surprised by how calmly she took her father's death. When Solomon died, her grief had been wrenching, but at her father's funeral the predominant feeling she had was one of peace. She thought: he's a good man, that's why he was blessed with an easy death.

They decided to bury Jacob without waiting for his son to arrive. The journey from Nuwara Eliya would take too long. As she looked upon her father's face for the last time before the casket was sealed, Charity was struck by something. In all my years, she thought, I have not once thought of my father by name. By custom and tradition I have used honorifics to distance and revere him – I need something more. The assembled mourners saw Charity's lips move and thought she was whispering a prayer, but all she said was, 'Jacob, Jacob Packiam.' The name sounded rusty and unfamiliar in her mouth but she repeated it over and over again, and even as she named her father she made him her own in a way that she had never quite done before. The loss hit home, and she broke down and wept by his coffin.

A fortnight later there was another death to mourn. Rachel died giving birth to her third child, a daughter who didn't survive her mother by more than a few hours. Charity was beside herself with grief. Ramdoss had recently accepted an offer from Daniel to help with the expanding business. He had been in the process of moving to Nagercoil when disaster struck. The sight of Rachel's beloved children, already confused by the move and now without a mother, made Charity push her own grief to the back of her mind. She must not let her grandchildren down; she must not let her daughter down.

Through all this, Aaron's capture and arraignment formed a grim backdrop. Daniel, pitched into the unfamiliar role of head of the family after Jacob's death, tried his best to get to see his brother. He wrote to every person in authority he could think of, asking for help. His greatest hope was his father's friend Chris Cooke in Madras. But Cooke pleaded his inability to help. The Government was making no concession to the conspirators. They were determined to make an example of them. Aaron was accused of being an accomplice to the murder of an official of the state and there would be no leniency. Still Daniel hoped ... that there had been a miscarriage of justice, that his brother had been wrongfully detained, that he was innocent. When Aaron was sentenced to prison, the family's grief grew so vast and intolerable that it exhausted them of every emotion. They went about their daily routine mechanically, and the cottage grew still and cold. The children forgot their natural exuberance and crept around the house like small sullen animals, and even Miriam didn't throw a single tantrum, pitching in as best she could with her mother and sister-in-law. Visitors who came to condole left as soon as they could, shocked by the immensity of the family's sorrow, and secretly glad that it hadn't been allotted to them instead.

When Aaron began his jail sentence, Charity finally broke. For a dozen years, her estrangement from her son had been a hard knot of pain at the centre of her existence and now it expanded and blotted everything from her world. Daniel first became aware that something was wrong when she woke him one morning with his coffee. As was usual, he was already awake, although his eyes were shut, milking the last drops of sleep. Instead of leaving the coffee by his side and going her way, he suddenly heard her call out, her voice viperish, 'Begone, chaatan. Get away from that window. Leave my surviving son alone.'

Daniel woke up with a start and said, 'What is it, amma?' She didn't look at him but continued to glare furiously at the locked and shuttered window. She spoke fiercely once more. 'Get thee behind me, Satan. How dare you think you can enter this house of the Lord?' Daniel leapt up, hastily secured his lungi and gently shook his mother, asking her what the matter was. She told him in a harsh, strained voice that there was a sinister little man, dressed all in black, squatting on the window-sill. Daniel looked to where she pointed but there was nothing. He led her muttering back to her room, unrolled her sleeping mat, and gave her a potion to sedate her. He told Lily to take over her chores for the day.

After the incident of the demon on the window-sill, Charity's behaviour became increasingly bizarre. She would wander up to whoever was in the room and begin talking to them in a guttural voice of the huge evil she glimpsed behind their eyes and how it would need to be extinguished if the world were to be a better place. At other times she would address the person nearest her as Aaron and begin weeping and asking for forgiveness for being such a heartless mother. Lily began to fear for the children's welfare and would never leave them alone in their grandmother's presence, although Charity showed no signs of violence. Her hair, still black in late middle age, started turning white.

Daniel became seriously concerned when she took to going out in the evening, as the lamplighters began to light up the town, to accost strangers and warn them of the hell-fire and plague that would consume them if they did not give up their sinful ways. He began treating her the siddha way, pooling oil on her head to cool her fevered mind, making her inhale the vapours of herbs, massaging her with therapeutic oils. When none of these seemed to help, he reluctantly agreed to follow the advice of Lily and the padre of the Home Church (who had prayed without any discernible result over Charity for weeks) that he should take his mother to the church in Ranivoor town, a day's journey to the northwest.

Charity didn't protest when Daniel announced they were going on a trip. Two days later, they were in a jutka whirring along a narrow road that ran like the spine of an open book through fields of emerald rice. Eventually they arrived at their destination, St Luke's Church, whose patron saint was famous throughout the district for his success in curing people possessed by spirits. The church proper was a little outside the busy town of Ranivoor, the second biggest in the district. Their route took them past the crowded main bazaar, a scattering of imposing government buildings and the squat, forbidding Sub-jail. A little further on, the crush of buildings thinned out and soon they were on the outskirts of the town. St Luke's loomed up before them.

A small settlement, two rows of houses and shops, had grown up around the massive building. Makeshift kiosks sold rosaries, crucifixes, pictures of a pink-faced St Luke, rings, amulets, chains, roasted peanuts and gram. The streets were filled with the families of those who had come to seek the help of the saint. Every community was represented – caste Hindus, and those beyond the pale of caste, Muslims, Christians – and every slice of society: poor labourers and farmers mingled with landlords and townspeople dressed in expensive cottons and silks. Finding lodgings in one of the houses that catered to travellers, Daniel settled Charity in and ventured out in search of food and provisions.

Near one of the shops, he heard a clanking behind him, and looked around to see a man of medium height with frizzy hair walking along the road, his eyes wide and staring. He was conservatively dressed, but wore no shoes. With a peculiar thrill, Daniel realized that his ankles were bound together with two crude hoops of steel. There didn't seem to be anyone minding him, and after staring vacantly at Daniel for a while, the madman shuffled off, his dragging gait raising little puffs of dust. Now Daniel began to notice that a fair proportion of the crowd possessed an empty gaze. Many seemed to have been left to wander by themselves as their families took a break. He presumed these were harmless lunatics. The townspeople were obviously used to having them around. Making inquiries, he learned that the exorcisms would begin in the evening, after a special church service.

The brief evening service, a daily affair, was conducted with the minimum of ceremony and ritual. The priest, a harassed-looking man, with exophthalmic eyes and an unruly beard, made a practised sermon, obviously one he had been delivering for years, on Jesus casting out devils. Drawn from Luke, the text centred on the madman whom the Son of God encountered in the country of the Gadarenes.

And Jesus asked him, 'What is thy name?'And he said, Legion: because many devils were entered into him.

The priest talked about Christ's numerous encounters with the many forms of Satan. He cited the power Christ gave to his seventy disciples:

'Behold, I give you power to tread on serpents and scorpions, and over all the power of the enemy.'

His voice grew animated.

And that is the power the Lord Jesus gives all those who call upon him with a humble heart.

He blessed the congregation and retreated swiftly.

When they filed out of the church, volunteers funnelled the crowds into an open area around a pillared hall, roofed, but without walls. On the floor was a thick layer of sand. The hall abutted a grotto that had a terracotta statue of St Luke painted in garish colours. The statue of the saint was protected by an iron portcullis. A steady stream of devotees filed past the likeness. Every inch of space around the pillared hall was packed with people, a large proportion of them villagers dressed in lungis and cheap saris, out for an evening's entertainment. Peanut vendors hawked their wares, skilfully wending their way through the patient crowd. A few torches flickered dully here and there, scarcely illuminating those closest to them. In contrast, the pillared hall blazed with the light of dozens of lanterns like a spotlit stage on which the actors would presently arrive.

On cue, a nondescript young man who had been strolling around on the fringes of the crowd gave a huge roar and headed for the statue of the saint at a dead run. With a loud wail, he leapt into the air and crashed head first into the iron bars with a sickening thump. His fettered hands clinked against the saint's cage. He rushed at the saint again. A long, ecstatic sigh escaped the crowd – this was what they had been waiting for. Behind Daniel, a man was talking to his neighbour. 'Did you see that? If you or I had hit our head against those bars they would have cracked open like coconuts. It's the devil inside him that keeps him from injury. The devils can't stand the saint, that's why they try to attack him.'

'I've never seen anything like it.'

'Yes, yes, it's quite a spectacle. I've been coming here for nearly seven years, at least once a month. It's better than any therukoothu or villupaatu.'

And so it was. The roaring man was now joined by two beautiful young girls dressed in their best saris, their faces expressionless masks. They cavorted around the hall, bouncing up and down as if on steel springs, moaning deep in their throats. Then, taking long run-ups like well-jumpers, they soared into the air in unison, turning perfect cartwheels before landing on the ground with a thud.

'Did you see their saris? Even when they were upside down, they didn't fall down around their waists. It's the devils which keep them glued to their bodies,' the knowledgeable villager said. And indeed it did seem incredible that no matter how frenziedly the girls threw themselves about, their carefully plaited hair and their clothes remained unruffled.

Daniel was sickened by the carnival atmosphere. He hadn't brought Charity here to be made a spectacle of. She had remained quiet throughout the evening, only glancing up occasionally if there was an especially boisterous man or woman on the lighted stage. Not wanting to risk exposing her to the statue, Daniel took her the long way round to the room in the church where the priest was receiving supplicants. When their turn came, Daniel explained the situation, while Charity sat impassively. The padre tried talking to Charity, but she would not reply. Giving up quickly, as the crowd pressed up against them, he said a short prayer, sprinkled water on her, made the sign of the cross and gave Daniel a slip of paper on which was written a verse from the Bible and a cheap copper pendant bearing a vague likeness of the saint. The exorcism was over. 'Bow before the saint. The devils in her will be challenged.'

'Will she be cured?'

'Depends on her faith in the Lord. She could be cured right away or it could take a while.'

Daniel was going to ask more questions but the priest had already turned to the next visitor. Nervously he shepherded Charity into the queue of devotees filing past the shrine. As they approached the statue, Daniel's anxiety increased, but he needn't have worried. The demons within his mother weren't perturbed by the presence of the saint. Charity walked silently past the statue.

They returned home the next day. Daniel reverted to siddha ways of treatment. As the months went by and Charity didn't get any worse, he began to worry less. Then her sorrow manifested itself again, in a quite unexpected way.

46

The beggars of Nagercoil were an organized lot. Although there were dozens of them, they had worked out a very professional system by which all the members of their fraternity would benefit. Territories for each beggar or group were clearly mapped out, so they didn't compete unfairly with anyone else. Some would stake out temples and places of pilgrimage, others would haunt cremation grounds and cemeteries, and the majority would criss-cross town, arriving at certain streets on predetermined days, taking care to keep the frequency of their visits low so that the good housewives of Nagercoil didn't tire of them.

Very early one morning, the old wall-eyed woman who had been taken on to help around the house when Charity had fallen ill came rushing in to Lily's room screaming, 'The kitchen is on fire, the house is on fire.'

Lily hastily accompanied the servant to the kitchen where she found the earthen stove wreathed in flames. It had been stuffed so full of firewood and coconut husks that a portion of the kitchen did seem to be on fire. A large container that was full of something that smelled like stew sat on the burning fuel. Charity calmly watched the fire. It was three in the morning.

Lily went up to her mother-in-law and anxiously asked her if everything was all right. Charity muttered something. Later, Lily would tell her husband that it sounded like 'hunger must be fed', but she wasn't sure. For now, she helped Charity make the chicken stew. There was enough in the container to feed at least two dozen people, but Charity had no answer for why she had cooked so much. From that day onwards, the hearth in the little kitchen would devour massive amounts of fuel from morning to night as Charity and the crone cooked and cooked, churning out an astonishing variety of food – appams, thin, soft and papery, towers of puttu, liberally laced with grated coconut, athirasam crumbling like moist, fragrant earth, hillocks of idiyappam, light and diaphanous as spiders' webs, basins of stew and sweetened coconut milk, neimeen kolambu, shrimp curry and vast mountains of biryani that perfumed the house and the neighbourhood.

Unsurprisingly, the family could eat barely a fraction of these monumental feasts, so the beggars benefited. The regulars paid a visit every Saturday, rattling tin or coconut-shell receptacles against the bars of the gate to alert the household to their arrival. As soon as Charity's cooking binge began, word spread that there was food to spare. Within days, the cottage became a daily stop at lunch-time for scores of beggars who waited impatiently for their share of heaping portions of biryani, spiked with succulent chunks of mutton or chicken (for some reason Charity never cooked a fish biryani), or platters of dosai or slabs of halwa, glistening like polished granite, or tamarind rice, or whatever it was that Charity had decided to make that day.

Sometimes the food would taste strange: onion-flavoured halwa, for example, or sweet biryani, as Charity carried experimentation too far. But by and large, the beggars ate well. Some wouldn't even do their daily rounds, preferring to camp near the cottage so as to have to make the minimum effort.

It was an expensive business, but Daniel decided that so long as it was therapeutic he would finance his mother's passion. Gradually, Charity's labours grew less frenzied, to the great disappointment of the beggars. A couple of months later, the clattering of their vessels at the gate drew no reaction from her. It appeared that the vast grief that had unbalanced her had finally been dissipated by her furious activity. Still, Daniel was cautious. A fortnight passed, and then a month, and still she behaved normally. He slowly relaxed his vigilance. But it was evident that the long road back to sanity had taken its toll. Her speech was slower, her mannerisms deliberate, and her hair had turned completely white. To restore her fully would take something more – perhaps the safe return of Aaron. Daniel redoubled his efforts to try and persuade the authorities to allow him to visit his brother.

47

The skirts of the Great War brushed past India. Over one hundred thousand Indian soldiers were killed or wounded at Mons and Verdun, Ypres and Gallipoli, but the subcontinent itself was threatened only briefly. Soon after the war started, a sleek whippy German battle-cruiser, the *Emden*, appeared off the coast of Madras and began shelling the sweltering city. The effect was remarkable. Around seventy thousand people, almost a quarter of the population, panicked and began streaming out of town. But a brave, or foolhardy, throng gathered on the Marina to get a closer look. To their disgust, the German warship decided that shelling Madras was poor sport and moved on to the Southeast Asian coast where she was eventually dispatched by the Australian battle-cruiser, *Sydney*. Three people died and thirteen were wounded as a result of the *Emden*'s brief foray into Indian waters, but she had made a powerful impression: for years to come, a bully anywhere in the Presidency was known as an Emden.

But the war had other, more far-reaching consequences. For a start, virtually all the political organizations previously opposed to the British closed ranks solidly behind them. The country's new-found support for the rulers contributed to the collapse of the Extremist struggle in the south. Violent revolution continued for a while elsewhere, but in Madras it was only a matter of time before it was relegated to the status of a minor historical footnote.

In his spacious office overlooking the Marina, Chris Cooke was thinking about the revolutionaries and Aaron Dorai in particular. He wondered whether he would have been able to prevent Aaron's involvement if he had revisited Kilanad district and Chevathar, as he'd promised himself he would. The thought made him feel guilty.

Although he had managed to obtain a transfer to the districts after his first stint in the capital, he hadn't served in Kilanad. Marriage and two children later, he had actually applied for a transfer back to Madras. His wife loved the city. There were better schools. And he'd begun to enjoy his work and the diversions of the metropolis. He made new friends, took part in amateur theatricals, enjoyed his excursions to Ooty in the summer – his life began to take on all the hallmarks of a privileged colonial.

When he'd received news of Ashe's murder he had been horrified. But he had also felt for the star-crossed Dorai family. First Solomon, now his son. When would their troubles end? It had saddened him to have to refuse Daniel's requests, but there had been nothing he could do. Until very recently.

The administration of British India was under pressure to feed the war chest and it had occurred to Cooke that this was the opportunity he'd been looking for. On the day that he'd received the circular from the Revenue Secretary asking him to step up his efforts, Cooke had written to Daniel. Aware of the other's prosperity for some time now, Cooke wrote that a substantial contribution to the war effort might help Aaron's case. He wasn't promising anything, but ... Perhaps it would be best if Daniel came to see him in Madras to discuss the matter.

A few days later, Daniel made the journey to the capital. When his assistant ushered him in, Cooke broke with ceremony and embraced Daniel warmly. How the serious young boy he remembered had grown! His face and bearing had acquired gravity, his manner was confident. He looked every inch the wealthy upper-class Indian gentleman that he was. Cooke thought: If for every one of us there is an age that suits us better than any other, Daniel, in his mid-thirties, was in his prime. But the strain of coping with Aaron's tragedy was telling on him. He looked worried and anxious and Cooke felt for him.

Their business was concluded swiftly. In return for a large donation, Aaron's status as a prisoner would be upgraded and the Government would even consider letting him off a year before he was due to finish his sentence. Daniel agreed promptly to the terms.

Cooke invited him to stay a couple of days longer when he learned that this was Daniel's first visit to the capital.

48

Indian vs Indian. We're brilliant at it. Differences of caste, community, language and religion have split our society for thousands of years. All the more surprising, then, that in modern times we've acquired the wholly undeserved reputation of being a tolerant people, exemplars to the rest of the world on how to make a plural society work. In truth, we're only happy to 'adjust' when it suits us, and our behaviour generally shows that we're unable to handle the vast diversity that invests this nation. If we're not actively intolerant we're inert. This makes us fair game for loathsome casteists and communalists (usually priests and politicians) who are always willing to exploit the envy and resentment we nurse against each other.

When the British united India in the nineteen century, they didn't take away our essential Indianness – of which one definition would be the most total inability to make common cause with one another. Instead, they exploited our fatal flaw as it made us easy to control and rule. South of the Vindhyas, they latched on to one of the longest-running feuds in the country, that between Brahmins and non-Brahmins. In the past, the Brahmins had victimized the non-Brahmins but by the twentieth century there was the beginning of a backlash. Most of the leading lights of the independence movement were Brahmin, which earned them the displeasure of the rulers. Quick to seize the opportunity, some powerful non-Brahmin politicians decided to collaborate with the British. Their aim: to advance the cause of the repressed communities by seizing political power. The best known non-Brahmin party was the Justice Party, inheritor of the mantle of organizations like the Madras Dravidian Association, which had its formal baptism on 20 November 1916 with around thirty non-Brahmin leaders meeting in Madras to form the South Indian People's Association. One of the favourite haunts of the Justicites in Madras was the Cosmopolitan Club in which Cooke had found rooms for Daniel.

Daniel had been invited to Cooke's home for supper on his last evening in town. He had decided to wear European clothes, in fact a suit which he had worn only once in his life before, on his wedding day. He had allowed plenty of time for mastering the intricacies of knotting a tie but to his surprise he did it quite easily. He spent a few minutes walking around the room, getting used to the clothes, and then decided to practise his English. He knew the language well enough in a bookish way, but hadn't used it for years. He had found his conversations with Cooke a trial, and was apprehensive about the evening. He muttered English phrases for a while, although he felt slightly foolish saying 'How do you do?' to an empty armchair. Then he wandered down the stairs to the vast lounge near the club entrance, where his host had arranged to pick him up. He ensconced himself in a comfortable chair, and picked up a copy of the *Mail*. As he was idling through it he became aware of someone staring at him. He looked up to see a remarkably ugly man, with fountains of hair jetting from his ears.

'You are new here, sir!' the man said when Daniel caught his eye.

'I'm a visitor. I'm waiting for someone. Mr Cooke.'

'Yes, yes, Mr Chris, he's a good man. The British are good people. Are you liking the British?'

Daniel hadn't really considered the matter and wasn't expecting to be interrogated about it, least of all by a stranger, so he took his time to answer. Not very interested in politics to begin with, the demands of the clinic, family and his growing business had further eroded the attention he paid to the political events of the day. But he supposed he did approve of the British in a distant sort of way. They had brought stability and discipline to the country. His grandfather Jacob, like many Indian Christians, had admired them, especially the missionaries, for their efforts to alleviate the misery of the lower caste groups. Further, his childhood friendship with Father Ashworth had predisposed him to look favourably upon the white man. Aaron's arrest by the British had dismayed him, and for a while he had begun to read the papers diligently. But the tragic developments within the family had pushed everything else from his mind. When he had resumed his efforts to see Aaron, the intransigence of the authorities had irked him considerably, but his meeting with Cooke had succeeded in partially restoring his faith in the British. On balance, it would seem that he didn't mind them at all. Realizing the stranger was waiting for an answer, he said, 'I don't think they are too bad.'

'Very good, sir, very good. May I be knowing your good name?'

'Dr Daniel Dorai.'

'Christian? Andavar Christian?' Although it was quite cool, there was a sheen of sweat on the man's jowly face.

'Yes.' His interlocutor was speaking in English so Daniel, not entirely comfortable with the language, decided to keep his replies short.

'Myself Vardaraja Mudaliar.'

'Pleased to meet you, sir.'

Just then a thought occurred to his new friend. His brow furrowed. Daniel watched as a drop of sweat collected in the frown and meandered into a bushy eyebrow.

'You are not by any chance the famous Dr Dorai? All my family is using your thylam, sir, and I'm also planning to use it.'

When Daniel admitted his identity, Mudaliar retorted, 'You are knowing who I am?'

Daniel said he did not.

'Sir, my name was mentioned in a report of the Justice Party, in the paper that you are reading.'

When he saw Daniel hesitate, his brow furrowed again, this time in irritation. 'You are not knowing about the Justice Party?'

Daniel was glad to say that he had indeed heard of the party.

'We are engaged in a most important task, sir,' Mudaliar said. 'We are committed to breaking the conspiracy. You are knowing?'

The experience was unnerving. Daniel was glad to practise his English but his rather tenuous grasp on politics and current affairs made him feel completely out of place in Mudaliar's company. A reply was expected but as he didn't have the faintest idea of what conspiracy Mudaliar was referring to, Daniel took the safe option.

'I don't know,' he said.

'You must know the fucts,' Mudaliar said. 'Without the fucts the truth will never come out.' It took Daniel a moment or two to work out that his companion was referring to 'facts'. Not that it mattered, for Mudaliar was paying no attention to him. He was suddenly filled with an intense desire to get out of the other's clutches. He glanced down covertly at his watch, but before he could see what time it was, Mudaliar's sweaty hand took hold of his.

'For thousands of years the Brahmins have conspired to keep us down, Mr Daniel,' he said passionately. 'I will restrict myself only to the fucts to prove it. Kindly allow myself to place them before you.' He raised a thick finger. 'I'm telling you, sir, these fucts are unimpeachable as they have been compiled by the Government of Madras. In 1912, the latest year for which figures are available, there were three hundred and forty-nine Brahmin tahsildars and deputy tahsildars compared to one hundred and thirty-four non-Brahmin Hindu tahsildars. Christian and Muslim even less. Brahmins had over seventy per cent graduates. You are Christian, Mr Daniel, do you know what the Christian percentage was? five point three per cent! How could this happen? Same with law colleges, teachers' colleges, everywhere nothing but Brahmin, Brahmin ... Sir, let me quote an illustrious Justicite who said in a statement to the Royal Public Services Commission in Madras, "The Brahmin has been for thousands of years the custodian and object of all intellectual culture, and the other castes have in consequence been placed in a very disadvantageous position intellectually."

He released Daniel's hand to mop his brow with his shoulder cloth. A couple of large and prosperous-looking men greeted him and he introduced them to Daniel who folded his palms in a namaskaram. They grinned broadly back at him. Vardaraja Mudaliar heaved his capacious bulk out of his chair and made to go. 'You are not a member of our party, sir?'

Daniel shook his head but Mudaliar wasn't finished. 'But you will be soon,' he said. 'All right-thinking people must join the fight. As the great poet Subramania Bharati, himself a Brahmin, has said, "Now that India is actually awakening to a New Age it will be well for my Brahmin countrymen if they voluntarily relinquish all their old pretensions, together with the silly and anti-national customs based on such pretensions, and lead the way for the establishment of liberty, equality and fraternity among Indians ..."' Vardaraja Mudaliar looked at Daniel meaningfully. Daniel was tempted to reply that he had no quarrel with Brahmins but was spared any further discourse with him, for Cooke had arrived in their midst. The three men were preparing to draw Cooke too into the conversation when he slipped smoothly out of their clutches, much to Daniel's admiration. 'We're late for a dinner appointment, gentlemen. Now if you'll excuse us.' He steered Daniel through the chairs and out into the portico where his car and driver were waiting.

As the car pulled out of the driveway into the bustle of Mount Road, Cooke turned to Daniel. 'What did you think of our friend Vardaraja?' He pronounced the name 'Werderja' and for the first time Daniel did not feel as diffident about his English.

'Oh, he's very passionate. But I'm not comfortable with politics and more so caste and religion. I've already lost my father and brother to it. In fact ...' He stopped, embarrassed, as he realized that Cooke had merely been making polite conversation and hadn't invited an outpouring of the soul.

'Yes, I understand,' Cooke said diplomatically and Daniel's embarrassment deepened. Why did he feel so out of place in the city? He looked out of the window and was dazzled by the crowds, the traffic, the lights, the wealth, the glitter ... He thought of when he had first arrived in Nagercoil. He had found the pace of town life unnerving but this was of a wholly different order. And yet, despite everything, he had the curious sensation that the entire edifice was nothing more than a thin pulsing rim of light and froth on top of a greater darkness. A major cataclysm and it would be gone, leaving behind the timeless rocks and sand.

The car moved through the great commercial districts of the city and his host pointed out the famous stores and establishments of what had once been the first city of the country: Spencer's, Whiteaway Laidlaw, P. Orr & Sons, Higginbotham's, C. M. Curzon & Co. They stopped at a couple of shops and Daniel bought a set of earrings encrusted with pearls for Lily, a Singer sewing machine for Charity, and some toys for the children. But he was not much of a shopper and gratefully accepted his host's suggestion that they go for a drive before supper. As they motored through Mount Road, Cooke pointed out further landmarks – the Lyric Theatre, the D'Angelis hotel, the *Hindu* building, the *Mail* offices.

They left the main artery and drove through a web of small lanes, the car inching its way through the throngs of people on the roads and pavements. Everywhere Daniel looked there was busy and colourful activity. Once again, he felt a sense of disorientation. He wondered how the people who lived here could cope with the city's activity, its enormity, its absoluteness.

After some time, they crossed a bridge over a sluggish river and were driving down a broad road with light traffic and hardly any people. The familiar smell of the sea filled his nostrils. Lamps cast their dusty light for a few metres of the beach but beyond there was only the night stretching over the limitless sea. The crowded city might never have existed. He turned to look out of the other window and was staggered by what he saw: a cliff of buildings, dozens of feet high, pricked with lights. He realized that this was where he had come to meet Cooke two days ago. The buildings had been impressive enough during the day, but now they were truly resplendent, a triumph of man's ambition and power.

Cooke said, 'Tremendous, aren't they? I don't know why we ever decided to abandon Madras in favour of Calcutta.'

'I've never seen anything like it.'

Cooke laughed. 'Part of our strategy, old boy. We couldn't bring London here to impress you chaps, so we decided to build our own palaces to show that we could be as grand as any maharajah, zamindar or mirasidar. They are a jolly impressive sight, aren't they? I often drive home along this road to marvel at them.'

He murmured the names of the buildings as they rolled by – Chepauk Palace, the university buildings, Presidency College, Senate House, the PWD building, the Ice House looking like an oddly risen cake. They left the long line of buildings behind and entered the quiet neighbourhood of Adyar where Cooke lived, in a sprawling bungalow on the banks of the river.

In the high-ceilinged drawing room, they had a quick drink with Cooke's wife, Barbara, a tiny woman with startlingly blue eyes. As they went in to supper, Cooke put his arm briefly around his wife's shoulders. They make a handsome couple, Daniel thought – Cooke, tall and athletic, his brown hair barely flecked with grey in early middle age, and his lively petite wife. The Cookes' two small children, a boy and girl, came and wished their parents and their guest goodnight before trailing away in the wake of their governess.

Supper was an enjoyable meal and Barbara, who was something of an amateur historian, regaled Daniel with stories of Madras. The food was excellent. As the meal progressed, Daniel found himself somewhat envious of the Cookes. He could have a house like this if he wanted, he supposed. He had the money. But innately modest, he had never had any ambition for a grander house in Nagercoil. And besides, what would he need such a big house for? Come to think of it, what did the Cookes need such a big house for? There were only four of them.

His musings were cut short when Barbara rose to leave, summoned by the governess to the side of her daughter who had not been well that day. Cooke suggested they retire to the veranda for coffee and cigars. Daniel declined the cigar.

'Are you sure? It's a Spencer's Light of Asia. Haven't smoked a better brand.'

'Quite sure,' Daniel said. They sat without speaking savouring the quiet of the night. A fragrance of frangipani wafted over them.

'Are the frangipani still flourishing in Chevathar? I remember I used to anticipate their fragrance long before I actually got to them.'

'I haven't been ...' Daniel hesitated. His host wasn't interested in his family's troubled history! 'There are still a couple of trees, but the rest are gone.' The remark triggered a cascade of images and he longed fiercely to be in Chevathar.

'Pity. But I suppose change has its own consequences. I hear Meenakshikoil is booming.'

'Yes, it is.'
'And your own business? You are a wealthy man, Daniel. Your father would have been proud of you.'
Memories of Solomon, Aaron, Chevathar welled up in his mind, and he pushed them away, fighting to keep his composure. They sat in silence for a bit after that. Cooke puffed out a luxurious cloud of smoke, then asked casually, 'Why did Aaron get mixed up with those terrorists?'
'I don't know, Mr Cooke. Perhaps he believed in their struggle.'
'Killing an innocent man just because he was doing his job?'
'That was wrong,' Daniel said. Yes, it was, Cooke thought. It was.
'You said you weren't interested in politics, Daniel?'
'Not really ...'
'You're like Barbara then. She's banned politics at the dinner table,' Cooke said with a laugh. Then he asked: 'So how did Vardaraja Mudaliar get you to listen to him? Hypnosis?'
Daniel opted for diplomacy. 'He's a forceful speaker. I found his views on the Justice Party fascinating.'
'Ah yes, our friends the Justicites. Appears they are the only friends we have left ... They have their own objectives, but at least they're willing to work with us. Montagu is a good and decent man, but he has to contend with a bewildering variety of pulls and struggles. The Indian nationalists must realize that. The reforms he is proposing, the areas in which he suggests that Indians be part of decision-making, are the best he can do. Why doesn't Congress see that?'
'Mr Mudaliar was saying something to me about Brahmins. He reeled off a lot of facts and figures.'
'Oh, yes, that's old Vardaraja for you. He was a mathematics teacher, you know. But that's the principal agenda of the Justice Party. They feel they must fight for the rights of tens of millions of non-Brahmins who have been unfairly kept down by the Brahmins. Can't say I blame them.' Cooke's cigar had almost burned down to the nub. 'Sorry, I'm boring you with politics.'
'No, it's quite fascinating.'
The Englishman wondered whether this was the moment to tell Daniel what he had been keeping to himself. But his guest was leaving the next day and he wouldn't have another opportunity.
'There's something I've been meaning to tell you,' he began, trying to keep his tone light. 'After I wrote to you I wired Superintendent Rolfe who runs the Melur jail, and he wired back to say that Aaron is ill. Tuberculosis, I'm afraid.'

'How bad?' Daniel asked.

'Not too bad, apparently, but instructions have been sent through the relevant channels that he be moved to Ranivoor. There's a better equipped Sub-jail there with a brand-new infirmary.'

'I'll leave immediately for Ranivoor.'

'No, give it a fortnight or so, I'll need to get all the paperwork in order.'

'But my brother is not too bad?'

'I've been assured that he isn't, but I should also tell you that in allowing you to go to Ranivoor I'm doing so in express disregard of Aaron's wishes.' Cooke's voice grew gentle. 'I hope you're able to see your brother, Daniel.'

There was nothing more to be said. Shortly afterwards Daniel was driven back to the club. All the way there he stared unseeing out of the window as the city shut down for the night. The unlit buildings crowded down on the vehicle. He thought they looked like tombstones.

The car swerved to avoid an old man clad only in a tattered lungi who had stepped suddenly off the pavement. Daniel was jerked out of his reverie. He asked the driver to slow down, then settled back into his seat. His conversation with Cooke had only served to confirm what he'd suspected but still the revelation that Aaron did not want his family to visit him was deeply depressing. Why did his brother hate them all so much? He remembered how much he'd been wounded by Aaron's rejection of him, but this tragedy had overwhelmed everything else. Now all he wanted was his brother back, for himself, for Charity! He smiled sadly as he remembered his mother telling him about the time Aaron was born. Until the new arrival could walk, Daniel had been his most zealous protector, constantly hovering around the baby, but the minute he took his first tottering steps, he would look for every conceivable opportunity to knock him down. 'Quite the little terror you were. We had to watch you constantly to ensure the little one didn't suffer any permanent damage,' Charity had said. Was that where the breach had been born? How absurd, he thought.

As the car rolled down Mount Road, he began checking off everything he would need to restore Aaron to full health. If the TB wasn't too far advanced, it should be easy enough to control. All it needed was the right diet, plenty of fresh air and water. And if all went well, Charity need never know, for the disease would be under control by the time Aaron had finished his sentence. His mind grew calmer as he grappled with the practical aspects of his brother's present situation. As the car pulled into the driveway of the Cosmopolitan Club, he thought, I do not believe that we cannot be one family again.

49

Superintendent Rolfe had lied. Aaron Dorai was critically ill with TB when he was transferred to Ranivoor Sub-jail. He had instructed the prison doctor to prepare a report for Madras that hid the prisoner's true condition and quickly arranged to transport Aaron to his new destination.

He personally delivered news of the transfer. Aaron was in the infirmary, a hot airless box with seven beds next to the kitchen. Paan stained the discoloured walls and the room smelled of vomit and shit. The Superintendent, who rarely visited the infirmary, stood by the door and shouted: 'Dorai, you are to be transferred tomorrow. God help you and don't die on me, you little shit.'

The prisoner's eyes opened and a light glowed deep within his pupils. The skin stretched across the bones of the wasted face moved, and with a mounting sense of incredulity Rolfe realized the prisoner was attempting to smile. Rage swept him. He wished he could pound the hated face to a pulp, extinguish the life within that skeletal body, erase this abomination from the face of the earth. But the threat of retribution from Madras was too strong. He turned and walked out of the door.

Aaron Dorai was transferred seventeen times in his first five years in prison. This was because the Government was determined to prevent the growth of popular centres of resistance around the revolutionaries. Also, to break their spirit, they were treated very badly, whipped and put into solitary confinement on the slightest pretext and given the dirtiest tasks to do. In some prisons, the Superintendent was more humane than others, but Aaron was always given the worst jobs, the worst quarters, and was punished for the least infraction. In Coimbatore jail, he was made to draw the heavy oil press; in Palayamkottai jail, he was given the dreaded jute-cleaning detail, where the skin was literally flayed from his palms; in Sivakasi jail he was set to breaking rocks like a common labourer. But it was in Melur jail that he almost died.

Superintendent Rolfe hated the new prisoner, the only one of the conspirators to be transferred to his jail. He despised natives anyway and the fact that they had dared to take the life of an Englishman enraged him. If he'd had his way, every one of the conspirators would have been tortured before they were shot. He would have done more, he thought; he would have instantly executed a hundred Indians and ordered every native to crawl on his belly when they approached within a hundred yards of a European.

When he had first set eyes on the skinny prisoner, eyes enormous and feverish in his drawn face, he was taken aback. How could this rodent have taken on the English? He soon found out. He had him whipped thrice in his first week, and immured him in solitary confinement throughout that time. But no matter how hard he tried, he couldn't break the prisoner's spirit. Rolfe didn't give up. Every morning, he would have Aaron brought to his office for a little sport. He would taunt and abuse him, and try to devise new methods of abasing him. Aaron would remain impassive and unflinching through the torture and ridicule, further stoking the fury of his tormentor.

One morning, Rolfe walked across to him and slapped him hard. 'I want you to go out on the street, with the warden here, and publicly announce that you are a son of a whore ...' For the first time during his sessions at the Superintendent's office, the prisoner spoke without being forced to. He said, 'You're mistaken, Superintendent. It isn't my mother you are thinking of, it's yours.' If he'd hoped that such a provocation would quickly end it all, he wasn't far wrong. Rolfe beat him furiously but methodically, before finally turning him over to the prisoners whom he charged with meting out suitable punishment to obstreperous inmates. In his jail, as in some others in the Presidency, these prisoners were called Black Caps and were usually the most violent and sadistic. Rolfe told them to be careful. He had almost fallen for the oldest trick in the book, he thought, but Aaron wouldn't escape so easily. And besides, he had explicit instructions: political prisoners were not to become martyrs to the cause.

A huge lifer called Sethu, in jail for murdering his wife, seven children and in-laws, was given the task of carrying out Superintendent Rolfe's implicit orders. Aaron was cornered in the canteen. His feet were swept from under him, and two rapists pinned him down. They stretched his good leg on one of the metal tables and Sethu, with the delicacy of a surgeon, broke every bone in it. His tool was a length of metal pipe. Aaron's screams only stopped when he passed out. A half-hour later, when the prison doctor examined him in the infirmary, his verdict merely reaffirmed Rolfe's faith in Sethu's expertise. The skin on the foot wasn't even broken, but Aaron would never walk without assistance again.

He was assigned to the cumbly-weaving section, where wool was immersed in lime, then treated, carded and woven into coarse blankets. The prisoners worked in a large, dingy, room where wool dust hung in the heavy air. One day Aaron collapsed, spitting blood. The prison doctor diagnosed tuberculosis and prescribed rest and better food than the cold lumpy kanji and pickle that was the usual prison fare.

Rolfe disagreed. 'Just make him well enough to get him back to work.' As soon as Aaron was able to leave the infirmary, he was issued with a pair of wooden crutches, and on the first day of his release the Superintendent was delighted to see his crutches knocked from under him whenever Sethu and his fellow inmates needed to amuse themselves. Aaron never complained. His eyes would blaze with anger but he would say nothing. He was assigned once more to the weaving section.

In less than a month his condition had deteriorated so much that he was coughing almost continuously. The prison doctor told Rolfe bluntly that the prisoner wouldn't last more than a couple of weeks if he weren't given an easier job. Rolfe assigned him to lavatory detail.

The lavatories at the Melur Central Jail had become so noxious that the panchama prisoners, whose responsibility it was to clean them out, had gone on strike. They had refused to yield to any blandishment or threat. Finally, Rolfe had hired scavengers from outside to do the job. He had no option but to pay them five times their usual rate, so he economized by cutting down the frequency with which the lavatories were cleaned from once a week to once a month.

The lavatories stood at the farthest end of the prison, a row of six sheds with a cement hole in the centre of each. They had been built for the needs of sixty prisoners, but the jail now had seven hundred inmates. The smell that emanated from them had spread to every corner of the prison. From a distance, all you could see was a moving black carpet of flies that crawled, buzzed and flew over the excreta that coated the floor of each shed. As it had been some time now since they had last been cleaned, they were, without exception, inches deep in urine dotted with turds like islands. Indeed the lavatories were so filthy that the prisoners had taken to defecating outside, leaving little hillocks of excrement all over the place.

Superintendent Rolfe dispatched a warden to fetch antiseptic from the infirmary. He and the warden dipped handkerchiefs in the antiseptic, wrapped them around their noses and went to see how Prisoner No. 114301 was doing in his new job.

They found Aaron sitting with his back to a wall, staring blankly ahead, his crutches by his side. Flies crawled over his face, eyes, mouth and hair, but he made no attempt to brush them away. The stick broom, his only implement to clean the filth, lay in a pool of urine.

'Get him back to work immediately,' the Superintendent screamed, the rage in his voice somewhat muted by the cloth covering his face. The warden picked his way delicately through the excreta, then swung a foot at Aaron. 'Start working, you miserable bastard,' he yelled.

Aaron did not react.

The warden kicked him again, so hard that he toppled over on his side. He lay there for a moment, then slowly righted himself. He made no move to pick up the broom. The warden's foot lashed out once more, but Aaron seemed as indifferent to him as to the flies that clouded his face. In a fury, the warden began working him over, crashing kicks and blows on his meagre frame. When he had beaten him into a stupor, he and the Superintendent unbuttoned their trousers and urinated on the unconscious man.

While Aaron was recovering in the infirmary, Superintendent Rolfe received the transfer orders. The prisoner was allowed a good bath, his hair (that was almost white with lice eggs) was shaved, and he was given a set of clean clothes before beginning his journey to his new home.

50

Daniel was saddened, then infuriated, when he saw Aaron in the Ranivoor jail infirmary. The place was airy and new all right, but this wasted human being was on the verge of death, not slightly ill with TB. He conferred with the Superintendent and the young prison doctor, who was clearly in awe of him, and it was decided that while Daniel was in Ranivoor, he would be in charge of his brother's treatment.

For some time after he'd arrived in the infirmary, where Aaron was the only occupant, his brother continued to sleep, his breathing rough and tortured. Daniel sat by his bed, his mind a whirl. He'd waited for so long for this moment, there had been so much that he'd wanted to say to his brother, but Aaron's condition had completely unsettled him. He'd wanted to tell his brother how much he loved him, how much his family wanted him back, but he'd also intended to reproach Aaron for the pain he'd caused them, especially Charity. Now there could be none of that. This man needed all his skills as a physician if he were to survive, although deep down, Daniel knew that his efforts would probably be futile. He knew when a patient was too far gone. It made him despair, but he fought the feeling; it wouldn't do for him to give up. If he did so, Aaron would have no chance whatsoever.

He didn't know how long he waited, but he suddenly realized that his brother's eyes were open. He recoiled inwardly from the hate in Aaron's gaze.

'Get out. Let me die in peace.' The effort of speaking led to a bout of coughing. Blood speckled the cloth Daniel used to wipe his lips. With great difficulty Aaron spoke again. 'Why are you here? You abandoned me, so why come now?'

'I never abandoned you. Appa sent me away.'

'Thank God. Or we'd be licking the dust off Muthu Vedhar's feet.'

'Thambi, if we had appealed to Muthu Vedhar's good sense, maybe we could have bought time. Avoided the battle.'

'Avoided it. Are you mad? And will we get rid of the British that way too?'

Aaron closed his eyes as he tried to control a cough. When he opened them, Daniel said, 'You shouldn't talk. I'll go now, but if you need anything I'll be close by.'

'Why are you suddenly feigning concern? Get out, you disgust me.'

A great storm of coughing racked his skeletal frame. Daniel beckoned frantically to the prison doctor who had just entered the infirmary. A quick-acting sleeping draught was administered to Aaron. He should come back another time; he knew his presence was agitating the dying man. Reluctantly Daniel left the infirmary soon after his brother had fallen into a restless sleep.

At the cheap boarding house, which he had chosen for its proximity to the jail, he tossed and turned and then, giving up the idea of sleep, went and stood by the window, looking out at the refuse-strewn alley below. Daniel couldn't remember Aaron and he fighting much as children, yet there had been little common ground between them from early on. They were different, so unlike each other that it was hard to believe they were born of the same parents. But had they actually disliked each other all their lives, hated the fact that they were united by blood when it was evident that nothing else bound them? No, no, it couldn't be so. Daniel had always loved his younger brother, even when Aaron wanted nothing to do with him. It was evident Aaron still hated him, but surely it wasn't impossible for them to come together? Oh Aaron, he thought sadly, I've been denied you all our life; now, God willing, perhaps we can forget our differences, begin again. There was so much they could do, the sons of Solomon unleashed upon the world. They had both travelled great distances in their lives, suffered defeat and tasted victory, and they would be unbreakable! They would put the past behind them. They were both strong enough and together they would take on every challenge, big and small. Thank you, Lord, for bringing Aaron back to me, Daniel thought. Your ways are inscrutable but please grant us one chance at a future together.

He was at the tall steel gates of the prison as soon as they opened the following morning. He managed to get the Superintendent to agree to his seeing the prisoner ahead of visiting hours. For much of the day Aaron lay in a stupor, his breath rattling in his throat like dry leaves shifting in the wind. Looking at his wasted body, Daniel shuddered at the torture Aaron must have been subjected to. What had they done to him, this strong, beautiful youth, someone he remembered as being so impossibly fine that it seemed life couldn't leave even the slightest scratch on him? But they hadn't been able to touch his spirit, that much was clear from his brief encounter with his brother. No, they could do whatever they wanted, but they couldn't destroy the steel that invested men like Aaron, like his Joshua-chithappa ... What was it about such men that in their fleeting span they shone so brightly that everyone else was cast into their shade? And why did they last so briefly? Did their Creator embed some fatal flaw in them so that they were destroyed before they were forced to the level of ordinary men? Was it ordained that they lived and died heroically so they were forever perfect in the eyes of all who beheld them?

Late that afternoon, Aaron opened his eyes, struggled to focus them on Daniel. The hate flared. When he spoke, his voice was so soft that Daniel could barely hear him. 'Why are you still here?'

'I've come to get you out of here, thambi. Get you well again. Bring you back to the family.'

'What family?' Aaron hissed. 'Abraham-chithappa told me a long time ago what this family was all about. I've no use for any of you.' The weak voice was contemptuous. Slowly and painfully, Aaron turned his back on him.

Suddenly furious, Daniel wanted to shout, 'Do you know how we've suffered? Do you have any idea, you miserable little wretch? Do you know that amma went mad when she heard you'd gone to prison? Do you know Rachel is dead, thatha is dead? Do you know the terrible time we've been through ...' To his horror, Daniel realized that he hadn't just been thinking the words in his head, in his anger he'd actually said them. He fought to control himself. What did he want to do, kill Aaron? Was there nothing he could do right, where his brother was concerned?

Aaron turned back to him, his eyes huge and bright in his wasted face. 'What did you just say?'

'Nothing, nothing, I didn't mean the words to slip out, sorry, thambi, I didn't mean to upset you ...'

'Amma ... Rachel ... Thatha ...' The pain in Aaron's voice was unmistakable.

'I'm so sorry, thambi, I'm such a stupid fool. Please ... we'll have all the time in the world to talk when you are better. You mustn't exert yourself, rest ...'

Aaron interrupted him, 'Is there more? Tell me, is there more?'

'Thambi, we can talk later. Please ...'

The bruised lips formed a short sentence: 'No time!' And then Aaron said, struggling to get the words out, 'I wish I'd known, I wish I'd known, all these years hating amma ... you ... my God, anna!'

A great joy flooded through Daniel's anguish when Aaron used the honorific for older brother. He leaned forward, took his brother's hand, bony and with the knuckles abnormally pronounced, in his own. 'Rest, thambi, you must rest ...' Daniel said, tears spilling down his cheeks. 'We'll all be back together very soon ...'

'What have I done ...' Aaron began, when he was overcome by a coughing fit.

'Enough, thambi, we'll talk later, this is doing you no good. Here, take your medicine ...'

Aaron waved the medicine away. 'Let me finish, anna, I don't have much strength left.'

Tears continued to drip down Daniel's face. He made no effort to wipe them away.

Aaron said, 'So many regrets ... little I can do about them now. I wish I could see amma, Rachel ...'

'But you will ...'

'I don't think so, anna, not them, not my beloved Chevathar.' Aaron paused, then pressed on. 'You know, one of the things I thought obsessively about when I was in prison, the only thing which kept me going, was memories of Chevathar. I had no use for my family, chithappa had seen to that, but Chevathar, oh Chevathar was always with me, it kept me alive. It's ironic, I kept running away from the place, but it grew to be the most important thing in my life ...' His voice tailed off as his energy ebbed away. Over Daniel's protests, Aaron struggled to speak again, finish what he was saying. 'Isn't it curious how we always realize the important things when it's too late? Perhaps that's His way of reminding us how useless and insignificant we really are.'

As a long bout of coughing shook the sick man, Daniel swiftly administered the sleeping potion; Aaron couldn't be allowed to exert himself any more. As it took effect and his brother's ravaged face began to relax, Daniel leaned back.

Just then Aaron's eyes opened. 'You should go back, anna, take our family back to where we belong,' he said slowly. 'Don't have the regrets I do. You may not be much like me, but you're the last of us ...'

Aaron slept the rest of the day. Daniel persuaded the Superintendent to let him spend the night in the infirmary. He lay awake, listening to his brother's laboured breathing, praying that he would recover. In the early hours he nodded off. He thought he heard his brother say 'Jayanthi', and watched the woman, young, beautiful, with eyes so black they seemed to absorb all light, go to him ...

In the morning, when he awoke, Aaron was dead, the beginnings of a smile on his lips.

51

A few furlongs from Chevathar, the landscape unfurling outside Daniel's jutka matched exactly the landscape kindled in his memory. The road was a shimmering blue-black stripe scored in the red soil. Small clusters of huts rose from the living earth, punctuated every so often by a more pukka construction, blue, green or white, all shawled and swathed by the dull green of coconut, and the duller olive of areca nut. Deep emotion swept him as he absorbed the familiar details. Lord, how could I have stayed away so long? Aaron was right, Chevathar is where we belong. He leaned as far as he could out of the carriage to take in everything that offered itself up to his remembering eye.

They passed into an uninhabited stretch. This rock- and scree-strewn landscape possessed a beauty that owed nothing to nostalgia. The hand that had painted this landscape of God had, from time to time, daubed a brilliant mad contrast to the sober earth tones of the background – the jewelled red of a coral tree, spliced with the violent vermilion of flame of the forest, the yellow slash of laburnum, mellowed only by the soft violet of jacaranda. Each new vista that he soaked in affected him more powerfully than the one that had preceded it.

'I will recover Chevathar for you, Aaron,' he vowed, 'I'll recover it for all of us. I'm only sorry it took me so long.' As he had often done, he wondered now if a return to Chevathar was the restorative that his mother needed. His mind went back to the immediate aftermath of his brother's death. When he had returned to Nagercoil he had kept the news from Charity; he didn't know if she'd be able to cope with it. She had asked him how Aaron was, and he'd told her that he was well, and she'd seemed satisfied. Three days later, as he was preparing to go to work, she came up to him. 'I dreamed last night that Aaron was with his father in Heaven.' When Daniel looked at her, thunderstruck, she said, her voice eerily flat, 'You're a good son, Daniel, but you shouldn't lie to me.' He'd been terrified that she would have another breakdown but she had grieved so much, it seemed to have exhausted her of all emotion. It hurt him to see her empty eyes, her lack of interest in her grandchildren and the family, but he was also relieved that she was doing no damage to herself. As the weeks slipped by, and her condition showed no signs of deteriorating, he began to make plans for his journey to Chevathar.

Meenakshikoil, which he reached in the short twilight hour, was a revelation. Slabs of light from the busy vegetable market revealed a town that had stretched and grown. The road through town passed two schools that hadn't existed when Daniel left Chevathar, a brand-new jail and a profusion of shops. They finally came to the old bridge that led to the village.

As the jutka rattled over it, Daniel strained to take in every sight, absorb every smell and sound. The village seemed much the same, except that there were a few more houses of brick and mortar, and it seemed dustier and dirtier than before. A medley of dogs snapped at the jutka for a couple of minutes, then the horse pushed through and they were rolling past Anaikal and the acacia wasteland, from which the smell of ordure wafted as of old. The Murugan temple had been spruced up, he noticed. A few more minutes and they were at the Big House.

Daniel was disconcerted by what he saw. It was as if the vitality and grandeur he had associated with his old home had been sucked out. The great neem and rain trees, the profusion of palms, the teak that grew behind the house, all outlined in black against the grey fur of the sky, seemed positively malevolent, dead spirits threatening the house they had once sheltered. Even in the half-light, Daniel could see that the house itself was in an advanced state of disrepair. The roof had lost half its tiles, windows hung from their hinges, it obviously hadn't been whitewashed in years, and dead leaves and other detritus clogged the courtyard. He walked around the house. The place seemed lifeless, and then a dark shadow came leaping out of the gloom and he evaded the dog just in time. He picked up a stone and flung it, and the animal took off with a yelp. He wandered around the house, pounding at windows and doors, and finally a weak voice quavered, 'Who is there?'

For much of the journey, his uncle's perfidy (for even though Aaron had taken his secret with him, it had been easy enough to work out) had alternately enraged and mystified him. Why had Abraham done it? Why had he and his wife turned Aaron against his family? He could easily imagine the broad strokes of their campaign, the detail was unimportant now – Abraham and Kaveri filling Aaron's confused mind with carefully invented facts about his mother and himself abandoning Chevathar and the soil of their ancestors for the dazzle of Nagercoil, their prosperity and their neglect of him. Aaron's pride would have done the rest. And it was all so unnecessary. Neither he nor Charity had asked Abraham for anything, not even remonstrating with him when he had failed to send them the annual pittance he had promised them. And his brother? Why hadn't he bothered to check? Daniel thought of the last words his brother had uttered. Was this what Aaron wanted him to return to? Or had he been gone too long to see the house in this dilapidated state?

He was taken aback by his first sight of Abraham Dorai. His uncle had always been skinny, but now the bones leapt out of his face and chest. Clad only in a filthy dhoti, he looked like a mendicant. He blinked at the man in front of him, not recognizing Daniel for a long instant, then a grimace stretched his features.

'Daniel-thambi, is it really you? Vaango, vaango.' He raised his voice in a shout for his wife and then came forward to greet his nephew. Kaveri emerged and greeted Daniel as effusively as her husband had. And then for a time they stood around, unsure of how to proceed. Daniel was astonished to see how husband and wife had grown to resemble each other – their features had settled and arranged themselves in patterns that could have been lifted from an identical mould. He remembered how they had been. Kaveri, short, plump and fair, and Abraham, tall and dark. Now their faces were lined, hair white. Decades of a childless marriage could do that to you, Daniel mused. He found the thought unexpectedly humorous. But there was nothing funny about the way they had conducted themselves. Through their avarice and selfishness, they had divided his family, dishonoured Solomon, brought about the death of his brother and the madness of his mother.

Grimly he agreed to stay the night. He refused dinner, asking only for a glass of water. Kaveri brought him a tumbler of buttermilk and left to prepare a room for him to sleep in. He drank it sitting on the veranda, as his father had often done, and listened as Abraham began to talk about how hard times had been. All the villages had been sold or taken over by the Government for non-payment of dues, and now he owned only thirty acres of land here and in a village to the north. That was the reason he hadn't sent Charity the regular remittances of baskets of mangoes and rice, as agreed.

'You are evil people,' Daniel said. 'I spoke to Aaron before he died and he told me everything.'

Kaveri had just come out on to the veranda and she began weeping noisily. 'Oh, that poor misguided boy. How much we loved and looked after him, and now he's gone, Jesu have mercy on his soul. When will our sorrows come to an end, after all the sacrifices we've made ...'

Daniel cut in, his voice cold. 'The only sacrifices you've made are for your own personal gain. If half the things I've heard ...' That was all it took. His aunt and uncle, tears seeping down the rills and furrows on their faces, bent to touch his feet, at which he sprang up in horror. They asked him to forgive them. It was only their poverty and indebtedness that had made them behave so badly. They spoke long into the night as mosquitoes and other insects whined about their ears. As he listened, Daniel grew at first furious, then sorry. He pitied their miserable lives, and the covetousness and insecurity that hadn't given them a moment's peace. When they began to get repetitive and dramatic he stopped them, and pronounced judgement. He had first thought he would punish them but had now decided otherwise. He would pay them three thousand rupees, exactly what his mother and he had received from them for the house and land, and they would leave Chevathar for ever. The old man and woman began to cry as soon as he said this, and Daniel was persuaded to revise the terms a little: the compensation would be the same, but they would be allowed to keep a couple of acres of rice and coconut, and build themselves a small house in the village to the north of Chevathar. 'I'm showing you more mercy than you ever did to my mother, or to me. I hope to God I'm doing the right thing,' Daniel said, before dismissing them from his presence.

The next morning he was up early, the sounds of the dawn renewing in him the feeling that he was finally home. He walked to the mission compound and was saddened to see the blackened ruins of the church. In the cemetery, he spent a long time by the graves of his father and Father Ashworth. He thought about nothing, just letting his senses flow with the crackling of the breeze in the coconut palms and the deep thudding of the sea on the deserted beach. Memories swirled in, the episodes of family history most deeply etched in his mind rose up, and he allowed them to take him over ... When he finally rose to go, he was exhausted from experiencing afresh the tragedies and triumphs of the Dorais. But it had been a necessary act of remembering, for it had helped him make up his mind. He now knew without a doubt what he had to do next.

52

Daniel Dorai was thirty-five years old, and one of the richest men in Nagercoil, when he decided to re-establish himself on his ancestral soil. His family, with the exception of Charity who was neither for nor against the idea, was alarmed by his new obsession. When Lily and Ramdoss, his brother-in-law, taxed him with it, all he would say was, 'Chevathar has always had a Dorai. With my father and my brother gone, it's time I returned. I've become a stranger in my own land and I would like to get to know it again.' They tried everything they could to change his mind, but he wouldn't budge and so they left him alone, hoping that pressure of work would eventually divert him from his course.

It was not to be. Although it would be years before Daniel finally returned to Chevathar, he stuck to his resolve. Meanwhile, there were more pressing demands on his time. He had to keep an eye on the business, which was expanding at a furious rate; there were the usual importunate relatives and friends whose demands had to be dealt with tactfully; the children, both his own and Rachel's, had to be looked after; and finally there was Miriam to be settled.

His pampered sister had painfully dragged her way through a Home Science degree, never once losing the opportunity to tell whoever would listen to her that her life was being ruined. If she grew to be an old maid, she would know exactly who to blame. During the family's difficult days she'd had the good sense to behave herself and once the year of mourning for Aaron was over, Daniel set about arranging her marriage. He had worried that Charity wouldn't involve herself but although his mother didn't take on the entire responsibility, as she would have done in the past, she began to show an interest. After sifting through scores of proposals, for there was no dearth of parents willing to give their sons in marriage to Dr Dorai's sister, Charity and Daniel settled on a young advocate in preference to the scions of landowning families. Arul's family was prosperous, but Daniel was impressed with the young man's determination to build a career. He married his sister off with a rich man's pomp. The celebrations lasted nearly a month and the bride's dowry included, in addition to the traditional gifts and money, a brand-new Ford Model T Raceabout.

But despite the myriad duties that occupied him in Nagercoil, Daniel would often drive to Chevathar. In a couple of years, the stately progress of his latest acquisition, a laburnum-yellow Oldsmobile, through the dusty streets of the village was no longer remarked upon. On these trips he was always accompanied by Ramdoss, and by a distant cousin of Charity's called Santosham who had helped him build the factory where his patent medicines were manufactured. The three men would patiently seek out the dozens of smallholders who owned property in and around Chevathar and negotiate to buy their land. Usually, the farmers were only too willing to sell, for Dr Dorai offered almost double the market rate. Often the lands acquired had once belonged to Solomon. The acres slowly added up. By the end of 1918, Daniel owned four hundred and twenty-seven acres in Chevathar and Meenakshikoil.

On New Year's Day 1919, he wrote to the head of every family in the Dorai clan. One hundred and twenty-three letters were dispatched, outlining a simple proposition. He wanted to start a family settlement in Chevathar. He was willing to give each invitee to the scheme an acre of land (those who wanted more could have it, subject to availability) at a fifth of the market rate. The only condition was that they settle in Chevathar for, at the very minimum, their own lifetimes. And if their heirs wanted to resell, they could only do so to the family. After repeated reminders, he received eighty-eight positive replies. Some of the others thought it was a hoax, some had died and the rest were not interested. There were questions, clarifications, a veritable mountain of detail, but infused with the zeal of a new convert to a cause, Dr Dorai patiently resolved every problem that was thrown up.

He began to make the necessary arrangements. He hired assistants to run the Nagercoil clinic and factory, and set a date for the move two years in the future, 27 September, Aaron's birthday. On his next trip to Chevathar he initiated work on his own house. He had decided it would be where the Big House stood. Modest by nature, Daniel Dorai decided that he would go against the grain and build the most magnificent building in the whole taluqa, perhaps even the district. 'The glory of the Dorais has been eclipsed for far too long. I want to have a house that will last a hundred years and be a fitting testament to my father and brother,' he declared to Santosham and Ramdoss. The only room that he would retain of the old structure would be the room his father had used.

53

The scraggly acacia tree at the edge of the marsh cast a scanty shade. Santosham had sat under it for over six months now, overseeing the efforts of a couple of hundred men who laboured from dawn to dusk on Daniel Dorai's 'thousand years' house', as it was known locally.

He was a small cheerful man with a big shapeless nose and had been one of the first beneficiaries of Daniel's new-found obsession with family. A failed engineering graduate with a flexible attitude to life, he had acquired a basic understanding of the building trade from a Nagercoil contractor. What Santosham did not know about floating pediments and poured concrete, he more than made up for with his capacity for hard work and ability to come up with unorthodox solutions to seemingly intractable problems. Daniel had been satisfied enough with the jobs Santosham had done for him, and had no misgivings about appointing him to build the house.

As soon as he had selected his site and his contractor, Daniel had visited Madras to pick his architect. He had interviewed twenty-three before settling on Colin Snow, a third-generation disciple of Mad Mant, the eccentric inventor in the mid-nineteenth century of the Indo-Saracenic style that fused Indian baroque with English common sense to produce a wondrous new hybrid. The only thing about Indo-Saracenic grandeur was that it required an enormous amount of money, and even Daniel's considerable fortune would have been stretched. His architect and he decided to settle for something a little less opulent. They criss-crossed the city for a week before finally deciding on one of the grand garden houses on the banks of the Adyar river as a model for the Dorai home.

Putting down a deposit, Daniel had invited Snow to visit Chevathar as soon as he could. The architect had arrived in the village a few days later, to survey the site that had been chosen for the monumental edifice: seventeen acres of land by the river, including the spot on which the Big House had stood. The only problem was that over the years the Chevathar had altered its course and a fair amount of the land on which Snow was expected to build was marshy, home to a seething mass of mosquitoes. He had suggested finding another site but Daniel would have none of it. Nor would he consider a smaller building. His instructions to his architect were clear: enshrine within the edifice the unquenchable spirit of the Dorais and proclaim to the whole world the magnificence of the family.

Snow prided himself on his ability to incorporate elements of the surrounding environment into his design. But what could you do with a marsh?

The architect and the contractor debated the practicality of laying a pile foundation, still a relatively new concept in the building industry, but decided against it in the end. It would have meant bringing everything, with the exception of chunam and brick, by rail and cart from the district capital or even further afield. In the end, Santosham came up with a solution that displayed to best effect his native shrewdness: they would dig a series of shallow wells across the marsh into which channels would drain the water. Once emptied of the water, the wells would be filled with broken tiles, sand, pebbles and crushed stone, packed in tight, so they would be baked as hard as granite by the fierce Chevathar sun. On these, the foundation would be laid. Snow's estimation of his colleague rose a hundredfold, for Santosham had just proposed doing what Scottish engineers had done a century earlier to drain the marsh on which the magnificent St Andrew's Kirk now stood in Madras. When Snow mentioned this to him, Santosham looked at him blankly – he had never seen the great church, and he knew even less about how it had been built.

The work was slow and tedious, and seven months after he had begun, Santosham had dug only eighty shallow wells, just over half of what was needed. Daniel was growing impatient so he doubled his labour force to four hundred men, but it was hot, difficult, dirty work. The labourers, wearing only skimpy loincloths, worked half submerged in the water. As they dug deeper, the water would cover them completely; still they would dig, holding their breath for a short time, before surfacing, gasping and spluttering. As the months passed, the marsh remained resolutely soggy. Santosham despaired often. And then, all at once, in the ninth month, dry land surfaced, and then spread rapidly.

The chattering of sparrows, mynahs and crows was drowned by a new sound – the tick-tick-tick of hundreds of crude hammers as the women on the workforce began the arduous task of breaking down boulders into piles of tiny chips that would be used in the construction. Smoke poured from brick kilns and every day bullock carts creaked in, bearing all manner of building materials.

Once the foundation was laid, the walls of the mansion rose rapidly. And then, during one of Daniel's lightning visits to Chevathar, he fell out with his architect. He had recently visited the nearby princely state of Mysore and had been very taken with the intricate bargeboards and canopies that rose like pointed hoods over the windows and doors of the palatial bungalows he had seen. He wanted Snow to incorporate these distinctive monkey tops into his design, but the Englishman, who loved the lines of his building, refused.

'Dr Dorai, you must understand that while this is your house, and you are paying for it, I have to be in complete charge of the model you approved, or it simply won't work. If you want a great house, you must let me do things my way.'

Daniel looked at the architect reflectively, then said, 'I thank you for the trouble you have taken, but this is my house and I will have things done my way. That is the only way it will work.' Snow left the same day, cursing his client, his temper somewhat soothed by the generous severance gift he had received.

To Santosham's astonishment, he now found himself in charge of the whole project. Within days, his limitations showed. An enormous bedroom would rise, only for the contractor to discover that he had omitted to put in any windows. On one of Daniel's periodic inspection trips, he walked around the building until he came to a halt under the imposing porte-cochère. He studied the frontage of the building for a long moment, the glistening columns of Pallavaram gneiss, the deep bay windows, and then turned and yelled at Santosham who had been following him nervously, 'You donkey, you've spent a year and a half building this house and look what you've done!'

'What, anna?'

'You've forgotten to put in a front door.'

'But we have always entered through the side door, anna!'

'What would you like to do, idiot, turn the house around ninety degrees?'

'No, anna, I'll put in the door.'

'Be sure you do, and I'm going to get you some help.'

Within a fortnight, another English architect arrived, this time from Mysore. Samuel Brown had built several bungalows with the distinctive monkey tops Daniel craved. The work speeded up.

Brown was charged with creating a suitable garden for the mansion. In a land where dust and rock predominated, he was determined that the building would float on a sea of green and riotous colour. He laid out a vast lawn; arbours of bougainvillea sprayed upward like pink and white surf, and climbing roses, yellow as egg yolk, punctuated the green. He planted a windbreak of casuarina, and created interesting features around the few ancient banyan, pipal and neem trees that had survived years of neglect. Some of the looming giants acquired anklets of hibiscus and croton, others shaded wrought-iron benches and tables. The red earth of Chevathar was mounded into gentle hillocks here and there, and decorated with seashells and flowering shrubs, sculptures and fountains.

Even before work on the house had begun, an army of gardeners got to work restoring the ancient mango groves. Grafting, pruning, layering, fertilizing and replanting, the new mansion soon had an elegant collar of Chevathar Neelams, two acres deep and several acres wide, following the contours of its semicircular back veranda and filling the grounds between the house and the river. In the centre of the front lawn, a great mango tree was carefully transplanted. The head gardener was given special charge of the tree, and warned, on pain of instant dismissal and worse, to keep the showpiece tree ever healthy, ever beautiful. He took his job seriously. Every second day, he had the hundreds of leaves on the tree washed by hand. The fruit, in season, would be buffed and polished, and two little boys from the village kept them from the attentions of squirrels and crows.

54

On the outskirts of Meenakshikoil, just before the shops began, was a large maidan of gritty red earth, scattered with tussocks of dried grass. One half of it was taken over by a school for its sports ground. Most days it would come alive with the ragged cries of schoolboys attempting to cope with the uneven bounce of their playing field as they pushed a hockey ball around.

One evening, Ramdoss, Santosham and Daniel got into the Oldsmobile and drove to town. As they passed the hockey ground, Daniel noticed a blazing fire near the far goalposts. A large group of schoolboys stood around it in their underwear. Astonished by the sight, Daniel ordered the car to be stopped and sent Santosham off to investigate.

The contractor returned with a boy. The lad, though somewhat awed at finding himself in the presence of Daniel, confidently responded to his questions. They'd refused to attend school, he said, and had made a bonfire of their clothes, in response to an appeal by Gandhi-thatha.

'What's this all about?' Daniel asked Ramdoss.

'His latest initiative, anna. It's called the Non-Co-operation Movement,' Ramdoss replied. After Aaron's death, Daniel's antipathy towards politics had deepened so profoundly that he refused even to read the newspapers. He relied on Ramdoss to keep him informed. And though Gandhi's presence had by now grown so pervasive that even Daniel had heard of him, he had little knowledge of the Non-Co-operation Movement. Ramdoss quickly filled him in. Gandhi had promised to free the country of British rule within a year, and had called on his countrymen to stop co-operating with the British. Students were to leave schools and colleges, and lawyers were to boycott law courts. Foreign clothes were to be burned and toddy stops picketed.

'And he expects this to happen?' Daniel asked dubiously.

'It's already happening, anna, this boy is an example right before your eyes.'

'Do you know why you are doing this?' Daniel asked the boy sternly.

'We have to boycott school and foreign garments, aiyah,' the boy answered stubbornly.

'You and your friends will return to school immediately,' Daniel ordered. 'Without education you will all become loafers.'

Without waiting to see if his instructions were carried out, he got back in the car with Ramdoss and Santosham and ordered the driver to proceed. 'Must report this to the tahsildar,' he said irritably. 'This is an outrage and I hope Narasimhan can do something.'

*

P. K. Narasimhan, the tahsildar, was someone Daniel had a lot of time for. Born into a family of Tanjore scholars, Narasimhan had an encyclopaedic knowledge of the classics as well as of current events. He could always be relied upon to provide a stimulating discussion. He had been helpful and efficient when Daniel had begun establishing the colony, and he had come to enjoy his visits to the tahsildar's office. This time, however, when Daniel demanded he do something about the truants, he said he was helpless. He spoke in English, which he was apt to break into from time to time, especially when he needed to think and formulate his thoughts carefully. Daniel had initially found this disconcerting, but in time he had grown used to it.

'Government's orders are not to do anything,' Narasimhan said. 'We don't want to be repressive, especially after Dyer's outrage in Jallianwala Bagh and the Punjab troubles.'

'But Punjab is at the other end of the universe,' Daniel countered. 'Why can't we keep our boys in school?'

'Anna, Meenakshikoil isn't the only place that's affected. The whole country is in a ferment,' Ramdoss said. 'It's not just a couple of issues they are protesting against. None of the Crown's recent measures, the Rowlatt Act, the Hunter Committee recommendations, nothing seems to have gone down well ...'

'I'm afraid that's true,' the tahsildar said. 'Our latest reports say that over ninety thousand students have left their schools and colleges, there are bonfires of foreign cloth on every street. There is no way in which we can stop this thing. All we can hope for is that it will die down of its own accord.'

'But, according to Ramdoss, Gandhi wants your masters out in a year,' Daniel said.

'So he says,' the tahsildar said with a sigh, 'but not even Mr Gandhi always gets what he wants.' He continued, 'I think you'll find Mr Gandhi's methods very interesting.'

'Oh,' Daniel said.

'If you have some time, I'd be very pleased to discuss them over coffee.'

Daniel nodded. Santosham went off to do the paperwork that had brought them to the tahsildar's office, while Ramdoss and Daniel settled into the hard wooden chairs. Narasimhan rang for coffee, then asked: 'Do you know the story of my namesake in the *Bhagavatam*?'

Daniel knew the tale vaguely, although he didn't know what it had to do with Gandhi. But he had time on his hands and the tahsildar always told a good story. 'He's one of Lord Vishnu's avatars, isn't he?'

'Very good, sir,' the tahsildar said. 'He is indeed, and this is how he came to be.'

The ill-starred Hiranyakashipu, the tahsildar began, was a man of more than ordinary ambition. He wanted to be unquestioned Lord of the three worlds, invincible in battle, but most of all he craved immortality. In order to realize his goals, he performed years of extraordinary penance to Lord Brahma. Anthills and weeds grew and covered him from view as he sat lost in meditation on the Mandara mountain. He was so devoted and single-minded in his penance that Brahma had little option but to grant him anything he wanted. Hiranyakashipu wanted only one boon: the gift of immortality. The creator of the three worlds said it was not within his powers to grant him his request because he himself was not immortal, but he could certainly grant him immunity from virtually anything that could ordinarily cause him harm.

Hiranyakashipu tried to think of every contingency, the tahsildar said. He paused as the peon handed around the coffee. Once everyone was served he continued his story.

Hiranyakashipu asked that none of the creations of Lord Brahma be the death of him, neither weapon, nor man, nor animal, nor any living or non-living thing. Brahma agreed. Hiranyakashipu went into greater detail, trying to think of every possible danger that might threaten him. He asked to be protected from Gods, demons and every form of disease. The request was granted. He said that he should not die inside his house nor outside, neither during the day nor during the night, neither on the earth nor in the sky. Brahma acceded to all this as well. Finally, his steadfast devotee asked to be ruler of the universe, with a fortune that would never diminish. To this, too, Brahma consented and then he disappeared from the Mandara mountain.

The ages passed and everything that Brahma had bestowed upon Hiranyakashipu ensured that he became the unquestioned ruler of the three worlds. Unfortunately for his subjects, his ambition was matched only by his tyranny. Gods, demons and ordinary mortals prayed to Lord Vishnu to rid them of the monster.

Hiranyakashipu had one thorn in his side, the tahsildar said: his son Prahlada who, to his father's consternation, was an unflinching devotee of Lord Vishnu, the only God the tyrant feared. Hiranyakashipu had tried every form of persuasion to deflect his son from his steadfast devotion, all to no avail. He had then tried to kill him. Wild elephants were made to trample him underfoot, cobras, kraits and vipers were set upon him, he was thrown off cliffs and buried alive, he was poisoned and set alight. He survived every frenzied attempt to do him in, further incensing his father. Finally, Hiranyakashipu decided to kill him with his own hands.

One day he was haranguing his son as usual. Prahlada refused to bend. To a question from his father, he said Lord Vishnu was everywhere. The furious Hiranyakashipu pointed to a pillar in his council hall and asked whether it contained the Lord. His son calmly said that it did. 'Very well then,' the tyrant said, 'I'm going to kill you now. Let your Lord come out of the pillar and save you.'

So saying, he advanced upon his son with a drawn sword. The pillar cracked with a thunderous sound, and an astonishing being blocked the path of the enraged tyrant. It had the head and powerfully muscled torso of a lion, but from the waist down its form was human.

Hiranyakashipu looked into the terrible eyes of the apparition and realized his hour was upon him. But he was not a coward. Raising his sword he attacked the man-lion. His puny challenge was brushed aside, and he was picked up and carried to the threshold of the palace. He was neither outside his house nor inside it. It was dusk, neither day nor night. He was in the clutches of a creature that was neither beast nor man. He was caught up in its grip and was therefore neither on the earth nor in the sky. The man-lion was certainly not a creature of Brahma and the only weapons it was about to use were its own claws and teeth. As his entrails were ripped out of him, Hiranyakashipu understood that no one could be mightier than the Lord.

'That was exceedingly well told, Narasimhan,' Daniel said. 'But what does it have to do with Gandhi?'

'The ingenuity, sir, the ingenuity,' the tahsildar said. 'Faced with an astonishingly complex problem, the Lord came up with a solution that was intricate, unusual and supremely effective. And that's what Mr Gandhi is doing, and it's driving Government crazy.'

'You sound as though you admire the man, Narasimhan.'

'No, his methods. I don't think Government has ever faced a bigger threat than this. Mr Gandhi seems to have a deep, almost mystical, grasp of what it takes to weld our fractious countrymen into an effective fighting unit.'

'Do you think he might overthrow British rule?' Daniel asked quietly.

'I cannot answer that question, sir,' the tahsildar said. They sipped their coffee in silence. After a while, Narasimhan said, 'But what I must repeat is that never have I seen a more serious threat to the Government than the one Mr Gandhi has mounted. He meets violence with non-violence, deception with truth, our efforts to suppress him with non-co-operation. What do we do with such a man except wait and hope he makes a mistake?'

'I wish you luck with him, Narasimhan,' Daniel said, getting up to leave. 'But get those students back to school. If Gandhi does succeed in kicking the British out he'll need educated men and women to run the country.'

'Oh, I don't think the British will leave in a hurry, sir. They'll find an answer to Mr Gandhi yet.'

'Perhaps you're right, Narasimhan, but I have no time to worry about that, I have a colony to build. And if there's one thing I'm sure of, it is that it will have no politics to disrupt its working.'

After a year or so of the Non-Co-operation Movement, Government began to get tough with the protesters, especially as the future king of England had decided to tour India. His visit was greeted with demonstrations and black flags as the Indian masses voiced their displeasure. None of this had the slightest effect on Chevathar, where Daniel's total ban on any form of political engagement ensured that work on his mansion proceeded smoothly. Working from dawn to dusk in three shifts, Brown and Santosham finally completed their mammoth project, only two months behind schedule. The house was a curious hybrid, but it worked. Seen from above, it resembled nothing so much as a giant palmyra-leaf fan, its fifty-eight rooms radiating backwards in a wavy cone from the *porte-cochère*. The walls were coated with a mixture of eggshell lime, river sand, milk and fermented kadukka-and-jaggery water – the famous Madras-mirror finish – so that they gleamed like polished marble. Surrounding the house were groves of blue mango trees.

The house was inaugurated with due pomp and ceremony. After a brief thanksgiving service in the new church that had risen on the ruins of the old, the congregation moved to the mansion. The new priest intoned a blessing and Daniel made a short speech. 'I regret that we couldn't move here on my brother's birth anniversary because it was he who finally made up my mind about returning to Chevathar. But I know Aaron will forgive us for being slightly late, for this magnificent mansion has been worth the wait.' He paused and sought out Brown and Santosham and congratulated them publicly on their masterpiece. Then he said, 'The naming of anything we hold important has to be done with care. This house represents the fruit of years of toil by my family. I've spent months now trying to find a name that would aptly represent our hopes and aspirations, and more importantly capture the essence of this place. Finally, after much time spent in thought and prayer, I've come up with the name I think most appropriate, a name that honours the memory of our revered ancestors and this place from which we have sprung. Brothers and sisters, aunts and uncles, members of my esteemed family, it is with great satisfaction that I formally announce that this house will be called, from this time onwards, the House of Blue Mangoes, Neelam Illum.'

55

The new settlement sprawled for miles by the Chevathar and provided a striking contrast to the existing village, more than half of which it had swallowed. Instead of twisty straggling paths it possessed ruler-straight avenues of beaten red earth, lined with ashoka, jacaranda, gulmohar and rain trees. The roads were neatly signposted: Solomon Avenue, Aaron Crossroads, Ashworth Lane. Some landmarks were carefully preserved. Daniel had a grove of trees planted around the well Aaron had jumped, both to beautify it and to ensure that nobody ever attempted it again. The Murugan and Amman temples remained, but the acacia forest was cleared to make way for elegant farmhouses and kitchen gardens. However, the great forest giants were not cut down, Charity saw to that. Her love of trees undimmed, she had hundreds more planted on the newly cleared land. Village urchins were paid handsomely to water the fragile saplings and chase away the cows and goats which would have made a meal of them. As Daniel had hoped, Chevathar was beginning to heal his mother.

Soon after his return, Daniel had thought long and hard about whether to take over as thalaivar of the village: a Dorai had held the position for as long as anyone could remember. In the end he decided the family colony had a greater claim on his time. He let the village elder he had appointed when he had sent Abraham away continue in the job. Ramdoss would supervise him. To run the settlement, Daniel constituted a committee of elders drawn from the twenty-three founding families. A fortnight after they arrived, the committee met to frame the rules the colony would live by. They drew up twelve commandments, of which the most contentious was the one which banned all political activity within the colony. A couple of cousins objected, but Daniel used his chairman's veto. 'I've seen politics up close and find it abhorrent,' he said. 'I've already lost a brother to it, and I will not lose any more of my family if I can help it.' But even Daniel had to concede defeat on the proposal he mooted to remove all traces of caste from the family. 'Christianity does not recognize caste, and we have all seen the dangers of caste conflict,' he said. 'I would like to suggest that all of us drop caste names and only retain the birth, marriage and death rituals of our caste.' He didn't find a single supporter for the idea and even Ramdoss demurred. 'It's all very well to abolish caste in this community, anna,' he said, 'but we are also part of society at large. It gives us our identity. You cannot change the entire world.'

Unable to move his family on the issue, Daniel had to content himself with a minor consolation prize. From this day onwards his immediate family would drop its caste suffix, Andavar. 'If you want to be tied down by your caste affiliation, I respect your wish,' he declared to the council of elders, 'but I have a great desire to be free!' The final item on the agenda was the naming of the settlement. Daniel was inclined to let it remain an anonymous part of Chevathar but Ramdoss stepped in again: 'The world needs to find us, anna. We need a name.' Daniel was immediately persuaded. They named their colony Doraipuram.

A month after they moved to Chevathar, Lily gave birth to their third child, a boy. No strange stars appeared in the skies, no poisonous snakes spread their hoods over him, none of his organs – nose, ears, eyes, throat, penis, head – were abnormal, and he possessed no extraordinary powers or faculties, but the settlers were overjoyed. This was most propitious. Especially as the child was the son Daniel had always craved. Forty-one days after the baby was born, the family visited the church for the infant to be blessed. Daniel had a name ready for his son, one he'd thought of a while ago. He had toyed with the idea of bestowing it upon his daughters, but Lily had been opposed to the idea and he'd given in. This time, surprisingly enough, the resistance came from Charity, whose involvement in family matters, while greater than before, wasn't yet strong. 'Too unchristian,' she'd muttered when Daniel asked her what she thought of the name Thirumoolar, one of the greatest siddha saints. But this time he was determined to have his way, and the baby was baptized with the name. However, it was Charity who ultimately prevailed. Kannan, her nickname for the baby, soon became the only name he responded to. Within months, the only person who called him by his given name was his father.

The baby revitalized Charity, consuming all her time and energy. As soon as he was weaned, he seemed to take up permanent station on his grandmother's hip. He went with her everywhere – to the kitchen, where she began to supervise, as she had done many years before, the cooking of enormous meals, for long walks through the mango groves and gardens of Doraipuram. They became a familiar sight – the diminutive old lady dressed all in white, with the enormous baby on her hip (so large in fact that she had to lean all the way over to keep her balance). She crooned lullabies to put him to sleep and sang songs to make him eat. The song he seemed to like best was a little ditty about blue mangoes:

Saapudu kannu saapudu
Eat my beloved eat
Neela mangavai saapudu
Eat the blue mango
Onaku enna kavalai
You have no cares or worries
Azhakana mangavai saapudu
All you need do is eat the beautiful mango
Parisutha maana devadhuta
Angels from the heavens above
Un ulakathai kaaval
Watch over your world
Saapudu kannu saapudu
Eat my beloved eat
Neela mangavai saapudu
Eat the blue mango

At first Lily was put out by Charity's obsession with her baby boy. But over time she grew reconciled to it, and even welcomed it. Kannan was not only a powerful restorative for her mother-in-law; the fact that he had Charity looking after him virtually every waking moment gave her the time she required to meet the constantly expanding needs of Neelam Illum.

Having refound his family, Daniel would go to extraordinary lengths to satisfy its every whim. The fifty-eight rooms, most of which were converted into makeshift bedrooms within months of their moving in, were almost always full of relatives. In addition, there were children, ranging in age from five to fifteen, who had been entrusted to Daniel the moment he had volunteered to take care of some need or other. Lily and Charity, when she wasn't preoccupied with Kannan, supervised the cooking of meals and other domestic arrangements for nearly a hundred people every day.

56

'Do you really believe the Chevathar Neelam is the best mango in the world?' Daniel asked Ramdoss.

'I believe it's the best I've eaten.'

'I wonder what makes it so remarkable,' Daniel said thoughtfully. 'Could it be the soil?'

'Probably. But certainly there was some grafting done a long time ago.'

It was the summer of Daniel's second year in Doraipuram and Ramdoss and he were supervising the harvest of blue mangoes. It was four in the morning, the time at which the Chevathar Neelams were traditionally picked to ensure their sweetness was retained, and that they ripened evenly.

'I'd like to decide for myself,' Daniel said abruptly.

'Decide what?' Ramdoss asked.

'That the Chevathar Neelam is the best mango in the world.'

In his years with Daniel, Ramdoss had learned that when his brother-in-law was enthused by a new idea it was very hard to deflect him. 'What did you have in mind?' he asked.

Daniel didn't reply for a while, silently watching the men harvesting the mangoes flit like ghosts through the pre-dawn hush, gently picking the fruit with what looked like giant butterfly nets and depositing them in cane baskets filled with straw.

'I'd like to taste the finest mangoes available to satisfy myself that the Chevathar Neelam is the best!'

Ramdoss's heart sank. The time, the cost, the travel! 'But, anna, Doraipuram needs your guiding hand, we can't wander the world tasting mangoes.'

'India has the world's greatest mangoes, there's no need to leave its shores. I've always wanted to eat Alphonsos, Langdas, Chausas and Maldas. There's no point trying to make me change my mind, Ramdoss, it's made up and we're going.'

He was as good as his word. The great mango yatra began in Kerala, where Daniel, Ramdoss and the four gardeners who made up the party tasted the Ollour, a fruit with thick yellow skin and flesh and a faintly resinous after-taste. It was a fruit they were all familiar with, as it was found in the bazaars of Nagercoil and Meenakshikoil.

As summer progressed, dozens of varieties of mangoes began to ripen. The group from Doraipuram trailed through the fruit markets of the south, making the acquaintance of many well-known mangoes such as the regal Jehangiri, named for an emperor, the Banganapalli with its sweet, pale, whitish-yellow pulp, and the rare and delicious Himayuddin with a taste in the upper registers of the palate. In the fruit markets of Madura, they ate Rumanis round as cricket balls and so thin-skinned a baby could peel them, Mulgoas so enormous that they often tipped the scales at three kilograms and the highly prized Cherukurasam.

Then they had to hurry west, for the fruiting season of the Alphonso was at its peak. Deciding that it was not practical to journey to Ratnagiri, Bulsad and Belgaum, where the celebrated Alphonso orchards perfumed the air, even infusing the rice paddies, they headed instead for Bombay. Straight off the train, they made for Crawford Market. Long before they caught sight of the country's most famous mango, they could smell it, its scent rising above the odours of rotting cabbage and corn, sweat and kerosene. They turned a corner and suddenly there they were – row upon row of gilded Alphonsos arranged in tiers behind gesticulating, yelling mango traders and their equally vociferous customers. Daniel ate his first Alphonso, and as the taste – a touch of tartness, a spill of honey, a profusion of fresh, light notes on a deep bass foundation – sank into his palate he understood why it was so coveted. He would have liked to have lingered longer in the west, but there was still much ground to cover during the short season, and they were soon on a train heading east, their last memory of the great western mangoes being a glass of juice, thick and sweet as clarified sunlight, made from that other classic, the Pairi.

As they made their journeys, Daniel steeped himself in mango lore. He discovered that the mango grew nearly everywhere on the subcontinent and that there were over a thousand recognized varieties. Ramdoss successfully dissuaded his friend from even thinking about sampling them all, suggesting instead that for practical reasons they limit themselves to the most renowned. He learned that *Mangifera indica*, to give it its proper name, had evolved somewhere in the mysterious northeastern corner of the country over two thousand years before, and had been spread by travellers and other carriers throughout Southeast Asia, China and the Malay archipelago. Greedy Portuguese traders and adventurers were the first pale skins to encounter it in the early years of the sixteenth century. Immediately falling under its spell, they had introduced the fruit to Africa and South America. About the same time, it had travelled by another route to the West Indies, the Philippines and thence to Mexico. In the nineteenth century, it had appeared in the orchards of California, Florida and Hawaii.

Everywhere they travelled, there were fascinating stories about the fruit, a delicacy so prized among connoisseurs that it drove its admirers to all sorts of excess. The Mughal emperor Akbar's romance with the mango made even the Dorais' obsession with it pale in comparison. Never one to do things by halves, he had ordered an army of malis to raise an orchard of a hundred thousand trees in Darbhanga. Even more dedicated to the cause of the fruit was the Nawab Wajid Ali Shah of Lucknow who was fêted throughout the land for the excellence of his mango orchards where nearly thirteen hundred varieties were raised; the prince's mango marriages were famous, as were his mango parties where, to the sound of tabla and santoor, the nobility gathered in pavilions constructed in the orchards, and tasted mangoes plucked from trees by women specially selected for their long tapering fingers, the better to grasp the fruit.

They spent a week in the east acquainting themselves with the finer points of the Malda, also called the Bombay Green, which had a subtle taste that seemed almost anaemic until it expanded to fill the senses. They sampled the exceedingly sweet, thin-skinned Himsagar and the Bombai, not to be confused with the Bombay Green. And Daniel was thrilled to be invited to a mango-tasting festival by an ageing Murshidabad nawab. Graciously inviting his guests to take their places at the head table, the Nawab showed Daniel how he ate the fruit. He first munched on a spicy, coarsely ground kabab so that his palate was completely fresh and then delicately picked at a little of the heart flesh of the Gulabkhas, a mango that tasted of roses. 'Truly, an unusual way to eat the fruit,' Daniel remarked to Ramdoss. 'Why didn't we think of something like that?'

They had one other major mango-growing region to visit before the long journey home. Daniel had heard a lot about the Malihabadi Dussehri, and when he tasted it, he was quick to accept its claims to greatness. But he discovered that its claim to being the finest mango in the country was by no means secure, for there were those who would bestow that honour on the Langda, which according to legend was first grown by a lame fakir from the holy city of Benares. When Daniel encountered it, he was overwhelmed by its qualities – the pale green skin, the orange-yellow flesh and above all the taste: a distinctive sweetness balanced by a slight tartness. They decided not to wait for the late-fruiting Chausa to arrive in the markets: Ramdoss managed to persuade Daniel to abandon his plans to visit Lahore and Rangoon and they took the train home. On the way back, Daniel discussed the dozens of varieties they had tasted. He referred to the notes he'd made, he recalled their distinctive qualities, and he tried as fairly as he could to determine the greatest mango he had encountered in the course of his yatra.

A week after he'd returned to Doraipuram, Daniel still couldn't pick the winner. That evening, when he and Ramdoss took their daily walk, he said, 'You know, Ramu, we've spent months trying to find out whether the Chevathar Neelam is finer than any other mango.'

'Yes,' Ramdoss said cautiously. But Daniel didn't pick up the conversation for he was lost in a reverie. He saw himself reach up to pick a Chevathar Neelam from his father's orchard, the fruit invested with the golden light of the sun. He tore at the warm fragrant skin with his teeth, then bit down into the flesh, the nectar running in yellow rivulets down his face, neck, even his arms, its unmatched flavour overwhelming him. 'Ramu,' Daniel said slowly, 'we went a long way to know what I've always known. There's no question that the Chevathar Neelam is the greatest mango in the world.' Then, to Ramdoss's disquiet, he added, 'Now that we know that, we need to proclaim its glories far and wide.'

As always when in the grip of an obsession, Dr Dorai worked single-mindedly in pursuit of his objective. He lavished money and attention on the mango topes, enriching the soil, guarding against common diseases and infestations. Startled stem-borers and mango hoppers, shoot-borers and blossom midges died by the thousand as an army of gardeners attacked them, with their bare hands if necessary.

By the time the next fruiting season came round, Daniel was ready to inaugurate Doraipuram's first Blue Mango Festival. The finest mangoes had already been carefully harvested and left to ripen in enormous storerooms at the rear of Neelam Illum. On the appointed day they were taken from the densely scented rooms and carried to the pandal that had been erected on the banks of the Chevathar. For the celebrations, Daniel had copied many details from the mango-tasting ceremony he had attended in Murshidabad, but there were some touches that were unique.

He had commissioned the legendary weavers of the region to weave a hundred mats with a special mango pattern, and these covered the red earth of the river bank. The Collector, who was the chief guest (the Murshidabad nawab had been unable to make the journey), sat at the head table along with Daniel, Ramdoss, Narasimhan, other local dignitaries and the heads of the founding families. A band played soft music and lamps lit the mango groves. As the heart flesh of the Neelam was ceremoniously served on small plates, each guest munched first on a hot vadai (a variant that Daniel was rather proud of) before tasting the fruit. Once the formal tasting of the Neelam was over, other varieties were presented, seventy-seven in all. The Collector gave up after tasting twenty-two types of mango, Narasimhan managed twelve more, and only Daniel and Ramdoss tasted them all.

The formal tasting was only a part of the festivities. The mango groves echoed with laughter and excitement as the settlers and hundreds of visitors participated in mango-eating competitions and other feats of skill, endurance and frolic.

When the party finally concluded at two in the morning, queasy stomachs notwithstanding, it was declared a great success. 'We must do this every year,' Dr Dorai said to Ramdoss and Lily as he bid goodbye to the last guests. They received the news in silence, which Daniel chose to interpret positively.

57

Doraipuram continued to grow. New families poured in and by the end of the third year of its founding, the settlement was home to over a hundred and fifty people, some of whose links to the clan could best be described as tenuous. The brother-in-law of the husband of a third cousin, for example. There were retired airmen, geologists, doctors, engineers, accountants, clerks. Once in Doraipuram, they threw themselves into farming with a fervour that was commendable, except that their enthusiasm masked a woeful lack of experience. Rats ate their seed, crops withered, fruit rotted, and plants died due to excessive watering. Undeterred by this, the settlers hatched even more ambitious schemes. Cost was no consideration, for Daniel funded most of the projects.

An uncle, who had retired from practice as a dentist, decided to grow tulips, after having read about the craze for the flower in the seventeenth century when a single bulb could fetch more than a painting by Rembrandt. Half the expensive bulbs he imported from

Holland were eaten by bandicoots, and most of the others did not sprout. Barely half a dozen shoots struggled out of the red earth, to wilt under the hot summer sun. Unfazed, the former dentist went the next evening to Neelam Illum, where Daniel parleyed daily with the elders of the settlement. He had a couple of new proposals to put forward: raising ostriches for meat and crocodiles for leather. Sitting in his cane easy chair, Daniel's eyes gleamed with excitement. He liked both ideas and asked how much they would cost. The dentist was vague, but Ramdoss, who was present, was not. 'Too much. It'll cost too much,' he said firmly.

Daniel said, 'But they seem very promising. And very profitable.'

'Like the tulips?'

Daniel looked annoyed. Nobody else would have dared contradict him in public, but Ramdoss had grown to be his most trusted friend and confidant.

'The settlement is haemorrhaging money, and your funds are not inexhaustible,' Ramdoss said, drawing Daniel aside.

'My family is important, Ramu, I don't care how much money they cost me. Besides, what are you complaining about? We've had three good monsoons in a row, sales of our products are booming, God is looking after us.'

'God isn't going to make tulips thrive in Doraipuram,' Ramdoss said calmly. 'He has more important things to worry about than the crazy schemes of the Dorais.'

Grumbling and fretting, Daniel allowed himself to be dissuaded. He put an end to the wilder schemes, and began to spend more time in his laboratory doing what he was good at – combining various herbs and metals and potions to come up with a new line of patent remedies. He had neglected his business for almost five years and although his whitening cream continued to sell well, Ramdoss's concern had sprung in part from the fact that sales had flattened out. Now, within a year, Daniel launched five new products – a pimple cream, a tonic that boosted the body's vitality, a depilatory salve, a headache remedy, and a cure for indigestion. Posters advertising the new products as well as the rest of the range were printed in Meenakshikoil, and displayed at railway stations and on the sides of bullock carts. Business began picking up again.

The colony didn't stop consuming Dr Dorai's fortune but now there was a reversal in the cash flow as Ramdoss's prudence and Daniel's skills as a pharmacist began taking effect.

With his growing wealth and fame, Daniel became a magnet for

the importunate, the great and the good. Doraipura
tory stopover for visiting bureaucrats, elected offi
and Indian), holy men, aspiring politicians, v
reminded of their host's aversion to politics, and mino
was careful to keep the politicians and officials at a distanc
pride in his colony ensured that everyone who crossed the bridge ove
the Chevathar received a warm welcome. As the world came to him, Daniel rose to the pinnacle of his eminence.

There was another good monsoon that year. And the next. More families moved into Doraipuram.

58

Families thrive on gossip. It keeps the extended family connected and interested in the lives of its separate constituents. But it also has the potential to do great damage. One of the unexpected consequences of Daniel collecting his family together was the proliferation and concentration of gossip. In the past, whisperings about individuals were limited to the exchange of letters, rumours at family gatherings, weddings, births, funerals and visits. Sporadic and fleeting, it was handled easily enough. But now gossip grew to be a major problem. Almost half the families who had moved to the colony were over the age of fifty and had begun to look forward to retirement and the enjoyment of their grandchildren. Daniel's offer had given the men a new lease of life, but the older women were left high and dry. In their home towns they would have presided over joint families that would have kept them busy, but here, more often than not, they lived alone with their husbands. Domestic help was plentiful and cheap, and they found themselves with time to spare. Gossip rushed in to fill the vacuum. Squabbles broke out between families, relatives stopped talking to each other, and Daniel's glorious idea acquired a malicious core.

The queen of gossips was an enormously fat woman called Victoria. This particular aunt rapidly grew to be the most feared resident of Doraipuram, no mean achievement considering that when they arrived in the colony, she and her husband were the butt of ridicule. Her husband, Karunakaran, was only obscurely related to the family. He had somehow found out about the project and had been swift take advantage of his connection to the clan. Throwing up his job, e had arrived in Doraipuram with his wife and had almost immediately set about trying to make his presence felt. Desperate to impress, he had borrowed money from Daniel and bought a motorcycle. The only problem was that in his greed and haste, he hadn't spent time learning how to drive the machine. To the vast amusement of the settlement, he had hired a mechanic from Meenakshikoil to drive for him part-time. Whenever the couple went to town, Karunakaran would ride pillion on the motorcycle, while his wife followed in a bullock cart.

But the chortling soon turned to dismay, as Victoria showed just how dangerous she could be. Every morning, after eating a huge breakfast, she would drag her bulk from house to house, scanty white hair in as much disarray as the shabby sari she wore, imbibing as much poisonous gossip as she could from every household, which she would then spill liberally wherever she went. Over time she gathered a clique of women around her, and they wrought havoc among the residents of Doraipuram. The men, absorbed in their eccentric pursuits, were oblivious of the danger, but the women felt it keenly.

One evening, as dinner was being prepared in the great kitchen of Neelam Illum, Lily astonished Charity by bursting into tears. Charity took her to her own room, and asked her what the matter was. It transpired that Victoria had told her neighbour, who had passed it on to a cousin who had in turn mentioned it to Miriam who urgently whispered to Lily after church, that Shanthi had been seen kissing the Mangalam boy in the mango tope nearest the estuary.

'I thrashed Shanthi, mami, but she swore on Jesu, Mother Mary, her father and me that she had done no wrong. She's a good girl, I know she's telling the truth. It's getting too much, this gossiping and viciousness. I can't take it.'

'Have you told your husband?' Charity asked.

'No, mami. He's so busy, I feel it's such a frivolous thing to bring to his attention.'

'Not frivolous, not frivolous, this person could damage the whole colony and then where would our great experiment be?' Charity said. She paused for some time, then said, 'Don't worry, I'll think of something. You tell Shanthi to behave herself and not to take notice of anything that's said about her.'

A few days later, Charity cornered Lily in the backyard and said, 'I've found the answer to our problem. Good works.' When Lily looked mystified, she said, 'These women have too much time on their hands. Let's put them to work.'

Over the next months, Charity was a whirlwind of activity. Although she was in her sixties, and visibly worn down by the sorrows in her past, she seemed to be everywhere at once, chivvying aunts and grannies, cousins and nieces into a variety of tasks. One group was set to work teaching the labourers' children how to read; another was put in charge of children under the age of four; and the padre was deluged with groups of women holding charity raffles and Bible sessions.

For months, Charity kept the women busy, until work in their own homes, which swelled as the colony grew and matured, sucked them in. The upkeep of their houses, hosting of visiting relatives, and community weddings, funerals, festivals and church functions took care of any time on their hands. Soon, most of the women couldn't be bothered with Victoria. She would still drag herself from home to home, but her visits to her previous confidantes and co-conspirators were brief as they chafed to get on with their household chores. A few months later, even the familiar sight of her creeping progress through the colony ceased. She had grown so fat that her legs could no longer bear her weight. For a year or so she sat all day by the window while her husband roamed the colony, insinuating himself into the lives of others and gleaning food and information to share with his wife at home.

No longer the force she once was, Victoria even came to be pitied a little by the settlers. As for the few who still feared her, they soon had no more cause for concern when some months later her overworked heart, tired of pumping blood to her monstrous body, gave out.

Doraipuram had never witnessed a better funeral. All those who had dreaded her gave Victoria the grandest send-off she could have expected. On the sixteenth-day feast, Charity cooked her famous fish biryani, to Daniel's extreme puzzlement. After her breakdown she'd cooked it less and less, reserving it only for the most special occasions.

59

One morning Daniel woke at dawn in a panic. Looking out of the window he saw a ghostly procession of figures, clad all in white, walking slowly through the thin mist that sometimes descended on the area. Convinced that something terrible was about to happen to his mother, who had dressed in white for nearly thirty years, he ran to her room shouting her name. When he couldn't find her there he began looking frantically through the house before he finally thought to look in the kitchen. Charity was boiling milk on a stove.

'Amma, are you all right?' he asked worriedly.

'Of course, I am all right. Can't you see for yourself? What's the matter?'

'Oh nothing, nothing,' he said distractedly. The feeling of unease still hadn't left him, so putting on his chappals and drawing a shawl around his shoulders, he set off in pursuit of the processionists. They were some distance ahead of him, but Daniel, walking fast, managed to catch up. He kept a hundred yards from them, and watched astonished as, softly chanting prayers and mantrams, they filed past the salt-works and meandered across the beach, towards the swelling ocean. Perhaps they were all going to kill themselves, he thought in a panic. He charged after them. 'Stop, stop, I command you to stop. State your business.' Unhurriedly, the processionists continued on their way. A few feet from the water's edge, Daniel overtook them. 'Didn't you hear me shouting at you to stop?' he asked. A couple of them seemed familiar, but the rest were strangers.

'Only one agent of the Government,' an old woman said. 'Have you come to arrest us?'

Daniel looked at her as if she was crazy. 'Arrest?' he spluttered.

'No, he's not the Government, that's Daniel Dorai, the big doctor aiyah,' one of the familiar figures murmured.

'In that case, let's proceed with our mission,' the leader of the group said. As one, they moved to the water's edge, knelt and scraped up some of the salt-encrusted sand. Offering up a short prayer, they started back.

'Have you gone mad?' Daniel shouted, as he walked back up the beach with the procession. The leader, a youngish man clad only in a loincloth, and grasping a thick black staff, looked at him with luminous eyes. 'No, anna, we're not mad. All we're doing is following our sacred duty as laid down by the Mahatma. He is breaking the oppressive salt law of the British thousands of miles to the west, just as our elder brother Rajaji is doing at Vedaranyam. Would you like to make some salt as well?'

'No, I wouldn't,' Daniel said indignantly. 'What protest are you talking about?'

'The Mahatma's latest, anna,' the leader said gently, and he resumed his steady progress. Daniel watched them go, mystified. As always, he'd missed this latest development, especially as Ramdoss was away. He must go and visit Narasimhan, find out what was going on.

The next afternoon he visited his friend the tahsildar in Meenakshikoil.

'Oh yes, I've had to arrest them all for breaking the law. Government orders. But I must say that was a very clever move, very clever indeed. It was probably a bad idea for the Government to tax salt, it affects too many people, but what Mr Gandhi conveniently forgot to mention when he launched his agitation was that most other duties have been abolished. But he knows exactly what he's doing. It's all there in the paper. See for yourself,' Narasimhan said, handing Daniel copies of the *Mail* and the *Hindu*. He rapidly skimmed the reports which talked of the Mahatma's great twenty-five-day march from Ahmedabad to the little seashore village of Dandi. On 6 April 1930, the Mahatma and his followers had walked to the seashore to make salt. Wrote the *Hindu*'s special correspondent:

> The place selected was a marshy stretch about two yards square where there were patches of small deposits of shining sodium chloride, impure but all the same capable of yielding common salt. The sun had just risen over the eastern horizon and was casting its mild rays all around. A party of five hundred people had gathered to witness the historic ceremony. There was a deep silence and save for the click of cameras no sound was heard. Mahatmaji halted opposite the marshy tract. There were by his side, Mrs Sarojini Naidu, Miss Tyabjee, Shrimathi Mithuben Petit and Dr Sumant Mehta. Thirty minutes after six, Mahatmaji took a handful of salt deposit. His followers did likewise almost simultaneously. Into the enclosure none had been admitted other than Mahatmaji's volunteers nor did any dare enter. The great act had been done even before the crowd, which had gathered around and stood in a

reverential mood, had time to know that the salt law had been disobeyed.

When Daniel looked up from the paper, Narasimhan said with a smile, 'Impressive, isn't it? I don't know if my masters can stop this man.' And then, realizing how he must sound, the official quickly added, 'But if this continues, the Government will be forced to take extreme measures. Mr Gandhi should not be so irresponsible.'

'Why do I get this feeling, Narasimhan, every time we discuss him, that he's someone you admire, although he's on the opposite side?'

'Because he's a man of principle and honesty, and we have few such these days. But I'll probably have a chance to observe his methods very soon. I've just received my transfer orders, sir. I'm being posted to Melur.'

'You must come to the house, Narasimhan, before you go. Have a meal with me.'

Daniel's brief interest in politics was extinguished soon afterwards. Barely a month after he had witnessed the ghostly procession from his window, Charity was discovered unconscious in the outdoor privy. Her clothes, body and face were a moving, seething mass of black as tens of thousands of lightning-quick black ants swarmed all over her, attracted by the unusual sweetness of her urine. Daniel Dorai tried everything he could but she slipped into a diabetic coma from which she never emerged. Lily told him that a month or so ago, Charity had taken to her bed complaining of nausea and exhaustion, but the spell had lasted only a couple of days. Daniel had been touring and Charity hadn't wanted to bother him with her illness, which had seemed so minor.

The death of a parent leaves no one unmarked. Solomon's death had scarred Daniel, but Charity's death broke him. For a start, he blamed himself for her death. As a physician he should have noticed that all was not well. But more than guilt, Daniel felt the fear, pain and deep tearing sorrow of being truly alone for the first time in his life. He was grateful he had his wife and children around him, but it was only now that he realized the extent to which he'd depended on his mother. As head of the family he had coped as best he could with the passing away of Aaron and Rachel, but he wondered if part of the reason he had been so steadfast in the face of tragedy was because his mother had always been there to support him.

For weeks after her death, he would break off from what he was doing and stare blankly into space. It could be very disconcerting. At night he would dream. It was always the same dream: Charity, tiny and indomitable, dressed in a white sari, with a kerosene lantern in her hand, hurrying through a ravine in the deepest night. There was all manner of danger lurking in the shadows, but her step was firm and that part of her face that you could see, serene. Incredibly, the weak lantern kept at bay the malevolent fingers of the dark that probed at her. But the way was long and difficult. He would pray and try to reach out to her, goading her on, telling her to keep walking, looking neither to right nor left, just keep on, keep on. And she would ... just about ... to reappear in his dream the next night. Walking down the swart dusk of that valley, steadfastly, calmly, a tiny pinpoint of light.

Daniel was almost fifty years old when Charity died, but it doesn't matter at what age you've lost a parent, there is never anything you can clutch on to, to make it less grievous. He realized dimly through his grief that with both his parents gone he had no safety nets left, no possibility of retreat into sanctuaries, howsoever illusory. He was left with nothing but his own limited wisdom, talent and energy to see him through to the end of his own span. It was a daunting prospect.

He grew listless and disinterested in his work. No new products emerged from the lab, and to make matters worse, the monsoons failed that year, for the first time since Doraipuram had been founded. As the weeks lengthened into months, the family grew restive. They had respected Daniel's grief for as long as they could, but the truth was that their compassion and empathy were finite. They expected him to pick himself up and go on. Ramdoss and Lily tried to shield Daniel as much as they could, but they knew he would need to start taking an interest in the business and the settlement soon.

In the days of his grief, he spent a lot of his time in the little enclosed veranda behind his bedroom, reading and meditating on death. He read not only the Bible, but also the Upanishads and the Gita, and a couple of commentaries on Hindu and Buddhist scriptures that Narasimhan had left with him. Each text offered him something but there wasn't enough in any of them to remove the great sorrow that persisted in his heart. Ramdoss often came to sit quietly with him and occasionally he would bring up matters that needed to be attended to. Daniel's answer was unvarying: 'Do what you must.' He had no interest in discussing anything, although he would often tell Ramdoss stories about his childhood, every one of them featuring Charity.

60

All the weddings that had been planned in Doraipuram for the second half of 1930 were postponed until the official year of mourning was over. Among those affected was Shanthi. The groom had been picked, the dowry settled and the remaining arrangements were being finalized when Charity died.

The week after the memorial service that formally marked the end of the mourning period, Lily brought up the subject of Shanthi's nuptials with her husband. She had tried to sort out all the details, but had run into an unforeseen problem. As there were so many delayed marriages to solemnize, the family had run out of auspicious dates. Shanthi, as the founder's daughter, would of course have first pick, but it didn't seem right. There was no hesitation in Daniel's mind. 'I want my beloved daughter to be married off as soon as possible, so why don't we have all the weddings on the same day? The church is big enough and I'm sure we can get the padre some help.'

Doraipuram had never seen such activity. Guests poured in and were billeted wherever space could be found for them. There were clothes to be stitched, pandals to be erected, chickens and goats to be slaughtered, pickles and sweets to be prepared and stored, houses to be decorated, the church readied. Every household was drawn into some aspect or other of the preparations.

Having given his assent to the celebration, Daniel had withdrawn into himself once more, saddened by the thought that Charity would not be present. Lily and Ramdoss left him alone. His bedroom, where he spent much of his time, looked out on to an avenue lined with rain trees, Charity's favourite. She had personally supervised the planting of the saplings, but she hadn't lived long enough to see them bloom. This was the first year they were mature enough to do so and for weeks they had been clouded with flowers. Now they had reached the end of their flowering cycle, and the road under them glowed purple with fallen blossoms. One morning Daniel was watching a colony sweeper lazily pushing a broom around on the avenue. He would sweep the area and move on, only for it to darken again with falling petals. But the man was diligent and would return to clear the road, only for flowers to strew it thickly once more. One day, Daniel thought, the downpour would pare to a drizzle, and the broom would gain the upper hand. Wasn't his grief like that? For months he'd been paralysed, but slowly he was beginning to emerge into the light. He would get there, he knew, his sorrow diluted sufficiently for life to wash it away.

There was a knock on the door and Ramdoss walked in with Chris Cooke. Daniel couldn't believe his eyes. 'Thought I'd surprise you, old friend,' Cooke said. 'I'm due to retire next year and I thought this would be the perfect opportunity to visit all the places I might never see again ...'

'But if you'd told me you were coming we could have ensured that you were met and looked after properly.'

'Oh, Ramdoss and I have been planning this for some time. As soon as I received the invitation to the wedding, I knew I had to come. This was my last opportunity to see you all. But Ramdoss suggested that it would be even better if it was a surprise.'

'I cannot tell you how pleased I am that you're here,' Daniel said. 'And how well you look! India must be good for you, I can't believe you're to leave after, let's see, thirty years?'

'It'll be thirty-five years, actually, when they finally put me on the ship back home.'

After Cooke had rested and refreshed himself, Daniel and he went for a walk on the beach. The sun lay near the horizon, glowing an impossible red as it sucked the heat from the day.

'I don't think I've ever seen more extraordinary displays at dusk and at dawn than I've seen here,' Cooke said.

'Yes, Father Ashworth used to say that,' Daniel said. 'When I was a boy, he and I used to come this way a lot. He's buried overlooking the sea, you know.'

'He loved this place. It was a tragic business.'

'None of us will ever forget those days,' Daniel said sombrely.

'Any more caste trouble?'

'Not around here,' Daniel said. 'There are very few Vedhar families left, and they are a peaceful lot. Nationalist trouble flares up every time something big happens in the cities, but most of it takes place across the river. None of that sort of nonsense here.'

They walked in silence for a while, preoccupied with their thoughts, then Cooke said, 'I was very sorry to hear about your mother.'

'Thank you for your letter of condolence. I remember it still, especially the comment that her death only meant that she would now always be with me, living within, available whenever I had need of her.'

'I felt that way when my father passed away. That's one of the reasons Barbara and I decided to go back. My mother is ailing, and we'd like to be near her. Besides, the children are there now, so ...'

'Will you miss India?'

'Every moment, I think. I try not to think about leaving, and all else being equal, I'm almost sure we'd have retired here.'

'Aren't you worried by the political turmoil?'

'A bit, but nothing's insurmountable in my view. You chaps want your freedom. Fair enough. But I don't think you hate us enough to want to eject us completely. Even Mr Gandhi says he has nothing against us personally. I'm sure something can be worked out.'

'I hope so. Given the choice, I'd prefer the British to stay,' Daniel said. He had been surprised that his earlier liking for the British hadn't disappeared entirely. He should have hated them for what they had done to Aaron but after an unrelenting campaign against Rolfe which, because of Cooke, had been swiftly and successfully concluded (the jail Superintendent had been dismissed) he had simply chosen to reject politics altogether. The nationalists, in his view, were no better than the rulers. If Aaron hadn't been part of the revolutionary movement he might still be with him today ... And, if it came to a choice between the two, his more or less disinterested view was that the white man was less disruptive.

Cooke was saying, 'I think both sides could do things better. But with luck things won't get worse.'

'I certainly hope so.'

'Now that my time here is coming to an end, there's something I've been meaning to apologize to you about.'

Daniel laughed and said, 'But you've done me no wrong. On the contrary ...'

Cooke broke in, 'I'm sure it hasn't even crossed your mind, but for some years now I've been trying to get you on the King's annual honours list ... Given your contributions and support, it would've been the least we could do, but every time I've put forward your name, Aaron has come up!'

Daniel said, 'But how good of you, Chris, I'd never have thought ... In any case there's no need to apologize. Quite honestly I find such things meaningless.'

They ceased talking for a bit, wordlessly enjoying the sunset, then Daniel said, 'How are you going to occupy yourself when you leave?'

Cooke smiled. 'I'm sure I'll find things to do. We English say we retire to cultivate our garden.'

'Our version is that we give up everything and head for the forest, although I suppose we'd be lucky to find a decent forest these days,' Daniel said with a laugh. Cooke laughed with him.

They walked much longer than they had intended to, there was so much catching up to do. When they finally retraced their steps, their conversation exhausted, Daniel realized he would truly miss the Englishman, although for many years now their contact had been limited to letters and the exchange of gifts. Daniel would send his friend an enormous basket of Chevathar Neelams just before the annual mango festival – Cooke had always threatened to attend this, but had never managed to – which he would reciprocate with a bountiful hamper at Christmas. They should have done more together, he thought. He smiled to himself as he remembered how, at Cooke's urging, he had bought himself a handsome set of the collected works of England's greatest writers. These had remained, for the most part, decorative and unread in his library. We should have invested more in this friendship, Daniel mused, and now it's too late.

Two days later the five brides walked slowly down the avenue of rain trees, their saris fluttering like great white moths in the dusk. The sweepers had watered down the dust and their passage scarcely left any impress on the cool earth. Light streamed out of the windows of the church and shimmered on the estuary. Every available inch of space was taken, and the congregation roared out the songs and responses with a vigour never seen before.

Doraipuram is waking to life again, Daniel murmured to himself, just as I am. Amma would be glad. Later, in a gesture that endeared him to the other parents but dismayed Ramdoss, Daniel paid for a joint feast at Neelam Illum for all the couples married that day. The festivities did not stop until dawn ripped the sky apart. In the early light, the back of the mansion presented a hellish sight – all the stray dogs for miles around had congregated there to dispute the ownership of the pile of bones and scraps with the kites, squirrels and crows.

No such confusion marred the entrance to the mansion. Lily, who had impressed everyone with her unflagging energy and organizational skills, had one more surprise in store. Earlier that day Daniel's new Chevrolet had been sent all the way to Trivandrum on a special mission. The passenger who returned in the car was kept out of view until the time came for Shanthi and the other brides to depart in the late afternoon. Lily refused to let them go until they had participated in the final ceremony of the day – a group photograph under the spreading mango tree on the front lawn. It was the first time such a ritual had been introduced into a Dorai wedding and there was a lot of excitement among the assembled members of the family. But before the historic picture could be taken they drove the photographer to distraction. Every time he dived under the black hood and peered through the shutter, something or other would upset the composition – an aunt's extravagant pose obscuring Shanthi's face or a mischievous nephew having to be brought under control. Finally, after much giggling and whispering, the family was brought to order. At the photographer's command, the patriarch and the elders scowled obligingly for the camera. A blue flash, and the harassed photographer was done.

A month later, when the framed prints arrived at Neelam Illum, Daniel decreed that the picture of his daughter's wedding day would occupy pride of place in the enormous living room. 'Without Shanthi, none of this would have existed,' he said to Lily, as he supervised operations. 'Her name should have been Lakshmi.'

Just before the photograph was to be hung, Daniel called a halt to the proceedings, and then beckoned excitedly to Lily. Possibly due to the numerous distractions he was faced with, a small portion of the print had been over-exposed by the photographer. Daniel was having none of it. 'I knew she would be present. Lily, look at this,' he said, pointing to the light that misted the faces of the people immediately behind his daughter. 'How could Shanthi be married without her grandmother's blessing?'

61

When Kannan was born, Daniel had made a conscious decision not to treat him like the heir apparent. Mindful of his own solitary boyhood, and the oppressive weight of his father's expectations, he decided that his son should be free to enjoy the pleasures of a secure childhood in the midst of an extended family. Accordingly Kannan was left pretty much to his own devices. He dressed the same as his innumerable cousins, slept in the large room in the mansion that had been set aside for boys of his age and wasn't singled out for any special favours.

It was the best gift Daniel could have given him. Remote from the concerns of adults, and free of the pressures of his surname, life was entirely delightful for Kannan. For a year after Charity's death, communal celebrations were restrained but that didn't hold the young boys of the settlement back. They still had enough to keep them going: raids on the mango groves, swims in the river and the wells, re-enactments of Solomon's great battle on the beach – although Daniel had forbidden this. There were long bicycle rides under the sun that burnt them to an unnatural shade of blackness, fights, hunts for harmless water snakes in flooded paddy-fields, intense games of hockey and football. And during the migratory season, when water birds filled the sky and water, great shoots for duck and teal, the lakes and the river echoing with the thunder of shotguns and rifles.

One morning, a few months after his sister's wedding, Kannan woke up alone in his mother's room. He was recovering from the flu, and had been segregated from the other boys. He had slept late, and there was no one else about. He was a little weak but otherwise felt fine. Quickly bathing, and slipping on the combination shorts and singlet which was the standard garment for the younger boys when they were not in school uniform, he wandered out of the house with no set purpose in mind. All his friends were at school, and within a short time Kannan felt bored. It was a bright and sunny day, but the monsoon was about to break, and pre-monsoon showers had left pools of water in every depression in the ground. A large pool that lay just beyond the garden was full almost to overflowing and Kannan was intrigued to see hundreds of tiny shapes moving around under the surface of the scummy green water. Squatting down, he put out a hand and cleared some of the scum away. He could see the tadpoles more clearly now, ungainly creatures with enormous heads and ugly tails. He shifted position a bit, settled himself more comfortably and thrust his hand into the water. When he withdrew it, there were two tadpoles in his clenched fist. Kannan put them on a rock nearby and watched their death struggles with interest. When they had stopped moving, he prodded them with his finger to make sure they were dead. Then he turned his attention to the pond again. He caught only one tadpole this time, almost a frog with well-developed hind legs and a reduced tail. It took longer to die. By the time there were fourteen tadpoles on the rocks, stiff and twisted like burnt twigs, Kannan had begun to tire of the sport. The tadpoles offered no resistance, were much too easy to catch, and didn't even die flamboyantly. Rising to his feet, he wandered back to the house.

When he entered the driveway, he noticed that his father's Chevrolet stood alone and unattended at the top of the driveway, its driver Raju missing. Kannan couldn't believe his luck. Raju, who kept the lemon-yellow machine – all Dr Dorai's cars were yellow – in mint condition, was a terror none of them would face. That was the only reason the car had been spared the attentions of the dozens of small boys who were obsessed with it.

Every Sunday after church, Dr Dorai allowed three boys and girls, picked as fairly as possible, to accompany him on a leisurely tour of Doraipuram. It was an experience none of them forgot in a hurry. Kannan's third turn had come a fortnight ago, and he could still replay much of the journey in his mind. His irritating cousin Gopu, only six and therefore utterly without significance, had stood on the rear seat between Kannan and Mary, another cousin he didn't much like, terrified that the car would collide with something. Staring intently through the windshield, he would scream 'Raju, cow' or 'Raju, man' or 'Raju, neem tree' as these objects hove into view, at least half a kilometre away, on the die-straight roads of Doraipuram. After enduring this for as long as he could, Dr Dorai had snapped at his son to control Gopu. Kannan had been swift to comply, and had kept his cousin buried in the seat with a neck-hold, and hadn't allowed him to emerge until the Chevrolet had rolled to a stop. As he let Gopu out, Kannan had pinched him hard for spoiling his ride.

And now here the Chevrolet stood, a vast expanse of yellow trimmed with black, just inviting him to explore its multidimensional splendours without the distraction of strict adults or annoying cousins. He climbed cautiously on to the running board, unlocked the handle and quickly eased behind the steering wheel. He wasn't tall enough to see through the windscreen but it didn't matter, there was much that was thrilling within the car itself: the gigantic steering wheel, the dials with their mysterious numbers and symbols, the horn. For a while he just sat there, enormously pleased with himself, luxuriating in the car's embrace. Then he thought with a start that Raju might be back soon and decided to derive as much pleasure from the machine as he could before he was removed from it. He grabbed hold of the lower end of the steering wheel and swung it this way and that, making motor-car noises as he did so: 'Drrr-drr, drr-drr.' As he sank into the experience, he grew bolder, and began fiddling with levers and buttons. A lever fell and locked, and he froze, but nothing happened and he continued with his play. He noticed another lever that he hadn't seen before and tugged at it.

As he disengaged the handbrake, the car started to roll down the slight incline of the driveway. Kannan was shocked when the Chevrolet began to move. His first instinct was to open the door and jump out, but that was soon extinguished by the overwhelming terror he felt as the car began picking up speed. He frantically rotated the steering wheel, and pulled and pushed at various levers. He had observed Raju doing something with his feet when he drove, but the pedals were too distant. He slapped at the horn, and the Chevrolet blared once as it veered off the driveway and ran majestically into a neem tree.

Daniel was looking out of his window when he heard the sound of the horn and was horrified to see his new car sailing down the driveway with no one at the wheel. Quickly putting on his slippers he ran out, getting to the arrested machine just moments behind Raju.

'You donkey, where were you?' he shouted.

'I'd just gone to the servants' quarters to get a duster, aiyah. I'd left the handbrake on and everything, I don't know how this could have happened.'

'For your sake, I hope there is no major damage, otherwise I'll have you whipped.'

From inside the car, the men heard muffled sobbing. A moment later, Daniel had wrenched the door open to find a terrified little boy. He yanked his son out roughly, and his hand descended once, twice, three times and then again. Kannan twisted around his father to escape the blows but Daniel turned with him, trying to get in a few more licks, so for a time they resembled nothing so much as a carnival roundabout, whirling round and round. And then, deciding he'd thrashed his son enough, Daniel ordered him to his room. Kannan fled, sobbing.

Raju reversed the car back on to the driveway, and they examined the damage, which both master and driver were relieved to note was slight – a dented mudguard and a cracked headlamp.

Leaving the driver with instructions to make the necessary repairs, Daniel walked slowly back to the house. He hadn't liked thrashing Kannan, not that the rascal didn't deserve it, but it was not something he was used to doing. He knew that his wrath had been fuelled by more than concern over the car; it had also to do with the danger the boy had put himself in. How little I've seen of my son, he thought; what with one thing or another he's growing up without me, and in a couple of years I'll have missed his childhood entirely. He'd seen a lot more of Shanthi and Usha, and they were girls! And it wasn't good enough to argue that it had been easier to spend time with the children in Nagercoil. No, if he wanted to do it, he must make the time.

Daniel's approach to child-rearing was not very different to that of other men of his generation. Essentially, it consisted of keeping his distance. Children were to be looked after by their mothers and, if they were boys, they would occasionally connect with their fathers on shooting trips, family celebrations and the like until they were old enough to be treated like men. For all that he was different from his father and his other male cousins and relatives, Daniel too fitted the mould. He was awkward with children, and preferred to be a stern and distant father, quite content to limit the time he spent with children to things like joyrides and the occasional thrashing.

Kannan's weeping subsided almost as soon as he reached the house, for the blows Daniel had landed hadn't hurt him much, but it took some time for the shock to die down. He couldn't find his mother, so he went to his room and lay down on his mat, nursing his hurt. A short while later, footsteps sounded outside the door, and Kannan was appalled to see his father framed in the doorway. Frantically he looked around for a place to hide, but Daniel didn't enter the room. Instead, from where he was, he said, 'What you did was very wrong, Thirumoolar, and you know it. If I ever catch you near the car again, I'll give you such a thrashing that I promise you today's beating will seem nothing compared to it.'

There was only one response appropriate to this and Kannan made it, swearing that he would never go near the Chevrolet again. Then, to his surprise, his father said, 'Let's go out.' Instinctively, with the cunning of the young, Kannan realized the worst was over, and he got up from where he crouched and they set off.

Initially they were awkward with each other. It was all very new to both of them. They walked with no set purpose, Daniel asking Kannan about school and play, and receiving cautious answers in reply. After about half an hour, Daniel had exhausted every question he could think of, and began to wonder if the walk had been such a good idea after all. What now? He could lecture his son about the nature of the challenge that lay ahead of him as the male heir to the Dorai legacy, but he reminded himself sternly that there was time enough for that yet. How devilishly difficult it was to be a father, he thought. Although he knew he couldn't excuse Solomon for what he'd done, he felt a certain empathy towards him now, as he regarded his own son. They were passing the well Aaron had jumped, only partially visible behind the screen of trees, and Daniel took the opportunity to pick up the conversation. 'Do you know that your Aaron-chithappa cleared that well when he was only sixteen years old?'

'Yes, appa,' Kannan said quickly, 'everybody knows that. It's such a big well. Chithappa must have been a giant.'

Ah, Aaron, Aaron, thought Daniel, how wonderful it could have been. Together we could have made everything about Doraipuram work: little boys who needed their imaginations fired (Kannan even bore a physical resemblance to Aaron), dreams which needed to be managed ...

'Oh, yes, he was a giant,' Daniel said.

They lingered for a couple of moments near the well, and then carried on. After walking in silence for a few minutes, they came to the thicket of lantana scrub that had once been the ruins of Kulla Marudu's mud fort. When he had returned to Chevathar and had started laying out Doraipuram, Daniel had vaguely thought about restoring the fort, but it had never happened. Over the years, lantana, touch-me-not and other weeds and shrubs had almost completely overwhelmed the tumbledown mud walls. An old cobra lived in a deep crevice, and elsewhere in the tangle bandicoots and lizards thrived. The boys didn't go near it, it was too impenetrable and after a few desultory efforts to kill the cobra, they had left it alone.

'Do you know what that is?' Daniel asked, pointing.

'Oh, that's where the old cobra lives. It's become very cunning and shoots off to hide when it hears the slightest noise.'

'It's actually the remains of a fort,' Daniel said, 'from the time of Kattabomma Nayaka, nearly one hundred and fifty years ago.' He noted with satisfaction that he had the boy's interest.

'Were there battles and dead people?' Kannan asked.

'Yes, all of that. The fort belonged to a minor warlord called Kulla Marudu who proved to be a surprisingly tenacious fighter against the British. About a hundred men held off the famous Major Bannerman and his troops for a month.'

'Did he kill the Englishman, appa?'

'No,' Daniel said. 'A traitor within the fort opened the gates one night and Major Bannerman's troops poured in. After a short sharp fight Kulla Marudu was captured. As was common in those days, his head was cut off, mounted on a pike, and taken around all the surrounding villages to warn them against emulating him.'

'Do you think there are skeletons down there?' Kannan asked excitedly, all the nervousness and fear he had felt in the presence of his father wiped from his mind.

'I doubt it. Little boys have been playing here for over a hundred years and I don't think they will have left anything of interest. Besides, the British cremated as many of their victims as possible, not because they were respecting local custom but because they didn't want their remains to become objects of veneration.'

Kannan's enthusiasm for the fort diminished when he learned of the absence of skulls, but he was beginning to enjoy the walk. What new surprises would his father spring on him? He spotted an S-shaped mark in the dirt and pointed.

'Look, appa,' he yelled excitedly, 'there's the track of that old cobra.'

'What letter of the English alphabet does it remind you of?'

Kannan's enthusiasm vanished. This was unfair, he thought. Just when he was beginning to enjoy himself, how could his father put him in mind of boring old school?

'Is it a J?' he asked cautiously. It had been a long time since he had attended the weekly English class in his Tamil medium school. No matter how much he racked his brain, J was the only letter that came to mind.

'No, it's not J. Thirumoolar, what are they teaching you at school?'

'Lots and lots of lessons,' he said quickly. 'How about P?' he added, remembering another letter.

'It's absolutely not P,' Daniel snapped. 'If you can't answer something as simple as that, how are you going to pass exams, take your rightful place as the head of the family?'

All his earlier good humour gone, he looked at his son, taking in as if for the first time the grubby clothes, the badly cut hair that obscured much of the forehead, the scabbed and scraped legs, the generally raffish air of the boy. He began a tirade, but it was swiftly cut off by the memory of his own father's disappointment in him.

As he tried to restrain himself, Daniel hoped the unimpressive boy would somehow find within himself the spirit that would help him take on the responsibility of being a Dorai. It would be up to Ramdoss, Lily and him to nurture the boy's talent. But there's time enough for that still, he argued with himself. Let the boy be. He smiled at his son, unexpectedly ruffled his hair, and said, 'That was an S, son. You must study harder, learn English until it's at least as good as your Tamil. The English run the country, and it's always useful to learn the ways and tongue of the rulers.'

Kannan nodded. Although he was surprised he'd escaped a lecture, the fun had gone out of the walk, and the distance between them had re-emerged. Daniel felt the same, and cutting short their stroll, they made their way home.

That evening Daniel shared his concern about Kannan with Lily and Ramdoss.

'There's so much to be done. Every day brings with it new challenges, and I'm afraid that Thirumoolar may not be up to them. He looks and behaves like an idiot. Why, he couldn't even recognize the letters of the English alphabet!'

Lily was quick to spring to her son's defence: 'He's bright. It's just that he needs some coaching. I'll engage tutors for him. And we could transfer him to the new English medium school that's just opened in town.'

'Yes, that sounds like a good idea. And I should take a greater interest in him. After all, I'm his father and I feel I've been neglecting him. And let's not forget that the future of the family will depend on him in a few years' time.' He paused, then said, 'I wonder if my decision not to let him know what was expected of him as a Dorai was a good one. You never know with these things, do you?'

Ramdoss said, 'I think you made the right decision, anna. Give him a little more time, let him grow up normally. He's a fine boy and will make a fine leader.'

62

Ramdoss was right. As time passed, Kannan began to display the sort of qualities that augured well for the family's future. Although not too academically inclined or possessed of the remarkable sporting ability of his uncle Aaron, he was tough, confident and quite unafraid of taking on challenges.

These began quite early in his life, and had a lot to do with his surname. Despite his father's continued resolve not to single him out for favours, he was inevitably picked on by those who wanted to establish their claim to leadership in the group. Matters were not helped by Kannan's quick temper, which became apparent as he grew older. By the age of ten, he was getting into fights all the time. He was small for his age, but he more than made up for it with a ferocious determination not to yield. Everyone who knew him noticed this trait soon enough, and while she was still alive Charity would often say in exasperation: 'Just my luck that my favourite grandchild should have inherited the Dorais' most annoying characteristic. Every Dorai I've known was as stubborn as a donkey.'

One of the rites of passage every Chevathar boy had to negotiate was the art of riding a bicycle. This wasn't as easy as it sounds for there were no children's bicycles and the only machines the boys had access to were those belonging to an uncle or a parent. Consequently, learning how to stay on the bicycle became quite a challenge, for it often stood as tall as the boy did, and his feet didn't reach the pedals. He would need to balance the heavy, cumbersome machine upright, slide one foot under the crossbar on to the pedal on the side away from him, hop on to the pedal on his own side and then work both frantically to launch the machine on a wobbly course that usually ended in a spill. After adding several more dents to the already bruised machine and skinning his knees, the boy was miraculously able to stay upright, more or less, and it was a common sight to see large bicycles with small boys attached crabwise to them wavering along the dusty paths of Doraipuram.

The only problem was that the rider was still so precariously balanced that he was easy to unseat. One afternoon, a couple of weeks after he'd damaged his father's car, Bonda, an older cousin, pushed Kannan off his bicycle just as he was getting up steam. The machine and he came crashing down. Bonda stood over the tangle of boy and cycle smirking, but not for long. The minute Kannan had disentangled himself, he rushed at his tormentor.

The fight had been brewing for some time. Bonda, so nicknamed on account of his bulk, was the unofficial leader of the colony's younger boys. He'd realized he would never establish his leadership conclusively until he had put Kannan down. He needled and tormented him at every opportunity, but this was the first time he had humiliated him so publicly. Sensing the importance of the fight, the combatants were instantly surrounded by a gang of eager boys.

They fought grimly and silently, egged on by the jeering audience. By virtue of his size and weight, Bonda had the edge and within minutes he was smearing Kannan's face in the dirt. But the fight was far from over. With characteristic determination, Kannan ignored the pain and twisted and heaved until he had the bigger boy off-balance. With a hard push, he got him off his back and leapt to pinion him. Just then, an image of Charity rose in his mind, followed by an extraordinary feeling of loss and loneliness. It was the first time in over a year that he had thought of the woman around whom his world had once revolved. Tears started to drip down his cheeks. The cheers of his most vocal supporters were replaced by silence. But after that moment of extreme emotion, Kannan felt no grief, only a great desire to smash Bonda into the dirt. His opponent, who thought he had the battle won when he saw the tears, was startled by the redoubled ferocity of Kannan's attack. In a matter of minutes, he had given up the fight.

For the rest of his boyhood, the tears would flow whenever Kannan fought but by now his opponents knew that it signified nothing, except perhaps an even greater determination to win. Not once in all this time did Kannan reveal the cause of his weeping. He didn't want to be made a figure of fun. Paati's pet! He could imagine the heckling if people ever got to know.

By the time he entered his teens, Kannan was the undisputed leader of a group of cousins and hangers-on who were known as the Hockey Stick Gang because of their preference for settling all disputes with hockey sticks. From time to time, members of the group would be hauled up before Daniel by an irate parent or teacher for committing some offence. To Daniel's chagrin, the culprits would almost always have Kannan among their number. On these occasions he would grow alarmed and a spurt of sermonizing and vigilance over the boy's activities would ensue until Daniel was consumed by work once again.

During the summer break of Kannan's penultimate year at school, he was reported to his father four times for a variety of infractions. A week after he had chastised his son for stampeding an irascible cousin's cows, Daniel was very annoyed when Kannan and members of his gang were arraigned before him again – this time for stealing guavas.

The plaintiff, a small, meek-looking man, was growing more and more long-winded as he described the depredations of the boys, and finally Daniel could take it no more. 'I'll sort this out,' he said firmly, and turned a stern countenance on the culprits. He glared at his son, who was watching the little man's performance quite composedly, and was struck once more by how much the boy reminded him of Aaron. It wasn't so much the physical resemblance that Daniel was thinking about; it was the essential nature of the boy – impetuous, short-tempered, uninterested in school. It would be so easy for him to turn wild and unrestrained. Daniel had admired his brother's toughness and fearlessness and was glad they had surfaced in his son, but they would need to be tempered by restraint and responsibility.

There would be a lot of moulding to do. If only I had more time, he thought. But there was no point wishing for what he did not have. Kannan would need to learn, and quickly.

He handed down punishment that was fairly severe, given the nature of the offence – community service for a month, to be carried out under Ramdoss's supervision. Kannan looked at his father in disbelief, but there was no mistaking the grimness. There would be no reprieve.

That evening, after they'd eaten, Daniel and Ramdoss went for their usual walk. The subject of Kannan came up and Daniel said, 'I'm worried about the boy. I don't have the time to look after him and I fear he'll grow up like his uncle and half a dozen others I could name. It seems to be the hallmark of the Dorais. God gave us the sort of strength and stubbornness a monitor lizard would envy but He forgot to add self-control and prudence.'

'Between Lily-akka, yourself and me, we'll set him right, don't worry.'

'I know we will, Ramu, but what really worries me about Thirumoolar is that he has shown no interest in medicine, no interest in the colony's affairs. All he's interested in is hockey, shooting, cycling, or kicking up trouble to amuse himself.'

'He's still a boy, anna, he must have his fun, but I promise you that he'll be a source of pride ...'

'Oh, I'm proud of him, if a little disappointed. He's in the fifth form now. By the time I was his age I was already pretty sure of what I wanted to do. Look at your boy, Jason. Look what a fine engineer he is. I'm really proud he landed that job in Bombay.'

'You don't need me to tell you that we all develop at our own pace, and I'm sure ...'

Daniel interrupted, 'I think that perhaps he should be sent away. Separate him from his group, put him in a place where he'll be disciplined.'

Ramdoss absorbed this in silence.

'What do you think?' Daniel demanded impatiently.

'It might work,' Ramdoss said. 'What did you have in mind?'

'I'm not sure, but if he shows no aptitude for medicine, it would probably be wrong to put him in a medical college and expect him to survive. I'd much rather have him study something like botany so that he has some knowledge of plants and herbs, and we can teach him the rest here ...'

They talked of other things then, but as they were returning to the house, Daniel said, 'The more I think of it, the more I like it. Send the boy to a good college, and then build on whatever they make of him.'

They had almost come to the end of their walk when Daniel said, 'We must prepare him well, Ramu. He's got three more years: one year at school, two years Inter. He must make the best of college. Lily and you must prepare him. Spare no expense, he's our future.'

63

In Vedic times, when a king felt strong and powerful or just plain ambitious, he performed the Aswamedha or horse sacrifice. A magnificent white stallion was chosen and set free at the borders of the kingdom, there to wander as it chose. All the lands that it traversed would now automatically belong to the king. In theory, if the king was mighty enough, the horse would wander for ever, but in practice it was often stopped by some other ruler who didn't particularly feel like giving up his kingdom. This was tantamount to a declaration of war.

The Germans in the middle of the twentieth century had a different name for the concept – *Lebensraum*. Hitler did what the ancient Indian kings had done – he sent his tanks rumbling into the countries next door. After years of vacillation and appeasement, while country after country disappeared down the gullet of the Third Reich, Britain declared war on Germany.

This threw nationalist leaders in India into a dilemma. Mahatma Gandhi, the voice of the nation, was initially behind Britain as she fought to save the world from fascism but his support for the British grew rather less passionate when he realized that they still had no intention of giving up India in a hurry.

As with the other great movements of contemporary history, the prospect of a second global war left little impression on Doraipuram.

Kannan was in the second year of his pre-degree Intermediate course at the Bishop Caldwell College in Meenakshikoil. For the past three years, he'd been subjected to all manner of tutoring, all of which he'd found onerous. Lily or Ramdoss would engage teachers who would attempt to impart to him the unfathomable mysteries of mathematics, chemistry, history or whatever it was his father had decreed should be taught. Surprisingly, given his childhood failure at acquiring the language, he was quite proficient in English. Lily's decision to transfer him to an English medium school had paid off. Nevertheless, his English tutorials were continued, at his father's insistence. Kannan rather enjoyed them. Most of the other tutors didn't last very long, as the pressure of trying to get Kannan up to Dr Dorai's exacting standards grew too much for them. At these times, Lily would fill the breach, trying to teach him from textbooks. These makeshift tutorials would soon become storytelling sessions and it was at this time that Kannan was first introduced to the idea of Elsewhere.

Lily had always been somewhat distanced from her son, initially due to Charity's obsession with him and later because of the varied distractions of Doraipuram, and she was delighted at the opportunity to spend time with Kannan. Like any adolescent, Kannan would have much rather been out with his friends but he didn't have an option, given his father's determination to improve him. But his initial restlessness in his mother's company was soon displaced by the quality of the stories she told him. Stuck in hot humid Chevathar, she poured her longing for the misty tea estates of Nuwara Eliya into her elaborate tales. Every detail of her childhood acquired an exotic, enticing quality. She told of memorable parties held in planters' bungalows that floated like great ocean-going ships, full of light and laughter, through the deep black Ceylonese nights. She remembered in loving detail beautiful English ladies in crinoline frocks and gentlemen in dinner jackets dancing and dining, while she and a few other children from the staff quarters gazed entranced through chinks in the hibiscus hedges. She described the annual Christmas parties that the white planters threw for their clerks and native subordinates, and the soft white hands of the General Manager's wife as she distributed the presents.

These stories, and his English lessons, were the only aspect of his moulding that Kannan liked. For the rest, it was merely a matter of working out how he could get rid of the latest tutor. There would be a few weeks of reprieve before his father's attention focused on him once more and the cycle began all over again. The tutoring had intensified recently and he sensed that some new development informed his coaching schedule, for the teachers were tougher, demanded more of him and were not so easily thwarted. He hoped his father's plans, whatever they were, would allow him to continue at BCC. All his friends were planning to do so except Albert who wanted to study physics abroad. It would be awful if his father persisted with the idea of making him a doctor. Kannan didn't fancy the idea of cutting up cadavers and besides, from what he'd heard, medical college was too much work.

For now, what was uppermost on his mind was the hockey match his team had to win against Ranivoor Arts College, if they were to stay in contention for a medal in the District Championships. As he was emerging from his room, hockey stick in hand, he heard raised voices from his father's room. He paused to listen. 'To think I've nurtured kraits in my midst,' he heard Daniel roar. 'You come here talking of love and brotherhood and friendship and then you dare tell me that you would like to sell your land to an outsider. I never expected you to sink so low, Miriam. Have you forgotten the lakhs I spent on your wedding and dowry? And when you came begging to me, saying this rascal had squandered all your money, have you forgotten how I practically gave you the land and house you're living in? And now you want to sell! Let me make myself clear. If I hear another word from you about any of this, I will make you regret the day you ever brought it up. Get out, get out, I cannot bear the sight of you.'

There was silence, broken only by the sound of a woman's noisy weeping. Time to go, Kannan thought. He was just about to ease himself past his father's door when he heard footsteps and flattened himself against the wall. There was nowhere to hide and he was sure to be seen. The door was plucked open and first his aunt Miriam, fat and unsteady on her feet, rushed out followed by her diminutive husband. They looked neither right nor left, and he was sure he had escaped detection. He was congratulating himself on his narrow escape when a third person walked slowly out of the room. Ramdoss. His eyes met Kannan's but he said nothing and walked away.

The next day Ramdoss invited Kannan to go for a walk with him. They went past the mango topes and then strolled along the river to the estuary. Ramdoss asked Kannan how he was faring at college, whether he'd made any plans. Nervously, Kannan said no. A few boys were swimming in the calm water, their heads showing above the grey surface. They watched them in silence for a while, then Ramdoss said, 'You're old enough now to take up your responsibilities. I'm glad you heard the altercation yesterday because it's time you knew what things are really like here. Do you have any idea?'

'Some,' Kannan said cautiously.

'You should know everything. It's your father's wish.'

They settled themselves on the river bank, and Ramdoss began his story. He quickly sketched the history of Doraipuram's decline. He talked about the large sums of money that had been sunk into impractical schemes and sundry other expenses (dowries, marriages, births, deaths, bribes, gifts) and the declining returns from the patent medicines, especially the Moonwhite Cream that appeared to be reaching the end of its cycle. He told Kannan about the neglect of the business in the years that Daniel had spent nurturing the settlement, the brief period in which he had thrown himself back into it, Charity's death and how much it had affected his father. 'Daniel-anna never really recovered, thambi, and when he took charge again, his heart wasn't in it. The final perfidy was when the family he had given his life and fortune to proved less than grateful. You heard your athai yesterday, didn't you? That's only the latest example. For at least five years now, there have been periodic outbursts by members of the family who have accused your father of gross neglect, dishonesty, even criminal negligence of their best interests. You boys and girls are fortunate, you have your youth and its marvellous concerns to shield you, but the truth is, Kannan, your father has need of you. He's very tired and he wants to know that his dream can be transferred to his son.'

Kannan felt acutely alarmed by this. 'But what do I have to do?'

Ramdoss smiled at his reaction. 'Don't be so nervous, thambi. All you need to do for the moment is apply yourself where your studies are concerned.'

'I'll do my best,' Kannan said.

'Yes, you must,' Ramdoss said, rising to his feet. 'Your father says that you haven't shown any interest in medicine so he's decided to send you to one of the finest colleges in the Presidency. He wrote to his friend Chris Cooke in England a few months ago, asking his advice, and Mr Cooke recommended the Madras Christian College. It's run by a Scottish missionary order. I know you've picked English up well, but the standards there are very high so I'm doubling the time you'll spend in English tuition.'

'But why do I have to go so far away, mama ...'

Ramdoss held a hand up for silence. 'Let me finish. Because you have no interest in medicine, Daniel-anna has decided you should take a degree in botany. He feels it'll help you get a basic knowledge of plants and herbs, and the rest you can pick up when you start working with him. You'll be at the Madras Christian College a few months from now. We've already been in touch with the principal, Dr Boyd. What do you think?'

Fortunately a servant came running up to say Ramdoss was wanted by Daniel so Kannan, dumbfounded as he was by the abruptly revealed future, was spared the necessity of answering.

64

Kannan's first day at Madras Christian College in Tambaram was a disaster. Having deposited him at his hostel, Bishop Heber Hall, Ramdoss had left him. Within hours of his departure, Kannan had begun to feel alone and off-balance. He'd never travelled so far from home before and he found the experience disconcerting. Madras, where they had spent a few days before travelling on to Tambaram, had been the first major shock, with its enormous press of people and buildings and houses on a scale he could never have imagined. Before he could take it all in, he was transported to this new environment, and Ramdoss-mama, the last vestige of his old life, was gone. He remained in his room for a long time, slowly unpacking his holdall and big black steel trunk, trying to draw comfort from the contents. Most of his clothes were new, stitched by two tailors from Madras who had arrived in Doraipuram and worked around the clock for a week. Daniel had wanted his son's wardrobe to be in no way less than appropriate to the standards of the college. His mother had packed three bottles of homemade mango pickle and a few bags of murukku and sweets, and he arranged these on the shelf in his room. A bottle of hair oil, some other toiletries, and he was done. Still he didn't leave the room. He needed more time to summon up his usual confidence in these unfamiliar surroundings.

Towards evening he emerged from his room, walked rapidly to the bathroom at the end of the corridor, had a quick bath and returned. To his relief the bathroom and the corridors of the hall were quite deserted. He laid out a fresh shirt and lungi, carefully oiled and combed his hair, and then, just before he dressed, opened a bottle of pickle and inhaled deeply, breathing in Chevathar and the places and people he was homesick for. Then, steeling himself, he ventured down to the mess for supper.

The place was brightly lit, with long tables and benches. Serv boys scurried around, and a man behind a counter was bellow orders to the kitchen. The dining area was about half ful

number of the young men seemed to know each other, which made Kannan feel even more lonely. It had been quite dark when he'd left his room and this was the first time he was getting a proper look at the students he would be spending the next three years of his life with. The majority were in trousers and shirts. For a moment he wished he had decided on trousers instead of a lungi. He'd been put down for the European mess, another of Daniel's decisions to improve him, make him fit to be a success in British-ruled India. He asked a serving boy where it was and was waved to one corner of the hall. He headed for an empty bench. A couple of the students looked at him as he passed, but their gaze was incurious and he made it to the bench without drawing much attention to himself. As his confidence grew, he began to look around. The first-termers were easy to spot: they sat alone for the most part and ate without taking their eyes off their plates, while the others joked and laughed among themselves, catching up on their lives after the break. He tried not to make eye contact with anyone and waited for one of the serving boys to notice him. Eventually one of them came up and rattled off something in a mixture of Tamil and Malayalam; his accent was so pronounced and he spoke so fast that Kannan didn't understand a word of what he said, so he nodded. The boy seemed satisfied and went away. The mess was filling up quickly now, and he wondered who would take the seat next to him. He hoped it would be a new boy. By the time he had left Bishop Caldwell College, he had been the undisputed king of the student body. Here he was a nobody, the lowest of the low, a junior without connections. What a comedown, he thought.

'And what do we have here? A rustic from the mofussil with no manners!' A loud voice to his right. Kannan had been looking down and he decided not to look up. The owner of the loud voice sounded very irritated.

'Hey you, monkey-boy, I'm talking to you!' He felt the heat of the other's presence touch him and raised his head to see a hulking youth with a thick black moustache and longish hair. His brown eyes were furious.

'Don't you know it's impolite not to stand up in the presence of a senior? Especially if you're sitting in his place?'

'I didn't know these places were reserved,' Kannan said in genuine puzzlement.

'I didn't know these places were reserved,' the senior mimicked in a high falsetto.

Anger began to disperse Kannan's confusion. 'Look here,' he said,

'there's no need to insult me, I didn't know this was your place.'

'My, my, the village idiot is angry. Tip-top. How shall we soothe his anger?' the senior said, his voice mocking. 'Aha, I know how. Samuel, get me some special Tambaram grapes for our honoured guest.' One of the boys standing behind the senior ran out of the mess.

The place grew very quiet. Every clatter of cutlery was stilled, as was every voice. The serving boys froze where they were and even the man behind the counter stopped his orchestration of dinner. The boy who had left the mess returned with his fists full of unripe neem berries. He handed them to the big senior. Looking around to check that there were no lecturers or tutors present to thwart his plans for the upstart, the bully funnelled the berries through his hands on to Kannan's empty plate.

'Mr Lionel Webb presents his compliments, sir, and hopes very much that you will partake of his humble offering.'

Kannan stared at the yellow-green berries on his plate. Dirt stuck to some of them; twigs and leaves were liberally sprinkled among the fruit. Not even goats would eat unripe neem berries, they were so bitter and acrid.

He began to rise from the bench but Lionel slammed him back down. 'I said eat, you little pisser. This will teach you to play the fool with Lionel Webb.'

Tears started from his eyes, the familiar emptiness took hold of him, but this was not Chevathar, no one went in awe of his tears.

'Oh, the poor baby, maybe his mother needs to feed him our very special berries. I ...' but the senior didn't have time to finish the sentence for Kannan had erupted from the bench. Somehow he managed to push the long table in front of him aside and drive straight for his tormentor's body. He got in one good punch, but before he could land another, Lionel had recovered and had begun hammering him. Kannan didn't stand a chance. He went down. Willing arms secured him. Lionel deliberately picked up a fistful of neem berries from the floor, levered Kannan's mouth open, inserted the fruit and clamped his mouth shut. Kannan gagged and began spluttering. Abruptly, the pressure was released as Lionel said, 'Let him up. I think we've taught the little pisser his rightful place.'

Spitting the berries from his mouth, Kannan launched himself again at the smirking senior. Hard, hurtful blows to his face and body dropped him. Twice more he got up to fight, and each time he was put down, the last time so hard that he almost passed out. He tried to get up, but his left leg wouldn't quite support him. His tears were drying on his face, his body and head hurt, but there was no mistaking the anger that brightened his gaze. Watching him struggle to rise, Lionel muttered under his breath, 'Game little mongoose, aren't you?' When it was clear that it was all over, the hall hummed with the sound of nearly a hundred pent-up voices. His aggression entirely replaced by solicitude now, Lionel helped Kannan up from the floor and supported him to the nearest bathroom, where the blood on his forehead was washed away. His face felt puffy and painful, he had some difficulty speaking and his leg bothered him, but otherwise he was okay. Lionel took him to his room, settled him comfortably and left. Scarcely had he gone when there was a tap on his door and another boy he'd never seen before poked his head in. 'You fight well,' he said admiringly, 'I think that senior scarcely knew what to expect.'

Kannan grimaced and pointed to his mouth. The boy seemed to understand and said quickly, 'I'll let you rest now but if you want anything, just bang on the wall, I'm your neighbour. My name's Murthy.'

65

As summer approaches, the vast MCC campus lights up as its most distinctive tree, the peltophorum or rusty shield-bearer, begins to bloom in great gouts of bronze and gold. By the time the peltophorums began to flower in the summer of 1940, Kannan was completely at home on campus. That first fight with Lionel Webb had provided a short cut to acceptance and he did not look back. The Anglo-Indian boys, more clannish than most, were favourably disposed towards him. His proficiency on the hockey field helped strengthen the relationship. But he spent most of his time with Murthy. His friend's family owned a timber business in Coimbatore, and what began as a necessary alliance between small-town boys soon grew into a real friendship. They were both first-year botany students, inseparable in class where they formed the core of the back-benchers, and at the Hall where they took most of their meals together and spent hours gossiping and larking around. That summer when he went home for the holidays, Kannan discovered that he had already begun to grow away from those of his friends he had left behind, especially as his closest friend Albert had already left to study in England.

He was impatient to get back to college. He missed Murthy, he wanted to feel the excitement of inter-collegiate hockey matches, he craved the varied attractions of college life – trips to the city, evenings spent exploring the hundreds of acres of campus, late-night coffee and gossip sessions. Chevathar suddenly seemed dull and provincial.

His father was delighted that Kannan had taken so well to college but privately he confided in his wife and Ramdoss that he feared his son might find it difficult to readjust to Chevathar. But that eventuality was still over two years in the future, and it could be dealt with then.

66

Across the road from the massive gates of the college straggled an uneven line of shacks that sold everything that cash-strapped college boys would need: cigarettes, tea so strong that you could stand an iron bar upright in it, snacks and juices, calendars and stationery supplies. Nair's, the most popular of these, sold the best grape juice in Madras – black and thick as melted tar, and so sugary and concentrated that if you didn't have a sweet tooth it would give you a migraine. The entrance to Nair's shack was studded with flies. Most of them were so drunk from the juice that had spilled on the ground that they couldn't even fly and were crushed underfoot as customers entered or left. Nair, a genial, bulbous-bellied man, presided over a very utilitarian establishment. Besides the biscuits, fruit and juice he sold, all he provided for the customer's comfort were two roughly put-together wooden benches. These were occupied night and day.

One evening Kannan was at Nair's, drinking grape juice and gossiping with Murthy. Earlier, one of the leading nationalists of the city, the former Prime Minister of Madras, C. Rajagopalachari, had addressed a meeting in the college. As a result of Daniel's ban, Kannan was less than interested in politics, but Murthy was rather keen and certainly better informed about the rapid political developments in the country. Kannan had nothing better to do that evening so they had gone to the meeting. Soon, however, he was getting fidgety and suggested a grape juice at Nair's. Murthy had wanted to stay but Kannan had prevailed.

From talk of the meeting, their conversation moved to their fellow students. Murthy, who was always full of gossip, was narrating an absorbing story that involved Dr Boyd, the principal, the residents of Bishop Heber Hall and Tambaram grapes when Kannan chanced to look towards the road. He forgot about Murthy altogether.

A girl had just emerged from the train station and was walking down the road towards the line of tea shacks. She was walking fast, her feet seeming to float above the ground, and there was about her an unimaginable lightness. The muscles in the pit of Kannan's stomach contracted and his throat went dry. The hair she tossed out of her face, the pert nose, the slanting eyes: Kannan thought every detail of her was perfect.

'Helen Turner. Every man and boy from here to Egmore would like to get to know her better, so you might as well forget it,' Murthy said when he saw the look on Kannan's face.

'Tell me about her,' Kannan demanded. 'Who is she? Where's she from? Why haven't I seen her before? Why is she so beautiful?'

Delighted with the opportunity to gossip, Murthy launched into a description of Helen that was, to his credit, more factual than otherwise. The only child of a retired Anglo-Indian Posts and Telegraphs employee, who had built a small house for himself on the outskirts of the Tambaram Railway Colony, she had just started work as a secretary in an office in Guindy. She had hundreds of admirers but no one she went steadily with. She was best friends with a girl who was, if anything, more lovely than her, Cynthia ... There was more, and Kannan absorbed every word he could. Finally, even Murthy's powers of invention dried up, and he grew sick of the grape juice Kannan plied him with.

But Kannan had enough to go on. He had never gone out on his own with a girl before. The only girls he had even spoken to were his sisters and his cousins. But his obsession with Helen swept away all his inhibitions. He badgered every Anglo-Indian friend of his with the slightest connection to Helen, and finally managed to set up a meeting with her.

The encounter was an unqualified disaster. Kannan, who had been hoping and praying for a succession of miracles on the appointed day, was granted his first and last one immediately – there was no one at Nair's, no crowd of gawking, jeering college-mates. He was early, and before the bemused eyes of the proprietor, he carefully rubbed down the benches, arranged and dusted the various jars and tins in the shop. Finally, having nothing left to do, and finding it impossible to get rid of the doormat of flies, he sat down on one of the benches and stared down the road.

The girls, for Helen was accompanied by Cynthia, were punctual. They sailed through the eddying flies, bestowed smiles upon Kannan, agreed to have a grape juice apiece, smiled twice more at Kannan when he dared to catch their eye, finished their juice and left. There had been exactly nine words exchanged between the three of them in the fifteen minutes they had spent at the shack, including 'Hullo', 'Thanks' and 'Bye'. Kannan's contribution to the conversation, besides suggesting grape juice, was 'Erp' as he had tried and failed to get a dialogue going.

Things got better after that first meeting, partly owing to Cynthia's encouragement of the friendship, once she heard of Kannan's father's fame and wealth. Kannan did everything he could to ensure that Helen had a good time. He missed classes, he spent all his money on her and inevitably he failed all but one of his exams at the end of the year. The head of the department wrote to his father, threatening dismissal unless Daniel could guarantee an improved performance. He wrote disapprovingly about the 'extra-curricular activities' that he believed were to blame for Kannan's dismal record. To Kannan's good fortune, Ramdoss had had charge of Daniel's correspondence for some years now and immediately suppressed the letter. He provided the guarantee that the college sought, and wrote Kannan a tough letter, exhorting him to study hard. That summer, Kannan didn't return to Doraipuram for the holidays. Instead he pleaded with Ramdoss for money for extra tutorials, and stayed on in Tambaram.

In the 1940s, it was unusual for a young man and woman to go out together openly. But Kannan was too much in love to care what people thought. Tittering remarks, disapproving stares and unwanted advice were not about to deflect his obsessive love.

At first Helen didn't much care for the gawky boy and continued to hang out with the handsome Anglo-Indian boys who kissed so well. It was Cynthia who put things in perspective. If she wanted to get out of the depressing world of the Railway Colony that she was always grumbling about, she told her friend, she should take Kannan a bit more seriously. Helen accepted her friend's advice, but she was careful to let Kannan only slowly into her life.

The second year at college, Kannan once again failed two of his exams. This time the principal, Dr Boyd, wrote to Dr Dorai proposing a meeting to discuss his son's imminent exit from the college. Again Ramdoss intercepted the letter. He paid a visit to Tambaram, met with the principal and told Kannan that if he didn't stop seeing the girl and start passing exams, he would find himself on the next train to Doraipuram.

Kannan was not unintelligent. He learned to manage his time better, with Helen's encouragement. He cleared his exams and even received a letter of congratulation from his father, who usually confined himself to a line at the bottom of Lily's letters to him. But the thought of giving up Helen never seriously took hold. He could do nothing with the rest of his life if it did not include her. He continued to meet her clandestinely. How could he not? She filled him with excitement, with a sense of the limitless possibilities that life offered.

67

The mantram has enormous power. If you figure out the one that's right for you and repeat it incessantly, it will reach the very ears of God. Indeed, puny mortals are no match for the mighty mantram. As his battle with the British reached its climax, the Mahatma unleashed yet another of his unstoppable thunderbolts, the mantram 'Quit India'. As millions of mouths whispered, roared, warbled, chanted, carolled, bellowed, lisped, drawled, wheezed, trilled and stammered it out, it grew into a relentless force. The British, weakened by war and no longer entirely sure they wanted an Empire, were powerless before it while it lasted. Both sides knew it would only be a matter of time before they left.

Speaking in the cluttered and busy neighbourhood of Gowalia Tank in Bombay in August 1942, Mahatma Gandhi told a rapt audience that it was time for the British to leave for ever. Quit India. Then he added a deadly little subclause to the great explosive command that would ignite the land. 'Here is a mantra, a short one, that I give you. You may imprint it on your hearts and let every breath of yours give expression to it. The mantra is: "Do or Die".'

The Government acted swiftly. The top nationalist leadership was imprisoned but all to no avail. The genie was out of the bottle. Although the Quit India movement would fade in the face of British intransigence, as had all of the Mahatma's previous initiatives, it marked the beginning of the end of the Raj. The rulers didn't help their cause by making several tactical blunders. The move that infuriated the freedom fighters the most was the imperial offer to grant the country partial freedom as a Dominion of Britain, when what was demanded was total independence.

Politics finally invaded Doraipuram. Ramdoss was on an inspection tour of the settlement's outlying farmlands when he was horrified to see that a dozen palmyra palms had been amateurishly beheaded. He drove on, hoping to apprehend the culprits. He hadn't gone far when he found a small group of boys and girls clustered around two of their number who lay sprawled on the ground. One had a broken leg, the other had sprained his back. They were students from a nearby college who had taken the Mahatma's call to picket toddy and country liquor establishments a step too far by attacking the toddy palms themselves. One of them hailed Ramdoss: 'Aiyah, we need to get our friends to the hospital. One has broken his leg ...'

'He should have broken his neck,' Ramdoss said heatedly. 'Have you donkeys no respect for private property?'

'We are responding to the Mahatma's call. He has said we must all do our part to drive the British out.'

'Has he asked you to destroy your own country while doing so? I'd be doing an injustice to donkeys by comparing you with them. Come on, put your friends in the car.'

Daniel was unaware of the inroads that politics had made into the settlement. At about the time Kannan left for college, he had begun to retreat mentally into himself, tormented by the ills besetting Doraipuram. Physically, too, he had removed himself from view, disappearing into a suite of rooms – a bedroom, a room converted into a laboratory, a bathroom and a kitchen. He saw Ramdoss and Lily every day, and Kannan when he visited. He avoided the rest of the family. If they bumped into him by chance, they saw a dishevelled man, old before his time, with a straggly beard and bushy hair that sprouted from his ears and nostrils like smoke. He wouldn't speak or make eye contact with them but scuttled back to his rooms as quickly as he could.

More by accident than by design, a group of students arrived outside Daniel's rooms and began shouting slogans, denouncing the rulers and entreating him to join the agitation. Dr Dorai tolerated the din for as long as he could. When he could bear it no longer, he filled his arms with whatever he could find – cushions, slippers, test tubes, plates, knives – and began hurling them at his tormentors.

Having thrown everything he could at the students, whose alarm changed quickly to mockery at the famous doctor's bizarre behaviour, Daniel rushed out of the room to confront them. He never reached the boys. Before their frightened eyes, the wild-eyed old man crumpled to the ground. Ramdoss was there within minutes and Daniel was transported to the local clinic, where the doctor diagnosed a mild stroke. Two days later Daniel told Ramdoss that he wanted to see Kannan urgently. In fact, Kannan was already on his way home. No sooner had the Quit India movement begun to gather strength than Dr Boyd closed down the college. He informed the students that MCC would only reopen once the agitation had died down.

68

Kannan went to see his father straight from the station. He was pleased to hear from the young doctor attending him that Daniel didn't seem too badly affected by the stroke. He had some difficulty chewing, but was fine otherwise, he was told.

Daniel was delighted to see him. He smiled and whispered to Lily to get Kannan some tea.

'It's good to see you home, son. Doraipuram needs you.'

Kannan said, 'Don't exert yourself, appa. You must rest.'

'Nonsense, this is nothing. We siddhars know how to live for ever.'

But it was clear that talking tired him and Kannan left after a short while.

That evening, Kannan went for a long walk around the colony and was shocked to see how badly it had deteriorated during the year. Most of the houses needed to be whitewashed and the fabled mango groves were poorly tended and overgrown with weeds. He found Ramdoss waiting for him when he returned. He told a disturbing story. The troubles he had revealed to Kannan years before had spread. The farms and the other initiatives had continued to lose money. Some of the colonists had asked Daniel to make good his promise of compensating them for their land if they wanted to leave, and he'd had to sell his own land outside Doraipuram to pay for the land he bought back. These past months, Ramdoss said, Daniel had occupied himself with all manner of bizarre experiments. His manner had become increasingly eccentric and Ramdoss confessed that he had no idea how long it would take for Daniel to recover fully from the stroke and start taking an interest in the settlement again.

'You must come back soon, thambi, and help your father. Don't get involved in politics or any such nonsense. We're all depending on you,' he said.

'A few more months, mama, I'll be home and we'll take care of the problems,' Kannan replied. But he wasn't nearly as confident as he sounded. First there was the matter of Helen to be resolved, he thought. He was sure his father and mother would find her unsuitable. The daughter of a retired Anglo-Indian P&T employee, with neither money nor social standing, married to a Dorai! No, they would never allow that.

Two days later, Daniel sent for his son. He was propped up in bed, Lily and Ramdoss standing discreetly by. Instinctively, Kannan knew why he had been summoned. For just a moment he panicked, and then he was flooded with a strange calm.

'Son,' Daniel began heartily, 'Ramdoss tells me that the Government has locked up all those Congress leaders and is determined not to give in to their demands. I approve wholeheartedly. A few more months and you'll be a graduate and ready to take this burden,' he gestured around him, 'off my shoulders.' Kannan waited for the blow to fall.

'I'm old now and ready to rest. This is what I've always dreamed of: my son carrying on the line, taking charge of the family's fortunes, making sure the Dorai name doesn't lose its lustre.' Then came the announcement Kannan was dreading. 'It's time you settled down. Your mother and I have spoken to her cousin Isaac. He has a daughter of marriageable age. He's a modern man and has allowed the girl to finish college and learn Bharatanatyam. You will meet her when they come here for Christmas. Short engagement and you can be married by Easter.'

Dr Dorai smiled at his son.

Kannan's mind was a blank. Then he heard himself say, 'Appa, there's someone I want to marry.'

Perhaps Dr Dorai misheard him for he said, 'Good, then that's settled. You will like Shakuntala.'

'Appa, I have already decided to marry Helen.' He had said it.

Dr Dorai said irritably, 'Helen, who is Helen? What is her family? Do we know them? Which church do they worship in?'

Kannan answered slowly, 'Her father worked for the P&T Department. She's from Madras.'

'Are they related to us? What's her caste?'

He would have to say it. Better to do it quickly. 'Appa, you will like her. She's very fair and beautiful ...'

'That's all very well, but family is important. Is she an Andavar? God forbid she's a Vedhar!'

'She's an Anglo-Indian.'

'Ramu, go and cut a cane for me. My son has grown up but he thinks like a ten-year-old. I think I need to whip some sense into him.'

'Anna, steady, you shouldn't get excited.'

'Excited, excited. You heard him. He has told me he wants to marry some gold-digger he has found in Madras, and you tell me not to get excited ...'

Ramdoss turned to Kannan. 'Leave the room, thambi, we'll speak to you later.'

Not looking at any of them, Kannan left the room. The familiar sense of loneliness overcame him. Tears of anger, shame and humiliation clouded his eyes. As he walked away, he felt his unhappiness congeal within him. His misery dulled and settled. The tears stopped. He would no longer cry when he fought or found himself pushed into a corner.

A great anger consumed Daniel. How could his son let him down so badly, besmirch the dream he had given his life to, all over some scheming woman? Then, from deep in his mind, an image rose of himself at Kannan's age facing the wrath of Solomon Dorai. He had been haunted all his life by his father's inability to understand him, how could he behave exactly the same way towards Kannan? Other doubts crept in. He thought of his decision to drop the caste suffix from his name and was distressed that when it really mattered caste was still important to him. And so Daniel struggled with himself, as he attempted to see things from Kannan's point of view, tried to find a way out of his wrath. But the obduracy of the Dorais stood in the way of understanding. Although Daniel wrestled mightily with his nature it was unyielding and he gave up trying to fight it. He would not compromise. O Lord, he thought wearily, I am become my father.

69

Lily had a secret which she was quite sure she would take with her to her grave, and it was this: three years before she had married, she had fallen in love. The man she'd lost her heart to was a young Dutch creeper, a trainee manager on a tea plantation. He was briefly stationed on the estate where her father worked as head clerk and in that time Lily had absorbed as much as she could of him. From afar. Giddy with the excitement of a young girl who has never known a man, she would hide behind the luxuriant jackfruit tree in their garden, waiting for him to pass on his morning rounds. She would drink in the firm, clean-shaven jaw, the exotic eyes, the fine brown hair that flopped about his face, the peculiarly upright stance.

When he was transferred to another estate, she was not too upset for she hadn't expected anything to come of her infatuation. And, to her delight, she discovered that the man with the sea-blue eyes continued to visit her in her dreams as she waited for her betrothed across the Palk Strait to fix a date for their wedding. Her love was pure and chaste. What surprised her was that it remained with her for ever. Marriage, children, all the daily business of living, misted over the memory of the young Dutchman, but on the day of her son's revelation, it glowed in her mind again. Even though she was as alarmed as her husband by Kannan's declaration and hoped that his romance would fade, her heart was on his side.

Confronting her husband would achieve nothing. She wasn't even sure she was capable of it. But she wasn't disheartened. These situations occurred from time to time in every family and all it took was time, and subtle persuasion, to sort things out. Also, while her husband possessed the legendary stubbornness of the Dorais, she was aware that he attempted, as best he could, to temper it with fair-mindedness and objectivity, especially where the family was concerned. He would come round, of that she was sure, in a while.

She worried more about Kannan. In his case, the explosive rage which every Dorai was capable of was augmented by the volatility and emotional imbalance of youth. She tried to explain to him that his father's rejection of him was temporary, that peace would be made, that he should be patient. But Kannan would not listen. No amount of tears could budge him an inch. Knowing the effect his intransigence would have on Daniel, Lily grew frantic. She persuaded

Ramdoss to write to everyone she could think of, pleading for employment for Kannan, when, as now seemed certain, he was exiled from Doraipuram. Of the replies they received, the most promising was a letter from Chris Cooke in distant Surrey that arrived just before the college reopened. A friend of his ran a tea company and was looking for managers to replace his young English Assistants who were going off to war. Kannan might be just what he wanted. Cooke had already written to his friend and was also enclosing a letter of introduction that Kannan might find useful.

70

When Kannan's train reached Tambaram, he deposited his luggage in his room, washed and changed and went over to Helen's house. She wasn't in but her father was, already tipping back his second glass of rum in the warmth of the evening. 'Have a drink, men, it's good to see you back. Helen'll be here soon.' What wonderful people the Anglo-Indians were, he thought, grateful for the warmth of Leslie's welcome. Generous, open and full of life, how could anyone not like them? Why couldn't his father see them the way he did?

Helen returned in an hour or so. As he watched her walking up the road, a great happiness welled up within him, wiping away the misery of the past weeks. Helen's face brightened when she saw Kannan. She had grown fond of him and his unquestioning adoration was good for her vanity. She was quite sure she didn't love him, but that was all right because he was rich, and it always helped in a relationship if the less loving one was you. Cynthia had given her this last bit of advice.

'How's your dad?' Helen asked.

'He's well. How are you?'

'I'm fine. Have a rum, men,' she said, kissing her father.

Kannan settled for a small drink and they moved out on to the porch and sat down. Helen primly extended her hand and Kannan grasped it eagerly. In the two years and more that they had known each other, this was the only liberty she had permitted him. Kannan was telling her how much he loved her when she interrupted, 'How did your visit go?'

'Poorly,' he said irritably. 'I told my father that I was in love with you and wanted to marry you and he threw me out of the house.'

Helen jerked her hand away. A wave of anger and frustration swept over her. To think she had wasted her time on this insignificant fool. 'You didn't think I'd marry you, did you?' she stormed. 'Forget it, I don't want to ever see you again.'

Kannan flared up as well. 'Go and marry one of those stupid hockey players you used to hang around with before you met me then,' he yelled, his liking for the community vanishing for the moment.

'The least of them is better than you,' she screamed back.

'And to think I defied my father for someone as worthless as you,' he shouted, but Helen had already disappeared into the house.

For a week, the pure flame of his anger kept him going. For generations, the Dorai men had looked upon their women as pliant creatures, who would do their every bidding, and it was only his overweening infatuation that had changed the way Kannan regarded Helen. Now he raved and ranted to anyone who would listen, usually Murthy, about how stupid he had been to come to the brink of ruining himself on account of a woman.

Once his rage had died down, he discovered to his dismay that he was as much in love with Helen as ever. She filled his every waking moment and denied him sleep. Hating himself for doing so, but powerless to stop himself, he began to hang around her house, and was sometimes rewarded with a glimpse of her, the confident swinging walk, the small breasts, the shapely calves, filling his sight, his senses, with delight and pain. She would always ignore him and on the two occasions he actually summoned up the nerve to knock at the door and ask for her, she locked herself in her room and refused to emerge until Leslie told him gently to leave.

Kannan found himself brooding over his father's reaction. If he'd only taken the news differently, he thought angrily, none of this would have happened. Then Helen disappeared. When he inquired about her, Leslie told him that she had gone to visit relatives in the city, and that he had no idea when she intended to return. His days and nights grew even more oppressive. Now he didn't even have the prospect of seeing her.

One evening as he was returning to college, he saw Cynthia walking towards him. He hadn't seen her for days and was quick to accost her: 'Cynthia, I must see Helen, you know ...'

Something in his aspect must have touched her, because her

expression softened and she said quite kindly, 'Listen, men, forget Helen, she's not for you, there'll be other girls. Go make up with your daddy. It's not worth it.'

He made no reply, but his disappointment showed plainly on his face. She made as if to say something, then shrugged and walked on. He was moving away when she called out to him, 'Hey, men ...'

He turned, hope freshening his face, but Cynthia had little that was new to offer: 'You're a smart chap, go back home, make money, get married ...'

'But I want to, don't you see? To Helen. Will you talk to her, Cynthia, tell her I'll get a good job. We won't need my father's money, I'll make sure she'll live like a princess. I'm sorry I shouted at her, but I lost control of myself. You know, if she will only trust me, give me one chance, she'll never regret it in this life or in all her lives to come.'

Cynthia looked slightly bemused.

'Please, please, Cynthia, please tell me you'll talk to her, you're the only one she'll listen to. Please tell her that I'll do everything in my power to make her happy if she decides to stay with me.'

'Was she ever yours, I wonder?' Cynthia said.

'I don't know, but if she was mine, I'd make sure that she never regretted it.'

'And how would you do that, men?'

'I'll get a big job. I have a letter of recommendation from a very important man, Mr Chris Cooke, a senior ICS officer. I'll be better off than I ever could have been working for my father. Please tell her, Cynthia, I know you can do it ...'

'Well,' Cynthia said, looking dubious, 'I'm not promising anything, but I'll see what I can do.'

'Thank you, thank you,' he said fervently. 'Tell her that all I want is to talk to her. Try and convince her that things will work out all right.'

Two weeks later, Cynthia proved as good as her word. One of his hockey team-mates banged on Kannan's door early in the morning and said jovially, 'Wake up, you good-for-nothing son-of-a-whore. Cynthia wants to talk to you.' When Kannan opened the door, Philip said cheerfully, 'Eleven o'clock at Nair's,' and sauntered off.

Cynthia was sitting with some friends, but as Kannan approached, they got up and left with friendly waves. A burst of laughter, and they were gone. Had they been laughing at him? Probably, but he didn't care. Kannan ordered two glasses of tea with extra sugar, then turned eagerly to Cynthia. 'Will she see me?'

'Yes, I've persuaded her to see you, just the once ...'

'Cynthia, you're amazing. You've worked a miracle. How can I ever thank you?'

'By calming down and listening to me. I've got Helen to agree to talk to you, not accept you as her husband. Nothing might come of your meeting, so don't get your hopes up.' Their tea arrived, steaming hot in dirty-looking glasses. Cynthia looked at him, long and speculatively, then said more kindly, 'You're really in love with her, I can tell that much.'

'I would stop at nothing to please her. I'd strip the sky of its clouds and make a bed for her to lie on.'

'A poet,' Cynthia said with a smile. 'I believe you'd do all that and more. And Helen knows it. Probably knows too that you love her more than all the others.'

'There have been others?' Kannan said.

Cynthia's face took on a wisdom beyond her years. Despite his overwrought state, Kannan had a flash of insight. He saw the pretty nineteen-year-old two decades from now, a stout lady in a shapeless dress, with at least a dozen children but with a heart big enough to accommodate a thousand more. She would put up with a demanding husband, cantankerous neighbours, the myriad annoyances of a lower-middle-class existence in a poor country, but she would also be the backbone of her locality – a fund of wisdom and patience and tolerance. Cynthia didn't know it yet, but there was an unquenchable humanity within her that the world would crowd to.

'There will always be others for beautiful girls like Helen. The only problem in a hypocritical society like ours is that men have fantasies about girls like us, but never respect us. Some of you lust after us from afar just because we wear skirts and pants and go to dances, others whisper to us under their breath, or brush past us on trains. And then there are our own boys, people like Philip and Sammy and your friend Lionel, who are the sort of people that Helen and I will end up marrying, even if they will never be rich or famous, because they love us for what we are, beyond the lust they feel for us, and because they aren't hypocritical double-dealing Indian bastards.' Having delivered herself of this, Cynthia sat back, her nostrils flaring with anger. Kannan was stunned by her outburst, not least because of the profanity he had heard. From a girl!

Cynthia smiled, a smile that was much too cynical for her age, and said, 'Shocked? I'm sorry. You're quite decent for an Indian. And don't go thinking badly of me because of the bad words I use and because I said Helen and I have had other boys fall in love with us. We're both of us good girls, and we can't help it if boys keep asking us out. But we don't do bad things, as you Indians think.'

'Why do you keep calling us Indians? Aren't you Indians too?'

'No. We hate this country and we want to go home. To England or Ireland. My grandfather was Irish, and Helen's was a British sergeant posted here.'

'Have you ever met your grandfather?' Kannan asked.

'No. Yes,' she said, flustered. 'I mean, he's dead.'

'Have you ever been to Ireland?'

'I'm going next month, as soon as I can get my passage booked,' she said, then quickly changed the subject.

'Do you love Helen very much?' she asked.

'I love her with every fibre of my being.'

'Oh, yes!' Cynthia laughed, and then she turned serious.

'You adore her, Kannan, so you have elevated her to the position of a goddess, free from every blemish, but I'm her closest friend. I've known her since we were little girls playing in the alleys of a dingy government colony. The walls of our houses were so thin you could hear the neighbours fart. There is no privacy in places like that, Kannan, and when you're best friends ...' She shrugged. 'I want only the best for her. But I know her faults. I know when her breath smells bad, and she has said something stupid. I know her secrets. Things that you will probably never know. But this much I can tell you. Her deepest desire is not to end up in one of the colonies she grew up in. She would like, best of all, to live in England. Do you think you could manage that ...'

Kannan stammered, 'I ... I ... could ... try ...'

But Cynthia went on as though she hadn't heard him. 'Failing that, she would like to be married to a man who has status and money and a position in society. A nice house, a car, a job. You won't like me saying this, but that is why she encouraged you, because of your father's money and name. She's not a bad girl, and it's not a bad thing to want the things she wants, and she does like you a lot.'

'I will make her happy,' Kannan said, glad to be able to say something.

'How?' she asked. 'If you marry Helen, your father will never take you back, you're a college student with no money, no prospects. Nothing. Why should Helen accept you?'

'I'll work hard, get good marks. I'm sure I'll get an excellent job because of Mr Chris Cooke's recommendation.'

'Why has he given you a recommendation, if your father's so angry with you?' Cynthia asked suspiciously.

'I don't know.'

'Use it then. Study hard, get the best job in the world, and then maybe you'll have a chance with Helen.'

'I'll do it, just wait and see. You don't know about us Dorais,' he said.

'See you do. And now I suppose you'll want to know when you can see her.'

'Yes, yes, yes ...'

'Next week. But she will only see you when I'm around. And after this meeting, you are to communicate with her only through me ...'

Kannan hardly heard her as, his eyes shining and his heart thundering in his ears, he fell to contemplating his meeting with the woman who had given him no rest.

'Lucky Helen,' Cynthia said softly to herself.

71

The interview that Chris Cooke had set up for Kannan with Major Stevenson, the General Manager of the Pulimed Tea Company, had gone very well indeed. He would start work at the end of the year on their estates, located high in the central Travancore hills across the border. He would be the first Indian creeper the company had ever hired. On the train back to Tambaram, he thought how happy Helen would be. He could see just how they would be, in a very short time from now, splendid and certain of their place in the world. Then his mind flew back to the days in Doraipuram and the showdown with his father. If they hadn't fought, he was sure appa would have been proud of him, making his mark in the white man's world. And then it occurred to him that if his father had not rejected him, he would never have had this opportunity. And now there was nothing for Kannan to do but to strike out on his own, show his father what he was made of.

The train began to slow down as it approached the station, and his mood brightened. The future was opening up for him. For them.

BOOK III

PULIMED

72

The great German battleship, *Bismarck*, swirled rapidly down the storm drain, harried by her pursuers, the aircraft carrier *Ark Royal* and HMSS *King George V* and *Rodney*. 'Tishkwoo-tishkwoo,' went the *Bismarck*'s guns, but the waves of American dive-bombers were unrelenting in their attack, and the British gunners in the ships that followed fired with deadly accuracy. It was clear that the *Bismarck* didn't stand a chance. 'Krea-aagh.' The HMSS *Victorious* had just loosed off a torpedo. 'Brrhoom.' A direct hit. The principal architect of the *Bismarck*'s destruction, eight-year-old Andrew Fraser, pressed his second-in-command, Kannan Dorai, into service. 'You take the *Victorious*, Mr Dorai. I want you to move her to that side, and go "Krea-aagh".'

'Can't I make some other noise?' Kannan asked.

'No, you cannot,' Andrew said firmly. 'Krea-aagh is a torpedo noise, and you must make a torpedo noise because HMSS *Victorious* is firing torpedoes.'

'Yes, sir,' Kannan said, positioning his ship as directed. Satisfied, the little boy went back to the sinking of the *Bismarck*. His knowledge of World War II was encyclopaedic and Kannan had little doubt that the armature, guns, speed and tonnage of every ship, plane and support craft in the battle that was being enacted was absolutely correct.

'A little more to your right, Mr Dorai. Torpedoes away.'

'Aye, aye, sir,' Kannan said, making his torpedo noise. This was drowned by an even louder noise, as the *Bismarck* began to founder. A succession of tearing and wrenching sounds issued from Andrew's mouth and the 45,000-ton ship started breaking up. In moments it was over.

'Let's do it all over again. Maybe this time, the *Bismarck* can be the *Graf Spee*. I want to try and see if I can make the sound of her shells being fired.' Kannan was impatient to go for a walk, but he didn't really want to disappoint the little boy. He'd try and speed up the battle, that way he'd still be able to stretch his legs before they started for the club. If the rains held off, that was.

As Andrew began gathering up the ships, preparatory to beginning the next battle, Kannan wandered to the edge of the garden. Looking out across the mist-filled valley he could see that the monsoon had truly set in.

Kannan had never experienced anything like the rainy season in the hills. Up in the high tea country it drizzled most of the year anyway, but during the monsoon the rain spat continuously down from a sky the colour of chilled steel. Unlike the warm downpour of Doraipuram, the rain in the hills was cold. And it never let up. Day after day, he would struggle into clothes that never seemed dry and walk into a world where the sky hung low, grey and troubled. Great banks of cloud and mist (it was hard to tell where the one began and the other ended) were hurled across the cowering hills by driving wind and rain.

But, unlike most of the other planters, Kannan actually liked the monsoon. He wouldn't have minded his clothes drying faster and an umbrella that was designed to cope with Pulimed thunderstorms, but he enjoyed the cold and the wet, the constant sound of water echoing through the misty hills and valleys and the aqueous daylight. He didn't mind that he almost never saw the sun. And he was mesmerized by the mist. He loved the feel of it on his face, and its infinite malleability and movement. He could spend hours watching it, stirring restlessly or streaming noiselessly across the tea, standing still in the hollows or filtering smokily through the trees – a great ivory vastness that altered the material world he gazed upon, so it seemed he was in a dream. And then, abruptly, movement of water within air, a swift ever-expanding flurry, and the mist would lift from the quiet world, leaving it fresh-minted and refreshed, every colour burnished, every surface new. After the tired, dusty, heat-bruised plain, this was magic and he let it enter him freely.

He had arrived in Pulimed a little over six months ago and had been assigned as a creeper to Michael Fraser, the Superintendent of Glenclare Estate, the largest of the three estates owned by the Pulimed Tea Company. Glenclare had over a thousand acres of tea, constituted into two divisions. The Morningfall division's Assistant had gone off to fight in the Burma campaign, and if Kannan did well during his year as a creeper he would be promoted to that position.

He felt someone tugging at his sleeve. Andrew was impatient to begin the next battle. He had just got the little ships, skilfully fashioned out of bamboo, wooden clothes pegs and matches, ready for action and was demanding that Kannan join him at play. The storm drain was enveloped by the sounds of war once more.

After the *Graf Spee* was blown up, Andrew suggested they go and hunt for leeches in the old quarry behind the house, where the rain-water pooled during the monsoon. Kannan hated leeches but was saved from refusing the boy by the appearance of Andrew's father.

Michael Fraser was lanky, with a lugubrious cast to his face, and a wonderful smile that transformed his entire countenance. Kannan had taken to him instantly, as he had to Michael's wife, Belinda. And the liking was mutual. A lot of Kannan's colleagues had been unsure how to take the news of his appointment when the General Manager had announced it. For his part, Michael had been worried about how his wife would react to the announcement that he was bringing an Indian to spend a year in their spare bedroom. But it had all gone smoothly. Kannan was well-spoken and polite, and after his initial nervousness, had fitted nicely into the household. Michael was pleased that Belinda and Andrew had taken to his young Indian creeper. They led lonely enough lives, and it made a big difference to them to have someone else around.

As far as Kannan was concerned, if things hadn't gone so smoothly he doubted that he would have survived on the estates. Despite his liking for his superior and the weather, he'd been unhappy during the first couple of months in Pulimed. This was partly because he realized he might never see Doraipuram again, but had more to do with the reality of Pulimed. He was amazed at how white and 'foreign' the tea district was. He'd had English professors at college of course, but here India had been pushed to the margins. It had seemed that *he* was the outsider. Fortunately for him, he'd adapted quickly and had soon begun to enjoy the place.

'Who's winning?' Michael asked, as he walked up to them.

'We are, of course,' Andrew said acerbically. Grown-ups could be so stupid.

'Yes, we've got the *Bismarck* and now the *Graf Spee* in great trouble,' Kannan remarked.

'I wish you could work the same magic on the Japanese, Andrew. They're giving us a pasting,' Michael said.

'Do they have any big ships?'

'Yes, several. I'll give you details soon.'

'And planes?'

'Yes, those too. But at the rate the Nips are going, I won't have to give you the information, you'll soon be able to see them fly overhead.'

'Really?' Andrew said, his precious ships abandoned for the moment at this new and exciting prospect.

'Well, not yet. They're nowhere near us. Things are not that bad yet.'

They weren't, but they were bad enough. On the wall of his study, Michael had pinned a large-scale map of the Burma front on which he traced in red crayons, borrowed from his son, the progress of the Japanese divisions. They were now alarmingly close to the Indian border, bogged down in the thick forests of Burma by the monsoon. 'Time for dinner and bed, little man,' Michael said to his son. Andrew's ships gathered up, father and son went back into the house.

Leaving the boy in the care of the ayah, the Frasers and Kannan set off for the club. It had started raining again, a miserable drizzle that pattered on the roof of the Humber and thickened the mist that pressed in on every side. Michael drove very carefully, but the road was a familiar one, and there was no other vehicle about, so they made good progress. At the club, Michael and Kannan headed for the bar. Belinda made her way to the ladies' lounge, irreverently christened the Snakepit, especially when Mrs Stevenson presided over it.

Kannan disliked their weekly visits to the club. Its myriad customs and rules unnerved him. His usual practice was to shield himself from view behind Michael or Freddie Hamilton, the young Assistant at Westview, the other division of Glenclare Estate. He would stick as close as possible to Michael tonight, he resolved, as they pushed open the door and were immediately enveloped in a warm fug of cigarette smoke and whisky fumes.

The bar was comfortable, with well-padded armchairs, a bridge table in a corner, and a long straight bar of highly polished teak behind which Timmy, the ancient barman, presided. To the left of Timmy was a hatch through which the ladies were served their drinks. A log fire blazed in the fireplace. A worm-eaten leopard and a stuffed tiger graced the room, this last pressed into service as an extra chair on crowded evenings.

It was early and there were very few people in the room, to Kannan's relief. He found it easier to deal with the other planters if he was already settled in when they started arriving. They greeted their boss, Major Stevenson, who was seated at the bridge table, waiting for the other regulars to arrive. As Michael and Major Stevenson chatted, Kannan looked around for a place to sit. Spotting empty chairs next to Freddie Hamilton, he went across to greet him. Freddie was an amiable-looking young man, with bulging brown eyes concealed behind thick spectacles. 'Hullo there, Cannon. Looks like you need a drink,' he said with a smile.

'And here's our master,' he added in a whisper, as he rose to greet Michael. Drinks were ordered. Once they were comfortably settled, Michael said, 'Okay, spit it out, Freddie. I could see from across the room that there was some story you were dying to spill.' Freddie's storytelling skills were legendary.

'Oh, no, sir,' Freddie said, 'nothing new ...'

'You're going to have to change your preamble soon,' Michael said with a laugh.

'Gosh, am I getting predictable? That's worrying,' Freddie replied lightly.

Just then Patrick Gordon, one of the other Superintendents in the company, burst upon their group, and unceremoniously took over the conversation. It was clear that Gordon was upset. A scar, high on his cheek, glowed strawberry-red, a sure sign that he was in the grip of high emotion. 'Have you heard?' he began, slumping into a chair. 'The blasted coolie who assaulted Simon Raines has been let off with a slap on the wrist.'

The Raines incident had electrified the district just before the rainy season. A planter in Periyar, Simon Raines, had instructed his head gardener, an old man, to finish clearing a rocky, overgrown strip of land, where his wife intended to plant a bed of hollyhocks. Coming home early for lunch, he had found the old man dozing in the shade of a tree, the work on the plot barely started. In a fury, he had walked over and kicked him in the chest. The gardener had toppled on his side, blood oozing from his mouth and nostrils. When he was taken to the estate hospital, massive internal haemorrhaging had been diagnosed. He was given whatever medication was available on the spot, but had died during the night. The planter had tried to hush the matter up, but someone had reported it to the police. Hard bargaining by the white planters had managed to reduce the charge against Raines to simple assault, and it was only a matter of time before Raines, British and therefore entitled to have his case heard before a British judge in Madras, would walk free with a fine. But it wasn't to be so. Barely a week after the outrage, when he was relaxing on his veranda with a drink, a young coolie had walked up to him and split open his skull with a pruning knife before the horrified eyes of his wife and butler. The assailant had then thrown away the knife and calmly waited for the police. The blow had been a glancing one, and the best medical attention had saved Raines, though his speech would forever be slurred. In his defence, the coolie, the gardener's son as it turned out, had said only, 'What would you do if your father was kicked in the chest?' And now he had been let off with a small fine. By an Indian magistrate!

'In the old days, he would have been whipped to death. That's the only treatment these natives understand. If you ask me, the only good native ...' he stopped short, realizing Kannan was part of the group, and then continued, '... coolie is an obedient coolie, or a dead one.' He glared at Kannan as if he found the sight of him too distasteful to bear, heaved himself out of his chair, and left.

Kannan couldn't hide the discomfort he felt, and Michael was quick to speak. 'Don't mind Patrick, Cannon. His heart's all right. He's just a bit slow to change.'

At the bridge table, Major Stevenson and his regular bridge partner, a senior superintendent of the Travancore Planting Company, were also discussing the Raines incident.

'Shocking, I say. Wonder what the country's coming to?'

'What would you have done if someone had kicked your father in the chest, John, old boy?'

'But damn it, are you suggesting that a coolie get away with something like that?'

'No, I'm not,' Major Stevenson replied. 'All I'm saying is that the provocation existed, and in these changing times, it isn't entirely surprising.'

The other planter said sharply, 'Edward, do I hear right? Do you really think times have changed so much that puffed-up little natives can be insolent to Englishmen?'

'Of course not, but it's their country after all, John.'

'And look at what a mess they've made of it. Constant skirmishing, Hindu against Muslim, as if anyone cared, all those ridiculous maharajahs, and now a bunch of thugs posing as nationalist politicians.'

'Surely not, John. Nehru, Gandhi and many of the Congress lot have a first-rate pedigree.'

'Earned back home. And what do we get? Ingratitude. All of them should be left to rot in prison for life. The cheek of it, refusing to co-operate with us in the war. Where would they be without us? They'd have little yellow men telling them what to do. No, these Indians just don't know what's good for them. We offer them Dominion status, and what do they demand? Total independence! Total independence, forsooth, they'd go back to being the ignorant little heathens they were before we came along.'

'My word, John, I wouldn't have suspected that you nursed such strong emotions.'

His bridge partner looked slightly embarrassed, then guffawed and said, 'Look, let's forget this bloody country and get on with the game.'

Throughout the bar, as liquor flowed and tongues loosened, the voices grew louder and more boisterous. The planters took their club nights seriously, particularly now that the country was threatened by war. By the time they were ready to leave, Michael was slightly tipsy. He walked carefully out of the room, an anxious Kannan in tow. Belinda waited for them by the entrance. The cool night air seemed to sharpen Michael's focus. He scrambled behind the wheel of the Humber and they set off.

The rain had stopped but the mist lay thick and unmoving on the road, and Michael drove with great caution. They could see nothing beyond a couple of feet. An hour or so of this, and they were close to the biggest stream on their route. It had been christened Dhobi's Leap after a washerman was drowned in it one rainy season. Local legend had it that on moonless nights you could still hear the luckless dhobi's screams as he was washed away. Whether haunted or not, the sound of falling water, unseen in the mist and darkness, was a curiously desolate one. For all his love of the climate, Kannan shivered as the car slowly nosed forward. When Michael eased the car into the torrent and the water pushed at it, all three of them felt a moment of sheer terror. The Humber began to slide. But then the wheels gripped and they were safely over. The rest of the road back was easier, and they were home in half an hour.

Although he was very tired, Kannan could not sleep. A thump on the roof made him start. When he had first come to Pulimed, he had almost run out of his bedroom in panic when the noises had started up on the roof. Moans and thuds, a prolonged rumble as though something was being dragged along, a stealthy shuffle ending abruptly in a crash ... there had been a regular orchestra going on above his head. He had mentioned the noises casually to Belinda the next morning and she had laughed it off. 'Oh, rats. I mean, there are rats on the roof. And civet cats, probably an owl, a snake or two.'

'Snakes!' he had said.

'Nothing to worry about,' she'd said reassuringly. 'In the old days, the ceilings used to be made of cloth and there was a possibility something would fall on you during the night, but now there's no danger of that. You just have to get used to the noise.'

Over time he had come to ignore the commotion on the roof, but tonight it took on a new malevolence. Freddie had spent a lot of the evening telling spooky stories, and now these began to take effect. What if there were ghosts up there, along with the rats and the snakes and the owls? Damn you, Freddie, he thought. What possessed you to tell us horror stories on a cold misty night!

Rain started drumming on the tin roof of the bungalow, a rhythmic, immensely soothing sound. Sleep came finally. Just before it did, Helen appeared before him, as he had first seen her. Slim, tripping down the road in a long flowery skirt.

73

They were married six months later, in what passed for spring in Madras. Kannan was relieved to find he wasn't sweating in the heavy wool suit he wore. It had been specially made for the occasion by Pulimed's sole tailor, a genius at copying though his finish wasn't perfect and the insides of his suits sometimes made their wearers want to scratch themselves. Kannan's suit was an exact replica of one Freddie had bought in London four years ago. It had been quite in vogue then.

The wedding took place in the old church by the railway station. The golden light of late evening washed over Helen as she came up the aisle and the nervousness Kannan had been beset by all evening vanished, to be replaced by exhilaration. Beautiful women have such an advantage over cloddish men like me, he thought happily; they can rule the world by crooking their little fingers. It was evident God had created them to roam free and delight the world. Helen had agreed to be his, however, and he was so beside himself with excitement that he almost couldn't bear it.

Murthy, his best man, had been coached to take care of every eventuality by Helen's relatives and the priest. 'Be sure he doesn't bolt or pass out from sheer nervousness,' Helen's father had remarked cryptically. 'These things have been known to happen to men getting married.' The advice stuck in Murthy's mind, which was why he was quick to act when his friend swayed towards him, pincering Kannan's elbow with strong fingers. The bridegroom's world came back into focus and the wedding passed off without any further hitch.

Later there was dancing and music and tables groaning with food in the bride's house – great platters of mutton cutlets, a huge bowl of fried pork, mounds of rice, beef curry and railway chicken. There was scarcely a vegetable in sight. Murthy had to content himself with a little rice and potato gravy. But otherwise everyone had the time of their lives. No one knew how to enjoy themselves better than the Anglo-Indians, and they were determined to do their beautiful Helen proud. Everywhere you looked, there was laughter and music and gaiety.

The only still point in the room was where Lily, resplendent in a maroon Conjeevaram sari, and three of her Madras relatives stood. It had taken a lot of pressure and patience on her part to get Daniel's permission for her to attend the wedding, but he'd given in eventually, as she'd always known he would. In time the breach would heal, she was sure of that, if her husband's health held up, and her son's impetuosity was tamed. But these were things to worry about later; for now, she would need to be glad for her son and his bride. She'd intended to be present only at the actual wedding in church, but Kannan had insisted she come to the reception and she had allowed herself to be persuaded. She had come all this way for her son's marriage, and if she felt uncomfortable among people she didn't know, it was a small price to pay for his happiness.

But she was completely unprepared for the frenzied partying that had greeted her when she walked into the Turner house. The party was nowhere near its peak but it was still like nothing she had ever seen. She huddled together with her relatives, not making too much eye contact and evading all but the most necessary connections with the other guests. As the evening lengthened, her discomfort lessened, especially when she began to see how elated her son was. She watched him dance with his pretty bride, and reflected wonderingly about love and its effects. In our community it isn't given too much importance, she thought, it is accepted that the union of two families demands stronger bonds than those conferred by a fleeting euphoric link between two young people who lack any real experience of life. But she hoped that the great love her son obviously bore his wife would see him through the years ahead until she was able to bring him back into the family fold.

'Amma, do you know Murthy?' Kannan was standing before her with his friend.

'Yes, I do. You introduced him to me just before the service.'

'So I did, how forgetful of me.' Kannan looked happy and flustered and young, and her heart went out to him. May you and your bride be happy, she murmured to herself. My prayers and thoughts will always be with you.

Soon it was time for her to go. As the car taking his mother and her relatives pulled away, Kannan felt a momentary sadness. There would be no celebrations at Doraipuram. And then a wave of anger rose within him. If his people didn't care enough about him to overcome their misgivings, he wouldn't let that affect him.

After his mother had gone, Murthy and Kannan stood together, feeling a little left out of the proceedings. The party careened on as madly as before.

'These people really know how to have a good time,' Murthy said.

'Exactly what I was thinking. I don't think we fellows can keep up,' Kannan replied with a laugh. The music flowing from expertly strummed guitars and crashing maracas rose to a crescendo and blotted out any further idea of conversation. Cynthia whirled Murthy away, and Kannan hurried up to his bride. She smiled at him and the world reassembled itself into perfect order.

As the party intensified, old ladies, dumpy in crumpled frocks, took to the makeshift dance floor. Demonstrating an astonishing agility and quickness of step that belied their age, they waltzed and foxtrotted, twirling like faded parasols with partners as ancient as themselves in threadbare if neatly pressed jackets. Handsome boys practised being studiedly cool as they partnered brightly apparelled, noisy girls who were as self-conscious as the boys.

At midnight, the festivities showed no signs of abating. Leslie had retreated to his favourite armchair and lolled comfortably in it. 'She'll fix you, son. Now that she doesn't have to keep me honest,' he said to Kannan with a loud bellow of laughter. Helen pretended to glare at her father, and Kannan smiled.

He had wanted to leave for Pulimed immediately after the wedding but it took four days for Helen to say goodbye to all her friends, including, Kannan noted sourly, virtually the entire Railways hockey team. He tried his best to keep up with her, valiantly drinking rum by the glassful and even allowing himself to be persuaded to dance on one occasion. By the evening of the third day, however, he'd had enough of partying, and busied himself instead with preparations for their journey.

Lily had given him some money as a wedding present, and by

combining this with his scanty savings, he had scraped together enough to buy a motorcycle, the essential accessory of every young Assistant on the estates. He managed to get an imposing Norton, the king of motorcycles, for a good price. On the test drive, Kannan had enjoyed the feel of the machine, although the crowded Madras streets weren't the best place to get a sense of its power. That could wait until it was delivered to Pulimed.

At the railway station, where he had gone to confirm their tickets, he heard worrying news. Terrorist activity was anticipated on the Madras–Madura line, and there was a possibility that the train would be cancelled. Kannan was frantic. He'd only been granted a week's leave and they had to get to Madura on schedule. No guarantees, the stationmaster said firmly. Come tomorrow and check. Disconsolately Kannan motored home. As he left Madras Central Station, he saw a slogan emblazoned in foot-high letters on the wall of the building across the road:

THE BRITISH HAVE GONE TO WAR
TO PROTECT THE WORLD'S FREEDOM!

And below that:

WHY CAN'T THEY GIVE US OUR FREEDOM?

The last line was familiar:

QUIT INDIA!

By early 1944, most of the Congress leadership had been imprisoned by the British. But the agitation and demands for freedom continued. In the hills, however, all the planters seemed to care about was the war. It was as if the nationalist ferment was just a minor irrelevancy. India intruded, if at all, in the shape of the servants that every memsahib commanded; in the bearers and tennis markers at the clubs; the wretched coolies and tea-pluckers in the fields; the tea-makers and the factory workers. The more bigoted and uncaring planters could scarcely distinguish one from the other. Everything proclaimed the supremacy of the rulers – the princely bungalows with vast gardens and manicured lawns for the couples from Basingstoke or Dartford, the determined imposition of a rather overblown Englishness on the rhythms of India. What would happen to all this if nationalism suddenly rose up and swallowed everything? Kannan hoped revolution would hold off for a bit, though. He had to get to Madura tomorrow.

When they arrived at the station, they were relieved to find that their train was to leave on time. It was the first time they had been alone together, if you discounted the others in their second-class compartment – Leslie had pulled some strings to get them into a relatively empty compartment. Kannan was nervous all over again. He needn't have been, for Helen was so exhausted from all the partying she had done that she promptly fell asleep and did not wake up until the train reached Madura.

Michael's Humber and driver, on loan for the journey home, were waiting at the station when they arrived. Kannan wondered whether they should see the one obligatory sight the town offered, the Meenakshi temple, before they left, especially as he'd never managed to see it the couple of times he had passed through Madura. In the end, they decided to drive by it. They parked the Humber by the side of the road, ousting four cows, and gazed up at the intricately designed southern gopuram, the most imposing of the gateways of the temple. Helen soon tired of this, but Kannan was sucked into the mass of sculpture and design that writhed across the stone, even though he didn't understand the mythological implications and, moreover, had little or no interest in religion or art. What effort must have gone into the hundreds of thousands of carvings! Kannan felt a sudden desire to know what his life would be devoted to, what his life's work would be. Would he make his mark on the world that he had been plunged into? Would his exquisite bride be proud of him? He was young and strong and he had a lifetime to find out. But now was no time for philosophizing; he was impatient to show his bride his world.

74

The drive back to the estate was everything Kannan could have hoped for. No sooner had they left the brawling heat of the plains behind, than the hills began to place their enchantments before them. Forests quiet with rain, and valleys where clouds came to rest. A huge grey rock-face on which dozens of waterfalls unravelled like dirty white yarn, next to a piney hillside awash with great swatches of pink and yellow roses. The mossy smell, the hills helmeted with tea or forest, the sound of running water, the fresh cold breeze on their faces – every sense was pleasantly assaulted, all at once. They stopped for lunch by an ice-cold stream in which pale fish flickered like random thoughts. 'Oh Kannan, this is so beautiful, I'm so very happy,' Helen said ecstatically. Across from where they sat, a small rain had begun to fall while the sun still shone, dusting the hillside with a million glittering shards of light. 'So, so beautiful,' she breathed.

'You'll love the house too,' he said, so delighted by her exhilaration that the nervousness he felt at being alone with her disappeared. At least for a while. They stopped just once after lunch, to take in the view. As they got out of the car, Pulimed lay before them. It was a sunny day, and every detail of its beauty was sharply etched, though the mist had already begun smoking out of the crevices and crags of the hills, streaming across the tea bushes that democratically massed on every slope as far as the eye could see. Even as they watched, the world blurred, the tea, the hills, the tiny human settlements gradually disappearing into the watery maw of the mist, until all that remained was the occasional lake or tin-roofed factory gleaming like a polished silver incisor.

They reached Morningfall bungalow to which Kannan had moved barely a month ago, when he had been promoted to Assistant. As the Humber drew into the driveway, Helen reached across and gripped Kannan's hand tightly, her eyes gleaming with excitement. 'This is where we're going to live?' she gasped. He nodded.

The bungalow stood in a little clearing hacked out of a hill. Tall eucalyptus trees, their trunks grey and ghostly in the evening light, fringed the front garden, beyond which the hill fell away steeply. Against a backdrop of tea, hollyhocks nodded their heads in the breeze. Petunias, gerberas, camellias and phlox coloured the garden. Crag martins swooped and soared though the darkening air.

Helen jumped out of the car and hurried into the house, barely acknowledging the four servants who were waiting outside, hands folded in deep namaskarams. She gazed entranced around the living room with its deep bay windows commanding an extraordinary view of the valley. It was the size of the house, however, and its profusion of rooms that amazed her. What a distance she had travelled, she thought, from the grubby three-room houses in a succession of government colonies!

She had dreamed of marrying someone who could spirit her overseas to live the life of a memsahib but her imagination could never quite put colours and shapes into that dream. But this! She could touch, feel, see it, and it was hers. She fell to dreaming of the parties she would throw in the living room with its comfortable armchairs, its wine-red carpet, the matching drapes. It was all so rich, so confident. She couldn't bear it, she was so happy.

'Do you like it?' Kannan said behind her. She whirled around to face him. And then spontaneously caught him up in a tremendous embrace. 'I love it,' she shrieked.

Disentangling herself from him she raced from the sitting room into the passage, darted into the spare bedroom, their own bedroom, buried her face in the soft furry towels in the bathroom and then whirled into the dining room with its shiny polished teak table that could seat eight. A long roofed corridor connected the main house with the kitchen and the servants' quarters beyond.

By Pulimed's standards, Morningfall was a small bungalow, but it was more magnificent than anything she had ever seen.

'Did you do it up yourself?' she asked.

'No, no, don't be silly. Belinda has wonderful taste, and she was most helpful.'

'Who is Belinda?' his wife asked him. 'Is she some gorgeous English rose who has seduced my darling Kannan?'

He made an inarticulate noise, then managed to speak. 'No, no, nothing like that, she's the Superintendent's wife, Mrs Fraser.'

'Of course, silly,' she said, pouting. She didn't really care who Belinda was, although she expected she would have to, now. 'Are the Frasers nice?'

'Yes, very,' he said. 'They're having us over to tea on Sunday.'

'I'd love that,' she said. Real posh English people. And their bungalow must be even grander than hers. And she, Helen Turner of Tambaram, sitting and sipping tea with them like a proper English lady. She couldn't wait.

All at once she was overcome with the immensity of it all, the suddenness with which her life had been transformed, the speed with which things were happening.

When she was a little girl of maybe three or four, her father had decided to take her with him to work. She had been suitably impressed by the machines that whirred and spat out words like magic, but she had soon grown bored and Leslie had taken her off to the shunting yard, where he had arranged with friends to give his daughter a ride in an engine. Helen had clung to her father as they walked along the railway tracks, the noise and the confusion of the yard unnerving her. Massive black locomotives idled past like reflective whales, scarcely showing any of the strength and power they were capable of when they built up a head of steam.

'Over here, men,' her father's friend Uncle Kenny had shouted, leaning out of the locomotive that was puffing past, waving a red handkerchief that he often wore knotted around his neck to keep it from becoming encrusted with soot. A tortured squealing of brakes, locking wheels and roaring steam and the engine had groaned to a halt. Leslie had hoisted her up to Kenny, pulled himself up into the cab of the locomotive and the two men had grinned down at the nervous little girl. 'This is what Daddy's friend does! Want to go for a ride?' Uncle Kenny had said, while her father had nodded encouragingly.

The fireman, his face begrimed with soot and sweat, had said to her father, 'Pretty girl, Mr Turner.'

'Yes, Helen will make the boys turn cartwheels in a few years. Won't you, darling?'

It was incredibly hot and noisy in the locomotive's cab. The fire in the boiler leapt about like a great restless eye. The men were shouting above the noise and vibration – so intense it seemed it would split the thick iron frame of the engine apart. Uncle Kenny gestured and one of the men reached up and pulled the whistle cord. An enormous shriek ripped through the tangle of noise, and with a pronounced shudder the locomotive began to move. The experience had been so powerful that every detail of that morning had been imprinted on her mind, down to the little black smudge that her father had given her, right on the tip of her nose, as a parting present. 'You're all growed up, Helen darling,' he had said proudly, 'now that you've experienced my world.'

Even though she was nineteen now, a hard-bitten, experienced nineteen as she liked to think, she felt exactly the same way as she had felt that day – hardly able to believe the evidence of her eyes, unable to comprehend the difference, the alienness, of this world. It was something that she had yearned for, and now that it had suddenly yielded to her, she didn't quite know how to take it. And before her was the architect of all this – the person she had once disdained. She smiled at him.

75

That night, after the servants had tidied everything away and gone to their quarters, Kannan and Helen retired to their bedroom. Washed and changed, Helen in a full-length blue nightgown, Kannan in striped pyjamas, they sat on the bed without speaking or touching, looking into the fire with a not unpleasant excitement. The minutes passed. Kannan saw his wife (he had tried the word over and over again since they had married) smile and smiled back. He had no idea what to do, especially as his father or Ramdoss hadn't been around to explain a few things. The only previous sexual experience he could call upon was the mysterious thrill he'd felt when he and his gang had sneaked up on servant girls at home as they bathed in the Chevathar. Leslie had provided some advice that seemed useful, but had abruptly broken off his narrative. 'Can't tell you any more, young fellow. My daughter, you understand. But I'm sure all you young chaps know what to do once you're married, eh. Much more than we fellas used to know in our time.' Leslie had wandered away, and Kannan was left feeling as confused as before. How, he thought to himself, was he to convert the fantasy figure that Helen had been for so long into something human? Someone he could touch, be intimate with, cherish, make love to? He shrank from the prospect.

Kannan willed himself to look at Helen, escape the things that bound him. Perhaps she saw something in his face, for she looked down shyly. Her hair fell across her face and she brushed it back, tucked it behind her ear, and then delicately reached up and removed the little pearl earrings she wore. First from one ear, inclining her head in that direction, then the other, small movements. Helen's inclined head, the long expanse of neck, the cascading hair and her beautiful face, the odd vulnerability of the action, softened the world, changed something in the room. He hesitated, knowing that from this point on the idealized Helen would never be his again, and then he moved across the bed and took her in his arms.

For the first weeks, it was almost better than his most outrageous fantasy. As he gave himself up to the crushing weight of love, he lived his relationship with Helen more intensely than ever before. The neediness and ferocity of Kannan's love broke down some of her defences and resistance. Helen had always prided herself on being in control, even as she'd experimented with and experienced the joys and frustrations of teenage passion: furtive fumblings in a variety of awkward and uncomfortable places with Jimmy, the handsome hockey player whom she had once dreamed about marrying and loving for ever. Or either of the two others who had kissed her. Even now, as she allowed herself to succumb to Kannan, she did so at her own pace. But she was amazed by the speed with which she was being drawn into the relationship.

And so the weeks, chiming with light and love, sped by. They spent as much time as they could together, looked without pause into each other's eyes, went for long walks on the narrow paths that ran through the tea, drinking deeply of the sights that littered the path on every side – the beauty of a stunted tree on a wind-scraped hillside, new rain bright on the feathers of a dove that regarded them curiously as they walked past, hand in hand, the perfect scalloped symmetry of yellow-white tea-flowers on a field of green, a runnel of water brushed by the wind ... And with every day, their relationship grew more equal. Helen didn't love him yet, but even as she held back, she sensed it would only be a matter of time. Kannan didn't care; he could love enough for both of them. He told her so. She found this confidence very becoming and, as time passed, saw her earlier infatuations wither away in the blaze of this new and welcome phase in her life.

Intimacy begat intimacy. Helen at her dressing table, Kannan back from work. As they delighted in the sharing of their private spaces, they constructed an enclosed world that hadn't existed before for either of them. She became Hen and he was Ken, and their nicknames held a special meaning to them. They invented new names for each other that disappeared in a minute or lasted for days. They laughed, they fought, they grew comfortable in their skins.

Helen enjoyed her new life and Kannan's new self-assurance, the way in which he comported himself at the club or at the parties thrown to welcome the couple to the estates. She found Freddie delightful and even summoned up the nerve to invite him home. Supper would have been a disaster if Manickam, Kannan's butler, hadn't saved the day with the dishes he could never go wrong with, roast chicken and caramel cussard (as he insisted on calling it). Freddie had flirted mildly with Helen and Kannan had grown jealous until he realized that it was all right because she was his and Freddie was the interloper. Thinking about this late at night, after they had made love, he wondered if he felt so good because he was ascending in the white man's world, where something of his was the envy of those who had hitherto existed on a superior plane. It was as if he'd begun to belong, even if it was only his friend Freddie who had given him this sense of empowerment. This would only be the first step, he promised himself. Helen and he would soon rule this world.

76

Lily's brief excursion to Madras for Kannan's wedding was the first time she'd left Doraipuram in over fifteen years. When she came back, she saw the colony with new eyes and was filled with despair at the general decline. She was especially shocked by the deterioration in Daniel. She realized that she'd grown used to it but now she saw with great sorrow the scanty hair, the deeply lined face and lacklustre eyes. As she left his room, her eyes filled with tears. Only a miracle, it seemed, could revitalize him.

Ten-year-old Daniel, named after his grandfather, seemed to be the answer to her prayers. Shanthi and her husband had moved recently and until they were properly settled they had entrusted their three children to Lily's care. A few weeks after they'd arrived, Lily was mystified to hear sounds emanating from her husband's laboratory. It had lain disused for years now, although she had kept it spick and span in the hope that Daniel would recover an interest in medicine. When she looked in, she was amazed to see the old man and his grandson standing at the workbench, deeply engrossed in something that was bubbling away over a low flame. A servant stood by ready to help.

'Is everything all right?' Lily asked. All three heads swivelled towards the door and her husband said enthusiastically, 'Ah, Lily, do you know this marvellous boy?'

'He is your oldest grandchild.'

'Yes, I believe so.'

'Shanthi's son, she named him for you. Don't you remember?'

'Yes, I do, indeed I do, umm, he's the brightest young man I've seen in a long time. Lily, he has the interest, the passion, that I had at his age ...'

You were disappointed in your son, Lily thought sadly, but the feeling was momentary, swept away by rising hope.

'We must get the best tutors for him, Lily. His mind needs to be trained.'

Money was in short supply, as it had been for some time now, but with his usual ingenuity Ramdoss unearthed the necessary funds. The teachers began arriving at Neelam Illum. Lily's workday expanded, for Daniel had decreed that she would need to keep an eye on the tutoring. And so it was that she would spend an hour or so dozing with her eyes open as the boy was taught. After the tutorial, she was expected to present Daniel to his grandfather. She usually left them alone, returning periodically to see if her husband had grown tired or wanted something.

One evening as she turned to go, after ushering in her grandson for his audience, Daniel surprised her by asking her to stay. His interest this evening seemed not to be focused on the boy.

'I'm always amazed at how it's the women that hold the Dorais together,' he said unexpectedly. 'We men go off and do things that we are inspired to do but we've been fortunate in our women. Without them we would have accomplished nothing. You've done wonders for this child, Lily,' he said thoughtfully.

Somewhat taken aback, Lily protested weakly, 'I didn't do very much, he's very clever.'

'And as always you refuse to take any of the credit,' Daniel mused softly, 'always present, always self-effacing, always a rock. The Good Book was right: a man must leave his father and mother and cleave to his wife ... for she will do him good and not evil all the days of her life ... I forget how much you do for me sometimes, Lily, you must forgive me ...'

Realizing that today was not about her grandson, she hurriedly sent the boy off to play, and sat down next to Daniel's bed. Her husband regarded her affectionately. She had aged well. Her face was barely lined and there was still more black than white in her hair. A vagrant thought entered his head: her nose remained as delightfully tilted as when he'd first glimpsed her. Was the nose the part of the body that took the longest to grow old?

Aloud, he said: 'You're looking very well today.'

Lily didn't know what to make of this; it had been years since Daniel had paid her any sort of compliment and she had lost the knack of dealing with them. What came next did nothing to lessen her confusion.

'How's Thirumoolar?'

Lily was unprepared for the question. She wondered what sort of answer to give Daniel. If she said Kannan was happy, Daniel might feel angry; if she said he wasn't, he'd feel wrongly vindicated. She decided to feel her way into the conversation, and so said nothing.

'Is he happy in his job?' her husband asked.

'He seems to be enjoying himself.'

'That's very good, Lily. The British will teach him a thing or two. Discipline, hard work, the desire to strive for perfection in everything he does ...'

'He's had good things to say about the people he works with.'

'Excellent. He paused a while, then said, 'When was the last time you were on a tea estate?'

'Oh, years and years ago, for my cousin's wedding ...' she began wistfully but Daniel interrupted her. 'I think you should visit Thirumoolar, see how he is doing. It would be a good break for you. You work so hard.'

'But how will you manage?'

'I'll get by. Don't worry. There's Ramu and the servants, it's not as though you'll be gone for ever.'

A great joy filled Lily's heart. This was the first time she had any real sense of a breakthrough. Now it could only be a matter of time before her family was together again, and she would be able to welcome her daughter-in-law to Neelam Illum. There would be more grandchildren ... With an effort, she controlled her imagination. As she did, she felt a sudden impulse to hug her husband.

'I'll write to Kannan ...' she said.

'You must get up there and return before the monsoons break. I've heard the roads become impassable during the rainy season.'

'Yes, I'll do that.'

As she turned to go, Daniel called out, 'And don't forget to take him some mango pickle, it was always his favourite.'

77

Mrs Matilda Stevenson's Thursday afternoon teas were famous throughout the district. For a dozen years, ever since her husband was appointed Superintendent of Karadi Estate, she had presided over these monthly affairs, their prestige and mystique growing in direct proportion to her own place in society. And now that she was undisputed queen of Pulimed an engraved invitation to tea with her was a coveted prize. As time went by, Mrs Stevenson, who was acutely sensitive to nuance, became even more discriminating in her choice of invitees, and ever more fastidious in her arrangements. It was rumoured that the rarest teas to be had in India and China were served to her guests. It was common knowledge that the water that gave even the most ordinary tea its distinctive taste came from a pristine mountain spring that only Mrs Stevenson and one trusted retainer knew about. It was said that the tea service had been especially made for her by Spode, after which the pattern had been destroyed. The talk was that butter for the drop scones was churned from the milk of a cow used for no other purpose, and it was claimed that the gravel in the driveway was washed on the day of the tea, so it glittered to best effect. Mrs Stevenson, and the favoured few who constituted her inner circle, did nothing to deflect or dispel these rumours, and they grew ever more incredible. Every one of them served to further gild the occasion over which Mrs Stevenson serenely presided.

This Thursday, Mrs Stevenson and her closest friend, Mrs Wilkins, were ensconced in a small cluster of basket chairs in the western corner of the enormous front veranda, the traditional venue of the tea ever since the Stevensons had moved to Glenclare. They were discussing cannas. A great bunch of them shed cold yellow and orange fire on the lawns and their magnificence had attracted Mrs Wilkins's passing interest.

'Your cannas are looking fabulous this year, Matilda dear,' Mrs Wilkins said. 'Mine aren't even half their size, and my gardener can't seem to do anything with them. They're quite ugly flowers, don't you think?'

Mrs Stevenson nodded. 'My chap is using a new kind of fertilizer that he pinched from Edward's factory. Does wonders for cannas and hydrangeas.'

'Must send my gardener over to talk to yours.'

'Yes, yes, do, and he can take away as much fertilizer as he wants.'

There was a pause in the conversation as the butler arrived, magnificent in white turban, and trousers. He deftly whisked a damask tablecloth on to the table around which the chairs were grouped. -Eggshell-thin china, silver, and neatly pressed napkins were efficiently laid out, and he disappeared as silently as he had come. The conversation faltered, then died out entirely as they waited for the tea.

It was understood by all the participants at Mrs Stevenson's Thursday ritual that everything else was secondary to the actual partaking of the tea. No matter how stimulating or vicious the conversation, no matter how delicious the scones or the sandwiches (tomato, cucumber and, in place of watercress – a Mrs Stevenson touch – salted tongue), everything was expected to be forgotten when tea arrived. Experienced campaigner that she was, Gloria Wilkins knew the drill. She stopped discussing cannas as the food was carried in by the servants: small mounds of sandwiches carefully cut to the prescribed thickness, golden-brown scones warm and deliciously aromatic, clotted cream and strawberry jam, butter sculpted like a yellow rose (a little vulgar this), and a rich, inviting pound cake that Mrs Wilkins knew from past experience was so delicious that its taste lingered long after the last slice had been ingested. Mrs Stevenson graciously provided the recipe to whoever asked but none of the other wives' attempts succeeded: how could perfection be duplicated? The secret to its greatness was reputed to be Madaswamy, Mrs Stevenson's butler, who was almost as legendary as his mistress. He had perfected the pound cake when he first came to work as a kitchen boy for Mrs Stevenson over a decade ago, and he had continued to make it ever since. But even the pound cake was expected to be done with by the time tea arrived, and so Mrs Wilkins dispatched one slice with great decorum and skill, and swiftly took another that was pressed on her by her hostess. Her experience stood her in good stead, as she had just swallowed the last morsel when Madaswamy padded on to the veranda, bearing the tea tray.

Enormous and intricately carved out of teak, it was astonishing to see how effortlessly the slightly built butler carried it, shoulder high. As he neared the two ladies, it was possible to discern a vast array of objects on the tray: three teapots, a brown one of terracotta, an exquisite Stafford porcelain one and Mrs Stevenson's favourite, a Worcester teapot, part of the tea service she used most often. Four tea caddies, one of pewter, one of terracotta, one of tin and a fourth of heavy antique silver that no one had ever seen Mrs Stevenson open. Local gossip had it that within reposed buds of Yin Zhen, or Silver Needles, the exquisite white China tea from across the Himalayas, so rare and precious that it was plucked at dawn on only two days of the year provided the weather was right. Centuries ago, in imperial China, Yin Zhen was harvested by young virgins wearing gloves and using golden scissors. The joke was that when Mrs Stevenson was finally able to bring herself to drink her cache of Yin Zhen, she would find it had lost its flavour. Finally, a milk pitcher, sugar bowl, a saucer of finely sliced lemon, and two cups and saucers.

Madaswamy set the tray down on the table. Again from experience, and emulation (for which guest at Mrs Stevenson's teas had not experimented with their own versions of the ceremony?), Mrs Wilkins knew that all three teapots would have been warmed to just the right temperature by placing them in bowls of hot water. She knew exactly what each teapot was used for as well – the terracotta one for the strong Glenclare teas, the porcelain one for the lighter tea from Watson, and the Worcester one for Mrs Stevenson's favourite FTGFOP which was grown in one of the highest Darjeeling gardens. Among the world's finest teas, it was composed entirely of the golden tips that gave it its name. A friend of Mrs Stevenson in Bengal sent her a regular supply.

Another servant had followed Madaswamy with a tray on which a single china pitcher rested. Again from experience, Gloria Wilkins knew that the water had been plucked from the stove just as it had started simmering (if it had been allowed to boil, it would have gone flat) and had been instantly transported to the veranda.

Mrs Stevenson asked, 'Tea, my dear?'

'Glenclare for me, Matilda,' Mrs Wilkins said, and Mrs Stevenson gave her a brief smile and carefully spooned two teaspoons of tea from the terracotta caddy into the terracotta teapot. A minute for the tea's aroma to be released and then the servant with the hot water was at hand and she poured the water into the teapot.

'I think I'll have some Darjeeling myself,' Mrs Stevenson said, and her friend thought: At least there are some constant things in this world. Mrs Stevenson hadn't changed that line in a decade. A third servant had materialized in the meantime bearing an identical pitcher of hot water. Mrs Stevenson filled the Worcester teapot with two teaspoons of tea, then poured the water over it, shut the lid and sat back.

The two ladies did not speak for the time it took for the tea to brew. Mrs Wilkins stared with great fascination at the Worcester teapot as if she could look within to the fine cracks ingrained through long exposure to tannin that gave the teapot its own distinctive flavour. Every connoisseur knew that you never washed out a teapot, you merely rinsed it and left it to dry in the open air or in the boiler room during the monsoon. The minutes passed and the five people on the veranda were as still as in a frieze. Then Mrs Stevenson asked, 'Milk or lemon?'

Only two people whom Gloria Wilkins knew had asked for lemon and they hadn't lasted long on the estates. She was permitted a drop of milk, and a single level teaspoon of sugar. Mrs Stevenson belonged to the school of tea drinkers that believed the milk should be poured into the cup before the tea is decanted. She now poured the milk, and then gently added the strong honey-coloured tea. Mrs Wilkins helped herself to sugar, and then Mrs Stevenson poured her own tea, the colour of evening sunlight. Nothing marred its perfection, not milk, not sugar.

The butler scooped up the tray once the ladies had taken up their saucers, and the three servants left the veranda in a stately procession. They would mysteriously reappear when Mrs Stevenson or one of her guests wanted a second cup, for the tea was freshly brewed every time. Mrs Wilkins smiled to herself when she recalled one marathon session where Madaswamy and his entourage had come and gone seventeen times. It was a well-embedded part of the Matilda Stevenson legend.

After they had sipped their tea in complete silence for a while, savouring the taste, the colour of the light, the flowers, they began chatting once more. Mrs Wilkins thought her friend looked a bit strained but it was always hard to tell with Mrs Stevenson. And she would never dare ask. If Matilda wanted to tell her what was on her mind, she would do so, in her own time.

Both ladies were in their early fifties, but there the similarity ended. Mrs Stevenson was thickish with middle age but was neither plump nor fat. She was tall, and her quite elaborate hairdo made her look even taller. But it was her face – ridged, seamed, even cross-hatched, each wrinkle earned at great cost from worry, battle or inclement weather – that lent her distinction. It was said that once you were able to interpret the patterns into which the wrinkles in Mrs Stevenson's face arranged themselves you could tell in advance what was in store for you. Mrs Wilkins was short, plump and distinctly unthreatening. Large-lipped, with big cow-brown eyes, thirty years earlier she had been the object of many planters' fantasies. Four children had given her a comfortable motherly air. Although neither of them would have thought of it that way, Mrs Wilkins was the ideal foil for her friend. She did whatever Mrs Stevenson wanted at the shortest possible notice, and brought great patience and unmatched listening skills as well as gossip to the relationship. In return for all these, she was granted the privilege of being Matilda Stevenson's closest friend and had the right to call her by her Christian name, the only person in the entire district, apart from her husband, now allowed to do so.

'What a shame about poor young Camellia!' Mrs Wilkins said, gently setting her cup and saucer down.

'What about Camellia?' snapped Mrs Stevenson. Noting the other's peevishness, Mrs Wilkins lapsed into silence, for Mrs Stevenson's rages were legendary and Camellia Winston's travails could wait.

The butler materialized on silent feet and cleared the cups and saucers with scarcely a whisper. Mrs Wilkins admired his skill with a detached air. Even Mrs Stevenson's servants were the envy of the district.

'What were you saying about Camellia?' Mrs Stevenson said abruptly.

'Oh, nothing. The poor dear was quite cut up about something that happened the other day.'

Mrs Stevenson continued to regard her friend steadily over the top of her spectacles. It was one of the mannerisms that she had diligently cultivated. It came in very useful at the club, or the more prestigious parties, when she had to cow some upstart or bore into silence. She mourned the passing of the lorgnette, perfect for the imperious stare and the silent put-down. But she managed. She had no intention of trying to put the amiable Gloria Wilkins down; it was just, well, perhaps she was just practising for Friday week.

Mrs Stevenson softened the steely look in her eye and favoured Gloria with a smile. 'So, about Camellia?' she said.

Mrs Wilkins didn't need any further prompting. 'Of course, dear,' she said, 'as I was saying, there she was, stepping out of Spencer's, her arms piled high with shopping, you know how scarce things have become so you always stock up, and her driver had gone ahead to bring the car, when she bumped into an Indian man quite accidentally. He was most rude and said, "If memsahibs don't look where they are going, they will soon find themselves gone." Poor Camellia was so shocked at this impertinence, she didn't know what to say. She told her husband, of course, but then she couldn't describe the man, you never really notice Indians, do you now. All she could recall was that he wore one of those little white native hats ...'

'Yes, I know, a Gandhi hat. Absurd little hat, absurd little man.'

'Oh, really, dear.' Mrs Wilkins could see her story slipping away from her, but the steely look was back in Mrs Stevenson's eye and she didn't feel quite up to finishing it.

'I'll be running along then. Hope your party goes well.'

It was the worst thing she could have said. Barely repressing the irritation that flared up within her at the mention of the party she intended hosting for the Dorais ten days hence, Mrs Stevenson saw her friend to her car, and returned to the bungalow. What a stupid woman Gloria Wilkins is, she thought irritably. God knows how I've put up with her all these years!

78

Although Mrs Stevenson greatly valued her position as wife of the General Manager of Pulimed Tea Company, her unofficial position as queen of local society mattered even more. Neither had dropped into her lap, she thought grimly, as she watched Gloria Wilkins's car disappear down the driveway, and she would defend her eminence with every power at her command.

Mrs Stevenson had come over on a P&O boat in 1925, a strapping but plain thirty-three-year-old from Brighton, fearful of being left on the shelf. She had this in common with most of the other British women who constituted the Fishing Fleet, as the shipfuls of women who travelled to India to make a good marriage were called. She had spent three months with a distant aunt in Madras, and was about to sail home to a life of spinsterdom when Major Stevenson asked her to dance at one of the endless tea dances in the city. It was hot and stuffy and the headache she had woken up with that morning threatened to overwhelm her. The Major was not exactly young, and had a gimpy leg, and after the first dance, Matilda was ready to go home. But he danced with her a second and then a third time, and with a mounting sense of relief she realized she would not be one of the Returned Empties, as the Fishing Fleet rejects were dubbed. When he proposed two days later, she accepted. She knew nothing about tea-planting, only that it ranked high enough in Raj society to provide Major Stevenson with greater cachet as a prospective husband. Tea-planters ranked somewhere below the ICS but were deemed superior to the box-wallahs, whom the upper classes looked down upon, ostensibly because they were in trade but probably also because they were rich.

Mrs Stevenson soon discovered that the esteem that tea-planters were held in did not immediately confer upon them the sort of lifestyle you would have expected. When she had first arrived in Pulimed it was a dismal place. The dirt roads were impassable during the monsoon, which effectively cut the estates off from the rest of the world twice a year. The planters lived in miserable little shacks that were dark and musty. The unhygienic living conditions combined with malaria and periodic epidemics of plague and typhus regularly interred the British, especially women and young children, in the graveyard behind the little Pulimed chapel. The dreary, depressing weather required an astonishing degree of fortitude on the part of manager and worker alike. It was not unknown for a planter to kill himself and his family during an especially prolonged monsoon; Mrs Stevenson herself could remember two families who had succumbed during her time here. Drink often provided the only succour and many of the early planters, both men and women, were alcoholics.

Fortunately, the place had grown civilized quite rapidly. As the industry prospered, more acreage came under tea and the forbidding forests were rolled back. The roads improved and the bungalows grew more imposing. Their own situation was improving as well. Mrs Stevenson appeared to have brought her husband luck, for within a year of her arrival at Pulimed, one of the company's senior Superintendents took early retirement and Edward got his job. They moved into a comfortable bungalow on Karadi Estate.

There were other welcome developments in the tea district. The Pulimed Club opened in 1932. Lavish gardens and tennis courts were laid out, virtually one to a bungalow. The social life of the planters blossomed. There were tennis parties and picnics, costume balls and tea dances at the club. As tea-planting became more alluring, the pedigree of the planter improved. The occasional public-school boy was taken on and the rough-and-ready frontiersmen of an earlier era began to disappear.

Mrs Stevenson saw her opportunity. The couple were childless, and she had always fretted to herself that she didn't feel fulfilled enough. The rising gentrification of the district gave her a project she could devote herself to. Unlike the great stations of Madras and Bombay or even the bigger mofussil towns, Pulimed didn't have high-ranking ICS officials. The British Resident made only the occasional foray into the hills. And there was no army regiment with its Blue Books and rigidly defined conventions, precedence and other minutiae of social behaviour. So the opportunity to make up a set of rules to govern Pulimed society existed. Mrs Stevenson, with a couple of other planters' wives, soon became the social arbiters of the district. Then Mrs Hogg died, Mrs Buchan's husband was transferred to the Nilgiris, Edward received another promotion and Mrs Stevenson came into her own. She was forty-two years old. From then on, her word was law.

Not enough has been said about the role of the memsahib in India. Dozens of books have been written about the British men who first subjugated, then ruled, and finally lost India, but accounts of the white woman have been limited to a few autobiographies and a baker's dozen of cookery books and Raj memorabilia. This is a shame because, at the risk of oversimplification, it would probably be correct to say that these daughters of Birmingham grocers and Cheltenham schoolteachers played a not inconsiderable role in the departure of the British from India.

It was all a matter of attitude. For the first hundred or so years of his time in India, the white man was variously a trader, schemer, warrior and buccaneer. By the time Queen Victoria, Her Most Benevolent Majesty, accepted the homage of her Indian subjects, all three hundred and seventy-two million of them, the British had quite forgotten what they had originally come to the subcontinent for – i.e., plunder and the rapid generation of wealth. Now, in the grip of the imperial impulse, they believed they were ordained to rule a quarter of the world, and bring a civilizing influence to bear on the heathen.

By the middle of the twentieth century, however, the idea of Empire, even to the British, was fraying around the edges. Two wars had sapped their strength, the new generation didn't thrill to trumpets and bugles, and America was well on its way to dominating the world. The British had tried their best, but they would be gone soon from India just like every invader who had preceded them, leaving behind a few monuments – in their case, some excellent examples of Victorian architecture, the English language, the railways, a parliamentary form of democracy, a system of administration …

The Empire would probably have lingered a little longer, notwithstanding the best efforts of the nationalists, if Englishwomen hadn't begun appearing in India in large numbers. In the early years, the British had managed to achieve a fairly equitable relationship with Indians. By the beginning of the nineteenth century, this phase had begun to fade. The advent of muscular forms of Christianity coupled with imperfectly understood Darwinism equated colour and 'paganism' with inferiority. From that point onwards, matters deteriorated. The Englishman abroad, consciously or subconsciously, began to subscribe to the philosophy that the subject peoples (especially in the tropics) were a lesser breed; their civilizations were trashed and

British culture was exalted above all others.

But it was the advent of the flotillas of Englishwomen that confirmed the trend. Where some of the men were still prepared to seek out and understand the locals to some degree, providing both sides with the opportunity to build trust and occasionally friendship and admiration, the memsahib would not venture beyond her bungalow. Ill-prepared for the chaos and vastness of India, isolated by her lack of language, she could thrive only by rigorously excluding the enormous country at her doorstep, and this she did. Her bungalow was furnished just the way she might kit out a villa in Sevenoaks, her gardens drooped with pallid English flowers, and as she gradually drew her husband into this ersatz English world, it was only a matter of time before the handful of Britons in India began to lose the organic connection to the land. Soon they were burrs precariously clinging to the skin of India, that would be shaken off the minute there was a violent upheaval. Rare was the Englishwoman who was truly at home in India beyond the stockade, and Mrs Stevenson was no exception.

Matilda Stevenson would have been astonished if anyone had charged her with not knowing enough about India or Indians. She considered India home, even though she constantly grumbled about not seeing enough of England, and she believed she was genuinely fond of Indians. She relied hugely on her butler Madaswamy, and couldn't imagine life without him. But without her, as she constantly reminded him, he would be nothing, less than nothing. It was only because of her patronage and training that he had blossomed – to the point where he was solely in charge of the thirty-seven servants who ensured that the General Manager's Bungalow was always in good working order. Madaswamy, Velu the head gardener, Mani the driver, every one of them was an integral part of Mrs Stevenson's world. She showered kindness upon them, sending their children English toffees and small gifts at Christmas and Easter, in addition to the usual baksheesh, and she even allowed Madaswamy to do his share of skimming from the shopping and household accounts. No, Mrs Stevenson knew her Indians. But she would have been the first to admit that good Indians were Indians who knew their places. Mrs Stevenson had never met a maharani but she wouldn't have been fazed if she had. As the wife of the General Manager of Pulimed Tea Company, and as an Englishwoman, she was superior to any Indian.

Mrs Stevenson was deeply shaken when her husband hired Kannan Dorai. She would, of course, have never dreamed of telling him how to run his company, although she did it all the time, subtly and persuasively. But she hadn't seen this coming. It wasn't surprising, for she had no sense of history. She didn't read the Indian newspapers (and scanned only the society snippets in British-owned ones), in common with most of the Englishwomen in Pulimed, nor did she listen to the talk of her husband and his colleagues, except when it had to do with things that interested her such as promotions, demotions and marital discord. No Indians appeared on her horizon, save the staff, and when the trickle of London papers stopped on account of the war, she was completely cut off from the outside world.

As a result, she was unprepared when her husband began to usher in the sort of change she could not countenance. What could he have been thinking of when he had hired a native as a replacement for Joe Wilson? Of all people! Joe Wilson, her favourite. Joe Wilson, now fighting for country and for Empire. Joe Wilson, Old Etonian, marksman extraordinaire, a Cambridge blue in tennis, who let others win so skilfully that they never knew he controlled every point from the moment he arced back to serve. Joe Wilson's place taken by a native! By her own hand, no less, because Mrs Stevenson regarded her husband as merely an extension of herself. It was all too much to take. And what did it portend?

Mrs Stevenson's power in Pulimed had never been questioned in all the time she had ruled. Dining out required tails, boiled shirt, white waistcoat, stiff collar and white tie, twenty years after it had died out everywhere else in India – and only because Mrs Stevenson had so decreed. She knew *Mrs Beeton's Cookery and Household Management*, as she did Debrett's *Peerage* and the various other rule books that governed society. She watched people's accents, was keen to discover their pedigree, and never failed to detect vulgar blood lurking behind the most refined exterior. No one willingly crossed her, for there was only one possible outcome.

But Kannan Dorai disturbed her more than she cared to admit. He was properly respectful and seemed acceptable enough for an Indian. But was he a precursor of things to come? Some nights Mrs Stevenson would lie awake, visions of a suburban villa in a dreary English town, (such as Grantham) dancing in her head. She would shake the thought aside, but the unease remained. And now Kannan had shaken her composure again, by marrying a mixed blood. Someone who was completely beyond the pale. As the General Manager's wife, she was expected to be civil to the newcomer, and suitably dignified in the way she treated her. But it filled her with unease. She had always prided herself on being completely in control but these new developments had thrown her off-balance. However, this was only temporary, she vowed grimly; she knew exactly how to deal with them.

79

One morning, Kannan was in a self-congratulatory mood as he drove to the field. I've done things that I scarcely presumed I could, he reflected. I've imagined and reinvented my life in ways that I'd never have believed possible. I defied my father, went out into the world and made something of myself in a place that a couple of years ago I wouldn't have considered breaking into, no matter how highly I regarded myself. I've even managed to check my temper. I'm no longer callow and impetuous.

His thoughts turned to Helen, and here again there was cause for wonderment. He doubted that any Dorai he knew could have contemplated romance with a woman, let alone treated her as an equal. There had been moments when he'd doubted his own ability to do so, but he'd adapted, curbing his instinctual response to be dismissive and superior in order to cherish and adore his wife.

Feeling very pleased with himself he reached the field, where his supervisor presented him with an unusual gift. One of the pluckers had disturbed a hare and it had taken off, leaving behind a pair of leverets. These were given to Kannan. They looked pretty ugly, but he thought they would make the perfect present for Helen. For about a month or so now he had tried to take her some small surprise when he returned from work – a bunch of wild daisies, a lock of maidenhair fern, an interesting pebble that shone like gold. In the first flush of love the offering had always worked, but lately, he had begun to feel the need to get her something out of the ordinary.

Helen was overjoyed with the gift. She fussed over the ugly little babies and made a tiny bed for them out of cotton waste and straw that she placed on her bedside table. She soaked cotton wrapped around a matchstick in cow's milk and tried to feed them, but they refused every blandishment, and died two days later. Helen was inconsolable and wept loudly when they buried the tiny bodies under the camellia bush in the front garden.

She bounced back soon enough, and that Saturday took Kannan round the dance floor quite expertly. It was the first time he had danced at the club, and after his initial trepidation he began to enjoy himself. A waltz and a foxtrot, and his repertoire was exhausted, but he was so pleased with his performance that after the second dance, when Freddie asked her for the next one, he released her with only the merest twinge of jealousy. As he walked back to his seat, he chanced to meet Mrs Stevenson's eye. Her gaze was cold, but he smiled happily at her, and then moved on, out of her field of vision.

A new job, a new marriage, a fresh lick of paint on a peeling surface – in none of these does it take very long for fault lines to show. The first cracks in their idyll appeared on the day Kannan took Helen to the factory.

In April, life on the estates speeded up, as the finest harvest to be had all year, the first flush, was gathered in. Factories operated round the clock; managers, pluckers and labourers worked themselves to the bone, for this was the time of year that maximum profits were to be made. One Sunday, Kannan skipped church to do factory duty. The Glenclare factory had been shut for two days due to a breakdown of machinery, and to make up for lost time, Michael had decided the factory would work through the weekend.

Kannan woke up early as usual and watched a chink of grey light through the drawn curtains. By his side Helen slept on. He looked at her appreciatively. How defenceless she seems when she's asleep, he thought. Then he slipped out of bed, careful not to wake her. As he dressed, he wondered what he could do to make up for the previous night when he had begged off going to the club. He'd sensed her disappointment, although she hadn't protested. Now he'd be away for much of the morning, when they could have gone on a picnic, as they sometimes did on Sundays when the weather was good. As he finished shaving, an idea struck him. It seemed so excellent that he didn't know why it had never occurred to him before.

He took in her morning tray himself. By her teacup lay two sprigs of tea – the famous two leaves and a bud that are picked when tea is 'fine'-harvested. He kissed her and hovered around as she slowly came awake. He watched her examine the tea-leaves on the tray in some puzzlement and then said lightly, 'I've got a wonderful surprise for you, Lady of My Life.'

'And what might that be?' she asked sleepily.

'It just occurred to me that I've shown you everything about my life here – tennis parties, dance nights at the club, dinners at my colleagues' bungalows, every nook and corner of the estate – except for one thing. How those leaves by your plate become the tea in your cup. Today, my love, we're going to the factory.'

She looked at him as if he were mad, not sure that she had heard correctly. Was her husband really proposing to take her to that huge tin-roofed barn that they had passed dozens of times on their way elsewhere but had never actually entered? She didn't have the slightest interest in visiting it; there were some things in life you knew you had no use for. But in the face of Kannan's enthusiasm she gave in. He was slightly deflated by her lack of excitement, but put it down to the fact that she was half-asleep. She would be fascinated by what she was about to see, he was sure of that. Especially as so few planters' wives had actually seen a tea factory in operation. If he had been somewhat less overwhelmed by his own genius he might have had cause to wonder why not.

A message was dispatched to the tea-maker and Kannan roared off on his motorcycle to ask Michael's permission to take his wife to the factory. When they arrived, the tea-maker, a middle-aged man with discoloured teeth, was waiting for them at the factory entrance. Inside, the air was scented with tea, and they were assailed by the continuous clatter of machinery. Kannan and the tea-maker held a shouted conversation, and then he smiled and pointed to a rickety ladder that disappeared into the upper reaches of the factory. They skirted piles of tea and thundering machines and a number of men clad only in dirty khaki shorts and singlets, who paused in their work to stare silently at Helen before the tea-maker gestured them back to work. Up the ladder they went, the tea-maker first, followed by Helen and Kannan. In the withering loft it was quieter, but warm. In long troughs with wire-mesh bottoms, freshly plucked tea-leaves were spread thickly. Kannan took a couple of the leaf stalks that lay in a trough and passed them to his wife. 'Remember that day when the pluckers were working in the field next to the bungalow? You said the sound they made while they worked was like cows munching grass?'

Helen did remember. The women who plucked the tea had seemed as delicate and colourful as butterflies. She had walked out on to the lawn, and they had pointed to her and giggled and made remarks about her that she couldn't make out. A supervisor had walked up to them, and they had resumed plucking.

'This is what they pluck,' he said. 'When they pluck fine, they take the tip of the stalk, the bud, and the two leaves beneath it, but most of the time they pluck coarse, the bud plus three or four leaves. We get more cuppage that way.'

They started back the way they had come, Kannan still explaining the mysteries of the manufacturing of tea. 'The tea-plant is one of the most obliging cash crops known to man,' he said proudly. 'It virtually does all the work when it comes to converting itself from the leaf on the bush to the tea we drink; all we do is help it along.' He explained the five stages in the manufacturing process, of which withering was the first. Hot air was passed through the leaves, as a result of which they lost their moisture; the effect of the heat catalysed the first of several internal chemical reactions.

He showed Helen where the leaves were sent down a chute to the rolling room, the noisiest section of the factory. Here, among the thunder of iron Britannia machines that stood as tall as her, Kannan shouted that the leaves were rolled until their cell walls shattered and the oils within rose to the surface. The rolled leaves were placed in a dark room in which they began to ferment, following which they were taken to another section of the factory and put into a huge machine that dried them by passing a current of superheated air over them. Firing done, the tea was now ready to be sorted into various grades that would then be packed into crates and shipped out of the factory.

He stopped and picked up a handful of tea, black and intensely aromatic, from one of the piles in the sorting section and held it out to her. 'Just smell this, nothing can match the aroma of freshly manufactured tea.' Helen gave him a wan smile, and sniffed. It smelt like tea. She let it dribble away and waited for Kannan to finish talking to the tea-maker. Her enthusiasm, already at a low ebb by the time they had reached the factory, had dwindled all through the tour and now all she wanted to do was go home. But Kannan wasn't finished. 'Come on, Hen, Shankar here has got everything ready for the tea-tasting.'

Helen didn't know what a tea-tasting was, but she was sure she wanted to go home. 'I'd like to go home now, if that's all right,' she said quietly.

Kannan didn't appear to have heard. 'You know Churchill said that the British soldier could fight on without ammunition, but not without his daily cuppa. And most of that tea comes from here. Makes one feel proud, you know, those merchantmen braving U-boat packs to get this precious stuff to England.' He was walking off with the tea-maker when he realized she wasn't following. 'This way, Hen, it's an eye-opener to see how these chaps decide whether the tea is of the best quality or not.'

'Do you mind if we skip the tea-tasting? I'm really tired.' She saw the enthusiasm on his face fade, replaced by puzzlement and a little hurt. She felt guilty, but she'd definitely had enough.

'It's all ready. It'll only take a little while.'

'Do you really mind if we do this another time?' she asked, wondering, even as she spoke, whether it was worth being so stubborn. After all, it was just another step in the stupid tea-making process, and if she'd been able to endure a whole morning of it, surely she could put up with another half an hour.

'Well, all right then, if that's the way you want it,' he said stiffly, and she realized he was angry. This annoyed her. Suddenly she wanted to get free of the stifling atmosphere of the factory. The entrance was only a short distance away and she began walking towards it. She had almost got there when she heard quick steps and Kannan caught up with her.

Outside, he said grimly, 'You might have had the courtesy to wait until I'd finished talking to the tea-maker, making my excuses.'

'I didn't want to come in the first place. It was your idea,' she said.

'Oh, really! You should have said you didn't want to come.'

'So this is all my fault, is it?' she said, her anger growing.

A couple of workers were coming up the path towards them, and Kannan said quickly, 'Look, not here, please. If you want to say something to me, say it at home, not in front of the whole world.'

She suppressed the sharp retort that sprang to her lips, and walked away to where he'd parked the motorcycle.

The silence between them lasted as long as it took for Kannan to drive to the house, park the motorcycle and lead the way into the bedroom. He shut the door firmly behind him. And then they went for each other, systematically targeting every weak spot in the other's psychological make-up, determined to cause the maximum damage. All the things that had been swept aside by the force of their love returned, swelled their anger, made them implacable.

'I've never been so humiliated,' Kannan began. 'Have you gone mad? Shouting at me in front of the factory workers!'

'I never wanted to go to your stupid factory, it was your idea. Wait, let me see if I can recall the exact words ...'

'That's it. I'm never going to take the trouble to think up things for us to do. Not only do I have to slave, I've also got to provide entertainment for missy amma, while she lolls around the house.'

'That's because there's nothing to do here, you stupid ass. You're so caught up in the romance of tea that you don't seem to see that this place is dull, so boring I could cry.'

'Yes, yes, I see, of course I see,' he said, his voice ominously calm, 'you'd much rather be dancing in your Railway Institute with your boyfriends, you cheap little ...'

A mirror from her dressing table came flying at him. 'How dare you call me cheap!'

'How dare you call me boring?' What on earth had possessed him to marry this awful woman? How dare she talk to him like this? He couldn't remember his mother or any of his aunts or cousins even making a mild complaint to their husbands! Why, none of them even addressed their husbands by name! The fight lasted over an hour. She told him exactly what she thought of him, his friends, his job, and he reciprocated in kind, telling her exactly what he thought of her, her friends, Tambaram Railway Colony and whatever else he could throw in. Gradually the heat left their accusations and finally, tearful and remorseful, they made up. Kannan allowed himself to give in, something she was grateful for. She had never seen him this angry and it frightened her. She wondered whether she was as much in control of the relationship as she had thought. She shelved her unease. They made love, promised not to hurt each other. They meant it when they said it, but both knew that certain things had been said and could never be locked up again. To avoid a repeat of the ugliness that had left them both diminished, they took care around each other, trying their best not to give offence, to recapture the perfect unscarred love they'd had.

Five days later a uniformed servant from the General Manager's Bungalow turned up at Morningfall bearing one of Mrs Stevenson's famous invitations, not to tea but to dinner. They had just finished breakfast, and Kannan opened the envelope, read the engraved card and passed it to Helen, saying, 'At long last, an invitation from the Dragon Lady. I was beginning to wonder whether it was going to come at all.'

'Why?'

'Oh, nothing.'

'Tell me, please, please, *please*.'

'No, seriously, it's nothing.' He hoped she wouldn't persist. He thought about his own preparations for the party Mrs Stevenson had thrown for him when he first arrived. He had spent a fortnight observing everything the Frasers did – the way they sat, ate, drank, wielded cutlery and glasses. Even then he had almost collapsed from the strain of trying not to come up short during the course of that long evening. He had made it through somehow. How was Helen going to cope? He was sure she would bridle if he tried to coach her, so what was he to do?

'Penny for your thoughts?' she said brightly.

'Just thinking that this will be the grandest party you'll have seen yet.'

'Oh, I'm so excited. I've heard they live in the most magnificent bungalow.'

'That they do.'

She frowned. 'Do you think Mrs Stevenson likes me? She seems so forbidding.'

'That's the way she is with everybody. She's actually very nice.'

'I hope so. I haven't exchanged a word with her yet, she looks so ... so ... headmistressy!'

'She's the perfect hostess,' he said, thinking, provided we're the perfect guests.

'I've nothing to wear,' Helen said, making a face.

'Look, let's go over to the Frasers'. I'm sure Belinda will be able to help.'

'Fine, let's do that,' Helen said. 'Now I'm really excited. I think I'll wear the earrings Dad gave me.'

His heart went out to her. For all her city ways, she was still so naïve, such an easy target.

80

Major Edward Stevenson didn't consider himself an especially daring man. He had fought in a war, even shot a tiger before the beasts became scarce, but if he were asked to describe himself, the adjectives he would have chosen would have been dependable, unexcitable, cautious, solid. He had two more years to go before retirement, and he was looking forward to the time when he could retire on a pension, perhaps in England, perhaps in one of the other colonies. Canada possibly, no, that would be too cold, maybe Kenya, where there would be servants and a pleasant climate. Perhaps even here in India, if those pesky nationalists would only calm down a bit. He had thoroughly enjoyed his life on the estates, but when the time came he would be quite happy to go.

He knew that Matilda dreaded his impending retirement. And had known for a long time that she camouflaged what she truly felt about most things. But even so, he had been disconcerted by the scene she had created the previous Friday when he had said that they should invite the Dorais over soon. It didn't seem quite good form if the young couple weren't welcomed to the district with a party at the General Manager's Bungalow, especially now that virtually everyone else had had them over.

She had said, 'It's pathetic to see a foolish old man trying to do something daring.' She had said a great many other things, and it had shocked him because they hadn't had any real disagreements for as far back as he could remember. In the manner of couples who have been married for a long time, they knew how to manage their life together so that it offered the maximum benefits with the minimum amount of discomfort, so her outburst had left him dumbfounded. The moment he had mentioned the Dorais she had let him have it. She had accused him of letting the side down, she had screamed that he was undermining her position in society. It had all spilled out in a great torrent of emotion. She had quickly dammed up what remained, but the damage had been done. In his patient, methodical manner he had absorbed everything, waited for her to calm down, accepted her fervent apologies and left the breakfast table attempting to understand her outrage.

After her husband left, Mrs Stevenson had stayed on at the table. She was furious with herself. She hated it that Edward knew how much Kannan and Helen bothered her. This had never been her style. Now she had ruined everything by verging on hysteria. He would do everything he could to ensure that she was nice to the Dorais. And when he dug his heels in, it would be sensible to go along with him.

Oh, the pity of it, she'd thought miserably, in the days following their disagreement. Have I learned nothing in the years and years I've been married? It would take every ounce of skill she possessed to win him over. And it would be a long, slow process, but there was no way around it. She should start at once. It wouldn't do to let things fester. Whether she liked it or not, she was going to have to throw the grandest party the district had seen in a long time.

On the morning of the party, Mrs Stevenson carried out her customary inspection of the bungalow. The servants lined up on the veranda after breakfast. Mrs Stevenson sailed down the line, inspecting a button here, a discoloured shirt there. Madaswamy shuffled along at her side, proffering explanations and trying to deflect the memsahib's wrath by shouting even louder than she did. Today, the dog-walker and the junior polisher of brass – doorknobs, pot holders, vase holders, sconces – were sniffling in a noticeable way and Mrs Stevenson sent them back to the servants' quarters that sprawled behind the house. The senior polisher would have to take over. It would mean a very long working day, there was so much brass in the house, but there was nothing she could do about it.

She paused then, right in the middle of her inspection, as the servants waited nervously, struck by the contrast between the palace she lived in and the house that Edward and she had lived in when she had first moved to Pulimed. It had been little more than a three-room shanty, and although she had lived in it only briefly, she could still recite from memory the list of possessions she had taken charge of from the old man who served as the bungalow's cook, major-domo, butler and polisher of brass. There had not been much brass to polish except the front-door knob. This he would spend over an hour gently rubbing in an alcoholic haze, the fumes of metal polish and cheap country liquor mingling in the air. The shanty's inventory wasn't large. The list was obviously the work of the man who held it out to her:

1) 1 copey of *Inge Va* (This Tamil–English phrase book was considered indispensable for planters in south India and Mrs Stevenson still possessed her first copy. Tattered and torn as it was, she held on to it, although she was not sentimental by nature.)
2) 2 chares
3) 1 tabile
4) 1 materes
5) 1 bad
6) 1 cummod
7) 1 beeg tabeel
8) 1 baath
9) 2 pillos
10) 1 wodrobe
11) 1 badside tebel

Thinking about it now, Mrs Stevenson smiled. She even recalled thinking how odd it was that table had been misspelt three different ways. The memory of her first house always put her in a good mood, and she swiftly completed her inspection, dismissed her servants and walked out of the house into the mild morning sun, glorying in the magnificence of the General Manager's Bungalow. It spread over much of the cutaway top of a low hillock, its walls of brick and stone covered with honeysuckle and climbing yellow roses. The driveway, gleaming white after its customary wash on party days, wound its way down what remained of the hill to Major Stevenson's offices. Azalea and camellia bushes lined the driveway and when these were in bloom, they perfumed the air with a subtle scent. Massed phlox and fuchsia, gerberas and zinnias, irises and petunias painted the flower-beds in front of the bungalow in iridescent swatches of purple and blue, red and yellow, white and pink. The cannas clumped on the lawn, the hollyhocks that bordered the live hibiscus hedge, the *Gloriosa superba* that crept along the ground, spilling its dramatic flowers on to the lawns that marooned the house in a lake of polished green ... everywhere that Mrs Stevenson looked, something pleased her.

She walked back into the bungalow to inspect the rooms, a task that would take her until mid-morning, given her standards of perfection. The counterpanes on each of the beds in each of the eight bedrooms would be scrutinized to see that not a wrinkle marred their surface. The flowers in each of the seven bathrooms would be minutely examined; the seven baths would be looked into to see that no circles of dirt ringed the plughole. Mrs Stevenson was nothing if not thorough.

By the time she had finished her rounds, she was ready for her elevenses. But before that she would need to hand out the stores for lunch. Having done this, she dismissed the butler, rang for tea in the smallest of the bungalow's three living rooms, and reluctantly allowed herself to think about the evening ahead.

81

Kannan wheeled his motorcycle to a stop, and Helen clambered off. Although they were exactly on time, there were already vehicles in the driveway – the Frasers' hulking Humber and Freddie's Norton, green to Kannan's blue. His friend must have just arrived, for he could hear the ticking of the motorcycle's engine as it cooled. Helen took off her wrap, and the two of them stamped their feet on the gravel to get the circulation going and walked up the shallow steps that led to the veranda. Major Stevenson met them at the front door, heartily exclaiming, 'Ah, Dorai, Helen, wonderful to see you. You, my dear, look smashing!' She was looking her best. The lilac dress that the old tailor had copied from a six-month-old copy of *London Weekly* in two days flat was an excellent fit and set off her perfect complexion. She wore her only good piece of jewellery – sapphire and diamond ear studs that had belonged to her mother and that Leslie had produced with a flourish the day before her wedding, bringing tears to her eyes. The earrings glowed a deep mysterious blue as they passed into the great lamplit drawing room where Mrs Stevenson waited.

The room was made to hold forty people comfortably and Mrs Stevenson, whose taste was impeccable, had decorated and redecorated until it was perfect. A grand piano, dark as night, stood in a corner; dotted around the room were two or three intimate clusters of sofas, their rich carnelian fabric (the room was done in tones of russet) lent depth by the lamps that stood adjacent to them. A chandelier blazed above an oval coffee table on which an enormous arrangement of roses and iris stood. Mrs Stevenson had spent hours that afternoon supervising the huge floral confection and it was a triumph, the perfect counterpoint to the waterfall of brightness from the chandelier. The rest of the room was softly illuminated by the roaring fire in the grate, which spliced its light with that of small lamps on exquisitely carved and polished occasional tables. Mrs Stevenson sat on one of the long sofas that faced the door, Belinda Fraser on one side and Freddie Hamilton on the other. As the Dorais and her husband entered the room she broke off talking to Belinda and looked at them impassively. Not a muscle twitched, not a smile.

'Well, here they are, dear. Your guests of honour. Isn't the young lady looking terrific?' Kannan wondered fleetingly whether that was a note of unease he heard in his host's voice. As if from far, far away, he watched his wife being received by Mrs Stevenson: the one imperious, calm, even cold, the other lighting up the room with her beauty and freshness. A moment, two, and then Helen said, 'Pleased to meet you,' and everything in the room imperceptibly flattened. Kannan devoutly wished he had overcome his fear of a skirmish and at least been able to tell Helen the 'Pleased to Meet You' story which had acquired legendary status in the district. The previous summer, a young English nurse, up from Vellore to spend the summer on a neighbouring estate with friends, had run into Mrs Stevenson at the Pulimed Club. She had greeted the other upon being introduced with a bright 'Pleased to meet you' and had been instantly cut dead. If you were an Englishwoman of the Right Sort you simply did not say 'Pleased to meet you'. Or 'Cheerio'.

Freddie Hamilton, who had told Kannan the story in the course of a long, drunken evening at his place, had ranted on for several hours about how boring it was that tiny incidents were blown out of all proportion by the dragons who ruled Pulimed society. The story had shaken Kannan. Who knew what gaffes he was committing? After he had passed the test set by Mrs Stevenson's party, he had been rather lax about observing and mimicking the English; following the evening at Freddie's he'd renewed his assault on Englishness, determined to possess it. He began to pump his friend discreetly on all manner of things, observing him and other pukka Englishmen at work and at play, copying their gestures and perfecting them at home, learning a word a day from the *Oxford English Dictionary* (a tip he had learned from Freddie, who had confessed that he had done it all through his first six months on the estates in a bid to improve his memory as well as his vocabulary, before he had given it up as a bad joke) ... Kannan's period of study and self-improvement had been temporarily suspended when Helen joined him but now, as he recalled it, he knew exactly what was to happen next. Helen was about to experience the implacable way in which the English put down someone not quite in their class.

'How do you do?' said Mrs Stevenson icily. 'Belinda and I were just talking about the way standards are falling everywhere. But times change, and we must cope as best we can.' She was being less rude than she could have been, still mindful of the fact that she needed to placate her husband. Fortunately for Helen, the snub didn't register.

Major Stevenson stepped in smoothly. 'What can I get you to drink, my dear?'

Another hurdle, another fall. 'Why, a rum would be fine.'

The disdainful look Mrs Stevenson had perfected slid into her eyes.

'Yes, of course, a rum ...'

Unable to contain himself any longer, Kannan said, 'That'll be for me, sir. Helen will have a sherry.' Helen turned to him, and with a great effort he summoned up a smile.

'A good choice,' Mrs Stevenson said pointedly. Then she gestured for Helen to sit. Kannan would have preferred to sit next to his wife but the Major steered him to another cluster of armchairs, to which Freddie Hamilton had moved. The sounds of vehicles straining up the hill came to their ears and Major Stevenson excused himself and went to meet his other guests.

'So, how did the first formal encounter between our Mistress of Pulimed and young Helen go?' Freddie asked quietly.

'Oh, well. She seems to like Helen,' Kannan said.

'Really now, that's unusual. Maybe the Dragon Lady is getting soft.'

Major Stevenson came back with the new arrivals. Patrick Gordon and his wife Agnes, Geoffrey and Susan Porter of Empress Estate who came accompanied by their Assistant, a shy young Scotsman called MacFarlan with whom Kannan had exchanged little more than polite comments about the weather. Gordon's Assistant, Driscoll, was down with a fever. Mrs Stevenson had decided her party for the Dorais would be limited to the managers of the Pulimed Tea Company and their wives.

As Major Stevenson bustled about getting everyone their drinks, and the new guests settled into their sofas, Kannan watched his wife out of the corner of his eye. He would have done anything to help her, but there was nothing he could do. He grimaced as he took a sip of his drink. He hated rum, but the thought that he was doing it for Helen cheered him up. Just a little, for his wife looked miserable, the effervescence with which she had greeted Mrs Stevenson long gone. She was hunched over in her chair as if Mrs Stevenson was about to attack her. And even though her hostess's onslaught was muted, Helen was soon on the defensive.

'I've seen you dancing at the club, my dear. Those Anglo-Indian institutes must have been quite a good training ground. Never been to one myself, but my husband says they were popular with the British Other Ranks.'

Gordon snickered and Belinda looked contemplative. 'But I'm sure the ones you frequented were all right.'

Anywhere else, Helen would have fought back, but here she felt alone, unsure, on the point of breaking down. Mrs Stevenson knew exactly where she had her victim, and she eased up, just the tiniest bit. It wouldn't do to have Helen weeping. But she wasn't just showing a beautiful young pretender her place, she was also battling something she but dimly sensed, a feeling that everything she held dear was about to be swept away. It was bad enough that fools like her husband thought Indians could be their equals, but to think that she had to entertain a mixed blood, whom even Indians discriminated against, in her own sitting room ... Mrs Stevenson had hated the idea of Englishmen consorting with native women when she had encountered the occasional light-eyed urchin in the Pulimed markets in her early days in the district. Thankfully, the waves of young Englishwomen arriving on Indian shores had braked the rate at which miscegenation took place. Suddenly, she felt very tired. She looked across at the knot of people surrounding her husband. If only that darkie was replaced by handsome, blue-eyed Joe Wilson. Every time she thought of him, she fervently hoped that the war would end soon, and he would return to enliven life on the estates.

Helen excused herself to go to the bathroom. Probably going to have a cry, Mrs Stevenson thought with satisfaction. Maybe she would even decide to leave Pulimed. She caught young Freddie Hamilton watching Helen leave the room and frowned. It was time the young knave found a wife.

Across the room, the talk was of the war. The news from the north-east was not good, although the planters tried to take heart from the fact that everywhere else the tide had turned in favour of the Allies. 'Should get that blasted corporal any day now,' Major Stevenson declared. 'Wish I could've bagged a couple of Boche myself. Got my first one in St Lo and I forget how many thereafter.' The Major's war exploits were famously boring, but there was nothing his listeners could do to escape and he began to retell them now with gusto.

'Cow or bicycle?' Freddie mouthed at Kannan when he caught his eye. 'Ten to one it's moo-moo,' he mimed.

'Do you know,' the Major began, 'what struck me the most about the war was not the brains spattered over the faces of soldiers, the flies clustered thickly on the blood that encrusted almost everything on the scene of the battle, the unexpected sight of an arm or a leg dangling from the trunk of a tree or the window of a house ...'

Freddie winked at Kannan and said soundlessly, 'I won!'

'No, none of these,' the Major continued. 'Almost thirty years after my first battle, the thing that still remains with me is the smell of dead cows. It was a big dairy farming area that we were fighting in, and there were bloated, rotting animals lying around everywhere. And the stench ... it went through your body like a fever. Some of the men would have a laugh at first, puncturing the swollen bellies of the dead animals with their bayonets, but the odour that was released was so concentrated and intense, they quickly stopped. And ...'

But the Major didn't have time to finish because just then Helen walked in. Freddie hailed her, saying, 'Over here, Helen. Can't have the most beautiful woman in the district monopolized by someone else.'

He was the only one there who could have dared face down Mrs Stevenson. As one of the few young Englishmen left, he was a constant reminder to the planting community of the charm and youthfulness of their own kind, a talisman that kept them all going. He was an especial favourite of the women, and that pretty much ensured he could do as he pleased. They put up with his pranks, and his flirting. But Freddie was aware of the limits to what would be acceptable. He took these equably, as he did most things, for he was an uncomplicated, energetic man who loved the outdoor life.

Patrick Gordon, whom both Freddie and Kannan shared a dislike of, said with a brogue that Kannan found very difficult to understand, 'These Nips in Burma are a worry, surely. Could overrun India, if we're complacent. Just like they did Singapore and Rangoon and Mandalay.'

'Oh, I wouldn't worry about the little yellow men. One of our Tommies is worth ten of them!' Major Stevenson said confidently. 'It's all strategy, I'm sure.'

Freddie said with a smile, 'They're little, they're slit-eyed, they're almost yellow but pound for pound they're the best fighters in the British Army ... Guess who they are? ... The Gorkhas, of course,' he said when he received no answer.

'Better than the Black Watch ... or the Highlanders?' Gordon said slowly, rubbing his chin thoughtfully. He was slow in everything he said or did and could be tremendously irritating.

Freddie butted in, 'With due respect, sir, we can argue about that another time. We have a beautiful young lady with us, and by Jove, we must entertain her. Anyone heard the joke about the Gorkha and the Kraut?'

Without waiting for a response from his audience, Freddie began. 'Well, this Gorkha and a big lumbering German sergeant met on a battlefield in France, let's say Rheims. They had exhausted all their ammo. The German had heard all about these little warriors and their prowess with their razor-sharp khukris, so he advanced cautiously, his rifle and bayonet extended well before him. The Gorkha was the first to attack, ducking in under the German's guard, his khukri whistling through the air ...' Freddie paused and looked at his listeners. It's peculiar how eyes of every hue glitter in lamplight like bits of polished glass, he thought. Feels like talking to a bunch of stuffed animals. But he had everyone's attention, for the story was new. 'Nothing happened for a moment. The German gave a mighty, belly-quivering laugh. "You missed me, little man, my head's still on my shoulders and now you're going to die." "Not so, you beeg white peeg," the Gorkha said. 'If I were you I wouldn't turn my head too fast."'

Everyone laughed, and even Helen managed a small smile. Only Gordon looked a little puzzled.

'Well, sir, the Gorkhas' khukris are supposed to be so sharp, and cut so cleanly, that the victim doesn't even feel his head parting company from his neck.'

82

The tinkling of a little silver bell announced supper. The dining room looked magnificent. A lace tablecloth with intricate embroidery covered the teak dining table, crystal shone at every place and a turbaned bearer stood behind every chair. Major Stevenson looked at the scene with satisfaction. Matilda was a wonder, he thought; even the Governor, why, even the Viceroy, would be hard-pressed to put on such a show, especially in these difficult years.

Kannan didn't quite see the scene the way the Major did. The grand table with its flowers and spotless napery, the rows of polished silver and the shining crystal, filled him with dread. Even his months of training could founder here, he realized. Surreptitiously he moved next to his wife and asked in a whisper: 'Are you all right?'

'Yes, I am,' she whispered back, but it was clear that she wasn't. At least she would be spared the attention of Mrs Stevenson during dinner, he thought. At a signal from their hostess, soup was served.

It was unusual for such an elaborate supper to be served during the war, if only out of a sense of guilt. Although the shelves of Spencer's were virtually bare, and the catalogues of the Army & Navy Stores and Harrods of London were suspended, the planters didn't really feel the pinch as much as others did. They grew their own vegetables, there was enough game to be had, and liquor was still freely available. Even so, an old-fashioned six- or seven-course meal, patterned on the great feasts of the 1920s and the 1930s, was rare.

But it all fitted perfectly in Mrs Stevenson's mind. Her party would be the talk of the district, and not even Edward could blame her if, incidentally, a few of the guests were discomfited by the array of knives and forks and spoons. She realized she was rather enjoying herself.

Kannan was certainly not. He tried very hard to eat his soup skilfully, but his spoon clattered loudly against his hostess's Royal Doulton and he slurped up the tomato soup, no matter how hard he tried. Helen did better than he did.

There was baked river trout to follow, with parsleyed new potatoes and green beans. As the meal proceeded without mishap, Kannan began to relax. Fish was followed by an entrée of veal and olives, which was succeeded by a magnificent glazed duck, brown and gleaming in its skin of Calvados and honey, accompanied by rice and sausages in a nest of red cabbage. There was a clatter across the table and he saw Helen's portion of duck fly off her plate and land on the table. Major Stevenson was quick to go to her aid, but her face grew tighter. For an instant, Kannan felt pure hate towards Mrs Stevenson, and then he sternly reminded himself that if they were going to do things the English way, they would have to learn to cope with all this. Duck was followed by pudding, an enormous custard quivering and shaking in its dish, all brown and gold and ivory. After the sweet came the savoury: cold venison paste spread thickly on toast. The servants bustled about, the dishes appeared and departed as if by magic, and the discomfort Kannan had felt at the beginning of the dinner was replaced by a growing sense of weariness, and finally an overwhelming desire to go home. Their ordeal ended with the arrival of Major Stevenson's zealously hoarded Madeira port and Trichinopoly cigars. Mrs Stevenson rose, as did the other ladies, and the men settled down to enjoy their cigars.

An hour or so later, everyone was on their way home, and the Stevensons were preparing to go to bed. As he undressed, Major Stevenson said contentedly and a little drunkenly, 'That was a very nice evening, my dear. And the Dorais showed up rather well, don't you think?' In his mind's eye, he lingered appreciatively on an image of Helen, beautiful and young, her complexion faintly flushed from the drink and the glow of the nearest candles, laughing at some witticism of his.

'Yes, it did go rather well,' Mrs Stevenson said, as she struggled out of her long evening dress. Helen featured in her reflections too. Only this time, she was covered in confusion, having inadvertently broken one of Mrs Stevenson's exquisite fruit baskets. The butler had created a magnificent tiara of spun demerara sugar for the brown crystal baskets on which the fruit reposed. As she'd reached for a pear, Helen had dislodged the sugar cushion. In trying to save it, she had knocked the fruit basket to the floor. Apologies, confusion, and the deep burning shame that had suffused her guest's face – these had been sweet to behold. The spectre of an India damaged beyond repair, that the Dorais' arrival had raised in Mrs Stevenson's mind receded – for now. 'A very good evening indeed,' Mrs Stevenson repeated and the Major wondered if he was missing something.

83

Lily's visit to Pulimed almost didn't come off. She was scheduled to arrive barely a fortnight after the débâcle at the Stevensons' and Kannan toyed with the idea of asking her to postpone the visit. He wasn't sure if Helen would be up to it. But in the end he decided it would be a good thing for her to have a companion for a few weeks, especially someone as caring as his mother.

In the weeks leading up to Lily's departure, a vast variety of sweets and savouries were prepared in the cavernous kitchens of Neelam Illum – murukku, oompudi, athirasam, munthirikothu, halwa and thenkuzhal – and packed away into boxes. Three steel trunks held yards of shimmering Conjeevaram silks. She presumed the house would be well furnished so she omitted the traditional gifts of pots and pans and furniture but she did include two sacks of new rice and two large jars of mango pickle. Kannan had asked her to pack some woollens, it could get quite cold, so one trunk was devoted to sweaters borrowed from a cousin who had moved to Doraipuram from Ooty. When she'd finished she had twenty-seven pieces of luggage, which Ramdoss managed to whittle down to eighteen, including a case containing bottles of Dr Dorai's Moonwhite Cream (Helen was very fair, but you could never be too fair) and other unguents. There was some family jewellery to be passed on, gold earrings and chains; and she had a thali specially made at the best jewellers in Meenakshikoil for her son's bride. Finally, all was ready with two days to go. On the evening before she was due to leave, she looked in on Daniel. 'I'm sure Thirumoolar will like the mango pickle,' he murmured.

She could hardly sleep that night for excitement and she was already exhausted when she climbed into the Chevrolet in the morning. The driver and his helpers managed to wedge in fifteen pieces of luggage (two boxes of sweets and one sack of rice were left behind) plus six people. In addition to Lily and the driver, there were a middle-aged couple whom Ramdoss had nominated as her travelling companions till Pulimed, and two servant boys to assist with the luggage at the station.

Despite the crush, and the rigours of the journey, Lily managed to sleep in the car and on the train. At Madura the group shed the two servants and four pieces of luggage. The rest were somehow fitted into the Humber, which Michael had again loaned Kannan for the day. Having washed and eaten, they set off, a pickle jar wedged tightly between Lily's knees. Her travelling companions, unused to the twists and turns of the ghat road, were mildly car-sick, so having produced some limes for them to suck on, Lily was pretty much left to her own devices. With every passing mile, as the air grew chillier and the world sheered away from the road in great forested ridges, her excitement grew. Michael's driver had warned them that they might run into wild elephants, an ever-present danger on the ghat, but the only wildlife they saw were dozing langurs suspended in a tree like exotic black fruit.

Higher and ever higher they rose, and the houses and trees of the plain shrank from view. They entered a dark, dank stretch where forest giants met overhead. Water dripped from the leaves and stained the road. The driver switched on the headlamps and they went on with exaggerated care. From the darkness came the sound of a solitary bird. Its song, liquid and sweet, tripped a switch in Lily's mind and in a flash she was back in the estates of her childhood. Those hills in Ceylon were different to these jagged slopes, their pleasantly rounded contours furred with pine and tea, and studded with English villas and most prominently the Hill Club to which, naturally, she was not admitted. And yet there was something that yoked them together – the cold, the damp, and once they reached the cultivated area, the fragrance of tea. There was a club in Pulimed, she knew that from Kannan's brief letters, and she couldn't quite believe that she might soon be part of a world she had glimpsed and coveted from afar.

Higher still, and the first mists of the day slid in, ageing the trees along the road. An hour or two of this and they were near the end of their journey. Her companions had dropped off, and Lily thought now about Helen, and how they would get on. She had spent very little time with her at the wedding, and she wondered how she would build bridges with her pretty daughter-in-law. She would have to win her trust, paper over the hurt caused by Daniel's rejection, show her how to please her man and manage her marriage. In other words, she would need to be the right sort of mother-in-law. As the car rolled towards Morningfall, she thought, as she had often done in the past weeks, of how exceptionally good her own mother-in-law had been. The circumstances were somewhat different, but she was sure everything could be worked out. First she'd need to get a sense of Helen's world. It had seemed so different from her own during her brief glimpse of it. No matter, there was bound to be common ground. All she had to do was find it.

It was not to be. The tyranny of the oppressed is much too potent to be deflected by mere goodwill. Helen had been wounded twice. First by Daniel and then by Pulimed society. And she was too mired in her own hurt to extricate herself. Even if Helen had been able to ignore the feeling of being wronged, Lily and she were too dissimilar to even begin putting the semblance of a relationship together. For a start, they didn't have a language in common – Helen's Tamil was as poor as Lily's English.

Trouble broke out almost as soon as Lily arrived, when Helen turned her nose up at the gifts her mother-in-law had brought. 'Is your mother mad, men?' she stormed at Kannan the night Lily arrived. 'Expecting me to wear those ugly saris and jewellery? And all those awful sweets. I don't want them. Give them to the servants if you wish.' Kannan had been infuriated by her contempt and they'd fought through the night, neither making any attempt to make up. There were other points of conflict. Lily had objected mildly to Helen addressing Kannan by name and this had set Helen off again. Two days later, Helen discovered that Lily had been teaching the servants to cook food Kannan had loved at home, and she had angrily ticked off her mother-in-law.

Lily did not fight back. It would only make things difficult for her son. After the first few days, she retreated to her room. She wished she hadn't sent back her escorts, she would at least have had someone to keep her company. She ate in her room, the homesick Tamil servants from the plains cosseting her and secretly cooking her favourite foods. But she put on a brave front for Kannan's sake. All the advice she had rehearsed for weeks remained unsaid. It wouldn't have been understood anyway. Perhaps it was for the best that her son had brought his wife to live on the estates, she thought. How would Helen have fitted into Doraipuram and the traditional role of the daughter-in-law?

For his part, Kannan rued the day he had ignored his impulse to put off his mother's visit. Every time he thought this, he was consumed with shame, for he knew how much his mother had looked forward to this holiday. At such moments he would hate Helen for bringing things to such a pass. Why, he would think bitterly, he'd even been embarrassed by the bundles and bags of home-made sweets and pickles Lily had turned up with. How could he have brought himself to think that way? But he had, and he continued to do so, hating himself for it and growing in his dislike of his wife and his own weakness. At other times he would try and look at things from Helen's point of view. She had suffered. It wasn't right that she'd had to put up with so much. It didn't last, though, and he'd grow angry with her again.

For a few days he tried to make peace, but it was an impossible situation. He grew irascible. Finally, he took to leaving the house early and returning as late as he could, anxious to have as little contact as possible with the combatants. When he did have to be home, he would divide his time between his wife and mother, for Helen refused to be in the same room as her mother-in-law, let alone speak to her. By now all three of them were desperate for the visit to end.

Lily never got to the Pulimed Club. Kannan offered to take her, but she refused quite emphatically. All she wanted to do was return to her own house, and her ailing husband. She had tried her best; there was nothing more she could do. Her son would have to manage his life as well as he could. If she had been able to leave earlier than scheduled she would have done so, but it would have been too much trouble, and Lily didn't feel she could impose any more.

The day she left, Helen didn't come to the door to see her off. Kannan hugged his mother, his affection charged with guilt. But Lily was beyond caring. She pretended she'd had a good time. She pressed small gifts of money into the hands of the servants. When she reached Manickam, the butler took his present, folded his hands in a namaskaram, and said sincerely, 'Amma, all the servants want to thank you for the delicious mango pickle.' The words filled her with a deep sadness.

84

Every time he received an update on the Burma campaign, Michael Fraser would chart it on the big map of India in his study, where red tinged the northeastern frontier. This morning there was news of heavy fighting and he stared at the map for a long time. The fine cross-hatching of lines that depicted the contested area dissolved in his mind into thick green forest infested with leeches and murderous snipers. He wondered how Joe Wilson was doing. Giving the Japs a bloody nose, he was sure. Joe had never given way in a fight. Would that there were more like him, Michael thought, as he worriedly surveyed the spreading pool of red that marked the enemy advance; if we don't stop the Japs soon we'll be in big trouble. It frustrated him immensely, not being able to serve at the front. There was nothing worse than sitting around, listening to news of British reverses without being able to do anything about it. Too young to fight in the Great War, and too old to shoulder arms in this one! But at the rate the Japanese were racing through Asia, he wouldn't need to go to the front; it would come to him.

By March 1944, the campaign in Burma was spilling into India. The Burma Army, a mixed bag of British, Indian, Burmese, Chinese and American forces, had suffered defeat after defeat at the hands of the Japanese. Rangoon had fallen, as had Mandalay, and now the enemy was threatening Imphal, Kohima and Dimapur. If these towns were taken, India would be vulnerable to the invading army and even China would be threatened. It was a battle the British could not lose, for they weren't sure who the vast mass of Indians would support, should the Japanese achieve a breakthrough. The Congress leadership continued stubbornly to demand independence for India as a condition of its co-operation, and the Japanese were already talking vaguely of a Greater Asian Co-Prosperity Sphere, a partnership of Asians against the white man. Moreover, the Japanese had already won over one of India's most charismatic nationalist leaders, Subhas Chandra Bose, so it was anyone's guess how the chips would fall if the British were thrashed at Kohima and Imphal.

If it was a war the British could not lose, it was a war the Japanese had to win. The Russians had repulsed the Germans at Stalingrad, the Americans had battered the Japanese navy in the southwest Pacific, Allied bombers were carpet-bombing the industrial heartland of Germany, and already forces were massing to retake France and advance to the bloodthirsty corporal's lair. Their supply lines stretched, the Japanese had to swiftly conclude the opening battle for India.

This they were confident of doing, for hadn't they smashed the British at Singapore and at every other point in their campaign in Burma? They were the better fighters in the jungle, their planes had ruled the skies, and their tactics this far had proved superior to those of their opponents. And so the forces met on the Imphal plain, and the future of India hung in the balance.

The fierceness of the battle reflected the crucial implications of victory. And of defeat. Both sides reached deep for courage, ingenuity and fortitude. The Japanese would cut off the water supply to a beleaguered garrison, the British would respond by having their planes drop the inner tubes of car tyres filled with water for their thirsty men. The British would seize a position, only to have waves of Japanese soldiers swarm all over it, uncaring of what it cost in terms of men and *matériel.* The British forces were probably better officered, for the Japanese general, Major General Sato, had acquired the reputation of being a stolid, unimaginative soldier who was a stickler for carrying out orders, with little regard for strategy or common sense. If General Sato was ordered to take a feature, he would try to do so even it meant the death of every soldier in his command. The British, looking for the smallest advantage, were thankful that it was him they were up against. But his forces were fierce, courageous, well equipped, and for a long time monumentally superior to the defending army.

The rest of the world may have had little interest in the war in Burma, but to the British non-combatant in India, it was the only conflict of consequence. They had cheered Allied victories in El Alamein and Monte Cassino, they had drunk to the spirit of the blockade runners of Malta, they had celebrated the sinking of the *Bismarck,* the *Tirpitz* and the *Graf Spee,* but they had never lost sight of the war on their very doorstep.

The Pulimed planters were as anxious as every other white man in the country. No aeroplanes overflew the tranquil hills. Life went on much as before. But there was a hysterical edge to their actions as the battle grew closer. Planters would pull rifles and shotguns from cupboards and closets, keeping them close at hand, almost as if they expected screaming Japanese hordes to erupt out of the tea.

One of the fiercest battles for Kohima took place in the garden of the District Commissioner's Bungalow. Once an elegant residence, the bungalow, which overlooked the strategic Kohima crossroads, was now a blackened ruin. The two opposing armies were dug into bunkers on either side of the tennis court at the bottom of the DC's garden. Hurricane and Vengeance fighters wheeled and darted overhead, tanks churned their way up the dirt tracks leading to the scene of battle, but in the District Commissioner's garden the fighting was hand to hand. Neither side would give in, as the possession of the bungalow and the tennis court had acquired a symbolic significance. On the night of 29 April, the Japanese launched a desperate attack to clear the scene of British forces. Joe Wilson, a platoon commander (of 6 Brigade in the 2nd British Division), had just lobbed a grenade at the advancing Japanese when a bullet caught him in the chest. He was removed to a makeshift field hospital where he died three hours later.

85

The memorial service for Joe Wilson at the Pulimed church was packed. The Reverend Ayrton, more focused than anyone had ever seen him, reached outside the Bible for the central idea of his sermon, Petrarch's observation that a good death does honour to a whole life. He spoke of the love and esteem the brave young man was held in, he talked of the loss to the community, and he spoke of how Joe had brought glory to Pulimed. In one of the front pews Mrs Stevenson's shoulders shook silently as she wept.

After the service, the congregation wandered out into the spacious grounds. The ladies of the church committee had organized tea and biscuits, served under the shade of a venerable cypress tree. The morning was clear and bright. It was a day that should have witnessed the sound of laughter and song, celebrated the beauty and vitality of life, but the mood among the congregation was disconsolate.

Kannan collected tea for Helen and himself and walked across to the small group of people she was with: the Frasers, Driscoll and a planter who had driven over from Peermade for the service. They stood in the shade of a late-flowering spathodea, its purple flowers littering the ground. The conversation was desultory; there wasn't much that anyone seemed to want to say. All they wanted was to be left alone with their memories of Joe Wilson. Kannan thought he would have liked to have known the man. He must have been quite special to have affected so many people. Belinda blew her nose in her handkerchief, her eyes red-rimmed. Joe had been her bridge partner and a close friend. The noise seemed to release them from their silence.

'He promised me a Jap bayonet as a souvenir,' Driscoll said.

'Oh, Joe was irrepressible. He promised one to every planter in Travancore and he would have done it too,' the planter from Peermade said.

'Where's Freddie? They were close, weren't they?'

'Yep,' Michael replied, 'poor chap's down with malaria. I can't imagine what he must be going through.'

'Remember that time Joe went and distributed medicine in the coolie lines during the cholera epidemic? He shamed us into going and helping,' Belinda said. It was the first time she had spoken since they had come out of the church.

'Yes, he was the whitest Englishman this district has ever seen,' her husband said sombrely.

Helen was silent, and Kannan wondered what she was thinking of. Ever since Lily's visit her unhappiness had escalated. Her squabble with his mother was only a part of the problem though, and as time passed, an increasingly minor one. With incredible speed but completely wordlessly, the message had reached every corner of Pulimed and the surrounding estates of the way in which Mrs Stevenson had ordained she was to be treated. On the only occasion they'd been to the club in the recent past, Helen was cold-shouldered and ignored by all the women, except Belinda, and she'd wept when they got home, from the sheer humiliation and hopelessness of it all. Kannan had never seen her cry before. From then on, she found some excuse not to accompany him to the club and to parties at the other planters' homes. It wasn't good for his own career, he knew; the planter and his wife were expected to participate jointly, and enthusiastically, in the community's social life. But he understood her pain and tried to cover up for her. Others tried to help, Freddie, the Frasers, and slowly they achieved a precarious equilibrium. Helen even began venturing out occasionally. He hoped she wouldn't feel too out of place in this gathering.

Everywhere murmured voices retailed stories of the young planter – Joe racing his Norton up a steep rain-soaked hillside in pursuit of a wounded boar, exceedingly dangerous when provoked, after he'd collided with it. Joe boldly grabbing the tails of ratsnakes and cobras as they disappeared into their burrows, whirling them around his head and snapping them like a whip so their spines were dislocated. Joe's silken touch at tennis. Joe's greatness as a planter. It was as though, by remembering him, they could keep at bay the grim future which the death of their golden boy portended.

'What a bloody waste this Burma campaign is turning out to be,'

Michael Fraser said deliberately. 'Thousands of England's best and brightest sacrificed to a stupid, thankless war.'

'We don't want the Japanese to have India, sir,' Driscoll said.

'Well, why not, do you think they'll be any worse than us? And who are we to deny it to them anyway? Didn't we acquire an Empire for exactly the same reasons that prompted the madman who started this war ...'

The public anguish of the quiet man, the one who has always minded his own business, is both disquieting and strangely compelling. Belinda put a hand on her husband's arm.

'If you think about it, all this started because poor bloody Hitler wanted to be just like us. What the fool didn't realize is that the age of Empire is over. It galls me that a fine lad like Joe should have died in a hell-hole called Kohima, for an idea that is no longer important.'

He glared at them all as if daring them to challenge him. No one said anything; the outburst had taken them all by surprise. Finally, the planter from Peermade said, 'But sir, Kohima is simply part of the larger war. Do you mean to say we should have let the Krauts walk all over us?'

'Not at all, we should certainly have gone to the aid of our neighbours and defended Britain to the last man. It's this role as the world's guardian that I object to.'

'It's our responsibility, sir. We govern a quarter of the world.'

'But do they want us to guard them, never mind govern them? Do you think Joe's sacrifice means anything here, except to people like us? The vast majority of Indians would much rather be free. What difference does it make to them whether the colonial ruler is British, German or Japanese? Sorry, Cannon. I'm just making a general point ...'

Any further perceptions Michael might have wished to share were drowned by the clatter of teaspoons on saucers and the Reverend Ayrton's deep baritone. When he had secured their attention, he announced that the annual tennis week that was due to start in four days' time would henceforth commemorate Joe. The Stevensons had donated two trophies, one for the men and one for the ladies, both of which would be called the Joe Wilson Cup. Details of the tournament would be posted on the noticeboard of the Pulimed Club.

86

Fever shook Freddie Hamilton and he groaned. It had been over two years since he had contracted malaria, but every time he began shivering and shaking with an attack it was as though he was experiencing it for the first time: the chill that burned though to his vitals and sapped his strength, the weakness that made it an ordeal even to visit the bathroom. At such times all he could do was thank God for his butler, Kumaran. The rascal took every opportunity to swindle him out of chakrams and cash, but he cared for him as he would for a baby when he was knocked flat by the fever. Kumaran came into the room just then with a handful of quinine tablets and Freddie indicated to him that he wanted to visit the bathroom. The butler helped him out of bed and supported him across the room. Freddie hung on to the doorjamb of the bathroom, trying not to collapse. 'Thank you, Kumaran, I'll call for you when I'm done.' The butler shuffled off and Freddie somehow made it to the commode. But he should be okay by the evening, he thought. It was astonishing how dramatically you recovered from malaria – once you had taken the medicine. Freddie had often felt the old-time planters were crazy to establish estates in the malarial belt. If he had been a planter here before the advent of quinine, he was sure he'd have sucked on a shotgun a long time ago.

Back in bed, he found himself thinking of Joe Wilson, as he had, over and over again, since Michael Fraser had brought him news of his friend's death. The fever lent a surreal glow to his imagination as he tried to recreate Joe's final moments. It must have been hellish, but it would have brought out the best in Joe. Under the neighing and screaming of shells he must have rallied his men. Michael had sketched out the scene of the battle, the darkness, the shattered bungalow, the tennis court, the bunkers, the planes roaring overhead, and his imagination had supplied the rest, the screams and groans of dying men, the heat, the smoke, the harsh chatter of Brens, the great glow of flames, the grunting and cursing of men. A time for heroes. A time for Joe. Indeed, his death was of a piece with his life. Joe had scripted the perfect exit. The image broke and faded under the renewed onslaught of the fever and Freddie drifted into an uneasy sleep.

By afternoon he was better, but he doubted whether he would

be well enough for work the next day. He hated this phase of any illness, when you were not sick enough to have lost all interest in everything and not well enough to rejoin the living. Then he heard the faint mutter of a motorcycle and perked up. Michael had said that Kannan would drop in after church. That would be him now.

The English planter valued a house with a view, which is why every bungalow on the estates was perched on an elevation. Freddie's house was an extreme example, situated on a hill and reached by a steep road that was a nightmare to negotiate during the monsoon. There was a blind corner that turned at almost a right angle just short of the house. There was only one way to get through without mishap – by motoring with infinite slowness up the slope and round the corner. Kannan, like every other young planter, was irritated by the crawl up the hill to Freddie's house. But he didn't mind today for he was still preoccupied with Michael's outburst at church. Michael's anger had been more than disquieting. It had, in some way, permanently altered the way in which he regarded the white man and his world. For a brief moment he had seen despair, inadequacy, uncertainty, where there had always been strength, composure and authority, and it hadn't been a pleasant sight.

Kannan was taking a long time to turn up, Freddie thought, and then he realized that he must be driving more slowly than usual because Helen was with him. He was pleased at the prospect of seeing her again. Lucky fellow, Kannan. What a trophy! He wondered what it would be like to be married. For a start it would mean being looked after by someone other than Kumaran when he fell sick. But where was he going to find a bride? The war had stopped the Fishing Fleet and it looked like India would be lost anyway. If not in five years, then in ten. And what Englishwoman would want to live here if she couldn't queen around like that awful Mrs Stevenson? Christ, he thought with some alarm, what if he ended up with someone like Matilda Stevenson? Maybe all he needed was a woman. The resourceful Kumaran could organize a plucker, as he had always done before. Freddie never asked about his method. He had no idea if the women were married or single. He simply paid the money the butler asked for and took his pleasure. The face of a pretty young plucker he'd had his eye on for some time swam into his mind, as did images of firm breasts, huge black nipples, pretty eyes. Did he prefer black nipples to pink ones? It had been so long since he had slept with a white woman. Christ, what the hell was he thinking? This fever really fixed you; it unstoppered the poisons in your mind.

Kannan walked into his room just then and Freddie managed a smile. He was genuinely pleased to see him and had often wondered if they could develop the sort of friendship Joe and he had shared. Would the colour of their skin and the absence of any shared history be an insurmountable barrier, a retardant that would advance their friendship thus far and no more? He hoped not. He sensed that Mrs Stevenson didn't approve of their relationship but that didn't bother him too much. Good planters were thin on the ground, and he doubted that she would be able to prevail upon her husband to get rid of him.

'You look awful,' Kannan said, by way of greeting.

'No worse than you, old chap. And at least I'll get to look better when this boring fever passes. Christ, what was God thinking of when he created mosquitoes?'

'Freddie, I'm really sorry about what happened.'

'Yes, what a waste. We'll all be the poorer now that Joe's gone. You never knew him, did you? You would have liked him, he won people over so easily.'

They continued to talk about Joe, or rather Freddie talked and Kannan listened – the laughter, the crazy bachelor stunts, the wild death-defying rides through the tea, hunts for boar and junglefowl, all-night bridge and brandy sessions ...

'Joe could light up any room, bring people alive. Yes, he was a good sort, the best. All this, and a hero too. How many heroes do you know, Cannon?'

It was an unexpected question, and he didn't know how to answer it.

'What sort of hero do you mean?'

'Well, you know, people who possess such great gifts that they seem to be able to do things without worrying about their own lives or fortunes, as weedy little people like us do?'

Kannan thought for a while. Kumaran came in with tea and biscuits.

'I had an uncle who died fighting you chaps, and my grandfather died in a battle long ago. I didn't know either of them, but I guess they would qualify as heroes ...'

'Joe was certainly cast in the heroic mould. You could have added him to your pantheon. Where's Helen?'

'Couldn't come. She had some work to do,' Kannan said lamely.

Something of his discomfort must have shown on his face, because Freddie asked, 'Everything all right?'

'Yes, I suppose so,' he said slowly.

'Aha, the well-known perils of married life.'

They laughed together.

'Hey, what's this?' Kannan asked, picking up a book, *The Man-Eaters of Kumaon,* from the bedside table.

'Oh, Michael brought it when he came to visit. Apparently it's a big bestseller. He had it mailed from Bombay.'

'Has he written anything else?'

'I don't think so. Cracking stuff. He goes after a man-eating tigress which has killed four hundred and thirty-six people, and only just escapes being killed himself.'

'I'll ask Michael if I can borrow it after you.'

'Yep, put in your claim quickly. I'm sure there's going to be a long queue. Every bloody planter here thinks he's God's gift to shikar.'

'Have you ever taken a shot at a tiger?'

'None left,' Freddie said with a grimace. 'That's the problem with the planting life today, you know. When I was growing up, there was an exotic figure in my life, a distant uncle who owned a tea estate in the High Wavys. I used to look forward to his visits home. Tigers, panthers, elephants, a day scarcely seemed to pass when my uncle wasn't fighting for his life. Ripping *Boy's Own* stuff. It really fired my imagination, I can tell you that!'

'And nothing since you've been here?'

'Not really. There's no big game any more, not unless you count the occasional elephant. But somehow I've never warmed to the idea of shooting elephants. It's prohibited anyway. But there was that time when Joe and I saw a black panther that Harrison had shot. Remember Harrison? That maverick planter I told you about who went native, God knows how many years ago, and virtually dropped out of sight?'

Kannan said, 'Harrison?'

'Come on, I'm sure I've told you about him. Best shikari the hills had ever seen, until toddy claimed him. Anyway, he'd been called in to shoot a panther that had been prowling around the old bungalow at Empress. Last time I saw him, incidentally, wonder what he's doing now … but listen, this story is about the panther, not Harrison … I remember that the dead beast looked pretty pathetic, a tangle of legs and a disproportionately large head. It's only when I took a closer look that I began to have an idea of its terrible power, you know, teeth, great yellow eyes.'

'I remember reading somewhere that the grunting of a charging leopard can stop an elephant in its tracks.'

'Wouldn't that be grand to see? A black panther charging out of the black night, only to be stopped at the last possible moment by the crack of Freddie's rifle that takes it right between the eyes ...'

'How on earth are you going to shoot a springing black panther on a pitch-dark night?' Kannan asked, smiling.

'Oh, between the whites of the brute's eyes I expect, or should it be the yellows ...'

'Bet you'd be shaking so much your quivering would put the poor panther off its aim.'

'Speak for yourself. The Hamiltons of Lincolnshire are known for their nerve,' Freddie said with a laugh. 'What a pitiful time we're having of it,' he went on after a while. 'No tigers, no leopards, nothing that gives you the thrill of going after a dangerous animal ...'

'Wild boars are dangerous ... the first time I shot one I couldn't get over how sharp its tusks were. And Michael was telling me about the poacher who was gored by a boar a few years ago. He died, Freddie, bled to death, he was too far from civilization to get medical help.'

'But they're pigs, Cannon. Swine. Nothing ennobling about them. This wasn't what I was after, if truth be told, when I signed up for the glorious life of the estates.'

'Well, you could always be at war.'

Freddie flushed.

'I'm sorry,' Kannan said quickly. 'I shouldn't have said that.'

Their conversation dried up. Kannan felt awful. How could he have been so insensitive? It had slipped out, and he had certainly meant nothing by it. Freddie's voice jerked him out of his remorse.

'You know, I know this sounds disrespectful, but when I think of Joe blazing through his life so fast, just eating it up, it seems right that he went so quickly. He would have made a miserable old man. I can't see him at seventy, white-haired, wrinkled, a garrulous old drunk ...'

Freddie seemed to go off to sleep after that, so Kannan got up to go.

'Thanks for coming, Cannon,' Freddie muttered sleepily. 'Really appreciate it. We'll get together, tomorrow, the day after, when I'm better.'

Kannan was almost at the door when he remembered.

'Oh, Freddie, I forgot to tell you, the annual tennis week will henceforth be played in honour of Joe. There's to be a Joe Wilson Cup and everything.'

'Good. Now all we need to do is win it for Joe!'

87

There's nothing quite like playing tennis in the hills. The ball travels through the air with great clarity and when it is struck it sings off the racquet with tremendous velocity, the sound and the action resonating through the cold, thin air. That summer, the thwock-thwock of tennis balls took on a greater urgency as the planters prepared for the Joe Wilson Cup.

The women's matches were played first. Agnes Webster of Chenganoor Estate, who had taken part in Wimbledon before the war, easily outclassed her opponents to capture the ladies' trophy. The redoubtable Mrs Webster had no obvious counterpart in the men's draw. The majority of the younger assistants and superintendents were overseas with their regiments, and of those who remained there weren't more than a dozen fit enough or proficient enough to wield a racquet. Sensing her tournament losing much of its gloss, Mrs Stevenson persuaded her husband to contribute a crate of hoarded Famous Grouse to the spoils that the victor would take away. Eight more planters entered the fray, but most of them were so decrepit or unskilled that it made no difference to the eventual quarter-final line-up.

Kannan was astonished to find himself in the last eight. He hadn't touched a tennis racquet until a year ago, but under the tutelage of his Superintendent, who was a keen if erratic player, he had become fairly good at the game. He had acquired a decent first serve, covered the court well, and made up for a non-existent backhand with his best shot, a running forehand drive that curved wickedly away from his opponent. The two men he had faced during his run-up to the quarter-finals were planters in their fifties, with neither the stamina nor the strokes to hinder his progress. His third opponent hadn't even bothered to show up. A walkover.

Today would be different, Kannan knew, as Freddie and he walked towards the courts from the clubhouse. His opponent was no pushover. He had never seen Hemming play, he was an owner-planter from the far north of the Periyar district, but Freddie had filled him in.

'Looks and plays like Big Bill Tilden,' he had yelled in Kannan's ear as they motor-cycled towards the club. 'Same high serving action and penetrating ground strokes.' The great American was Freddie's ideal. Kannan preferred the fighting Englishman, Fred Perry. While their games couldn't live up to those of their heroes, the young assistants mimicked their every other action – the way they held their racquets, the way they shook hands, their positions on court after they had executed a shot. If passion alone could have improved their on-court skills, Hamilton and Dorai would soon have been champions. But, as things stood, they were no more than enthusiastic club players, with Kannan having the edge over Freddie simply because the latter was the most uncoordinated athlete the district had ever seen.

'You can win this tournament, my friend,' Freddie said as they got to the courts. Through the high wire mesh that enclosed the playing area they could see the first two matches getting under way. Robert Cameron vs Stuart Webb and Alec Cameron vs Graham Court. The sun was pleasantly warm on their shoulders, and the tea fields pooled gold and green all around the playing area.

'You're mad,' Kannan said. 'Have you forgotten the dreaded Camerons? And Hemming?'

'You'll beat them. They're all old enough to be your grandfather.'

'But they'll wipe the court with me.'

'Don't worry. If all else fails, I'll throw rocks at them at critical moments.' To Kannan's disgust, Freddie started whistling. He felt nervous, almost nauseous, as the tension gathered in him.

He watched the Cameron brothers walk to their serving marks, their slow, smooth swagger subconsciously reflecting the arrogance of players who ruled the court. They swatted the ball a couple of times across the net to their opponents, their racquets travelling in lively controlled arcs that Kannan had practised a thousand times on his own but could rarely replicate. Within moments, both brothers had settled into a lovely rhythm, as they swung the ball to their opponents on the far side.

'No bets on who is going to win. Cameron Redux.'

'Yuh.'

'Hullo there. George Hemming.' Kannan turned sharply. His opponent was a tall man, in his late forties, fit and with a strong grip. 'See you around later. Have a good match,' he said to Kannan in an accent he couldn't readily identify and was gone.

'Definitely like Bill Tilden. The height. And those shoulders.'

'Come on, Freddie, you're making me nervous.'

'Sorry, old boy,' Freddie said with a smile.

And then they went silent, for Alec Cameron was preparing to serve the first ball of the day.

Kannan didn't know where Cameron had learned his tennis (although it would have been easy enough to find out from Freddie, who seemed to know everything about everyone) but wherever he had picked up his game it had given him a service action that was unique. Turned sideways on to the net, he glanced quickly at his opponent, then bent seriously to the task at hand. He bowed carefully, piously almost, over the ball, and then went quiet like the sea at rest. The world waited with him, the red tennis courts veined with white, the light-suffused tea, the tall silver oaks that lined the playing area, the stepped flower-beds, the ballboys, the umpire, the six spectators, his opponent. There was nothing static about the second or two that Alec was stooped over the ball. No, this was a powerful dynamic moment, full of implicit violence and grace, all his splendid and varied talents merely counterbalancing each other. A few seconds more and Cameron was arcing back, a wave gathering power, before exploding forward, his legs rocketing him upward like pistons towards the gently falling ball. The moment of contact between racquet and ball was unbelievably violent, the twisty downward smashing motion of the serve spiralling the ball forward from the strings with immense speed. Cameron's opponent took a half-step forward but was way too late, the ball had arrowed down the centre of the T, paused for a moment at contact, then skidded wide. An ace. Fifteen-love.

Within no time at all, Cameron was three-love up and looked on the point of breaking his opponent's serve again, holding three break points against him. The hapless Court, who seemed to have been battered into submission, chose that moment to assert himself. He strode purposefully to the service line and banged in a winner. One break saved. He served another excellent serve, which Cameron barely managed to reach; Court put away the short ball easily. Two break points saved. The tide was beginning to turn. It was then that Cameron chose to create a moment of magic.

Great athletes, like musicians and artists of genius, have it in them to create works of art, perfectly executed plays that leave spectators and opponents awestruck and linger on in the memory long after they have lit up the scene of battle. Court's next serve was very good, but Cameron was ready for it. He lunged for the ball as it swung out wide and managed to return it deep to his opponent's forehand. Court scrambled for it, and with every ounce of skill he possessed, he contrived to hit the best shot he could, a searing forehand cross-court that landed on the line. Incredibly, Cameron was there, and he began to put together a point that all those watching would remember for a long time to come.

Off-balance, he dispatched Court's thunderbolt back to him, scrambled into position, and when the ball was returned, loomed over it like a deity, and struck it with a backhand of great beauty and violence. The ball sped to the far corner of the court. An exhausted but valiant Court managed to get to it, but only just. For the first time that afternoon Cameron came to the net, and put away the easy volley. Four-love. Every spectator present applauded, the umpire restraining himself but only just. The poor courts, old Slazenger racquets, worn-out balls (the war had made new tennis balls impossible to find), shabbily dressed urchins who functioned as ballboys ... all these had, for just a moment, been gilded by the beauty of the play.

Court applauded too; after that perfect point, all the fight seemed to have gone out of him, and he handed the first set to Cameron six-love.

Kannan and Freddie, who had been transfixed by the action on court, found voice. 'By Jove, that was astonishing, monstrously brilliant,' Freddie said with awe. 'Budge would have played like that, Borotra ...'

'I'm going home,' Kannan said. 'Best to give my opponent a walkover. Rather than shame myself.'

'Nonsense, man. Who knows, you might be able to give this Hemming a run for his money. He's no Cameron. And if you make it to the final it will be an achievement in itself. Who knows, maybe old Alec C will have the flu or malaria on the day.'

'Let's stop pretending. I'll go and shake hands with Hemming, honourably leave the scene of battle.'

'Not so honourably, old boy. For Christ's sake, do you think Joe would have walked away?'

'No, he wouldn't, but sometimes you know that no matter what, you can't win ...'

'Come on, Cannon, you've got to do this. If for nothing else, do it for Helen.'

Ah, Helen, Kannan thought. Yes. He should think of Helen if he wanted to lose the match. Or then again, it might make him so angry that it would propel him into a different zone of court craft and skill. Kannan had done his best, but his efforts weren't enough. Helen had grown more and more unhappy. They squabbled daily, and it had become an effort to be civil to each other. She blamed him for everything that had gone wrong at Pulimed, kept at him to take her back to Madras. Finally, even though it tore at him to think that the marriage he had invested so much in was disintegrating so swiftly, he said they'd go to Madras at Christmas. That had brought a lull for a few days, but soon the squabbling had begun again. He hoped, of course, that over time she would stop being so bitter and frustrated. There was nothing else he could do. He had simply run out of ideas. But, come to think of it, a victory over an Englishman might taste sweet to Helen, redeem him partially in her eyes. Except it wasn't going to happen.

'I don't stand a chance, Freddie,' he said disconsolately.

'Wrong attitude, my dear fellow, absolutely wrong. Can't have this sort of thing, you know. Would a stiff brandy and soda help?'

'Probably fall asleep on court. Look at the pummelling Court's getting.'

A flurry of strokes descended on the hapless Court like a fleeting monsoon shower and the second set was over six-one.

It was his turn now. He stepped on to the court with Hemming. The tall planter's face betrayed no emotion as he called the toss. Hemming won and elected to serve. 'Good luck,' he said to Kannan, and they went to their respective positions and began practising. Hemming's clean, compact strokes, the way he moved on court, his unfussy service action – Kannan knew that he was a better player than he could ever hope to be. All he had on his side was youth, quickness around the court, and resolve. It was not enough. Hemming easily held serve, and broke Kannan just as easily. The games went with serve thereafter, and before he knew it the set was over six-four.

'Excellent, excellent,' crowed Freddie, 'you lost just one service game. You can take him. The next set is yours, he's tiring, mark my words.'

'Freddie, easy now, let me get my breath back.' He was so tired from trying to run down every last one of his opponent's expertly placed shots that he could hardly breathe. Gradually, the world came back into focus, his breathing eased. He sipped at the glass of lemonade Freddie brought him, and looked over at Hemming, who was talking to a friend.

'You have to break him, at least once, Cannon, you mustn't think he's invincible. He's an old man. He's tiring, now is when you should go for the kill. Get focused, run down every ball, show some daring.'

Freddie's exhortations had a positive effect. Kannan battled for every point when play resumed, and slowly the set began to swing his way. He was nowhere near as good as Hemming, but he compensated for his deficiencies by grimly refusing to yield no matter what his opponent threw at him. In the crucial seventh game, with the honours even Hemming served, an excellent kick serve to his backhand, but luckily Kannan had guessed which direction to go, and was well placed to return it. He tried a sliced backhand, the only backhand stroke he could play with any measure of confidence. Hemming returned the ball, Kannan hit it back and then Hemming tried to lob him as he stood in mid-court. This was Kannan's moment. He was in motion as soon as he saw Hemming's intention, tired legs pumping the earth, raising him way above the court, racquet back, ready to bludgeon the ball. The racquet fell, the ball skidded past a stunned Hemming and all at once, the outcome of the set was wide open.

Having astonished Hemming with his effrontery, Kannan took the set. Unfortunately for him, he couldn't sustain that level of play. And it is axiomatic in tennis, as it is in life, that when you have an opponent cornered, you must put him down. Give him a second chance and he will come on stronger.

Which is what happened in the third set. With craft, guile and experience, Hemming took the game away from his younger, less skilled opponent. Forceful drives were returned with the power that had driven them, smashes were met with dink and slice. The brute arrogance and strength of youth were cleverly turned to the older man's advantage. He found the angles, tried Kannan's patience, and held his nerve when Kannan stormed the net or tried to find the level he had played at in the second set. After he had lost four games in a row, Kannan tried an ambitious passing shot and saw the ball balloon yards wide of the sideline. Suddenly, the enormity of what he was trying to do engulfed him, and he felt very alone. What was he trying to do: take on the white race all by himself, far from family and friends, isolated by an embittered wife, his brownness, his lack of skill? As he disconsolately paused to collect himself, a favourite story from childhood eased into his mind – wouldn't it be just marvellous if he could be a God in disguise, like the infant Krishna, just a nondescript cowherd until, confronted by the terrifying rakshasa, he'd opened his mouth and deep within it stretched worlds, planets, universes, life itself? Wouldn't it be fabulous if he were to be suddenly transformed into a combination of Lacoste, Borotra, Budge and Perry, and storm his way to an improbable victory? He committed a double fault instead. Distracted now, and already beaten in his mind, fourteen minutes later he had lost the last set six-two.

'Well played,' Hemming said simply as they shook hands. 'That smash in the second set was perfection itself.'

The praise did little to lift Kannan's spirits. He morosely accepted Freddie's offer of a beer and they wandered up to the bar. 'You tried everything and you almost got him,' Freddie said. His cheeriness seemed forced.

'He won, and that's what matters. All that rot about it's not winning or losing that counts, take it from me, it's all bosh.'

'Got to be something in it, old boy. I've never won a game in my life.'

'Yes, but it's different for you. I can just imagine Mrs Stevenson's face when she hears about today's results. I know exactly what she'll say: "You can't expect better from an Indian." It's all so depressing.'

'It's all right, Cannon. It's only a tennis match ... say, game for some jugged hare?'

'Why not, this bloody racquet needs to be good for something.'

'No, not your playing racquet, I've got an old one.'

'Yes, but you drive. I'm hunting. I'm in the mood to crack a few heads.'

They finished their drinks, signed chits and made their way to where the motorcycle was parked. Freddie took an old racquet with a cracked frame and sagging guts from his saddlebag, and handed it to Kannan who took a few experimental swishes with it.

Hare hunting with tennis racquets was great sport among the young planters on the estates. The hunters would roar along the narrow tracks at dusk, their headlamps rooting the unfortunate creatures to the spot until they were dispatched.

Soon after they left the club, they startled a tiny owl from its perch on the stump of a pruned tea bush. It swooped ahead of them, a dirty white rag in the wind, and finally managed to escape the magnetism of the headlamp. Three hares were not so lucky. The first jumped straight into the light, a few yards beyond Dhobi's Leap, and the old racquet swept down on it with crushing power, instantly extinguishing the light in its eyes. Kannan misdirected his blow at the second, and broke a leg. It limped out of the light, but they soon found it again and it was swatted to the ground. The third hare inexplicably leapt high in the air, and Kannan caught it a perfect forehand drive, hit with all his strength. The shock travelled all the way up his arm. By now they were within a kilometre of Freddie's bungalow, and decided they had enough food for supper.

'Stay for a drink,' Freddie said. 'I'll get my butler to skin the hares.'

About three hours later, a very drunk Kannan motored unsteadily home. As he was slowing down to turn into the road that led to his own bungalow, a gigantic hare lolloped into the glare of his headlight. Calmly it paused, then looked straight at him, its eyes gleaming red in the light. For a moment, Kannan was terrified. In these haunted hills, could the hare be the ghost of all its fellows, come to wreak vengeance on their killer? Kannan shouted and waved his arms at the animal. For what seemed a long time, although it was only a matter of seconds, it did nothing, and then it slowly came towards him. He almost fell off the motorcycle in panic. Nearer and nearer it came, then turned and slipped into the tea bushes.

88

Lily had little time to brood over her blighted holiday or the difficulty Helen would pose to the reunion of her husband and her son. For, within days of her return, Daniel's brief resurgence faltered. He suffered a second stroke that left him completely bedridden. This put an end to whatever little contact he'd had with the other residents of Doraipuram. He wanted only two people around him now – the devoted Ramdoss, and Lily, both of whom he failed to recognize from time to time. His wife had minded very much when it had first happened but when she realized that her husband wasn't doing it out of any desire to hurt her, but was only acting according to the dictates of his increasingly unreliable mind, she was quick to forgive him.

Her grandson Daniel was the only other member of the family permitted into the sick-room. Daniel barely recognized him. For a while, the boy drifted disconsolately in and out of the makeshift laboratory where he had spent so many happy hours with his grandfather, trying out various experiments on his own. Ramdoss put an end to that when an unanticipated chemical reaction flooded the lab and the adjoining rooms with the smell of dead lizards.

In the last month of his life, Daniel's world shrank to the room in which he lay. Without much expectation that it would ever be needed, Ramdoss had installed a fully equipped worktable along one wall in case Daniel should take an interest in pharmaceuticals again, but besides this, the room was very sparsely furnished. A shelf of siddha and religious texts, a couple of wooden chairs, a table for Daniel's medicines. On one of the walls was a picture of Charity, a garland of sandalwood shavings around it, and another of Daniel, Lily, and the children, taken when Kannan was born. There were no other decorations.

In his bedroom, Daniel would lie motionless and mute, day after day. Occasionally, he would immerse himself in one of the siddha texts that Dr Pillai had bequeathed to him, although it wasn't clear to Ramdoss or to Lily whether his infrequent expositions on siddha medicine had any basis in scientific reality or were simply deluded ravings.

In addition to Lily and Ramdoss, the people he communed with were Charity, Solomon, Aaron, Dr Pillai and Father Ashworth. It didn't surprise Lily or Ramdoss any more when they came into the room to find him locked in conversation with a dead person. Dr Dorai would solemnly introduce the visitor and would sometimes even invite Lily or Ramdoss to participate in the chat; this was always a trifle disconcerting, especially when they were expected to reply to some arcane question of metaphysics or medicine that had been posed by the dead person and had been diverted to them. At moments like these, a benign madness stared out from Dr Dorai's eyes. But at other times he was perfectly sane. On a couple of occasions, he spent long hours in happy reminiscence with his wife when he inquired especially after Kannan (he had no recollection of his marriage) and his namesake, Shanthi's son Daniel.

There were other times when he was full of anger. He would rage against an ungrateful world. Sometimes he would summon Ramdoss and dictate a letter to whoever had offended him, living or dead:

> Dear Priscilla, [he would write to a second cousin, deceased five years ago]
>
> I am duly in receipt of your letter dated 5 April 1938 which is just a tissue of poisonous lies and falsehoods and a series of mali-

cious insinuations and suggestions, interspersed with a lot of half-truths ...

Ramdoss would patiently take all this down, along with pages of accusations and allegations. He would have the letters typed up and sometimes Daniel would ask for them and sign them. More often, dictation done, the letter would be forgotten, and he would grapple with some other demon or delight.

As the days grew hotter, his condition deteriorated. Bedsores developed. He became weaker and his eyesight and hearing grew worse. The various specialists summoned by Ramdoss and Lily could do little more than prescribe new kinds of medication. The more honest among them corroborated with the family physician's diagnosis: after two strokes, at his age, every day was a miracle.

One day Daniel had an unusual request. Not once had he shown the slightest interest in leaving his room, but now he asked Ramdoss to arrange a car for him that evening. He wanted to go for a drive. The old Chevrolet was hastily taken to the workshop, and polished and waxed until it shone. Ramdoss had no idea where Daniel wanted to go but this was the first encouraging sign in a long time and he wasn't about to let it pass.

It was still very hot, although the sun had almost gone down when they carried Daniel to the car and eased him into the front seat. Ramdoss took the wheel. The sick man's favourite grandson Daniel and a couple of older cousins were rounded up, and they were all piled into the capacious rear seat along with a brace of shotguns.

Ramdoss drove slowly, and Daniel, more animated than usual, directed him with sure, precise directions. About an hour later they were parked in a thick stand of casuarina trees on a bluff overlooking the Chevathar. As night fell, the flying foxes began to float over them, wavering and slow. Guns popped and a couple dropped. Another wave, more fire and noise ...

From where he sat, Daniel's eyes filled with the clamour and joy of the past. He saw his father resting his arms on the cart, and firing carefully and steadily into the sky, the servants racing the enormous white Rajapalaiyams to the furry black bodies amid the sound and smell of gunfire. It was one of his few clear memories of his father. He hadn't retrieved it in a long time but now that it played behind his eyes, and was renewed in front of him, he felt a great calm descend.

He thought of his mother and the day she had gone. The dream that had filled his nights came back to him: Charity, small, indomitable, dressed in a white sari, walking down that dark, threatening ravine ...

'I'm ready to go home now, Ramu,' he said softly. His brother-in-law looked at him sharply, read the look in the tired eyes. He felt a powerful melancholy sweep over him.

On the way home, Daniel asked to stop in one of the blue mango topes that Solomon had laid down. It was almost too dark to see, the trees black and hulking in the poor light, the paleness of a few out-of-season mangoes only just visible. At the old man's request, Ramdoss crunched his way over the dry and brittle leaves to the nearest tree, and felt around, plucked a mango and brought it back to the car. In the back seat, the others were growing restive and Ramdoss quietened them with a gesture.

For a while Daniel turned the mango around in his hand, then spoke, almost to himself: 'When my son was very young, amma used to bring him down here. I remember she used to sing all sorts of lullabies to him, but his favourite was something she'd made up ...' He sang in a hoarse whisper:

Saapudu kannu saapudu
Neela mangavai saapudu
Onaku enna kavalai ...

'He'd want it sung over and over again.' Daniel gave a little laugh, and then nodded to Ramdoss to drive on.

When they reached the house, they carried Daniel back to his room, settled him on the bed, still clutching the mango. As Ramdoss turned to leave, Daniel said, 'Blue mangoes, Ramu, the pride and joy of our family as far back as I can remember. I recall appa going down to the river during the harvest and filling the first basket, the fruit blue as the sky, invested with streaks of sun. The Chevathar was full of water those days, and far below the surface we could see mangoes that had dropped into the river, glimmering mysteriously like the eggs of some rare sea creature ...'

He turned the fruit around in his hand, then said slowly: 'It's deserving of our commitment to it, Ramu. When I lived in Nagercoil, in my grandfather's house, I used to sometimes spend my free time on the veranda, looking out at a Chevathar Neelam. My mother had planted it and it stood tall and proud, the focus of the small garden. But, do you know, in all the time I was there, it didn't fruit once. Whereas here they are profligate, generous. I'm glad I'll die in

Chevathar ...'

'Anna, I'd like to call Kannan home ...'

Daniel didn't say anything for a long time. Then he said quietly, 'Yes, he should come home ... soon. I'll let you know.' Daniel rolled the mango between his palms, tilting it this way and that. Then he leaned back and shut his eyes. Thinking he had gone to sleep, Ramdoss was easing himself silently from the room when he heard him mutter, 'The maggot in the mango.' But he said no more. Gently, Ramdoss took the fruit from where it was loosely clenched in Daniel's hand, examined it for a moment, placed it on the bedside table, drew a sheet across the emaciated body and switched off the light. Just before he left the room, he turned and looked at Daniel one last time. He had a sense of things passing, and suddenly was afraid. Although he was very tired, he left instructions with the servant on the night shift that he was to be awakened if there was the least cause for alarm and went to his own room.

In the early hours of the morning, Ramdoss was shifting restlessly in bed when he felt a hand shaking him. The servant he'd left on duty whispered urgently, 'Lily amma is calling you. Aiyah ...' Ramdoss was instantly awake. Wrapping his lungi firmly around him, he rushed to Daniel's room. In the grey light, he saw Lily's sorrowful face and understood immediately. 'Take the car and get the doctor,' he said urgently to the servant who had followed him into the room. 'Quickly now.'

89

The pain had been unexpected, so intense that it had driven every other sensation from his body. Daniel didn't know if he was breathing, if he had screamed out in agony; all he could think of was that what he was experiencing was more than he could tolerate. And then, with the swiftness with which it had clutched him, it was gone, leaving behind only a feeling of great discomfort. He couldn't speak, he could barely breathe, a mist obscured his sight, but he wasn't afraid ...

The news of Daniel's decline spread rapidly through the colony. In less than an hour, the house was packed. The doctor would evict people from the sick-room, but they'd filter back. He lost his temper on one occasion and shouted, 'Get out, get out all of you. This man is fighting for his life, he needs air, he needs peace and quiet.' He turned to Ramdoss and said, 'Can't you get them to leave the room, and stay out of it! This man is too sick to be moved, otherwise I would have him taken to hospital immediately.'

The room was cleared at once, but nobody went far. The hot, airless corridors and passages of the mansion were clogged with people waiting with a variety of expressions, boredom, grief or the blank, unseeing look of people who have mastered the art of patiently waiting for nothing in particular. All through the morning more and more people trekked to the House of Blue Mangoes, drawn by a shared sense of grief at the imminent passing of the man who had been the dominant presence in their world as far back as they could remember. In the room where Daniel lay, there were still too many people, but Ramdoss and the doctor had at least managed to restrict it to close family and the priest. Two large nephews blocked the door, and politely but firmly refused everyone else entry.

The fog still filled Daniel's head, but his discomfort had lessened. He tried to use the breathing techniques enjoined by the siddha masters. Gradually his suffering eased. He sensed people around him, but couldn't make out individual faces. Nothing but blurry images in his vision, although in his mind's eye there was now some clarity – he saw Lily where he would have expected to see her, by his bed, her eyes shut in prayer; Ramu, tears running down his cheeks; Solomon and Charity; his sisters Rachel and Miriam, who had fought with him so vigorously; Aaron, such a beautiful youth; Thirumoolar, Dr Pillai, Father Ashworth. But why was everyone so sorrowful? He was at peace now, the pain was bearable; this passage was something he was prepared to negotiate, it was something he wished for.

He felt a pricking sensation on his skin, and then a voice that he couldn't understand came faintly to him. He tried to open his eyes but they didn't seem to be obeying his will. Better to concentrate on his breathing; if he could regulate that, everything else would fall into place.

The silence of the room was broken by a loud voice. Miriam, who appeared to have fallen into a trance, was shouting, sweat drenching her face and blouse, her eyes intense and bright, 'Anna, anna, can you see him now? Can you see our Saviour the Lord who is waiting for you?'

Galvanized into activity by the commotion, the people in the room surged forward. 'Clear the room. At once,' the doctor and Ramdoss were shouting, pushing people away from Daniel's bed. His grandson Daniel dropped to the floor and scrambled through the legs of the adults, an empty test tube in his hand; this he thrust under the dying man's nostrils and held for a long moment. Trace elements inside reacted to Daniel's breath and the inside of the test tube clouded over. The boy stoppered it swiftly and returned the way he had come. Miriam kept screaming, 'Anna, can you see the Lord?' Ramdoss continued to shove people out of the room, the priest murmured prayers and Lily stood by the bedside as if carved from stone.

A rumour snaked its way outside that Dr Dorai was dead, and immediately a high-pitched keening began, rising and falling in the thick humid air, setting the birds clumsily stirring in the branches of the large mango tree in front of the house.

Dr Dorai was oblivious to all this. He was walking down the beach in bright sunshine with Father Ashworth, looking not at the brittle surf, but at the sand at his feet where the shells left behind by the rushing water gleamed like polished stone. To his astonishment, the shells seemed to be moving of their own accord. Excitedly, he pointed this out to the priest. Father Ashworth picked up a shell and showed him the long fleshy feet of the mollusc, its imperceptible grip on his finger, its tenacious hold on life, amidst the thunder of the sea. A great light filled his head, an instant after the pain swamped him with an intensity he knew signalled the end ... then he was abruptly free of it.

All we can hope for, when the time comes, Ramdoss thought, as he watched the doctors try in vain to revive the man who was the centre of his universe, is that we die well, having overcome our terror of never again walking with friends, eating fruit off the trees, anticipating surprises ... That wasn't the only fear to be mastered, he realized the next instant – when we prepare to die, not only do we have to be accepting of what we leave behind, we also have to be prepared for what awaits us: a good place or a bad place, rebirth or union with the Divine.

Some weeks after Daniel died, Ramdoss found a copy of the Upanishads in his room, with some passages neatly underlined in blue ink. One of these was verse 13 of chapter 3 of the second Brahmana of the *Brhad-aranyaka Upanishad,* which maintained that when a person dies:

The speech enters into fire
The breath into air
The eye into the sun
The mind into the moon
The sense of hearing into the quarters
The self into the ether
The hair on the body into herbs
The hair on the head into trees
And the blood and the semen into water.

Another passage Daniel had underlined was the reply of Yajnavalkya, the Divine Teacher, to the question of what became of the self, the life force, when a person passed away:

As a goldsmith, taking a piece of gold
Turns it into another, newer and more beautiful shape,
Even so does this self, after having thrown away its body
And dispelled its ignorance,
Make itself into another, newer and more beautiful shape
Like that of the fathers, or the gandharvas, or of the Gods
Or of Prajapati, or of Brahma, or of other beings ...

Two further passages were so heavily underlined that the ink had soaked through to the other side of the paper. They compared a dying man to a king who was about to depart. Policemen, judges, soldiers, attendants, village leaders, other dignitaries cluster around the departing potentate. Just so do the senses gather around the self when a person is on the point of dying. The powers of the senses wane and descend into the heart ... the point of the heart lights up and by that light the self departs, either through the eyes or through the head or through the other apertures of the body. With the self go the senses, taking flight to another world. As his senses failed one by one, perhaps Dr Dorai thought of the image, as his living self fled up to the sun.

By the time Kannan arrived in Chevathar, having paused for neither sleep nor food since he received the telegram, the body of his father was washed and dressed in new clothes, and laid out on a block of ice in the great living room of the mansion. The room was filled with the smoky flame of a hundred and one candles.

It was almost twelve hours since Daniel had died, and the grief that had touched those closest to him had been replaced by a tired sadness. Ramdoss, normally an undemonstrative man, crushed Kannan in a surprisingly fierce embrace. His mother held him for a moment. Then the tears came. Kannan hadn't cried for as long as he could remember, but now he wept.

They buried Dr Dorai after a solemn funeral service. The young priest standing in for the regular padre, who'd been overcome by recent events and was in hospital, acquitted himself rather well and gave a short, moving sermon, before Daniel was interred in the family graveyard overlooking the sea, next to his father and his uncle Joshua. As one of the pallbearers, Kannan was surprised that what he most concentrated on was keeping his balance as they negotiated the uneven ground of the cemetery to the spot where the grave had been excavated. Even in the face of death, we have to pay attention to the small details of life, he thought. As the coffin was lowered into the ground, Kannan placed his lips against the sun-warmed wood for a moment, then drew back. The gravediggers began shouting instructions; they had seen plenty of grief in their time and there was work to be done. The family clustered silently around the open grave. The soft spill of flowers, then the clatter of sand on wood ...

A statue fleshed in stone would rise in Meenakshikoil; three streets would be named after him. Doraipuram would remember Daniel for at least a generation. And those who knew him would remember him too for a while. Barely two decades later, sun, sand and water would begin eroding the statue. His name would survive a couple of decades longer and then he would become just a landmark with no resonance – turn right at the Dorai statue roundabout and go straight to get to the Madras Ulundu Vadai Café.

90

A house in which a death has occurred is a very busy place. Mourners and visitors have to be welcomed and fed, each new arrival must be told by a member of the family about the events leading up to the death in elaborate detail. The death itself needs to be dwelled on at length; the funeral arrangements have to be made. All this gives close members of the family little time to grieve. It's only after the grave has been closed, and the supporting cast has begun to drift away, that the immediate family has the opportunity to be alone with memories of the one who is no longer with them. It's only then that they can grieve properly.

After the funeral was over, Kannan spent the rest of the afternoon wandering through the stifling house. Many people, several of whom he did not know, offered their commiseration, but their interest was already turning to other things and he didn't need to make any but the most perfunctory conversation. As he went from room to room, touching a table here, brushing off a cobweb there, pausing to examine a book, a painting or a memory, it occurred to him that a man's house resembled nothing so much as those fossil beds, in shale or sandstone, that preserve epoch upon epoch in neatly ordered layers. Here were a couple of rooms that Daniel had used as a clinic when he'd first arrived in Doraipuram. A little further on was the library from his English period, filled with rows and rows of heavy volumes: the *Encyclopaedia Britannica*, Dickens and Swift, Hazlitt and Burke. Most of the books looked unopened. Kannan picked up a copy of *Bleak House* and opened it. The page was mapped and embroidered by silverfish. The dust made him sneeze and he put the book back on its shelf and moved on.

As Daniel had retreated from life, he had simplified his needs, and the rooms closest to the day of his death were almost bereft of possessions. But the room he had died in was a muddle, like the tidewrack left behind by the departing sea. In the middle of it all was Lily. She was remarkably composed, given the distress and frenetic activity of the last few days. Kannan's mind flicked back to Pulimed, to her brief stay there. Helen should see her now, he thought, now she would realize the greatness of the woman she had tried to humiliate. They reminisced quietly about Daniel, then his mother got up to go. 'Towards the end, I know he'd forgiven you. Only his mind was no longer his to command, so ... but he never forgot you. You were his favourite.'

'Yes, amma. I wish I could have been here while he was still alive.'

'Will you be here for the reading of the will?'

'Yes, but I'll have to leave soon after.'

At the funeral, Ramdoss had announced that in accordance with his brother-in-law's wishes the will would be read the next day. Now the extended family wasn't sure whether to grieve or anticipate a windfall. Dr Daniel Dorai was a rich man and when the wealthy die, many strike gold. Or at least a few.

The next morning there were over twenty people in the drawing room. A fan barely stirred the air above them, but there was no fidgeting. Ramdoss, Lily, Kannan, Shanthi, Usha and Daniel's family lawyer and friend, a venerable old gentleman whose Brahmin caste marks and turban were in perfect congruence with the Western suit he wore, sat in a rough semicircle of chairs facing the rest of the family.

After greeting them sombrely, Ramdoss spoke, holding a sheet of paper in his hand: 'My respected uncles and aunts, friends and family, Daniel-anna was an unusual and great soul, and that is why even his will is rather unusual. Mr Iyengar has asked me to first read out a letter that he left behind. Some of its provisions are incorporated in the last will and testament that is in Mr Iyengar's office in Meenakshikoil. This was the way Daniel wanted things to be done, and Mr Iyengar and I are following his instructions faithfully.'

With this preamble he began reading out Daniel's last words. 'My family,' the letter began, 'when this is read out to you, I'll be dead. Thank God! For the last years I have wanted nothing more than to pass on to the next world, and God will have finally granted me my wish.'

Ramdoss paused, then read on: 'A dying man is supposed to be conciliatory, but I intend to speak my mind. I had withdrawn from the family, and I'm sure there has been speculation about it, and now I'll tell you why. With one or two exceptions I found my family a burden. When I was young and the sap of life flowed strongly in me, I believed, with all the passion at my command, that the family of a man was the greatest gift he could possess. But you aren't gathered here to listen to the ramblings of a dead man, so I'll dispense with the philosophy quickly, although I'm tempted to go on as it is one of the many privileges of the recently deceased to command absolute attention, perhaps for an hour, a day, a year, no matter, I know you'll be listening to Ramdoss with all the attention he needs.

'Long after I tried to vanish from the daily world of the living, long after I tried to empty my heart, mind and soul to grapple with the Infinite, I realized that my endeavour would not be wholly successful. We live, fully engaged, until we die. Pain, meditation, thoughts of God may distract us but we cannot subtract ourselves entirely from the world until we are dead. And so, while I no longer actively participated in the life of the community and of the family, my mind refused to let go. What did I think about? Mostly, I regretted the things I hadn't done, I thought about quarrels that hadn't been resolved, I thought about matters left incomplete. It's one of the paradoxes of life, and it is something that each one of you will discover, that your achievements, your successes, your crowning glories do not matter to you at the end of your life. No, no, no, if I leave you with nothing else, I leave you with this piece of wisdom – it's your regrets that stay with you till you die. And you, my family, whether you like it or not, are one of my regrets. I've often wondered why I slaved for you all my life when I could have lavished more care and attention on myself.

'As I write these words I think about the mango that has been our most prized possession for over a century. One fact about it strikes me powerfully and it is this: No fruit is more beautiful, yet the blue mango has a monstrous flaw. Every season a tiny insect, the mango fruitfly, lays its eggs beneath the skin of some of the ripening fruits. The eggs hatch and the maggots tunnel through the pulp, eating as they go. From the outside, the mango looks perfectly healthy. But when it is cut open, dark tunnels and headless maggots greet the eye. I do not need to extend the analogy to make my meaning clear. Every family has within it its maggots – greedy, dishonest, ungrateful people, whose worst qualities are magnified when they are gathered together. So, at the end of my life, my picture of Doraipuram is bleak. Outside, to the world at large, we are an example of just how a family should be. Inside, the rot is beginning to spread.'

Ramdoss asked for water. The silence in the room was broken only by the rustle of makeshift fans, the shifting of anxious bodies. A servant brought him a glass of water. He emptied it in one long swallow, mopped his face with a cloth slung over his shoulder, and carried on.

'Do I hear you shifting in alarm? Is some irrelevant advice the only thing the foolish old man has left us? Don't worry. For a family which has given me endless trouble, fights about land, about money, about prestige, about marriage, you should be grateful that I'm not an especially vindictive man. I have left you all something, although you will be surprised to learn that until very recently I had very little left of my former wealth. The empire I had created with my line of patent formulations was a shadow of its former self. People had begun flocking to inferior English medicines, which cost four times as much but were not even a quarter as effective, and business was bad. That didn't worry me for I was aware that I didn't have a great many years left. What concerned me was my family and how I could provide for it. *Kaka vuku thun kunjie / pon kunjie* – if even a crow thinks her chicks are golden, why should I be any different?

'And talking of gold, that's what I'm leaving you, my family, a fortune in gold, sixty-five kilos of it, that should keep all of you named in my will comfortable for the rest of your lives. You own the land you live on, that was my first gift. Now you don't need to worry about money ever again. This is my last gift.'

Ramdoss paused. Kannan noticed that he didn't look up. Instead his eyes were fixed on the sheet of paper he was holding. Kannan looked at his family: his mother, who sat with her eyes cast down, her head sheathed in the pallu of a white sari; his aunt Miriam, plump, sweaty and prayerful, her eyes fixed on the fresh-framed portrait of her brother garlanded by sandalwood and roses; his sister Shanthi, with a tired and lined face though she was barely thirty-five, her mousy little husband Devan behind her; his other sister Usha and her husband Justin, his eyes skittering over the crowd like light on water; his nephew Daniel, his father's favourite. Most of them seemed electrified by the news of the fortune that the patriarch had left them. Murmured conversation, the noisy exhalation of breath. Ramdoss held up a hand for silence. 'I'll be finished in a few minutes,' he said.

'When I realized my fortune had dwindled to nothing, this house, a few mango and coconut topes and rice paddies, three thousand rupees in the bank, my cars and the cottage in Nagercoil, I went back to the texts that Dr Pillai had left me. In them lay the secret that a great siddha mystic had succeeded in unlocking and which I knew would be mine if I had the patience, discipline and guidance from above to find it. I worked for a year and a half before I finally discovered the secret of the texts, a secret that will make you all very rich. For what the texts taught me was how to turn all tamasic matter into gold. Three months ago I had myself weighed, on my sixty-second birthday. I weighed exactly seventy-two kilos. After I die I want my body placed in a herbal bath, the exact formula of which is appended to this letter ...'

Ramdoss was reading fast now, ignoring the stunned incomprehension that was gradually overtaking his audience, anxious to get to the end of the bizarre letter he had tried hard to dissuade his friend from leaving behind.

'After two days, my body will have lost seven kilos, as all the tamasic matter leaves it. What will be left is sixty-five kilos of pure gold. I leave thirty-five kilos to my wife Lily and the children; the remaining thirty should be equally divided between all those who own property in Doraipuram. To make the division of gold easier, I have prepared a list of what each of my organs should weigh at the end of the transformation – my head should weigh ...'

'Stop this. Enough of this nonsense. My brother had clearly gone mad ...' Miriam shouted. Relieved, Ramdoss stopped reading. He had been wondering which of them would be the first to end the charade.

Miriam's outburst broke open the silence of the gathering. A few people started weeping noisily; the humiliation visited upon them by the dead man was more than they could take. Kannan looked around the room and caught and briefly held the gaze of Daniel; the boy's eyes had a strange expression in them – was it pleasure, was it pride?

91

Kannan sat by the Chevathar under the stippled shade of a tamarind tree, looking out over the river. It was hot, unbearably so. Was a short stint in the hills enough to make the heat so difficult to cope with? The river had shrunk to a few dirty pools, hardly visible through the rubbish and scum that covered them. Flies clustered thickly on what looked like a dead dog in an advanced state of decomposition. So was this what it all came down to, he wondered, the question that had haunted him ever since his uncle had begun reading the letter. Disillusionment, bitterness, revenge, unhappiness? He had looked up to his father, and even though they had parted bitterly, his respect for him was undiminished. He was aware of the conflicts within the family but he'd had no idea that they had affected his father so much that he was prepared to devalue his life's work entirely. Why did Ramdoss-mama have to read the letter? Why hadn't he let his father go in peace? But it wasn't his fault, Kannan realized the next moment; he would have suppressed it if he hadn't thought it important to Daniel, and everyone knew that Ramdoss's loyalty to his brother-in-law was unflinching.

The wind had shifted direction and the stench from the decomposing animal was blowing directly towards him. He got up and trudged back to the house, sweat running down his face into his collar. Why did a man need to fight to find a purpose in life, then spend his best years in its service, if all that waited at the end was regret and anger? Why couldn't he just flow with whatever came his way? Even as he thought this he rejected it. He recalled the last letter he'd received from Murthy. His best friend had written that he was thinking of leaving his father's timber business and throwing himself into the struggle for independence. He had urged Kannan to join him. Kannan smiled when he recalled his reply – he'd asked Murthy to holiday with them in Pulimed, get his strength up, before he bent to the task of getting rid of the British. But jokes apart, Murthy was right. Youth needed to think big, pour its considerable vigour and conviction into commitments that would never again seem as gripping or as essential. How could you give up on life's challenge before you had even begun? He thought of Helen, the woman he had fought to win. Perhaps he should have made the sort of marriage his sisters had, played safe, been retained in his family's affection ... He dismissed the idea angrily. And then his mind turned to Pulimed. He was beginning to carve out a niche for himself, the task he'd set himself when he broke away from his father. Would his striving have the same edge now?

His path home ran past the well his chithappa had jumped in his youth. The general decay that had overtaken much of the colony showed here too – the masonry walls were chipped and unpainted, the trees that surrounded it were unbarbered, giving the place a desolate air. It looked like nothing so much as what it actually was, an abandoned country well, one of thousands that dotted the villages in the area. But a young man had risked his life to jump across it! If he had contemplated the well's fate and his own, would he still have done it? He certainly would, Kannan decided, if all the stories he'd heard about Aaron-chithappa were true. Every man's struggle to make sense of life was his own. Look at his grandfather, dead in a conflict that no longer had any meaning except in family myth, but without doubt the most important challenge he'd faced. Or even his own father, doing his best to achieve his dreams ... No, no matter that he was disturbed by his father's dying declaration – there was no escaping the fact that it was a reflection of his father's disappointment – he would need to fashion his own goals, pursue them for all he was worth. He walked on past the well, heading back to the house. Wasn't it odd, he mused, that in the midst of death our thoughts turn so persistently to life, to the future.

When he reached the house, he found Ramdoss waiting for him.

'Is everyone still upset, mama?' he asked.

'Yes, they are,' he said.

'I was wondering why you read it out.'

'Your father asked me to. It was important to him, and that was good enough for me.'

'But surely you could have talked him out of it ...'

Ramdoss seemed about to reply, but when he spoke, he had changed the subject.

'You return tomorrow?'

Kannan tried once more. 'When did he write it?'

'He'd been working on it for some time. He dictated the final draft three months ago.'

'And he never had second thoughts about it?'

'He may have done, but I think his anger took care of any misgivings he might have had.'

'Tell me honestly, mama, what did he think about me, towards the end?'

'He was disappointed in you, but I think he had come to accept what you did. He loved you and always wanted the best for you, you must never, ever forget that.'

There didn't seem anything more to say, and Kannan was about to go into the house when something occurred to him.

'One last question, mama. Was appa happy?'

'I'd say so.' A faint smile appeared on Ramdoss's face. 'The day before he left us, we went for a drive ... Yes, he was happy.'

'He looked very peaceful when I saw him.'

'Yes, people do ...' Ramdoss looked pensive for a moment, then said, 'Are you sure you can't stay?'

'No, mama, we're short-staffed on the estate, and I couldn't take more than a couple of days' leave.'

'Are things going well for you there?'

'Yes,' he said without hesitation, 'I love my job, and ... and Helen is good for me.'

'Very well then. You must come home as often as you can. Lily-akka and I would like to see as much of you as possible. And maybe before too long you'll be able to return here. That was one of your father's dreams, you know.'

92

The monsoon broke with unusual severity, a fortnight after Kannan got back to the estates. Since his return, he had been trying to get on with his routine, but he hadn't reckoned with the devastating impact of his father's death. He struggled to divert the feeling of absence and loss into something that he could understand and lay to rest. He needed to talk to someone about Daniel, but there was no one to discuss him with, least of all his wife. Ramdoss said Daniel had loved him. But if he'd loved him so much, why had he rejected him? When things were going right, love could be a great uplifting blaze, but when it soured, its potential to do damage was just as awesome. Look at how things between Helen and him stood.

Helen tried to cope with the new situation as best she could. If she was being honest, she would have to admit that her first reaction to Daniel's death had been one of relief. One less pressure on this embattled marriage, she'd thought. Her own mother had died when she was barely two, so she didn't have the experience to know how Daniel's death might increase the strain on her relationship with Kannan. By dying, Daniel had drawn his son to himself. The marriage had been made more precarious. And all it took was the monsoon to reveal the strains that Daniel's death had temporarily masked.

Helen disliked the monsoon, the clammy weather, the endless rain that marooned her in the house, the smell of drying clothes in the bathroom and the boiler room, the leaks in the house that she vainly tried to combat and the cold dark walls of mist that shut out the light. To the long list of things that she abhorred about estate life, she added the weather. Her longing to be back in Madras took on a feverish intensity. She relived cherished moments: dances at the Railway Institute with her friends, drinking thick sweet grape juice at Nair's with Cynthia, saving up money to go to the Casino Theatre to watch Cary Grant and Greta Garbo, Humphrey Bogart and Vivien Leigh and the gorgeous world they inhabited. When she married Kannan, she'd thought she'd acquired a version of that world. But all she had got were miserable old men and women who hated her, a husband who couldn't defend her, and no friends.

A thud against the roof, and she began to drag herself out of the pleasant day-dream she'd been having. Jimmy and she had slipped out of Cynthia's birthday party, desperate to kiss and explore each other's bodies as they had recently started doing. They could never have enough of each other, and this evening had been no different, except it was Cynthia's party, and she would have been very annoyed if Helen had left early. Around midnight, drunk and desperate with lust, Jimmy had finally cornered her in the bathroom of the house, and they had kissed each other so hard and long, it seemed they would disappear into the wall they were leaning against. Someone rattled the doorknob, there was a wild cackle of laughter not too far away and Jimmy had frantically whispered in her ear, 'Let's get out of here. There'll be no one at the station. The last train has gone. We'll get back quickly.' She had been hesitant, she didn't know if she'd be able to prevent him going beyond the limits she had set soon after they had started going out, but she was hungry for him and she agreed to the plan. Nobody noticed as they slipped out of the house. The station was deserted, the tracks on either side of the platform gleaming and cold in the moonlight, the porters untidy snoring heaps on the platform. The attendant had been asleep inside the second-class retiring room. They had woken him up, and Jimmy had slipped him six annas. Sleepy and grumbling, he had opened up the first-class waiting room with its deep wickerwork planter's chairs and solid teak table and cupboards. The door had scarcely shut behind him before they were clasped together ...

The branch thudded against the roof again, and Helen looked at Kannan with a little alarm. The weather had been terrible throughout the night, thunder rolling continuously and lightning whitening the world. The creaking and rumbling in the house had kept them both awake, and the morning had brought no relief. The lawn was a lake. Virtually every plant and shrub had been smashed flat to the ground. Kannan hadn't been able to go to work for the second day in a row, and after breakfast they had adjourned to the living room, where they had sat, each absorbed in their thoughts, occasionally looking out of the window.

There was a loud crash. The old gum tree by the hedge had been uprooted. Fortunately, it had fallen away from the house into the tea. It was gusting so hard now that it was actually raining upward, the pelting rain interrupted in its downward passage by errant rills of wind which then bore it aloft, until a dense scurf of rain formed in mid-air; the knots of rain would last a brief moment, then dissolve, only to form again.

Lightning flickered soundlessly on the bare rock-face across the valley and the wind threatened to rip the roof off. Cold hard fists of rain slammed against the window. Kannan had never seen anything like it in his time in the hills. He wondered if the house would hold up. If the roof blew away, how would they get to safety? The gum tree had blocked the road. And even if they cleared that obstacle, he wasn't sure he could keep the motorcycle upright in the storm.

Towards lunch the weather grew calmer. Although the rain still crashed down, the wind had abated, and the thunder and lightning had moved away. The butler entered, announced lunch and went to see to its serving.

'I want to get rid of Manickam. He's a thief, and he's dirty. He coughs as though he has TB.' They were the first words she had spoken all morning.

'But why? Whoever you get will be worse. At least Manickam knows our whims and the bungalow like the back of his hand.'

'Exactly. He acts like he's the master of the house.'

'What? Has he been rude to you?'

'Not exactly, but you know how these things are ...'

He thought he knew what she was getting at. She had been angry with Manickam ever since Lily's stay in Pulimed. But that was no reason to get rid of him.

'What are you trying to say, Hen?' he said patiently. He didn't feel patient at all, but it was better this way, otherwise he knew exactly how the sequence of events would go – minor skirmishing would lead to bigger issues and then there would be an outright fight. He had begun to hate the time they spent together. You never knew when a furious argument would break out, angry thoughts and words creeping like dirty little animals from her angelic mouth.

Often when they fought, he would simply walk out into the rain, preferring the leeches and the wet to his cantankerous wife. He would have to sort out Helen's unhappiness somehow, he realized, and quickly, otherwise they should go their separate ways. That wasn't an option he was prepared to consider lightly, especially because admission of defeat in his marriage would be a massive blow to his pride, and Kannan was a proud man, but more and more it seemed the only way out ... She could leave when the weather improved, in September or in December. A few months in the plains would settle her, give him the space he needed to get over his father's death. And then perhaps they could start again.

Helen was screeching at him now, 'Kannan, hullooo, are you listening to me? Here I am, trying to bring something to your notice, and you seem to have gone wool-gathering! As usual! If only you'd take a look at how things really are, what we have to put up with here, then we wouldn't be leading such miserable lives.'

He tried hard to maintain his composure, to no avail. He reacted angrily. 'Now look here, nothing is as dire as you make it out to be. Just because some people are against you, just because you haven't been able to get the planters to swoon at your feet, then that is no reason to be hard on me. You're not one of them, and never will be, no matter how much you try.'

Helen's response was instant and splenetic.

'How dare you talk to me like that, you no-good beggar. Don't you see how they treat you? Every time I see you smiling and fawning on them, running around to do their every little errand, it makes me want to vomit. Don't you have any self-respect?'

'What are you saying, you pathetic woman? Don't forget that if it wasn't for me you would still be hanging around in your awful little colony ...'

'You miserable worm, if you had the guts you would stand up to these white buggers, instead of taking your resentment out on me. You Indians are all cowards, no wonder you bootlick so much.'

'Are you English? Is that why you are so miserable when the white man spits on you?' he said quietly.

Helen's face grew angrier. It's amazing how even the most perfect features take on a simian cast when angry, Kannan thought. At times like this we resemble nothing so much as the apes that preceded us.

Helen, who had been struggling to get the words out, began to scream at him. 'I hate you, I hate the day I let you into my life, I hate the day I married you, I hate you, I hate you, you miserable pariah.'

'If I am a pariah, what do you think that makes you?'

'Someone who'll always be a thousand times better than you ...'

'Oh really, and how's that, you stupid little fool?'

'Simple. Does anyone know the great Kannan Dorai's ancestry? Do you know how much your white colleagues would despise you if they knew?'

He didn't know where this was going, but it felt bad ...

'Who are you to look down on me, you bastard, when your own mother, the great lady who can't even speak English, is nothing but a head clerk's daughter?'

The words dropped like thunder. Even in their most bitter fights, they'd refrained from attacking each other's parents but Helen's rage was all-consuming. An image bloomed in Kannan's mind of his mother, the calm centre in the midst of the frenzy that had attended Daniel's death. How noble she'd seemed. And to have her spat on!

Helen's face looked almost comical when she realized what she'd done. She jumped up from the sofa, but Kannan was quicker. He got up from his chair, propelled by a fury so great that he barely registered his physical actions. He caught her, his fist raised to smash down into her face, to erase from his sight something that had suddenly grown hateful. At the last moment, diverted by the terror in her eyes, he pushed her from him and slammed his fist into the wooden mantelpiece. The hard unyielding teak absorbed the blow, the lone Wedgwood vase on it barely stirring. Weeping, Helen fled the room and Kannan slumped into a sofa, the future pitilessly clear. They were finished.

He moved into the spare bedroom that night and Helen didn't try to stop him.

All through that monsoon, they kept as far away from each other as they could manage, speaking to each other only when absolutely necessary, waiting for the moment when they could escape each other. When the rains thinned in September, landslips blocked the road to the plains. Finally, towards the middle of December, the rains gone, he drove her down to the station to catch her train. Their parting was perfunctory. He promised to send her things on as quickly as he could and they made polite talk about getting back together in a while, although they were careful to keep their plans vague.

Soon afterwards he wrote to Murthy, asking his friend to fulfil a long-standing promise to visit.

93

The decisive victory of the Fourteenth Army at the siege of Imphal was the worst defeat the Japanese had suffered since the Battle of Midway in 1942. It was Britain's greatest triumph in the region. The war began to recede from India. By the winter of 1944, enormous fleets of American Super-Fortress bombers took the war to Japan itself, a country that had believed itself under divine protection ever since the thirteenth century when the savage Mongol armies of Kubla Khan were scattered by great winds when they threatened the islands; this time, however, kamikaze, the divine wind, failed to protect Japan. Hundreds of B-29s under the command of Curtis Le May began to pound the country. The attacks generated firestorms that raised temperatures in the city to 1800°F and above.

As news of Allied victories filtered through, a mood of exultation grew in the estates. An invasion of little yellow men was no longer feared and the planters celebrated. In this corner of the planet, the war was over.

Even the weather gave cause for cheer. December was usually cold and gloomy, but this year the bright blade of the sun sliced through the mists, the temperature rose, and the high tea country became a place of enchantment. Everywhere you looked, the landscape was so green it hurt the eye. The sky was blue and unclouded, and the air so clear that every feature of the land stood out in sharp relief. After six months of rain, the world breathed again. It was a time of parties and picnics and serious bouts of drinking before roaring fires of eucalyptus wood.

Murthy arrived in Pulimed that month and Kannan swept his friend into a whirl of partying and clubbing. After three days, Murthy had had enough. On Sunday morning he asked whether they might not stay home for the day.

'It's been over two years since I last saw you, do you mind very much if we spend today catching up?' he asked.

'Of course not,' Kannan said. 'I hope you're enjoying the parties.'

'They're not what I'm used to but I'm having quite a good time.'

'If they get a bit too much, you'll tell me, won't you? I don't want to be accused of dragging my best friend all the way to Pulimed just to torture him,' Kannan said with a laugh.

'You know me better than that. If I have a problem you'll know immediately,' Murthy said, breaking off a piece of his dosai and dipping it into the sambhar on his plate.

They ate in silence for a while, Murthy with his fingers, Kannan manipulating a knife and fork. Determined not to repeat the mistakes that had attended his mother's visit, he had instructed Manickam to serve dosais, idlis and uppuma instead of his regular breakfast of eggs, toast and marmalade.

'If you think it's none of my business I know you'll tell me, but why did Helen leave?' Murthy asked after a while.

'There's not a great deal to say. We weren't right for each other, but you don't see that when you're in love.'

'Are you all right?'

'Yes, I think so. I go out as much as I can. Can't stand the empty house. It'll get better.'

'These things always do,' Murthy said wisely.

'What do you know about these things?' Kannan said with a laugh. 'You're not even married.'

Murthy looked nonplussed for a moment, then he smiled. The talk grew lighter, the years dropped away and they laughed and joked as they had in college. Finally Murthy asked, 'Why are you eating your dosai with a knife and fork?'

'Oh, just got used to it,' Kannan replied.

His friend said nothing and went back to eating his dosai. Just then, Manickam came in with a fresh supply. Kannan waited till he left, then asked, 'What did you mean by that question?'

'Nothing, nothing. I just found it a bit odd, that's all.'

'Come on, Murthy. Tell me what's on your mind.'

'No, really, I just found it unusual. I've never seen anyone do it before.'

'It keeps the fingers clean,' Kannan said as he raised a forkful of dosai and sambhar to his mouth.

Abruptly Murthy said, 'You've changed. You're not the Kannan I used to know.'

Kannan put his knife and fork down on his plate. 'What are you talking about?'

'Well, you know. Small things, like eating dosais with a knife and fork. Big things, like the way you behave around your English colleagues. You're not the Kannan I used to know.'

'We all change, don't we? You've changed. Why, you've even grown a beard!'

Murthy laughed and Kannan said, 'Enough about me. Tell me what's going on down in the plains.'

'A lot of action. Now that the war is almost over, I think it'll be only a matter of time before the Mahatma, Nehru, Patel and everyone else goes on the attack once again. I think the British are finished, Kannan. Three years, five years. That's all it's going to take before we're free.'

'Will that be a good thing?'

'What do you mean?'

'Won't there be chaos when the British leave?'

'It's easy to see why the British would think that. Things won't be easy. Jinnah is adamant about a separate nation for the Muslims. And the others are dead against it. Their positions are hardening. I fear it will delay independence, you know, give the British reasons to stay on.'

'What's the solution?' Kannan asked.

'I don't know. Rajaji fell out with the Mahatma and Nehru for suggesting that they accept Jinnah's demand in the larger interest of achieving independence, so that's a real stalemate. It's getting very messy. Every second day, some new party is formed, with neither accountability nor agenda, solely in order to take advantage of the uncertainty ... Sometimes politics makes you sick, all the cynical manoeuvring and opportunistic alliances and ...'

'So why do we want to get rid of the British? At least they keep it all in check!'

Murthy looked aghast. 'What are you talking about?' he said. 'I can't believe you just said that.'

'What's wrong with what I said?'

'Let me spell it out for you. If I sound dramatic, so be it. I don't know about you but I would rather die in poverty as a free man than be a prosperous slave.'

'That is rather a dramatic view, you know.'

'Absolutely not,' Murthy said excitedly. 'Do you know how disparaging Churchill is about the Mahatma? After the Quit India movement, he called him a miserable old man who had always been the enemy. Deep down, they despise us, all of us.'

'Political talk, Murthy. I'm sure our leaders have said bad things about them. I'm sure Churchill isn't racist.'

'He's certainly an old-style imperialist who believes he was created superior to all the subject races. It's no surprise his attitude rubbed off on people like Linlithgow, the worst Viceroy we've ever had! Think of the way he handled the Bengal famine! And do you know what he said about Gandhiji's fast? He said that if the Mahatma died, all that would happen would be six months of unpleasantness that would steadily decline in intensity after which things would go on as before. And Wavell is worse. He calls himself a simple soldier but he hasn't won a battle in years. And if he's a great general, tell me what he's doing here instead of fighting somewhere? And this man has the nerve to poke fun at the Mahatma. I read a poem he wrote about Gandhiji. It made me so angry I can still remember it word for word. It's a version of "Jabberwocky". Do you know the poem?'

'You know I was never much of a reader.'

'Well, it's from *Alice in Wonderland* and Wavell spoofed it like this:

'"*Beware the Gandhiji, my son*
The satyagrahah, the bogey fast,
Beware the Djinnarit, and shun
The frustrious scheduled caste."'

Kannan laughed.

'You find that funny?'

'Steady, Murthy, I'm not the enemy,' Kannan said with a smile.

'Sorry,' Murthy said a little sheepishly, 'I do tend to get carried away. But their attitude makes me really angry. Do you know that Britain fought a hundred and eleven wars in the last century and they were all funded by India? They are who they are because of us. Do you still think they're doing us a favour by giving us the crumbs from their table? They're bleeding us dry, and we're expected to take it? Sorry, Kannan. I'm no friend of the white man. I was surprised at how much you seemed to want to emulate them.'

'Michael Fraser is a good man, and Freddie is a friend.'

'Yes, he's a nice man,' Murthy admitted.

'And Major Stevenson and the others are not bad sorts. There are bastards, like Martin and Patrick, but you find them everywhere.'

'It's not that I hate the whites. Think of all our profs at MCC. What I cannot accept is imperialism.'

For a while they ate without speaking, then Murthy began again. 'You know, I find it a bit hard to accept that someone like you is not participating in the most exciting time of our lives.'

'There you go again. Flogging your pet peeve,' Kannan said with a smile.

'But can't you see it?' Murthy said passionately. 'We are living at this great moment in our history, offered an opportunity to transcend ourselves, be part of something that's bigger than us. The independence movement, Kannan, the greatest mobilization of people in recorded history, it's reaching its climax and you're not part of it!'

'I grant you it's very exciting. But do you think your own part in it makes any difference? The big decisions, the things that have an impact, are being made by people like Gandhi, Nehru, Jinnah, Rajaji ... How are we part of it?'

'Every one of us has a stake in what's going on. If the Viceroy takes a decision, if the Mahatma announces a programme, they are because of the actions of all of us. It's exciting to be an Indian, Kannan, more now than at any other time in the past or in the future ...'

'Am I less of an Indian for not being part of the struggle?' Kannan asked.

'You do seem proud to be a brown-skinned Englishman.'

'Because my boss said I spoke English as well as an Englishman?'

'I wasn't thinking of that, it was ...'

'I'm just trying to be good at my job, Murthy. Your father didn't throw you out of the house,' Kannan said, a trace of irritation in his voice.

'I wasn't trying to annoy you. It's just that I'm so caught up with the idea of the independence struggle that I'm a bit oblivious to everything else.'

Kannan accepted the apology. They sat for a while longer at the breakfast table finishing their coffee. Then Kannan said, 'Fancy a walk? It's a lovely day.'

'Excellent idea,' Murthy said and they got up to go. As they were leaving the dining room, Kannan said, 'I don't measure up?'

'It's hateful to be a subject race, Kannan. And that's what we are right now. It's something no one with a hint of pride in themselves could accept.'

'Are you telling me that I'm without pride, a toady of the British?'

Murthy hesitated, then said, 'No, that's not what I'm saying. When I first got to Pulimed I was amazed how little you or anyone else thought about the independence struggle. All the talk was of war, war, war. It was as though India never existed. Or if it did, only as an adjunct to the British cause ...' He broke off suddenly. 'I'm sorry, I'm haranguing you. Let's just go for that walk.'

Kannan smiled. 'I'm sure you'll go far in politics.'

'No more politics today. Okay. Not while I'm in Pulimed.' They walked as far as the fork in the road that led from the bungalow to the factory. And then, because the day was so beautiful, they walked some more. Everything the sun touched shone like polished glass: the blazing emerald of the tea, the water-wet hills and distant waterfalls, the silver-backed leaves of the grevillea trees as they turned in the breeze. Murthy said with a laugh, 'Long may you prosper in this place, Kannan. I know I'd want to come here whenever I needed to rest.'

They walked a while longer, letting the peace and enchantment of the place seep into them, then Murthy said, 'I'm sorry I never met your father, Kannan.'

'Yes, I'm sorry too, he was a great man. I regret now that I didn't get to know him better.' He smiled as a memory surfaced. 'He could be quite delightful, you know. Remember the Blue Mango Festival? I'm sure I told you about it in college. I was seven or eight and I was determined to win the children's competition. I'd eaten about ten mangoes and I desperately had to go to the lavatory, you know how it is when you eat too many mangoes. My father who was watching got so alarmed that he rushed up to me, caught me up and almost ran with me all the way to the house so that my mother and grandmother wouldn't find out ... That was the last one. There were no more festivals after my grandmother died.' Kannan was quiet for a while, then he said, 'I have so few memories of him.'

'We realize these things only when it's too late,' Murthy said.

'After he was gone, I found myself thinking of him all the time and I know that I will always regret that I wasn't able to mend fences with him before he died.'

'You shouldn't be too hard on yourself, Kannan. There wasn't anything you could have done, not really. Both of you were right in your own way ...'

'I'm glad he didn't live to see the marriage break up,' Kannan said sombrely. He slashed suddenly at a nearby tea bush, then walked on. By and by he said, 'Do you think you will continue in politics, Murthy? After India becomes free and all that?'

'I might, I might not. I know my father would like it if I went back. There's more work than he and my brothers can cope with. But I find politics a very exciting place to be in. What I'm most afraid of is that the seamy side of politics will gain the upper hand once the excitement is over. Corruption, nepotism, communalism.'

'You mean the sort of thing Jinnah is involved in.'

'I thought you didn't know anything about politics, Kannan.'

'I'm not a complete ignoramus.'

'Well, not only Jinnah, the Hindu right is as bad. They admire the Nazi drive for racial purity and that's just one of the distasteful things about them. All we need are some Christian, Sikh and Parsi fundamentalists to make things really interesting. No wonder the British think we can't rule ourselves.'

'You left out the Buddhists, the Jains and the animists,' Kannan said with a wry smile.

'Sorry, getting serious again,' Murthy said. 'Do you think you'll stay on here?'

'My mother and my uncle say I should go back to Doraipuram. But it's so hard to decide. I have a job here. And if the British start leaving in droves, there'll be opportunities.'

'Do you want to go back to Doraipuram?'

'I don't know. Sometimes I think I should, at other times I think I'd be a burden. I have no interest in medicine or the business.'

'But you like planting,' Murthy pointed out. 'You'd still be involved with agriculture and you could help with herbal formulations and suchlike.'

'I'm not sure what I want. For now, I'm just waiting.'

On the walk back to the bungalow they didn't talk much. It occurred to Kannan that they had barely discussed Helen. Perhaps that was the way it was meant to be – loss and unhappiness were sometimes best addressed indirectly.

In the four days that Murthy had left of his holiday they absented themselves entirely from Pulimed's social life. They spent the evenings and nights chatting and laughing and rediscovering their friendship. They had both changed, but they were relieved to discover that at heart their bond remained as strong as ever. In college, Kannan had been without doubt the stronger of the two, but Murthy had caught up. The fact did not discompose either of them.

On Murthy's last night they stayed up so late that they had difficulty getting up in the morning. The weather, unreliable as ever, had turned and they made the journey to the station through a grey and wet day.

94

A fortnight after Murthy's departure, the killings began.

The first victim died near the coolie lines on Kannan's division.

Kannan had just sat down to dinner, when Manickam, who was about to serve him, frowned. The kitchen boy, who normally never ventured into the rest of the bungalow after the morning's cleaning, was beckoning to him from just beyond the door of the dining room. Manickam continued to ladle out the corn. His frown deepened. But the kitchen boy didn't go away. Having served Kannan, the butler withdrew with great dignity. Kannan affected not to notice the sound of the cuff and the yelp that followed. There was some urgent whispering and then Manickam reappeared, this time with the boy, who was actually a middle-aged man, in tow. This was so unusual that Kannan stopped eating.

'Some peoples to see aiyah, this fellow is saying.' Manickam spoke in English. This was something he did when other servants or guests were present, a trait Kannan found amusing but did not discourage; he knew the butler would be offended.

'Can't they come to the office?' Kannan asked.

'I'm saying, aiyah, but these peoples they're saying that they are having some urgent things to be saying to aiyah just now only.'

Kannan was exasperated. But there was nothing to be done about it. When he stepped out on to the veranda, a babble of sound rose from the small knot of labourers who stood in the driveway. His kitchen boy shouted at them to be quiet, but Kannan signalled him to silence and asked the men what the problem was. They began talking at the same time and he told them sternly that only one of them should speak. They fell silent and stood there shivering in their lungis and cumblies, scant protection against the evening cold. Finally, the kangani, whom he took to be the leader of the deputation, found his voice. The man could be disrespectful and sly, but today he seemed genuinely upset: 'Aiyah,' he said slowly, 'a man was killed near the coolie lines tonight. A tiger, big as three jutka ponies, did it ...'

A tiger. A man-eating tiger. Everything else that clogged Kannan's mind blasted clear. An image rose behind his eyes of the dead panther that Freddie had spoken about, its lips drawn back. Stray passages from Jim Corbett's *Man-Eaters of Kumaon* came back to him. How thrilling it would be to stalk a savage beast through the jungle at night! Where would he put the head once the animal had been shot and mounted? Perhaps he could replace that indifferent painting of the gulmohar tree that Helen had put up in the living room. It would dominate the room. But the kangani hadn't stopped talking and Kannan forced himself to listen. 'I saw the monster as clearly as I see you, aiyah. Not more than ten feet away. One leap and poor Mayilandi was no more. His wife is a widow and his six children have no father. We beg you to get rid of it, aiyah, before it kills us all.'

Bidding the men to wait, Kannan hurried into the house, and made straight for the bedroom where he kept his Mannlicher .275 rifle. He had bought it in Mundakayam from a planter who was going to war, and thus far had used it only twice, against boar.

The coolies were squatting on the ground where he had left them. The sight of Kannan with his rifle seemed to infuse them with a new spirit, and they jumped to their feet, chattering excitedly. Somewhat self-consciously, Kannan walked down the steps. The coolies led the way, their weak lamp throwing a fitful glow into the night. As he walked, his eyes glued to the feet dwindling into the mist ahead of him, his initial thrill began to fade, and Kannan began to worry. The realization that he didn't know the first thing about shooting tigers, had never seen anything more threatening than a wild pig in the jungle, took hold of him, and he began to doubt the wisdom of what he was doing. He tried to recall what the great Corbett had written in his book about man-eaters and how they were to be dispatched. If he survived tonight, he would make haste to borrow Michael's copy again and acquire a tip or two on how to deal with rogue tigers. Meanwhile, he would have to make do with whatever his memory threw up. He hefted the rifle and drew some strength from its weight and feel. What did Corbett say about the best place to plant a bullet – the head, behind the shoulder, in the belly? Perhaps the head, no, no, it was probably the shoulder, or was that for elephants ...?

He should have sent a runner to Freddie's place. His friend had a monstrously powerful rifle: a .400/450 Winchester that could stop a rhino in its tracks. And it would have been reassuring to have someone else who could sit up over the kill with him, even if Freddie was as inexperienced as he was. Or perhaps he should have just waited until the morning? The man was dead, after all. There was nothing to be done for him. And if there was indeed a man-eating tiger about, it wasn't going to go away in a hurry. The thought didn't reassure him at all and he cursed his foolhardiness. He was an idiot! He shouldn't have been so precipitate. What was he trying to do? Commit suicide? But these men trusted him. He was the boss, after all.

'We're almost there, aiyah,' the kangani said, out of the night, and Kannan started nervously. The man had dropped back until he was almost level with Kannan. If a man could creep up on him without warning, what about a tiger! Concentrate on the job, he told himself sternly, and pushed his doubts aside. The decision had been taken, he was the man in charge now, and he would simply have to do the best he could.

The dead man lay at the edge of a dense patch of scrub jungle that grew along the path to the coolie lines. As they approached the body, one of the men in the group puckered his lips and called out in the peculiar way practised by the hill people. The sound would carry for miles. Learned at birth, it was impossible to emulate, no matter how much Kannan and the other planters tried. Presently, a group of men came up the path from the lines. When they noticed Kannan, they began vying with each other to tell him about the tragedy. After several minutes of incoherent babbling, it transpired that no one had actually seen the man struck down. Finally, a factory worker, with some experience of tiger kills because he poached, said that he was certain that this was one. He had seen the way the beasts dispatched their victims, and he had no doubt at all. He reconstructed the scene for Kannan: the tiger had waited for the man behind that clump of bamboo, it had sprung and caught him by the arm, which its teeth had severed cleanly, before it had got a better grip on his chest; then, even as the terrified coolie had screamed for help, it had closed its jaws around his throat. Kannan had noticed a village pye dog worrying at something that lay on the ground close to the body and suddenly he felt sick. Once again, he became uncomfortably aware of his boundless ignorance, but he was reluctant to press the poacher for more information. It would only diminish him in the eyes of the workers if they knew how inadequate their manager was to carry out the task at hand. He tried to act professional. First, he would need to select a place to sit up over the kill. Was it tigers that were active during the day, and leopards at night? Did tigers ever return to kills they had been disturbed at? There was nothing he could do about his inexperience now; he would just have to use his insufficient stock of information as best he could.

After rejecting a number of locations, he finally chose an enormous rock that fisted out of the tea. It was about twenty-five feet high, and from its summit Kannan had a good view of the kill. He instructed the men to leave and clambered up the rock alone. The sounds of the departing workers ceased quickly, too quickly, Kannan thought, as he sat on the rock. There was a fair-sized moon in the sky, but it was cloudy, and from time to time the world would grow very dark, increasing his edginess. He started at a rustle in the tea and ground the rifle into his shoulder, straining to align the foresight in the direction of the noise. Just then the moon was released from the cloud and he saw that there was nothing. He grinned, embarrassed, and lowered the rifle. Would the tiger return? He wished he had swallowed his pride and got more information from the poacher. Perhaps he should have asked the man to sit up with him. There was a steady breeze and the leaves of the shade trees stirred and rustled. He wondered if the tiger was out there, watching him, weighing its chances. He remembered reading about the fabled sixth sense that came into play whenever real hunters were threatened by a man-eater. He hoped he possessed it.

He recalled the numerous times Freddie and he had moaned about the lack of adventure on the estates. He'd got what he'd wished for all right, but it wasn't how he'd expected it to be. A nightjar drifted silently out of the bushes and Kannan almost toppled off the rock in fright. Easy, he told himself, nothing can happen to you, you are armed with an accurate rifle, the light's good, and besides, no tiger can reach you, you're well out of reach. As soon as he thought this, new doubts assailed him. How long was a tiger at full stretch? Ten feet long? Twelve? Weren't they able to spring twice their own length? He shivered and began to regret anew his foolish decision to sit up alone. If it attacked him, he was sure he'd freeze, giving it time to dispatch him at its leisure. How Helen would laugh if she could see him now. The thought shamed him and he scanned the country around him again. Nothing stirred.

The clouds had almost lifted and the corpse was clearly visible in the moonlight. He looked away, pushing it from his mind. All about him, the creaking of cicadas filled the air and the tea, silvery-black with night, was pricked by the brightness of fireflies. Gradually Kannan relaxed.

At a quarter to four, he decided the tiger wasn't coming and began to ease his stiff and aching body down from the rock. Halfway down, another vaguely remembered fact from his stock of shikar stories popped into his head. Sometimes tigers returned to feed in the early hours of the morning. He quickly scrambled back up the rock.

His recent activity brought him wide awake. He scanned the tea bushes alertly for a while, then his mind began to wander. He considered Murthy's brief visit. It had raised so many questions, challenged him so much that he wondered if he'd ever be wholly at ease in the estates again. He wasn't sure whether to be pleased or unhappy at the state his friend had left him in. At any rate, it had got him eating dosais with his fingers again. He wasn't sure Manickam approved. Managers should behave like managers. From there his thoughts drifted to Helen. Was it only a few months ago that they had been so in love? It was all too late now, but what a life they could have made together. The first Indian couple to ascend to high station in the Pulimed Tea Company. Although, after Murthy's visit, he wasn't sure that that was quite the distinction he had once felt it was. Did he love her still? It was a question he had asked himself innumerable times since she'd left. Yes, he did love her, although his love was now tempered with wariness and wisdom ... But wouldn't it be grand if he could shoot the tiger! He could already see the admiration in the eyes of his fellow planters, the love in Helen's eyes ... This would be much better than winning a stupid tennis match. Even Murthy would approve! He hoped the tiger would show up. He'd drop it with a perfect shot. He threw up the rifle, pointed it at the pathetic remains of the worker, and pulled the trigger in his imagination ... Phataak ... Phataak. Then, feeling exceedingly foolish, he lowered the rifle.

The first grey light was seeping over the clarity of the stars. Kannan gave it a few more minutes and then clambered down the rock and started for home.

95

The Pulimed Tiger, as the shadowy killer was instantly christened, was cause for no little excitement in the district. In the past decade only seven tigers had been shot throughout these hills, and none in the Pulimed area. This was a source of much discontent among white sportsmen considering that, as late as 1924, seventeen tigers had been shot in a single month in the district. In the adjacent hills, forty-four tigers had met their end and the Periyar region had acquired a reputation as one of the best places in the whole country to bag the animal. Unfortunately for everyone, the tiger didn't reproduce fast enough to be massacred at will, and by the 1940s, it was rare for anyone to see, let alone get a shot at one. Now every able-bodied man who possessed a gun had a real tiger to sit up for. And a man-eater at that. No persuasion was needed. All over Pulimed, rifles and shotguns were lifted off racks and pulled from cupboards as enthusiasts prepared to meet the killer. Their weapons ranged from peashooters like .22 rifles to elephant guns. Kannan sat up over the kill again the next night, but this time the rock was crowded. There was Freddie, who had his powerful rifle with him, and Driscoll, who made do with a double-barrelled shotgun loaded with buckshot. The tiger did not show up. Freddie and Kannan attempted to track the animal down with the help of the poacher, but there was little the man could do to decipher the two-day-old trail. The dead man's remains, which his relatives had been clamouring for, were cremated and the hills waited for the tiger to show its presence once more.

It did so with a vengeance. Over the next month and a half it killed six times – a postman; a plucking writer; two clerks making their way home from work, discovered with the backs of their heads stove in, and no other signs of violence (for a while, the police suspected that they had been murdered, but when they couldn't find a motive or a culprit, their deaths were attributed to the tiger, although no one could quite say why the backs of their heads had been bashed in and no part of them had been eaten); a kangani; and the tea-maker of Vayalaru factory, who met his end when he left his house at night to walk the short distance to the outdoor privy.

Fear slid through the area, twinned with excitement. Fifty-three sportsmen, all white with the exception of Kannan, sat up over the various kills. Although not one of them even glimpsed the beast, seven bullets were fired, dispatching quite needlessly three goats that were tied up as bait. It had been a long time since anyone had shot a tiger, and the inexperience was showing.

As the luckless sportsmen abandoned their vigils, the shadowy killer became the dominant topic of conversations everywhere – at the club, at work, at home – easily displacing the war, the agitation for independence, and even the incipient romance between Ralph Beattie and Margaret, the niece of Mrs Wilkins, who was visiting from Calcutta. Theories and rumours thickened and proliferated. People remarked on the fact that no native shikari had taken part in the tiger hunt, though they would, in the normal course, have taken near-suicidal risks to bag the animal, which now had a cash reward of five hundred rupees on its head. The talk was that no local poacher would take on the animal because they believed it wasn't a tiger at all but rather the spirit of an old vaidyan, who had been driven from the district by the planters for engaging in the black arts. This theory was dismissed by the planters, who put it down to ridiculous native superstition, but Kannan had no convincing answers for his butler who asked him one morning why, if the tiger was a normal flesh-and-blood creature, it killed only people in positions of authority under the planters (with the exception of the first victim), when the easiest thing in the world would be to kill pluckers or coolies who had no protection whatsoever; and why none of the victims, with the exception of the first, had been eaten (what tiger, even a man-eater, would kill purely to kill)? The theory of the ghost-tiger, it was evident, could not easily be wished away or dismissed. The only way forward would be to actually catch sight of the beast, and bury a bullet in its heart.

Freddie had managed to borrow Michael Fraser's *Man-Eaters of Kumaon* for two days (it was in great demand), and Kannan and he virtually memorized the great shikari's wisdom on the various means by which man-eaters should be dispatched. When a fortnight had passed and no further deaths were reported, Kannan suggested to Freddie that they emulate Corbett and track the tiger to its lair.

So it was that Kannan and Freddie found themselves in a strip of eucalyptus jungle around which a couple of the kills had taken place. After mulling over their stock of shikar lore, they had decided that this was the tiger's home territory.

There was still about an hour and a half of light left in the sky, and the jungle was quiet. Bulbuls flitted over the tea in quick jerky flight. A junglefowl began calling from the opposite hill and another one replied immediately from the dense undergrowth facing them. Koo-koo kooroo kuk kuk kuk. As the calls rang out from hill to hill, Freddie and Kannan looked again at the scrap of paper on which Kannan had scribbled Corbett's thoughts on calling up the Pipal Pani tiger. It was a short passage:

> You, who have spent as many years in the jungle as I have, need no description of a tigress in search of a mate, and to you less fortunate ones I can only say that the call, to acquire which necessitates close observation and the liberal use of throat salve, cannot be described in words ...

This was the problem. The idea of trying to call up the tiger was sound, but neither of them knew how to do it. However, neither wanted to be the first to admit how ignorant of jungle lore he was, and so they had gone ahead with their plan. Before the appointed day, they had separately attempted to draw out some of the older planters at the club, those who had actually bagged a tiger or bragged that they had, on how to call up the animal. In this they had failed, as none of the planters, even when fuelled with whisky or rum, had either the imagination or the knowledge to emulate a tiger's vocal range. One old soak had produced an awful croaking noise that had a couple of his neighbours looking at him anxiously. But the planter recovered soon enough and called for another whisky. There was one other possibility that had occurred to Kannan. Perhaps they should seek the advice of Harrison, the planter who'd gone native. If he had been the greatest white shikari the district had known, as everyone said, he might very well have a trick or two up his sleeve. Freddie was quick to shoot the idea down: 'No one has seen him around for years, we don't even know if he's alive. And if he is alive, why hasn't he made an appearance yet? News about the tiger has filtered to every corner of the district. No, I think we can safely forget about Harrison. Even if he's around, he's probably gone blind or insane from syphilis or country liquor or both.'

And so they had come full circle to Corbett. Why had he, always a writer of extreme lucidity and precision, left something as important so tantalizingly undefined? They had debated whether to engage a local shikari to call up the tiger, but even assuming that the natives were willing to get over their superstitious fear of the animal, they had independently come to the conclusion that their lack of experience should not be broadcast to the coolie world, always eager for news of the planters' inadequacies. Now here they were, without an idea of what to do.

They stood around for a while, feeling foolish.

'You go first. I'll stand with my back to that silver oak ready to shoot,' Freddie offered generously.

'No, no, my rifle shoots more accurately over a distance, so I should take the shot ...'

'Well, all right. You know, I'd have loved to have done the calling but I woke up this morning with a touch of laryngitis ...'

'I didn't know ...'

'No, of course not, but I was quite sure that we shouldn't call off the hunt, because you were an experienced caller as well.'

Kannan glared at his friend. He wished he had got in the bit about laryngitis before the other.

'There's no point standing about, let's get started,' he said briskly, though he felt none of the confidence he displayed. What if the animal actually appeared out of the scrub jungle? He had no idea of how he would handle it, reassured only by the thought that no self-respecting tiger would come within a hundred miles of him, once it had heard what he sounded like. He filled his lungs with air and cupping his hands around his mouth, he emitted a sound that was a cross between a loud throat-clearing and the barking of an amiable hound.

Freddie looked at his friend in disbelief. 'I didn't know tigers called like that,' he shouted.

'Well, you do it, if you know so much about it.'

'No, not at all. I was just being funny.'

'Don't be,' Kannan said shortly. He cupped his hands around his mouth and tried again, straining his vocal cords and attempting to throw his voice. This time his gargling call ended in a burst of coughing. Out of the corner of his eye, he saw that Freddie had put his rifle down and was shaking with laughter.

For a moment he was annoyed, and then the ludicrousness of the situation struck him and he too began to laugh.

'You sounded just like a constipated bear ...' Freddie said, shouting with laughter.

'Bet you don't know what a bear sounds like, you idiot,' Kannan replied.

'You were so damned effective, old chap, that you've even scared away the junglefowl. I was hoping to bag one for supper.'

'You have a nerve making fun of me. With that whacking great cannon you're carrying there wouldn't have been much of the junglefowl left for dinner.'

'Not much point hanging around here,' Freddie said, shouldering his rifle. 'By now that blessed tiger is probably halfway across Travancore.'

When they reached their motorcycles, Freddie said, 'Let's forget this nonsense and have a drink. Your house is closer, so you're it. Hope Helen won't mind us intrepid shikaris barging in.'

Kannan hesitated. Since Helen had left slightly over six weeks ago he'd managed to maintain the fiction that she was still around because he'd had no visitors with the exception of Murthy. There was no way he could prevent the servants gossiping but it would take a while before news reached the ears of his colleagues. But if Freddie came over ... He shied away from the thought of having to make explanations.

'Actually, Freddie, she's down with a migraine ... you know ... and when she's that way ... you know ... I'm not responsible for the consequences!'

'Christ, the problems you married chaps have. My place then.'

96

Three drinks later, he was telling Freddie about the parlous state of his marriage. He hadn't meant to share his marital woes with Freddie, especially after Murthy's diatribe, but the liquor dissolved his inhibitions soon enough. To mask his humiliation he adopted a light bantering air. Once he'd overcome the initial discomfort, Freddie's attentiveness and a couple more rounds of brandies ensured he spoke freely. After topping up their glasses for the fifth time, they were both quite drunk. They bemoaned the irrational, unstable ways of women. Then, to Kannan's delight, Freddie began to spout verse:

'She plucked one thread
of her glinting hair
and caught my hands

within that snare.
Laughing, I tried
To shake them free:
the hair, like steel,
imprisoned me.
A shackled slave,
I rue my laughter:
now, where she leads
I stumble after.'

'What was that all about?'

'Paulos. A nobleman at Justinian's court. About the first century. Christ, I'm sorry, old boy. I'm beginning to sound like my old don at Jesus, but one of my lesser-known claims to fame is that I read Greats before being kicked out of Oxford.'

'You know, Freddie, I've often wondered why you didn't try to become a writer or a poet.'

'The planter isn't expected to be a man of culture, shall we say!'

'Yes, I know, Major Stevenson asked me whether I read a lot, when he interviewed me. I said no, and he said, good, very good, planters are expected to get their boots dirty, not lounge around reading books.'

'Not a bad thing at all, if you ask me. One of the reasons I escaped England was to put an end to all those poetry-reading sessions and stuff. The only thing more boring was the old boys' get-together where a bunch of no-hopers from my old school would gather round to relive the old days, and keep the world at bay.'

'Yes, school can be stretched only up to a point, unless that's the only thing of consequence you've done in your life. But didn't you enjoy university?'

'I had a whale of a time! While it lasted. But once I'd had my fill, I wanted to get the hell out of that as well. Wild horses couldn't drag me back.'

'I spent most of my time at college chasing Helen and look how that's ended ...'

Freddie laughed and said, 'There you are. Speaking for myself, I'm glad that time is well behind me ... Burned my books a long time ago, but the ancient Greeks carved themselves into my mind when I was young and impressionable. How about this one by a rogue called Rufinus:

'If girls were nice
After lovemaking
No man could fuck them enough
But after bed
All girls
Are nauseating.'

Kannan's face darkened for a moment in embarrassment, then catching sight of Freddie's face he burst into laughter as well.

'Bet you made that up. And your language, my God, Freddie, my grandmother would have rubbed green chillies on my lips if I had used a word like that.'

'Ah, the pleasures of a public-school youth. Buggery, bad poetry and brio.' He turned serious. 'You know, I'm very fond of you both. I hope you're able to work things out.'

'I hope so too,' Kannan said as seriously. As with most drunken occasions, the lightness was beginning to alternate with maudlin emotion. 'I'm hoping to go down to Madras in a couple of months. Perhaps after Easter.'

'Yup, give things a little time to settle down. She seems a smashing woman, old boy, and I wouldn't give up on her.'

The tone of the evening lightened again.

'Women are so different, Freddie. You never know when they're going to go up in smoke!'

'You don't know the half of it. Probably why that Corbett fellow preferred man-eaters. Never married, you know.' Laughter broke out again, and Kannan thought Murthy might have been right about many things but some Englishmen weren't half-bad.

97

The next victim took all the fun and excitement out of the hunt. The Reverend Benjamin Ayrton was white, and a pillar of the British community in the hills. Everyone agreed that his sermons could have been improved but no one really minded his inadequacy as a pulpit-thumper. Indeed, for two decades, part of the Sunday morning ritual at Pulimed church was attempting to make some sense of what the pastor was talking about. It was common to lay a small bet on how long the old man would manage to stick to his chosen subject of the day before setting off on the first of numerous digressions. The record was forty-five seconds.

The dead man was found by a copse of pines that stood between the church and the parsonage. Pinned to his bloody cassock was a note that read: 'The White Ruler Is More Deadly Than Tigers! Quit India White Man Or Die!' The note was signed 'The Revolutionary Tigers'. His servants hadn't heard or seen anything.

The tea-planting district was shocked. Not only had the planters to cope with a man-eating tiger, now there were terrorists to contend with! They demanded effective action, something the local Pulimed police station, which usually concerned itself with harmless fights between coolies, was ill-equipped for. A message was telegraphed to the British Resident in Travancore. A deputation set off to Madras to meet the Governor.

Had it been terrorists all along? In their lonely bungalows, the managers and their families quaked at every unusual sound, kept a watchful eye on the servants, and hoped and prayed that the Government would send them a large force of soldiers to cope with the threat they faced. Unfortunately, their request for assistance was denied. There was a war on. And even though most of the top Indian nationalist leaders were in jail, there were enough law-and-order problems in the plains to keep everyone busy. The planters would have to fend for themselves.

Ten days after Reverend Ayrton's burial, one of the estate supervisors was carried off when he wandered off by himself to smoke a beedi. Not one of the labourers who had been pruning the field heard him cry out. It appeared that the tiger had stalked the man through the defile that bordered the field. With one huge bound it had been upon him, its jaws meeting around his throat. He had died instantly. Stripping off his clothes, the animal had picked up the dead man by the small of the back and had carried him for nearly two miles. The search party found the body at the edge of a thicket of eucalyptus trees. A small portion of the left buttock was eaten, but otherwise the kill was untouched.

Almost unhinged with fear, the people of the plantations, white and brown, barricaded themselves behind locked doors, only venturing out in large noisy groups when the sun was well up. An emergency meeting of all the planters in Pulimed and beyond was called to work out a plan to rid the district of the terror that oppressed them. A day before the meeting, another issue cropped up. The coolies had gone on strike, refusing to go back to work until they were provided with armed protection or, alternatively, until the killer or killers were caught.

98

All afternoon the cars and motorcycles roared and wheezed up the steep slope leading to the Pulimed Club. For the first time since its inception, ladies were allowed into the bar to attend the meeting. The estate wives who, until this afternoon, had had to be content with knocking on the service hatch if they wanted a drink looked around them with great interest. Even Mrs Stevenson, behind the stern face she wore in public, was excited at finally being admitted to this, the holiest of holies, the one place in her kingdom where she had no say. But after the initial excitement, there was an inevitable let-down: was this all there was to the club bar? The tiger had changed one more feature of Pulimed society for ever.

The President of the Planters' Association called the meeting to order. The bar was not big enough to hold all the invitees so the doors to the library and the Snakepit were opened and bearers bustled about arranging chairs. The President requested those who wished to speak to raise their voices so that those outside the bar could hear them.

Freddie looked around and was surprised to see that Kannan was missing. He leaned across to Michael and asked where he was. Fraser didn't know.

The meeting got under way and various planters got up and suggested ways and means of dispatching the tiger. But most of their proposals had been tried before with little success or were impractical.

'Let's organize a subscription drive and get that Corbett fellow down here. He's had some experience of shooting ghost tigers,' a planter from Periyar shouted. Nervous laughter broke out which the President quickly brought under control.

'I'm sure that the honourable member is aware that the deputation that waited on the Governor had attempted to get the Government to procure the services of Colonel Corbett to rid us of the menace. A message was sent to him but he declined, saying he was too old to shoot any more man-eating tigers.'

'Isn't there anyone else?' the same planter shouted.

'What about Harrison? He must still be around,' a voice called from the far corner of the room.

'You must be joking,' the planter from Periyar said in reply. 'Nobody's seen the old soak in decades, and I'll be damned if we're going to crawl under some coolie-woman's sari to find him.'

It suddenly dawned on the planter that there were women present and he stammered out his apologies. He was a portly man, with a fringe of dirty brown hair and a thick moustache. Freddie swivelled around to look at him. He decided he didn't like his moustache and from there his thoughts drifted to facial hair in general. Why did men wear moustaches and sideburns? It looked so unimpressive on most of them ... Where was Kannan? It was not like him to be late. Perhaps he was being held up by the striking workers. If that was the case he could be quite late. Freddie remembered the first time he'd had to deal with a strike, three hundred or more men against one, i.e. himself. He'd been waved to a stop on the road leading to the factory and surrounded by yelling, gesticulating men, some of whom brandished sticks and pruning knives. He had been terrified at first but, after about half an hour, had grown calmer when he realized the protesters didn't intend to harm him. Unless he did something foolish, of course. It had all seemed like some elaborately choreographed ballet: the workers would scream themselves into a frenzy, wave their sticks and knives threateningly at him, and then, unable to sustain the pitch, would begin to subside, until they gradually perked up again. They had finally let him pass, after demonstrating for about an hour, and he had driven straight to Michael's bungalow to tell him proudly that he had survived his first strike. It became something of an annual ritual: every year the workers would agitate for a day or two, usually demanding a higher bonus, and every year the management would give in, ostensibly with reluctance. It was just one of the things that were part of estate life. But this time, the flash strike was actuated by fear, and who knew what they were capable of doing? He hoped Kannan would be all right.

When Freddie tuned back in to the meeting, a Peermade planter was talking – the strike would have to be resolved quickly, the plucking must go on, the factories could not be allowed to remain idle.

'If we let this continue, the coolies will start deserting and then it will be impossible to get them back. Who knows how long this menace is going to be around? A few more months and the rains will start, the roads will become impassable and ...' The planter shrugged his shoulders.

'Perhaps we can give the supervisors guns. They could stand guard in the fields where there is plucking or pruning. At least ...'

'Damned bad idea,' interrupted a thin, weedy-looking planter, whom Freddie didn't recognize (probably an owner-planter from some small estate, he thought). 'You just can't trust Indians these days. Have you forgotten what happened to the padre?'

'I say, that's rubbish,' Fraser said, springing to his feet. 'You can't tar every Indian with the same brush. Indians died by the hundred in the Burma campaign just so that life for us could go on. Slim has said on the record that the Fourteenth Army couldn't have done what it did without its Indian troops and officers.' His outburst drew a couple of approving nods, but most of the planters displayed no emotion.

'I'm not saying that all Indians are not to be trusted,' the weedy planter said; 'it's just that these are difficult times ...'

'For Indians as well as for us,' Fraser retorted. 'I'm sure my Indian colleagues will bear me out.' He sat down, looking around as he did for Kannan, then for the Parsi planter from Peermade. But there wasn't a single Indian face in the room, apart from those of the bearers in their white jackets and trousers.

'Dammit, sir.' Freddie's anger was evident as he got to his feet. He had realized why Kannan was absent. 'I've just realized that there is not a single Indian planter in the room. Have they been left out of this meeting?'

'Mr Hamilton, the decision was taken in the best interest of everyone, including our Indian colleagues, so we could speak freely and arrive at some decisions that would benefit us all,' the President said quite calmly.

Freddie felt like flying at the man. When he found his voice, he said, 'You, sir, must surely realize that if the Indian Assistants were not to be trusted, if the vast majority of Indians were not to be trusted, we wouldn't be sitting around in our comfortable bungalows today. Actions like yours, sir, are driving our Indian friends from us. Damned bad form, I say.' Just then the enormity of what he was doing dawned on him. He, Freddie Hamilton, a junior Assistant of the Pulimed Tea Company, was standing up and accusing the President of the Planters' Association of being foolish and, furthermore, using the sort of abusive language that was rarely heard at PA meetings. His anger drained out of him. He looked around for support. Michael and Belinda Fraser looked sympathetic, but he did not see any encouragement on the faces of the other planters. Mrs Stevenson looked furious and Major Stevenson was gazing at the floor. Good God, he thought unhappily, what on earth have I done?

A chair scraped back and Michael Fraser got up. 'Mr President, I don't condone his language but I absolutely support my colleague's view that our Indian friends should not have been excluded.' The bar buzzed with excitement. Major Stevenson continued to look down at the floor. He would have to reprimand Freddie. There would be a scene, and he would have to be firm and explain away something that was patently unjust. And what if he resigned? And Kannan too? With two of his assistants gone, how on earth was he going to run the show? Why did everything have to be so infernally complicated?

99

Freddie gunned his motorcycle down the deserted estate roads, anger flaring inside him. His embarrassment and shock at his own impertinence had faded after a while, to be replaced once more by a sense of outrage. It was a glorious day, but Freddie didn't notice, he was much too distracted. Could he be fired for his outburst at the club? A junior Assistant quite simply did not abuse a senior planter in public. So what? He didn't care. If this was what planting was all about, then he was better off doing something else. Preoccupied with his thoughts, he almost missed the turn to the Morningfall bungalow. He slowed the motorcycle down, coasted to a stop by a wild guava tree. Its foliage was alive with screeching and squabbling rosy pastors. He watched them for a while. Until now, everything within him had itched to tell Kannan of the humiliation that had been visited on him, but now he began to wonder if he was doing the right thing. Perhaps he should just go on home. Kannan would get to hear of the PA meeting anyway, and would probably feel bad for a while, but these things happened in British India. More than likely he would find a way of accepting it. Then he thought of his friend trying to call up the tiger, and the anger rose up hotly again. Stupid, pompous bastards! How could they even think that Kannan was untrustworthy? He kicked the motorcycle into life and roared up the hill to the bungalow.

The butler led him into the living room.

'Hullo there, Freddie,' Kannan said brightly, 'unexpected pleasure.

I was thinking of going to the club, get in some tennis maybe, didn't want to waste a fabulous day. Then got a bit too lazy, you know how it is. Beer?'

'No, no. No, thank you. Tea will do fine, if you're having some.'

Kannan called for tea.

Now that he was here, Freddie didn't know how he was going to broach the subject. Kannan was the first to break the silence.

'How are we going to sort out this strike? I've been sitting around thinking about it, and short of giving the supervisors guns, there doesn't seem to be any way to get them back to work. The President of the PA should convene a meeting ...'

The tea arrived and Kannan poured. He should tell him now, Freddie thought. But how did you tell a man, whose sense of self-worth and pride were high, that he was less than he was, in the eyes of his fellows?

'I think we should put our heads together, hammer out a solution quickly, before things get out of hand,' Kannan was saying. 'The PA ...'

'The PA is of no use to you.'

'What do you mean?'

'That's the reason I came. There was a PA meeting to discuss the killings, and the Indian planters were excluded and Michael and I were outraged by it, and I protested ... and ... and that's why I'm here ...' Freddie said in a rush.

'I see,' Kannan said slowly. He didn't speak for a while, then said, 'Remember my friend Murthy?'

'Yes, I do, an intense man.'

'Yes, intense. And focused. He told me my desire to excel here, to make something of myself in the white man's world, was counterfeit. Nothing I'd ever achieve would stand up to scrutiny. He was right.' There was another long pause, then Kannan said gravely, 'It was really good of you to stand up for me.'

'It was nothing,' Freddie said.

'Now, if you'll excuse me, I have some thinking to do ...'

'Of course,' Freddie said. He got up hastily, almost dropping his cup in the process.

Some time after Freddie left, Kannan decided to get some fresh air. Around noon he found himself high in the hills overlooking his bungalow. It was a view similar to the one that had first entranced him in Pulimed. But he saw nothing of its enchantment for the rage that swept over him. What do you have against me, God, he stormed, that you trip me up at every stage in life, wreck my every safe haven? First appa, then Helen, now this.

Angrily, Kannan scanned the brilliantly lit panorama below. This had been the world he had escaped to; this was the foundation on which he was to rebuild his life. It had proved hollow ...

Something Murthy had said during his visit seeped into his mind.

When we are young, his friend had said, the truths we have acquired are pristine and pure, they admit of no other. Our heroes, our opinions, our convictions – we are passionate about these to a degree that will never again be felt with such intensity. When these are corroded, our disappointment is extreme; we are full of a rage that is so keen, so real, so vigorous that it takes us over completely. Middle age is tired, which is why it is tolerant. Youth is when we are most primed to act as our heart tells us. We are dismissive of our fears, ready to reject caution and advice, and willing to be what we most truly want ourselves to be. Murthy was right, Kannan thought, at this point he was willing to do whatever was necessary to attain his objective, which was to redeem himself in his own eyes. But what should he do? To whom should he turn for advice? For support? Helen was no longer available to him, nor was his father. Freddie (he was ashamed as he thought this) was white. The enemy and not to be trusted ...

In an attempt to purge himself of the anger and frustration, he began walking hard, trying to exhaust himself. An hour or so later, he had achieved a measure of calm, and had decided on a course of action. He would find and destroy the Pulimed Tiger or whoever or whatever was the killer, thereby erasing the suspicion in his colleagues' minds. And then he would show them what it meant to meddle with a Dorai. He would resign from the company and help his countrymen throw the white ingrates out. Brown would overwhelm white in a great surging wave; the oppressors would be nothing more than flecks of foam on a seething brown torrent.

100

The next morning he sent Stevenson and Fraser chits to say he was unwell, and wouldn't be at work for the next two days. Then he shut himself up in the small room off the drawing room that he used as a study, and drank. Kannan wasn't much of a drinker, and by noon he had passed out.

The butler found him stooped over his desk in the evening, and unsure of how to deal with the situation, went off and got him a pot of coffee. Kannan stared blearily at the man as he unloaded the contents of the tray on to the desk. The minute Manickam placed the coffee pot on the table, Kannan snatched it up and flung it out of the window, the savage gesture executed with scalpel-fine economy. Completely unnerved, the butler dropped the tray. Kannan instructed him to clean up the mess and dragged himself out of the study. The brief display made him feel much better. Then he felt sick. He took himself off to the bathroom and then to bed.

He began drinking again the next morning. All through that day and night he nursed his hurt with all the rancour and anger he could muster. All the other slights and setbacks he had received in his life, some as clear as the day they had happened, others only dimly remembered, pressed down and further oppressed him, and then, dimly through the anger, pain, confusion and bitterness, he began to perceive how he must implement the decision he'd arrived at ...

On the morning of the third day, tired and hung-over, Kannan was trying to get some porridge down when he heard the sound of a motorcycle. Freddie walked into the dining room, and if he was surprised to see the normally neat Kannan unshaven and dishevelled he didn't say so.

'Heard you were unwell, so decided to pop by after church.'

'The demon drink, old chap, otherwise I'm fine,' Kannan said with a wry smile. 'So what next? Am I to stand trial for seven, no, eight murders?'

Freddie glanced sharply at his friend.

'Things are not that bad, Cannon,' he said.

'Maybe not for you, but then you're white. I've just discovered I'm brown and no amount of soap and water will scrub it away.'

'Hey, easy on, old boy. No need to come over all shirty ...'

'I remember Belinda, or was it Michael, saying once: "He was the whitest Englishman I know." White, Freddie, for fair, brave, decent, courageous, heroic ... and brown, black, yellow, olive for revolting things that have crawled out of the dark.'

'Come on, Cannon, take it easy.'

'I'm sick and tired of taking it easy, Freddie. The day will come when we're all sick and tired of taking it easy and then where will we be?'

'Look, Cannon, I thought we were friends ...'

'I hope we still are ... What happened to your face?' Kannan had just noticed a slight thickening of Freddie's jaw. 'Got into a fight?'

'Nothing as fancy as that. Just clumsy old Freddie with two left feet. Slipped while getting out of the bath and the lip of the tub caught me a nasty whack,' Freddie said, getting to his feet. 'I'll run along then. See you at work tomorrow.'

'You're a poor liar. Tell me what really happened.'

Slowly and patiently, Kannan managed to coax the truth out of Freddie. Over the past couple of days, while Kannan had gloomed about his bungalow, a rash of crudely lettered posters, demanding in Tamil that the whites get out, had begun appearing on trees and walls around the district. The police had arrested a couple of labour leaders but the murder of the Reverend Ayrton hung heavy on the planters' minds and their suspicions weren't laid to rest by the arrests.

Freddie had gone to the club as usual on Saturday and after lunch had found himself in the middle of a group of people who were quite drunk and expounding a theory that he hadn't heard before: how was it, asked one obnoxious assistant, that none of the killings, with the exception of the first one, had taken place on the Pulimed Tea Company's estates? Was it because Kannan worked there? And why had the posters only started appearing when Kannan absented himself from work?

Did they know, he had asked, that Kannan's uncle had been imprisoned by the authorities for being a terrorist?

'Damned liar. He knew I was a friend of yours. It was almost as though he was daring me to take him on.'

'I don't know where he found out about my Aaron-chithappa, Uncle Aaron to you,' Kannan said. 'He was in prison for many years. He was one of the early freedom fighters. I wish I had known him.'

'The way Taylor put it, he seemed to suggest he was a criminal.'

'He certainly wasn't a criminal.'

'I didn't think so ...'

'And so you took the blighter on,' Kannan said with a grin.

'But you should have seen him,' Freddie said, adding modestly, 'He was much more drunk than I was. Nasty piece of work though.'

'Thank you, Freddie, I truly appreciate it,' Kannan said as he walked his friend to his motorcycle.

'Oh, I say, there's another piece of news that I almost forgot,' Freddie said. 'The police have taken someone into custody for the pastor's murder, a former sacristan who was dismissed for thieving.

Apparently he'd threatened to get even, and was considered quite capable of carrying out the threat while under the influence ...'

'But our friend yesterday and others like him would rather I remained the prime suspect. God, how they must hate me.'

'Spineless bastards every one ... But look, I'm off to Madras next week ...'

'Lucky devil, I know you had some leave coming, but how did you manage to get around Michael?'

'Well, with the strike and everything, he thought this would be the best time for me to slip away ...'

'How long will you be gone?'

'A fortnight, sixteen days actually. Is there anything I can do for you in Madras?'

'Not a blessed thing,' Kannan said.

'Why don't you drop in for a drink, Saturday? I leave early Monday.'

'I'll be there,' Kannan said.

When his friend had gone, Kannan went to his room, had a bath and changed. He was not surprised to hear that he was the subject of gossip and innuendo. It only strengthened his resolve. He thought: The world pushes, and it pushes, and then we push back, just a bit ...

That evening, contrary to protocol, he went across to the General Manager's Bungalow, without an appointment. The Stevensons were having tea when Kannan rode up, but he declined the offer to join them and asked to speak to Major Stevenson alone. Mrs Stevenson was none too happy at the request, and assumed her imperious aspect, but Kannan stood his ground.

As they strolled on the bungalow's vast lawns, Kannan made no reference to the events of the past days and asked only that when the next killing took place he be given a week's leave to bring the killer to book. And a guarantee that no one else would interfere in the hunt. Stevenson looked pensive, then nodded. He decided it was probably wiser not to ask any questions.

From that day onwards, every morning before he left for work, Kannan, who had never paid anything but lip-service to his faith, would offer up a fervent prayer. Please, Lord, let the killer strike again.

Nine days later his prayers were answered.

101

At the northern boundary of Morningfall division, the estate fell away steeply to a deep ravine, along the bottom of which ran a little stream. Beyond the ravine was an unusually shaped hill that split into two about halfway up. At certain angles the twin peaks resembled human faces, as a result of which they were dubbed Annan-Thambi. The valley between them was thickly forested, the scurf of trees extending well beyond the base of the hills. A footpath ran through the patch of jungle. The labourers on the estate used the trail as a convenient short cut to Pulimed town, which lay on the other side of Annan-Thambi. The alternative was a five-mile walk.

After the advent of the man-eater nobody dared use the footpath, unless a large party could be mustered to make the journey. The latest victim had made the fatal error of taking the short cut alone. His wife had come down with a high fever, and as it was barely an hour past noon he thought he could hurry across the hill to the small dispensary in town and get back before the light began to fade. He hadn't reckoned on the fact that a man-eating tiger, having lost its innate fear of man, will hunt both by night and by day. At a bend in the jungle road, the man-eater had sprung out on the unfortunate man and killed him. It had dragged the body to a small clearing, and after eating about half of it, had retreated deeper into the forest. The alarm had been raised when the man failed to reach town, and Kannan was at the kill within a few hours. With him he had the local poacher, a necessary evil, and a couple of his own men. The poacher interpreted the killing with only a minimum amount of exaggeration.

Casting around for a suitable place to sit up over the kill, they decided on a medium-sized jungle tree, shrouded by a thick screen of bushes. Instructing his men to build a machan some twenty feet off the ground, Kannan hurried off.

He had already informed Stevenson. The General Manager had granted him a week's leave and had spread the word that no one else was to interfere. Kannan wished he'd remembered to borrow Freddie's massive elephant gun before his friend left on vacation, but there was nothing to be done about that now. He got on his motorcycle and drove to the coolie lines on Connemara Estate, a largish plantation owned by the McCracken Tea Company, whose estates extended right up to the boundaries of Glenclare Estate.

He had never visited the coolie quarters on any of the estates since his orientation tour when he had first arrived. As then, the sight of the buildings depressed him: rows of long, low mud-and-plaster buildings roofed with tin, a dozen families to a building, a family to a room. Small, raggedly dressed children, their faces liberally plastered with mucus and dirt, were playing in the beaten earth before the houses. At the sight of him, the children ran screaming into the houses and the women hastily covered their heads with their sari pallus. Most of the men were back at work, at least some of the time, guarded by men with guns, either the managers themselves or local poachers with their fearsome weapons.

Kannan walked up to an old woman and asked where he might find Harrison. Lowering her head, she pointed to a one-roomed cottage perched on a slight rise near the lines. As he neared it, he saw that it was constructed in the same way as the other buildings in the quarter, except that it was roofed by country tiles.

In the open patch of beaten earth surrounding the cottage, four children were playing. They ranged in age from four to fifteen and all of them had the pale brown skins of mixed breeds. An enormously fat woman, dressed in a garish pink sari, gold bright against her nose and wrists, pounded grain in a stone quern, oblivious to the shrieking children who seethed around her. The children grew quiet as he approached and their mother looked up from her pounding and gazed at him with interest.

'Are you Mrs Harrison? I wish to see your husband,' Kannan shouted above the sound of wood on stone.

'Never married me, but yes, he's here. I'll see if I can get him.'

She stopped what she was doing, heaved herself to her feet, the sari slipping momentarily and affording him a glimpse of huge breasts. She waddled off towards the house. Over her shoulder she yelled at the children to go and play, then disappeared into the cottage. As he waited for her to emerge, he reviewed the little he knew of Richard Harrison.

He had never met the man, but then he'd gone native twenty years ago. After being fired for his excessive bouts with the bottle and pluckers, it was said that Harrison had simply packed all his worldly belongings into two empty kerosene tins and gone off to live with the coolie woman he had been sleeping with at the time. Since then, nobody had seen anything of him. This suited Kannan. All he needed was for the man to agree to what he had in mind.

The fat woman reappeared and told Kannan to go in. As he climbed up the steps to the house, he could hear the pounding start up again.

The first thing that struck him as he entered the room was the smell: the thick stench of unwashed bodies, stale food and drink, dung smoke and urine. When his eyes adjusted to the meagre light that filtered through the single dust- and smoke-stained window, he saw a gaunt old man sitting on a string cot, dressed in a lungi and a singlet. His disproportionately large head, which was totally bald and covered with liver spots, drew Kannan's attention. Realizing he was staring, he averted his eyes. He needn't have bothered, for Harrison did not acknowledge his presence but continued to sip from the brass tumbler in his hand.

Kannan took a quick look around. Pots and pans hung from pegs driven into the mud wall, as did saris and other clothes. Sleeping mats were rolled up in an untidy heap in one corner and there was a tin trunk and several empty kerosene tins along the walls. Harrison still ignored him, so he cleared his throat and began to speak, anxiously and fast.

'Mr Harrison, I'd like your help, sir. There's a man-eating tiger on the estate, and I hope you can help me get rid of it. The whole district's being terrorized by the animal and ...'

'Why me?' The voice was surprisingly deep and pleasant.

'Well, I thought ...'

Harrison didn't let him finish. 'Why don't you get those fancy bloody planters and their expensive rifles to get rid of your problem, Mr Dorai?'

Kannan was astonished that Harrison knew his name.

The old man laughed and took a swig of whatever he was drinking.

'Sir, I've heard you're one of the best shikaris in the district ...'

'And a drunkard and a bedder of a black woman to boot. Oh no, mister, you'll have to do better than that.' He laughed again, a disagreeable sound in the little room, and then his laughter was broken by a fit of coughing so prolonged that Kannan didn't know whether to go to his assistance or flee. When the cough finally subsided, Harrison wiped his face with a dirty rag, and said, 'Shall I tell you why you are here, Mr Dorai? It's because the white men think you are behind the killings. And you want to redeem yourself by killing the phantom tiger of Pulimed.'

Kannan said nothing.

'Let me tell you, mister, news travels in many ways here. And the answer to your request is, no. I have no desire whatsoever to help you or your masters.'

When Kannan spoke, there was a pleading note in his voice, to his disgust. But he kept on anyway. 'Please, Mr Harrison, I shall make this worth your while. Whether we shoot the tiger or not, I shall pay you a hundred rupees, no, two hundred,' realizing even as he spoke that it was over half his monthly salary.

The old man made no reply and seemed to have forgotten about him. Kannan was turning to go, when he heard him say, 'Your money does not interest me, mister.' This time when Harrison lapsed into silence it was evident that the interview was over.

Kannan had almost reached his motorcycle when he heard a child hailing him in Tamil. It was one of the older children he had seen playing around Harrison's house. The message the boy delivered was brief: his father wanted Kannan to visit him in the evening, when he would let him have a final decision. Kannan had no idea why the old man was reconsidering but he suddenly felt less dejected.

102

There were still a couple of hours left to sundown when Kannan and Harrison reached the kill. Harrison carried an old model .275 Rigby rifle, obviously well cared for, the metal parts oiled and gleaming, the worn stock lovingly polished, and Kannan shouldered his Mannlicher.

As they looked down at the remains of the victim, Kannan asked, 'Are you sure this is a tiger kill? I mean, this one's eaten a bit, but most of the victims weren't even touched. And not one of the shikaris has even seen it, let alone managed to get a shot at it.'

'So I've heard,' Harrison said drily. 'But if I were a bloody self-respecting tiger, I wouldn't show up with a bunch of bumbling jack-asses crashing about with bloody great guns around me.' He walked across to the machan, seemed satisfied with what he saw, and said to Kannan, 'I'll scout around a bit, see what I can find. Looks like we have a couple of hours of light left. Go home, get a couple of blankets and a good torch and be back within an hour. If you don't see me around, go straight to the machan and sit on it. I don't think the tiger is around yet, but if he's going to show up, I don't want anything spooking him.' As Kannan turned to go, he said, 'Oh, and bring a bottle of brandy with you.'

Kannan was at the machan at half past five. Soon after he had settled himself, he saw Harrison walking towards him. He wondered if the old man had watched him arrive; perhaps he'd had his rifle trained on him. He was suddenly nervous. He decided to watch the man carefully, try not to be caught unawares. Harrison nodded to him and climbed up into the machan. There was no conversation between them except for Harrison asking Kannan whether he'd brought the brandy. Kannan passed him the bottle and Harrison took a long swig. Then, capping the bottle, he settled himself more comfortably.

As the light began to leach from a sky crumpled and barred with cloud, the jungle around them came alive with sound. Cicadas whirred, birds chattered and rustled and once they heard a large animal crashing away through the undergrowth. The sound of a man singing eddied up to them. When there was barely enough light to see, they heard a log being struck rapidly with a stick. 'Barking deer,' Kannan heard Harrison say. 'The tiger's moving. In this direction.'

Excitement coursed through him. He forgot the pain of the past few days. He was alive only to the thrill of the moment. A man-eating tiger, the most dangerous animal alive, was approaching them ... The barking deer stopped calling. Night fell abruptly and slowly the excitement left him.

'Is the tiger still around?' he whispered to Harrison.

The old man's whispered reply was angry. 'Not one more bloody word out of you tonight. Comes of having bloody amateurs on a tiger shoot.'

'Look, Mr Harrison, this is not the first shoot I've been on ...'

'One more word out of you,' Harrison hissed, 'and I take no further part in this hunt, is that understood?'

Kannan clamped back the angry retort that rose to his lips and subsided into a sullen silence.

The landscape lightened as the moon came up. Beside him the old man sat so still and unmoving, Kannan wondered if he was alive. The pressure of the rough wood of the machan was uncomfortable, but he dared not move in case he provoked another outburst from Harrison. He craned his head to look at his watch. They had been almost two hours on the machan. Christ, it was uncomfortable! He could feel his legs beginning to cramp; the whine of mosquitoes increased in intensity and he felt a couple settle on his face. He itched to slap them, but his fear of Harrison stayed his hand. As time passed, the strain and the discomfort spurred him to anger. What the hell am

I doing in this place? he thought. I should just leave it to mad tigers, renegade Englishmen and bloody malarial mosquitoes. It's no place for normal people. He flexed his thighs unobtrusively and tried to ignore the mosquitoes. The anger leaked away of its own accord and a sense of resignation took over. He wondered whether he should tell Helen about his decision to resign. Would it make any difference to them, to their future together? Probably not.

His immediate priority was to show these damned white planters their place. He would try and link up with Murthy when he left the estates; he wanted to be part of the action when Gandhi, and the rest of them, sent the British hurtling back to their rain-ringed islands. He wondered what someone like Harrison would do if his countrymen were kicked out. Nothing, he suspected. Just stay in his cottage with his fat coolie woman and drink himself to death with arrack. God, he hoped the old soak would be able to shoot the tiger. Assuming there was a tiger. What if it was a ghost, would Harrison die of fright? Would he? He fought the urge to giggle, then every sense snapped alert as he felt Harrison's warning hand on his knee. The moon had gone behind a cloud and he could see nothing, but he knew that the old man had the stock of his rifle screwed to his shoulder. He held his own rifle aslant his chest but dared not move it. Now, even his untrained ears could pick up the sound of something moving cautiously towards them. The moon began to ease from behind the clouds and they could make out the shape of a large tiger astride the kill. The light grew in intensity as the moon sailed free of the cloud, and then Harrison's rifle crashed into the night. Instantly, the animal bounded up and away into the undergrowth. 'Don't know if I hit him, but I think I might have. He gave me a splendid shot and I don't usually miss at thirty yards. At least we know it's a tiger. Get some rest, we'll track him in the morning.'

Harrison sounded pleased and Kannan found that reassuring. The almost unbearable excitement that had enveloped him when they had first spotted the tiger began to fade, and their uncomfortable perch, the mosquitoes and the cold began to make themselves felt. But the tension and irritation were gone now. He laid his rifle down carefully, stretched, scratched luxuriously, folded himself into his blanket as best he could. As he dropped off he heard the bottle of brandy being uncapped.

103

A wounded man-eater is the most dangerous animal in the jungle. Where a normal tiger probably will not charge its tracker a day or so after it has been shot, especially if the wound is a surface one, and the pain and shock have subsided, there is no telling what a man-eater will do. The likelihood is high that it will go for the hunter. Mindful of this, Harrison and Kannan proceeded very slowly on the trail of the Pulimed Tiger.

At first light they had gone over to the spot where they'd seen the animal and the old man spotted the tell-tale cut hairs and splashes of blood that showed the bullet had gone home. Instructing Kannan to bring him a hat, sandwiches, coffee and a few other necessities, he had set about examining the blood trail. When Kannan returned, they set off at once.

At first they moved slowly, constantly checking every boulder, shrub or natural formation that was capable of concealing a wounded tiger. Wherever the trail wound through thick forest, Harrison sent Kannan ahead, for tigers do not like to charge head-on. They would inch along the jungle, keeping their eyes peeled for any sign. His every sense straining with the excitement he felt, but without the knowledge that enabled the old hunter to read the jungle with ease, Kannan saw the tiger everywhere – in a patch of grass dappled with sunlight, peering through a lantana bush, creeping over a carpet of dry leaves. Inevitably, this watchfulness took its toll and in less than an hour he was tired and was starting a headache. His body ached and spots swam before his eyes. He didn't see the root protruding a little above the path. His foot caught on it, and his tired body fell. He had the presence of mind to hold his rifle clear as he crashed to the ground. Harrison, who was leading, was back immediately.

'Clumsy bloody amateur,' he muttered. Without bothering to help Kannan up, he took his rifle, unloaded it, and handed it back.

'What did you do that for?'

'Take my chances barehanded with a man-eater any day before I'd have some idiot shoot me in the back.'

Kannan felt the anger take hold of him and he fought it. Today, for as long it took, he would hold his temper. He needed Harrison. Wearily, he got to his feet and followed the old shikari. He tried to shake off his tiredness, it was important to keep going. He was sure

Harrison would leave him behind if he felt Kannan was slowing him down.

Some time later, the blood trail was beginning to fade. At the first rest halt, Kannan asked whether that meant the wound was closing. The hunter shook his head and uncharacteristically volunteered additional information. He explained that as an animal's coat only loosely covered the flesh, when it was in motion the wound in the skin and the wound in the flesh did not match. As a result there was little blood spilled so long as the animal kept going. When it stopped, the blood would spill out as the skin aligned with the flesh. Fifteen minutes later, he proved his theory by pointing to a big splash of blood in a clearing where the tiger had paused to rest. 'Not a mortal wound. But not a superficial one either,' he said to himself, and then grew alert. Away to their left, a troop of black-faced langurs which had been feeding quietly suddenly began to call, khok, khok, khok, khokorrorr ... 'They've seen the tiger, it's on the move, come on, let's get going.' Kannan, who was sitting on the ground, his rifle propped between his knees, reluctantly got up. His calves, his thighs, even his shins ached. The sun was well up, and sweat sprung out on his body, further adding to his discomfort.

The tiger was moving faster now, judging by the punishing pace Harrison set. On they went, hour upon hour, under the mighty flail of the sun, through tea and eucalyptus thickets, dense sholas, up steep escarpments. Kannan staggered along, every step an effort. His rifle was monstrously heavy in his hands, his rucksack seemed full of rocks, and his thighs, calves and feet screamed with pain. Still Harrison kept on.

Towards noon they stopped by a small mountain stream. The clear cold water pooled in a natural grotto fringed with maidenhair fern and moss. Gratefully Kannan collapsed on the ground. Harrison carefully placed his rifle next to him, then removed his hat and splashed water on his face and arms. Idly Kannan watched the little silver and blue fish in the shallows scattering in panic as the old man washed, then ventured a question: 'Do you think we'll get him, Mr Harrison?'

He seemed not to hear. Kannan was about to repeat himself when Harrison said, 'The wound isn't bothering him too much. I'll have to try something else.'

They finished the sandwiches and coffee, and set off again. Around four o'clock, as they approached a spreading thicket of lantana, Kannan's tiredness suddenly fell away, to be replaced by a sense of terror. There was nothing out of the ordinary that he could see, but he knew that the thicket contained something terrible. Harrison had stopped dead, his rifle up and pointing at the bushes. The minutes stretched by and then the thicket erupted with roar upon stomach-turning roar. Kannan had his rifle to his shoulder in an instant, then, realizing it was unloaded, panicked. What would he do if the old man missed or was killed? Should he take the bullets out of the rucksack and load the rifle, or would that be unwise? Harrison had given him no instructions. The jungle echoed and thundered with the tiger's fury, then abruptly it was gone.

'It was waiting for us,' was all the old man said.

'Should I load my rifle?'

'No.'

'Look, Mr Harrison, I know that this is just a precaution that you're taking, but if the tiger stalks us again ...'

'I said, no. You said you would follow my instructions exactly, so do not argue with me! Now let's get going.'

About half an hour later, they entered a clearing in the forest. The sunlight slanted down through tall forest trees festooned with creepers. A lush carpet of grass was neatly bisected by a stream that flowed clear and with barely a ripple over a bed of smoothly rounded pebbles. Various birds that Kannan couldn't identify called through the green light of the glade. Jungle babblers rustled in the undergrowth. The old man, after pausing for the briefest moment to survey the scene in front of him, had gone across to a little isthmus of clear white sand by the stream. He studied the patch of sand for a long time, then beckoned Kannan over. 'We have a very hungry animal on our hands.' He pointed with his rifle. 'Here's where he stalked a sambhar doe, sprang, missed, and those tracks show how the deer got away.'

He paused in thought, then said, 'How badly do you want this tiger?'

'Very,' Kannan said simply.

'I have a plan that might work. But it depends on your complete co-operation. Is that understood?'

'Yes. What's the plan?'

'I'll tell you later. For now all I need to know is that I can trust you to do my bidding without question.'

Kannan nodded.

The old man regarded him for a long moment, then said, 'We've got just under two hours of good light left, and to have a chance of shooting him, we're going to have to do something out of the ordinary. If memory serves me correctly, there's a game trail that leads from here to the Kallan shola. After that, it passes along the Parallel Rocks to the Periyar river. My hunch is that our fellow is a Thekkady tiger and that is the route he'll take to get to the heart of his home range. Beyond the Kallan shola there's a big pool with plenty of cover and lots of game. He'll try and find some prey there, before he gets down to the river. We'll circle around and try to ambush him. Did it successfully with a tiger I was tracking in '24.'

Now that he had made up his mind, Harrison set a pace that stupefied Kannan. Where on earth did the old drunkard find the energy? Kannan lagged behind until Harrison snapped at him to hurry up.

They reached their destination as the sun began its descent. The great heat of the afternoon had mellowed. They walked through a mixed forest of teak and other deciduous trees, which ended in a ravine. The near slope was dense with scrub jungle which thinned as the ground got rockier. At the bottom of the ravine, a stream dropped in a series of rills and cascades into a deep pool with a broad shoulder of sand. As they got closer, they could see that it was pocked with the prints of all sorts of animals and birds. The far slope of the ravine was gentler than the one they had descended. It was sparsely covered with lantana and other jungle shrubs. Further up, there was more scrub jungle and then the forest proper started. A well-worn game trail ran down from the forest to the pool. The stream washed down the ravine to a rocky plateau, beyond which the ground fell sharply away into a bottomless valley, swirling with mist, in which there was an arresting natural formation: two huge columns of stone rising parallel to each other for hundreds of feet, their base obscured by thick jungle and mist. Kannan had never seen the Parallel Rocks and he was riveted by the sight. Harrison broke his reverie. 'Come on, we have work to do,' he said.

'I'm going to sit up on that rock.' He pointed to a boulder shaped like a lozenge. Scrub formed a natural screen in front and there was a steep drop behind to a small ledge that overlooked the Parallel Rocks valley. 'It'll give me an unrestricted field of fire. What I want you to do is start from the edge of the forest and walk slowly down the game trail to the pool, talking loudly as you go. I'll cover you every inch of the way. My rifle is dead accurate to two hundred yards.' For a moment, the import of Harrison's words didn't sink in, then Kannan said, 'Are you asking me to be bait for a man-eating tiger?'

'Yes,' was all Harrison said.

'You're crazy,' Kannan said. 'This thing has already killed nearly a dozen people and you're asking me ... you're asking me to be its next victim. Is that correct?'

'Quite correct,' Harrison said.

'I won't do it. I absolutely will not do it.'

'Fine. We might as well head back,' Harrison said, and he made as if to move.

Even as he protested, Kannan knew he was going to do as the old man asked: the killing of the Pulimed Tiger mattered so much to him. It was as simple as that.

Harrison's plan was uncomplicated. He would know of the tiger's arrival from the alarm calls in the jungle and would see every move it made from the moment it left the cover of the forest. The moment it showed, he would put a bullet into it.

'Remember, there is no danger from the front and I'm covering your back, every inch of the way, right down to the pool. If it doesn't show on the first pass, we'll try again, so long as there's enough light to see. Walk slowly, talk at the top of your voice, and keep your eyes on anything that might hide a tiger. Load your rifle. Now, be ready to snap off a shot at a moment's notice. If you hear a shot, stay where you are until you hear my call.'

They gave it half an hour. Harrison settled himself and then Kannan began to walk slowly down the game path to the pool, terror implicit in his every step. He had never been so afraid in his life. His vision blurred with concentration and fear turned his mind blank. What should he say, what should he say? How could he quarter every inch of ground in front of him, keep every sense alert, and still be able to talk and sing? Five steps, seven, nine, a dozen, and then, blessedly, the verse Charity used to croon to him in the mango groves of his childhood came to him. He began screaming it at the top of his voice, as if his childhood talisman could protect him from all the terrors of the adult world.

'Saapudu kannu saapudu
Neela mangavai saapudu
Onaku enna kavalai ...'

His grandmother's song unlocked the floodgates.

He sang snatches of songs half-remembered from his days of courting Helen, he composed speeches to Freddie, to his father, to his wife, he abused Harrison at the top of his voice, and recited all the nursery rhymes he'd read so often to little Andrew Fraser. Then terror seized him and corrupted memory. He fell silent, then, remembering Harrison's instructions, shouted out whatever came into his head:

'Jack and Jill went up a hill
To fetch a pail of water
Jack fell down and Jack fell down
And Jack fell down soon after.'

He had left the open ground behind him and reached a section of the trail where it ran through luxuriant undergrowth. The light was green and gloomy, and the horror of what might await him stopped him dead in his tracks. How did Harrison know that tigers never attacked from the front? Your job is not to second-guess tigers or hunters, he said to himself. Your job is to move ever forward, making noise. So saying, he forced himself to move. But his mind was blank again; he'd even forgotten his grandmother's ditty just when he needed it most. A memory of Pulimed church came to him and then, to his infinite relief, his mind flooded with Christmas carols.

'Away in a manger, no crib for a bed
The Little Lord Jesus lay down his sweet head
The stars in the night sky ...'

Concentrate on the bushes, that rock, what an odd shape it has, forget the shape, isn't that a red and yellow ... no, it's a dry branch. His throat felt dry, and he couldn't think of the words to the carol he was singing and began another:

'Jingle bells, jingle bells, jingle all the way
Oh what fun it is to ride on a one-horse open sleigh oh
Jingle bells, jingle bells ...'

He was halfway to the pool now, and the path curved. What if the tiger sprang on him as he turned the bend? He realized he had stopped singing, and began chanting:

'O little town of Bethlehem ...'

The shot was a sharp flat crack that drilled through the noise he was making. It was followed moments later by another. He heard Harrison's voice calling to him and then there was a third shot. His legs would suddenly support him no longer and he sank to the ground.

104

The Pulimed Tiger was magnificent even in death. Kannan marvelled at the superbly muscled forelegs, the massive jaw. And to think he'd put himself in its path! Blood clotted in the white hair of its underbelly. Harrison showed him where the first bullet, fired the previous day, had raked the tiger across the left flank, finally lodging low down in its front foot. The last three shots were within inches of each other and were centred on the heart.

Kannan marvelled at the old man's marksmanship. Harrison said, 'You were in no danger at all, you know. I saw the tiger as soon as he left the forest, and I waited till he got closer and let him have it.'

'Well, I'm relieved to hear that. But you won't catch me doing it again in a hurry.'

'You have an awful singing voice,' Harrison said, and Kannan looked at him in surprise. Was the old man warming towards him? But Harrison had already bent over the tiger and he couldn't see the expression on his face. 'Aha. Just as I suspected.'

He picked up one of the huge front paws and beckoned Kannan over. 'See how the hair has been completely licked off. Look closely and you'll see a number of holes in the skin. I'm willing to wager there's a broken-off porcupine quill under each of those punctures. The poor chap must have been in agony, no wonder he couldn't catch his usual prey.'

Kannan was nodding, when Harrison asked, 'Are you carrying your pruning knife?'

'Yes, in my rucksack.'

'Let me have it, I'll show you what I mean.' He picked up the great paw and made an incision. As the skin and flesh parted, Harrison pointed 'See? Quills broken off, but almost impossible to dislodge.' He dug out a couple of blood- and gristle-coated objects, cleaned them cursorily and held them out to Kannan. They were almost as thick as pencil stubs. He bent down, probed some more, and one of the claws dropped off. 'Everything else seems to be okay,' Harrison said, finishing his examination. 'It's the porcupine quills which drove him to find easier prey.'

Abruptly he stopped what he was doing, discarded the quills, and handed the knife back to Kannan. 'Cut a length of bamboo, about six feet will do, from that clump over there,' he said, pointing to a stand of wild bamboo that grew near the incline.

'Why, surely you are not proposing to tie the tiger to it and carry it back? Two men can't do it alone.'

'Remember, you agreed to do exactly as I said.' The old man's voice was hard. Perhaps he had just imagined the warmth in it moments ago. Kannan shrugged and, leaning his rifle against a rock, went over to the bamboo. Selecting a stout stem, he began hacking away at it with his pruning knife. Even though the sun had lost much of its power, it was hard work, and he was soon sweating freely. Crazy old man, he thought, but at least he'd got the tiger! He could just imagine the faces of the Stevensons and that bastard Taylor when he brought it in. The old man fully deserved his reputation as a great shikari. Who else would have anticipated the tiger's route? Pausing to rest, he looked over his shoulder to see what Harrison was up to and froze in disbelief. The old man had picked up Kannan's rifle. Even as he watched, Harrison casually sauntered over to the edge of the cliff and threw it into the teeming mist of the valley below. Kannan raced towards him. 'You crazy old fool, what the hell do you think you are doing? What the hell ...' He was almost upon him when Harrison spoke. 'No further or you get a bullet in your belly.' The calm voice sliced through Kannan's fury and he noticed, for the first time, the old man's gun pointing steadily in the region of his mid-section. He juddered to a halt, lowered the knife.

'Why the hell did you do that? Have you gone mad?' Kannan asked, his voice hoarse with confusion and anger.

'I've told you. No questions. Just do as I tell you.'

'I'll be damned if I will, you drunken lunatic. You've already made me walk into the jaws of a man-eater, now you've thrown away my rifle. What are you going to do to me?'

'Nothing, if you do as you are told!'

'Why should I obey someone who is crazy?'

'I can assure you I'm not crazy. However, if you don't cut that bamboo, I'm going to shoot you and throw your body into the valley. It doesn't matter to me if you live or die.'

'You've already made that plain.'

'Start cutting. I have work to finish.'

Fear began to mingle with Kannan's rage.

'What are you going to do?' he asked.

'You'll find out soon enough. Now cut that bamboo.' There was an edge to Harrison's voice. Kannan stared into his eyes, but there was nothing to read in them. He turned and stumbled back to the stem in a daze, and finally had it down. He trimmed the leaves from it and carried it, under Harrison's watchful eye, to the edge of the precipice.

'Now get hold of the tiger by its hind legs and drag it to the bamboo,' Harrison said.

'Why are you doing this? Please tell me,' Kannan said. Frustration mingled with rage and fear as he surrendered to the whims of the madman.

'It's just that I don't want anyone to know the tiger's dead.'

'What!' The statement drove everything else from Kannan's mind. 'What?'

'You heard. Now do as you are told.'

'No, I will not, you crazy bastard. Do you really expect me, after all I've gone through, to walk away from here and deny all knowledge of the tiger's death? No, Harrison. I'm going straight to the police to report you for threatening me. Then I'll come back for the tiger. You've gone too far, old man.'

He began walking away, but Harrison's voice stopped him. 'Walk any further and you're dead. I'm sorry, my dear fellow, you'll just have to think again. There's nothing to prevent me from disposing of the tiger, and you, and then shooting myself. I have nothing to live for. Think about it.'

Kannan turned to face the hunter. 'Why?' he asked.

Harrison didn't reply.

'Why, why? Why in God's name, why?' Kannan cried, almost hysterical now. Suddenly he knew. 'I'll tell you why, you bitter old sod, I'll tell you why. You want those smug pompous bastards to sweat it out for what they did to you. Isn't that it? But how are you going to keep up the pretence when there are no more killings?'

Harrison gazed at him impassively, his rifle held steady. Goaded on by the other's calm, Kannan shouted, 'You will kill and kill and kill, you monster. You were the one who put up the posters, you were the one who killed the padre. Admit it. Damn you. Admit it.'

The sounds of the forest filled the silence between them. When Kannan spoke again, his voice was steadier. 'You're going to kill me, aren't you?'

Harrison replied, 'Not if you do as you're told.'

'What do you mean, do as you're told? Why should I trust you?'

'You trusted me once.'

Was that mockery he heard in the other's voice? Anger began to build in him again. 'Look, if you don't let me go, I'll go to the police ...' His voice trailed away as he realized the utter futility of repeating the threat. He wondered if he could rush Harrison, reach him before he got off a shot.

'Don't even think of it,' Harrison said quietly. 'You'll be dead before you've moved three feet. Now, for the last time, will you do as you are told?'

Exhausted, his every gesture that of a condemned man, Kannan nodded. He walked over to the dead animal and grasping it by its thick hind legs began to pull it slowly over the stony ground. It was hard work, and the animal's rank smell filled his nostrils, but Kannan was beyond caring. Step by step he moved towards the precipice and, as he did so, a new thought formed in his mind – he would just keep walking until there was nothing beneath his feet ... Nobody would give him any trouble then ... He would never do anything he had hoped to do, he would miss Helen and his mother, but there was nothing he could do about that ... He would never see Doraipuram again, never eat blue mangoes by the Chevathar ...

Harrison snapped at him. 'That's far enough. Now take the pole and push the tiger over.'

Kannan ignored him and kept walking forward, dragging the dead animal behind him. The crack of the rifle and the whine of the bullet near his feet overlapped each other and whipped him out of his daze.

'I said enough,' Harrison said. 'One more trick like that and it's a bullet in the belly.'

Kannan picked up the pole, thrust it under the tiger, began heaving at it, then stopped.

'Why didn't you just let me walk over? Do you want the personal satisfaction of shooting me?'

'You will go unhurt if you do as you're told,' Harrison said.

'I'll make sure they get you.'

'You won't,' Harrison said with a thin smile, 'you won't rat on me. I can see it growing within you now, the realization that you can make them sweat, get your own back on the white man. Tell me I'm wrong.'

'I don't know what you're talking about.'

'Really! Since when have you become the white man's friend?'

'I've had enough encounters with good men, to know that all white men are not bad.'

'Have you now? And I suppose you'll tell me that the Englishman is brave, fair, courageous, honest, white ... You fool, don't you see that those are just myths assiduously built up to control you poor heathen natives?'

'Shut up, Harrison.'

'Watch how you speak to me, you young whippersnapper. Do you mean to tell me that you haven't spent your working life fitting into a straitjacket devised by someone else? You look like a fellow who doesn't put up with nonsense, so it must have been even more of a trial. Look at you, enunciating your words carefully, polishing your English manners, playing right into the hands of those who seek to keep you down. Why the hell should you not say Les-ester or Worsester or Chol-mon-de-ley when not one Englishman of my acquaintance can pronounce an Indian name correctly! And why should you not spit in public when the honking of a white man into his handkerchief would drown out a tiger's roar? And do you really think the English oak is sturdier than the banyan and the thrush superior to the bulbul? And that the lotus is inferior to the rose? Is Tamil less than English? Why don't these things make you angry?'

Kannan smiled ruefully at Harrison's remarks; they could have been Murthy's. He said, 'Because I'm not a bitter old man like you.'

'Forgiveness is for the birds. Forgive and forget is for the birds. You always need to seek revenge, it keeps you alive.'

'You're mad, Harrison, I'm not going to go your way.'

'Oh yes, you will, if you want to remain alive to your own potential. Discard what you've learned here, it's of no use. You can never be white, you've always known it, so why bother? Hope instead that you shake off the spell cast on you and wash away the white man in a roaring brown flood ...'

'It's funny you should say that.'

'What?'

'That we should sweep away the white man like a river in spate, it was a something that occurred to me ...'

'So you are capable of bitterness and rage! Life is not a tennis game. Nobody plays fair, and there's no winner or loser. Your enemies will be with you, your demons will haunt you as long as you live, and the only way you will be able to survive from one year to the next is if you take opportunities like this. This will keep me smiling through the rest of the wretched life that's left to me. Now push that bloody tiger over.'

Kannan bent over his task, then remembered something: 'But why are you killing the coolies? They're Indian. They've done you no harm.'

'I've killed no one. You're the one who is saying it.'

Kannan took the bamboo and began pushing. Slowly the tiger slid towards the emptiness beyond, then its forward motion stopped. Kannan took his hand off the pole and turned to face his tormentor. 'I don't trust you, Harrison, and I know I'm going to die. But, before you shoot me, I have one last question: Why did you agree to come with me to shoot the tiger?'

'It amused me to see if I could succeed where the other bastards had failed ...'

'But don't you see,' Kannan said, suddenly hopeful, 'you have succeeded. You're a hero now. You can pick up the pieces again, the bad days are over.'

'The bad days are never over, you young fool. My countrymen can never welcome me back because that would mean accepting someone who invalidates everything they think they stand for. And even if they did, what of it? A few months, a year of esteem, and then we'll go back to how we once were ... Enough of this.' There was steel once more in Harrison's voice. 'Push the brute over. Now.'

Kannan picked up the fallen pole, thrust it under the dead tiger, and pushed as hard as he could. The body slid, stopped, slid forward again. Only a couple of feet more and it would all be over.

From an enormous distance, his mind took in the scene: two men (one hunched over a dead tiger) in a little rocky amphitheatre, and beyond them the precipice with its endless shifting mist, the setting sun casting it into a fretwork of light and shade. One more push and the heavy body began to topple forward on its own. The mist rose up to receive it and then it was gone, the huge black-and-yellow body looping and twisting in a curiously graceful movement, down, down, down. Kannan sank to his knees, eyes barely registering the whiteness before him, waiting for the crash that would signal the end. Would there be any pain, he wondered. The minutes passed and when the shot didn't come, Kannan turned slowly, wearily, to look for his persecutor. Harrison, walking fast, had already reached the foot of the incline. Without pausing, the old hunter began to climb steadily into the closing dark.

105

By the time Kannan got back to Morningfall, the decision he had been mulling over was confirmed in his mind: he would leave Pulimed.

Now that he had decided, he wasn't sure what he should do. Join the freedom struggle or help with Doraipuram? Probably the latter. But there was time enough for that. First he must leave this place as quickly as possible. When he handed in his resignation to Michael, his Superintendent's attempt to get him to change his mind lost its power when he realized how solid the decision was. It was agreed that he would leave in a week.

He attended the obligatory farewell parties, of which there were mercifully only two: one at the Stevensons', which was strained and awkward, and the other at the club hosted by Michael, which was slightly more enjoyable although he greatly missed Freddie who wasn't due back for a week. He deflected all questions about the hunt, not that anyone pursued the subject with any enthusiasm. It had been widely assumed that his attempt would end in failure. He supposed he would have told Freddie the truth if his friend had been around but there was no one else to confide in. He'd toyed briefly with the idea of telling Michael but had decided not to in the end. He was especially pleased with his response to Major Stevenson. Kannan was leaving the General Manager's office after a brief interview on the day he'd resigned when Major Stevenson had said to him: 'Just a tick, Dorai, did you manage to get a shot at the tiger?'

He'd paused for a moment, and then savouring every word he'd said: 'I think it would be best if you checked with Mr Harrison, sir.'

On the morning of his departure he drove over to the Superintendent's house to hand over the keys to his bungalow. Michael invited him in for a cup of tea. They chatted for a while, and then it was time to go. Belinda, tired and flustered after having spent much of the morning arguing with the maistri who was building new furniture for the spare bedroom, paused to say goodbye. Michael saw him off at the door. As they shook hands, Michael said, 'So do you think being involved with the family settlement will satisfy you?'

'I think so, sir, my mother and my uncle have their hands full. It's time I helped.'

'But is that what you really want to do? I know things have been rough around here but you are a good planter, Cannon. You could have an excellent career on the estates.'

'I thought so too, sir, but sometimes you keep putting off the inevitable, knowing all the while that the decision has already been taken a long time ago, often without any conscious thought. It's always been there, you've just taken a few twists and turns in the road before you arrive at it.'

'Now you've lost me, with all this talk of destiny. What do you chaps call it, karma?'

'Not bad at all, sir,' Kannan said with a smile.

'You've never seemed more Indian to me than you did just now,' Michael said.

'But that's the whole point, sir. I am Indian, and I expect we just forgot that for a while.'

He found Andrew on the lawn throwing a tennis ball to Pixie, the family's fox terrier. The little boy interrupted his play for a moment to wave and Kannan beckoned him over. 'I have something for you,' he said, 'to remind you of me when I'm gone.'

'Where are you going, Mr Dorai?' Andrew asked.

'Far, far from here, Andrew. I have a big job to do that I've postponed for far too long ...' He could see that the boy was anxious to get back to his game, especially since the dog was frisking around his ankles, and so he slipped his hand into his pocket, withdrew the tiger's claw he had picked up after Harrison left, and gave it to Andrew. 'Keep it safe. It's a tiger claw,' he said.

'Gosh, Mr Dorai. Did it belong to a real live tiger?'

'Yes, it did.'

'How did you get it?'

'That's a long story, I'll tell you another time.' He ruffled the boy's hair and walked to his motorcycle. As he kicked it into life, he glimpsed Andrew tearing towards the house, the dog panting along behind him. The boy held the tiger claw triumphantly aloft.

There was one more thing he needed to do before he headed down the ghat road to catch his train. He pointed the nose of the Norton towards the factory on Empress Estate. It was a misty day and his spirits soared. He would miss this sort of weather in the plains. He slowed the motorcycle down, the better to feel the touch of the mist on his face. As the wetness wrapped itself around him, he gave himself over completely to the sensation of experiencing the world of the estates for what he was sure would be the last time.

And then he was at his destination, an old silver oak that was locally called the swing-in-swing-out tree. The mist was thinning and the tree stood, a lonely sentinel, on the hairpin bend that led to the Empress Estate factory. Beyond it was a sheer drop. It had come by its name because it offered an interesting challenge to anyone foolhardy enough to attempt it. The usual manner in which the hairpin bend was negotiated was slowly and with care, but one mad drunken night Joe Wilson had swung his motorcycle full-tilt at the tree and had miraculously pulled it out of the spin that would have sent him tumbling down to the rocks below. Nobody had succeeded in doing it since, always aborting the stunt at the last minute.

Kannan stopped the Norton short of the tree, then eased in the clutch and slowly motored around the bend. Turning the bike, he returned to the position from which he'd started. He emptied his mind of the consequences of failure and sat astride the motorcycle a while longer, gently revving the throttle, watching the mist swirl around the bend and the tree, allowing it to enter his mind. He let in the clutch, put the motorcycle into gear, revved the big machine and roared forward. Nearer and nearer the tree loomed, the vehicle and rider rushing at it. He aimed the nose of the Norton all the way in ... drawing all the rage and frustration of the past few months into himself, winding it into a tight burning knot, letting it inflame him. Swing in. As the machine began to skid towards the drop he fought gravity and the power of the engine to reverse direction. A moment of panic, the abyss yawning in his head, and then the motorcycle began to respond slowly to his touch, and then quicker and quicker. The tension and the fury exploded out of him, streaming away, freeing him from their powerful hold. Swing out. The road ahead stretched before him and he accelerated away.

106

So many of the members of the extended family descended on Doraipuram for the Christmas celebrations of 1946 that they ran out of sleeping space. At Neelam Illum, Lily, Ramdoss and Kannan opened up rooms that had been locked and shuttered for years. Makeshift beds and sleeping mats were unrolled in every room in every house in the settlement, and finally even the church was taken over. Pews were pushed to one side to make room for the hordes of first, second and third cousins and their families from far-flung corners of the world. Not since the memorial service for Daniel had Doraipuram seen such an influx, and nobody could tell exactly why everyone to whom an invitation had been extended had decided to show up, along with others who hadn't even been invited. Perhaps it was because the war was well and truly over. Perhaps they were drawn by the promise of freedom. Or perhaps they came because the twenty-fifth anniversary of the founding of the colony was less than a year away, and they wanted to make sure that they connected with Doraipuram, for who knew what the next twenty-five years would bring. And so they poured in, those who carried the place permanently in their hearts and those who had never set eyes on it – spoilt American cousins from Metuchen and Mississauga, British relatives with strange accents from Kensington and Birmingham, one family who made the journey from faraway Napier – all drawn to the colony on the banks of the Chevathar.

Within days of their arrival they had sunk into Doraipuram's embrace. The foreign cousins quickly lost their airs and accents, brushed out of their systems by the hard fists of the Doraipuram gang, and settled down to enjoy themselves. They scuffed bare feet in the red dirt of Chevathar and they wobbled around on bicycles that seemed to have been manufactured in some unimaginably ancient age. They gawked at the well Aaron had jumped and they poked around in the ruins of Kulla Marudu's fort, giving the old cobra, which was now almost blind and white with age, no peace at all. They swam in the sea and the river, they re-enacted Solomon Dorai's epic battle on the beach, and they wandered through the mango topes hoping against hope that the occasional tree might be fruiting out of season. The energy and resources of the eighty-three permanent residents of Doraipuram were tested as they tried to cope with the visitors, who outnumbered them two to one, but they rose to the occasion magnificently.

This was Kannan's second Christmas in the settlement since his return and he realized he was enjoying it much more than the first, feeling an integral part of everything that went on around him. He was delighted to meet many of his old friends although the closest, Albert and Shekhar who had emigrated to Vancouver and San Diego respectively, couldn't make it. Bonda, who was now employed by a bank in Melur, was one of the early arrivals and they spent hours reliving their childhood. All across the settlement old friendships were renewed and new ones forged, as the extended Dorai family gave itself over to a huge and tumultuous reunion.

Christmas Day was the culmination of days of frenetic activity and it began early. By seven in the morning the church by the sea was packed to overflowing, everyone impatient for the day to get going. Over half the congregation had had less than two hours of sleep, having spent the previous night tramping from house to house singing carols and wrapping presents and consuming vast quantities of food and drink that mothers and aunts and servants had churned out without pause. The moment the padre had finished his sermon, a group of teenaged cousins, under the leadership of Daniel, now in a senior class at the Government High School, broke out guitars and maracas and the church bulged with the sound of carols sung one last time that year with verve and enthusiasm. Spinster chithis and decrepit thathas clapped their hands and sang along, and even sour old Karunakaran could be seen tapping his feet to the music.

As he bellowed out the carols, Kannan looked around him: at his mother, Ramdoss-mama, his nephews and nieces, the dozens of well-loved faces, unselfconsciously revelling in the sheer pleasure of being alive and together. So long as we can summon up this spirit, no matter what the disadvantages and reverses, my father's dream will never die, Kannan thought. He felt a momentary sadness that Helen wasn't with him. But caught up in the optimism of the moment, he reckoned even that breach could be healed. I'll celebrate next Christmas in Doraipuram with my wife, he vowed.

The old tunes continued to roar through the church. Daniel was now leading the young people in a rendering of 'Hark the Herald Angels Sing'. Kannan was delighted that the boy who could have made a brilliant career for himself wherever he chose was determined to return to Doraipuram and the clinic once he'd obtained his medical degree. Together we can turn this place around, Kannan thought.

Scarcely had the service ended than the young people raced to the maidan by the Community Centre for the next event of the day – the hockey match between the Marrieds and the Unmarrieds. The youngsters won as they always did, although Kannan, the fleetest member of the Marrieds, was well satisfied with the goal he scored.

And so the hours sped by, and the great sprawl of the Dorai family forgot its worries and feuds, the future and the past, and concentrated on enjoying every moment of a very special day.

At the funfair, Kannan won a rather strange-looking rubber duck and narrowly missed winning another prize (a tin of Parry's sweets) for marksmanship, and then it was time for lunch. Poochie-chithi was in charge of the Lunch Committee and she had laid on a feast that would be talked about for years – three kinds of rice (tamarind, lemon and curd), two kinds of meat (chicken and mutton) and fish, sambhar and rasam, two kinds of pachidi (boondi and onion), five kinds of pickle (lime, nellikai, mango, chilli and brinjal), two kinds of kootu (cabbage and potato), appalams by the dozen and, finally, to top it all off, paruppu payasam that was served by the bucket. The family ate as well as it had sung and played. Then, their appetites sated and feeling very sleepy, the older Dorais went off to rest and prepare for the evening's activities, while the children sped through the mango groves and along the river, shouting and screaming and investing the slumbering rocks and ancient landmarks with their youthful exuberance.

The evening was, if anything, even more hectic. More sport and competitions, tea, a Bible quiz, and then the highlight for the children – the formal unveiling of the Christmas tree at the Community Centre. It was a rather spindly casuarina branch indifferently decorated with coloured paper and balloons, but nobody minded at all, especially the children, whose attention was riveted by the bright hill of presents that rose beneath it. As they fought to get at their gifts, Kannan said to Ramdoss who stood next to him, 'Appa would have been delighted. This is what he established Doraipuram for.'

'I agree,' Ramdoss said. 'Nothing beats a family in full cry. I hope Daniel-anna is watching.'

The tree gave up the struggle as the sea of children besieged it but by now the happy mob was completely beyond caring. The last present was snatched up and then there was more entertainment, amateurishly enacted skits, which nevertheless went down as well as everything that had preceded it. A short prayer to thank the merciful Lord and the founder for having bestowed Doraipuram on them all and the family wandered out on to the maidan where long tables groaned under overflowing containers of food. Dinner paled in comparison only to that magnificent lunch, but it was more than ample.

And then, just when it appeared that the hard-pressed organizers of the festivities would crumble, Christmas was over. The last guests rose from the benches, belching contentedly. The cooking fires were extinguished and lamps put out. Rounding up the children, who had stayed up long past their bedtime, the exhausted uncles, aunts and cousins who had made it all possible walked home under a sky scarved with stars.

Just before he turned into Neelam Illum's driveway, Kannan thought tiredly but happily of the day gone by. He had never felt so much a part of Doraipuram. It was quite extraordinary, he reflected, how from age to age, this piece of land by the river pulled people into its embrace – his grandfather, his father, his brother, himself ... At moments like this, any doubt that he might have felt about returning was stilled. This is the land of my family, he thought, it belongs to every one of us, we have made its hard red earth our own with our failures and our triumphs, our blood and our laughter. I'm glad I'm here, it is the place of my heart.

EPILOGUE

Time now for a final story, this one featuring Auvaiyar, the venerable Tamil poetess and saint who lived some time between the twelfth and fourteenth centuries. The old lady was walking along a road one day when she encountered a cowherd perched high in a nava tree. The boy was enthusiastically plucking and eating the deep black fruit that stained his lips purple. Auvaiyar was hungry so she asked him to throw her some fruit. Mischievously the boy, who was actually Lord Subrahmanya in disguise, asked, 'Would you like hot fruit or cold?' The saint was puzzled and faintly irritated. 'What's this about hot or cold? Can fruit on a tree be anything but cold? Throw me some fruit, you little scamp, I'm hungry.'

'All right then, paati-ma, here's your fruit,' the cowherd said with a laugh, and plucked a handful of fruit and dropped it on the ground. The poetess picked the fruit up and was blowing off the dirt when the boy shouted, 'If the fruit is cold, why are you blowing on it?'

Ways of seeing. Every reality is perceived differently, depending on who is doing the looking, so let's take the road ourselves to see what we can see. This road stretches back a couple of centuries to the time when the precursors of John Company came to India to trade and decided to stay. It has had numerous twists and bends, and is choked with the debris of a thousand battles and the unquiet spirits of the great and the good, but it is now coming to an end. A new road will need to be hacked out of the future and the implements to do so are in the hands of millions. Their leaders view the road ahead, each in his own way: the Mahatma sorrowfully, as the killings in Noakhali and elsewhere seem to presage the carnage that lies ahead; Jinnah inflexibly, he will make sure he gets his Pakistan before the terminal disease in his blood gets him; Mountbatten, the last Viceroy, guiltily, for he knows the mission he was charged with, the orderly transfer of power, is bound to end in costly failure with millions dead or displaced ... Virtually alone among the great ones, Nehru, though his heart is heavy, looks to the future with hope. It is he who will say, on 15 August 1947, the undying words that schoolchildren will memorize so long as there is an India: 'Long years ago we made a tryst with destiny and now the time comes when we shall redeem our pledge ... At the stroke of the midnight hour, when the world sleeps, India shall awaken to freedom ...'

And what of the people? When they walk the road to independence, what will they see, how will they feel? As they march along, bound in the opposite direction to the multitudes who will take over from them, some of them, like the soldiers of the 1st Cameron Highlanders, racist to the end, chant:

'Land of shit and filth and wogs
Gonorrhoea, syphilis, clap and pox.
Memsahibs' paradise, soldiers' hell
India, fare thee fucking well.'

But that is the minority view, even among the British. Most of them are beset by feelings of dejection, sorrow and fear, but what they feel, overwhelmingly, is relief that the years of uncertainty and ambiguity are about to end.

For millions of Indians, the horror of Partition will be the single overwhelming reality. Freedom for them is synonymous with grief, hatred, displacement and loss. For millions more, the most wretched constituents of the subcontinent, independence will not be an occasion for rejoicing, their lives will be as miserable as before. But what of our grandparents and parents, uncles and aunts, who have wrested a prize that has demanded of them every ounce of commitment, idealism, courage and talent they possessed, what do they make of it? No matter who or what they are, ordinary or extraordinary, rich or poor, high caste or low, humble or exalted, they look to the future with joy and hope. But embedded in the euphoria there are questions; no victory or triumph is ever unqualified. What exactly will freedom bring? Will its surging optimism cleanse the country of the noxious vapours of casteism and communalism? Will its currency buy the poor and the disadvantaged bread, hope and equality? In sum, will the country be equal to freedom's challenge?

LATE APRIL 1947. Early in the morning. It will soon be very hot, for summer has crept up on Doraipuram. Already the houses have begun to draw their cloaks of green – the dark green of mango and jack, the feathery green of tamarind, the lighter green of neem and ashoka, the green-black of palmyra, the slate green of casuarina –

tightly around them to ward off the blazing heat of day.

Deep in thought, Kannan makes his way down to the river. He has slept poorly, and hopes the cool morning will refresh him for the tasks ahead. The settlement is gearing up to celebrate the coming of freedom. Three months later there will be another celebration, for the twenty-fifth anniversary of the founding of Doraipuram is also upon them. He has spent the past week serving on various committees charged with co-ordinating the activities that are being planned for both occasions. It has been an optimistic time as the settlement prepares to honour events larger that its constituents' individual concerns.

But Kannan isn't thinking about the coming ceremonials. After the revelry is over, the problems that have kept him awake for many nights will inevitably resurface and it is these he is thinking about as he walks by the river. Miriam-athai and her sons have ganged up with Karunakaran and are threatening to sell out to a powerful builder who wants to build beach-front homes. There's a steady haemorrhaging of young people from the settlement to distant towns and lands in search of jobs and opportunities. The founding families who are committed to Daniel's dream are growing older. Will it be only a matter of time before Doraipuram is just a memory? He is not sure whether he is up to the challenge of ensuring that the settlement thrives for the next twenty-five years. It's easier to have a grand vision, he thinks, than to keep it going. But almost immediately he dismisses the thought as unworthy. Each generation has its problems. Daniel and the other founders dealt with their difficulties as best they could, we need to cope with our own troubles as successfully as our skills, passion, imagination and resolve allow. And then he thinks: I worry too much. Of course Doraipuram will survive and prosper because it was founded in love and hope, and these are the most vital and powerful impulses granted to our kind.

He is in one of the mango topes now, surrounded by rank upon rank of medium-sized trees with short straight trunks covered with fissured black bark. The arrowhead-shaped leaves are a beautiful dark green on top and a paler green below. They lie thickly upon the branch and effectively absorb the heat, dust and light, giving the orchard a hush that is broken only by the crackling of dried leaves underfoot. The Neelams are lovely to behold. Blue fruit on a field of green, it's as if the sky, the high blue-white sky of the Chevathar summer, has exploded and come to rest in this tope. Heavy as a woman's breasts, these are fruit to be fondled sensuously as you pick your way among the trees. Their fragrance fills the air. Kannan reaches up to a blue mango, caresses it, its heat filling his hand, and gives it the slightest tug. The mango comes away in his hand. Instinctively, he does something he learned from his father, and he from his father before him …

He empties his mind, concentrates the senses. He regards the fruit he has picked for a moment, then raises the mounded end, with the dimple in the centre, to his nose and inhales deeply. The bouquet explodes upon his senses: a huge delectable sweetness, overlaid with notes of freshness, lightness, sun and blue, counterpointed by a deep rolling melody of an almost corrupt muskiness. He holds his breath, lets the high and low notes invade every aspect of his being. The heaviness lifts from his heart.

AUTHOR'S NOTE

This is a novel, so the usual disclaimers apply – names, characters, places and incidents are either the product of the author's imagination or are used fictitiously, and any resemblance to actual persons, living or dead, events or locales is entirely coincidental. Having said that, there are a couple of things that need to be clarified.

One of my reasons for writing this book was to recapture memories of an idyllic childhood spent in places like the high tea country in Peermade, where my father worked, and my grandparents' homes in Nagercoil and Padappai. Also, my paternal grandfather Ambrose established a family settlement and this seemed such a splendid achievement that it marked the point of departure for my novel. However *The House of Blue Mangoes* is wholly invented. It is not autobiographical nor is it in any way family history masquerading as fiction. Solomon, Daniel, Aaron, Kannan and the rest of the Dorai clan are people I've imagined and bear no resemblance to anyone I know. The same is true of Doraipuram, Chevathar, Pulimed and Kilanad district.

For those who are interested in a little more information about these places, I can do no better than recapitulate my notes on them when they were first visualized. Kilanad is the smallest district of Madras Presidency, so small that in 1899 it had only two revenue sub-divisions or taluqas (one less than the next smallest, the Nilgiris district, which had three at the time). Shaped like a notched arrowhead, Kilanad's northern boundary is Tinnevelly district (now Tirunelveli); to the west lies the kingdom of Travancore (now the state of Kerala). It's rimmed to the east by the Bay of Bengal and to the south it narrows to a point two kilometres short of Cape Comorin (Kanyakumari). The Chevathar, a non-existent tributary of the mighty Tamraparani, bisects the district before debouching into the Bay of Bengal near the village that bears its name.

One further paragraph will suffice to encapsulate Kilanad's main points of interest. It has an area of 489 sq. miles with a maximum width of sixty-five miles and length of eighty-six miles, with three towns, forty-eight villages and a total population of one hundred and fifty-three thousand. Its chief town is Melur, with a population of eighteen thousand and ninety-nine on the Nanguneri–Nagercoil highway. It is where the Collector is based; it has a big Mariamman temple and a famous cattle fair is held there twice a year. The second biggest town, Ranivoor (population fifteen thousand two hundred and fifty), the headquarters of the second of the two taluqas, is almost equidistant between the district headquarters and the only other town in the district, Meenakshikoil on the coast. Ranivoor is famous throughout the district for a church dedicated to St Luke that is supposed to have miraculous powers of exorcism. Meenakshikoil, which became the headquarters of the taluqa of the same name early in the twentieth century, has an eighteenth-century temple dedicated to the Goddess Meenakshi built by Kulla Marudu, the last feudal lord of the area. Predating the Meenakshi temple is a small Murugan temple across the river in Chevathar village.

The entire district is sparsely populated and musters the lowest revenues in the Presidency. The chief cash crops are cotton, to the north, and palmyra products, jaggery, arrack, baskets and mats – these last are famous throughout the Presidency.

Of Pulimed, across the border in the central Travancore hills, there is little to add, except that it's an imaginary tea-planting district between Peermade and Vandiperiyar.

A word about some of the caste groups in the book. The Andavars (who bear no resemblance whatsoever to the contemporary followers of Andavan Swamigal, among others), Vedhars (not to be confused with Vedars, Vetans, Veduvars, etc.) and Mạrudars do not find a place among the hundreds of castes and sub-castes exhaustively surveyed by the Anthropological Survey of India in the People of India project, compiled and published in thirteen volumes by K. S. Singh (OUP, 1997). I invented three new castes because I did not wish to add fuel to the caste controversies that have raged for centuries now, to the general detriment of the country and the states of Tamil Nadu and Kerala which are my particular interest. All that needs to be said here is that the three castes share similarities with some of the non-Brahmin castes in the south.

Most of the historical incidents and personages to be encountered in the narrative are well-known and need little by way of explication. The only one that needs comment is the murder of Robert William d'Escourt Ashe. His assassination is a historically documented fact. Among those convicted of his murder were Neelakantha Brahmachari and Vanchi Iyer. Aaron Dorai wasn't among them.

Finally, I should point out that I've retained spellings from the period in which the novel is set – Tinnevelly for Tirunelveli, Madura for Madurai, Madras for Chennai and so on.

ACKNOWLEDGMENTS

Although this book is a work of fiction, I've tried to be as rigorous as possible in researching its historical, sociological and technical aspects. Of the dozens of books I consulted I found the following especially useful:

ON VILLAGE LIFE: *The Remembered Village* by M.N. Srinivas (OUP, 1976), *Fluid Signs: Being a Person the Tamil Way* by E. Valentine Daniel (University of California Press, 1984) where I first encountered an interesting version of the son of the soil theory and *Siva & her Sisters* by Karin Kapadia (OUP, 1996) which has excellent descriptions of ritual possession by villagers.

ON THE HISTORICAL AND SOCIOLOGICAL ASPECTS OF SOUTH INDIA: *Peasant History of South India* by David Ludden (OUP, 1989), *The Politics of South India, 1920-1937* by Christopher John Baker (Vikas, 1976), *Politics and Social Conflict in South India* by Eugene F. Irschick (OUP, 1969), *The Nadars of Tamilnad* by Robert L. Hardgrave, Jr (OUP, 1969) which is particularly good on caste conflict and *Land and Caste in South India* by Dharma Kumar (Manohar, 1992). I found *The Rajaji Story, 1937–1972* by Rajmohan Gandhi (Bharatiya Vidya Bhavan, 1984) useful and *National Movement in Tamil Nadu, 1905–1914* by N Rajendran (OUP, 1994) excellent for details of the extremist movement and the assassination of William Ashe.

ON THE RAJ: In my view James Morris's Pax Britannica trilogy, *Pax Britannica* (Faber, 1968), *Heaven's Command* (Faber, 1973) and *Farewell the Trumpets* (Faber, 1978), still remains the best account of the Raj, a quarter century after it was published. *Raj* by Lawrence James (Little Brown, 1997) is a good single-volume history and *Plain Tales from the Raj* by Charles Allen (Abacus, 1975) is an excellent gossipy account of the time.

ON THE INDIAN CIVIL SERVICE: *The Men Who Ruled India* by Philip Mason (Jonathan Cape, 2 vols., 1953, 1954) is the acknowledged classic, but the book I relied on the most sadly had lost both cover and title page so I had no means of ascertaining the author and publisher's name. No matter, *The District Officer in India* proved to be an invaluable work of reference.

ON SIDDHA: *Siddha Medicine* by Dr Paul Joseph Thottam (Penguin, 2000) is the best book on the subject.

ON THE INDIAN NATIONALIST MOVEMENT: I've relied heavily on *India's Struggle for Independence, 1857–1947* by Bipan Chandra et al (Viking, 1988).

ON THE PLANTING LIFE: *Above the Heron's Pool* by Heather Lovatt and Peter de Jong (Bacsa, 1993) is an excellent introduction to tea-planting in south India and *A Planting Century* by S. Muthiah (East-West, 1993) is a comprehensive history of the industry.

ON MAN-EATERS: On man-eating tigers, there is only one authority, the incomparable Jim Corbett. I'd recommend all his books.

TRANSLATIONS: I consulted several translations of the *Bhagavad Gita*. The lines that appear in this novel are an edited version of the Gita Press translation.

Finally Aaron's jump over the big well is a fictional retelling of an actual exploit in a south Indian village, narrated in the book by Amy Carmichael, *Raj, Brigand Chief* (Seeley, Service & Co. Limited, 1927). I must thank my father for drawing my attention to this.

*

Grateful acknowledgement is made by my publishers and I to the following for permission to reprint previously published material:

Oxford University Press, New Delhi: Excerpts from *The Principal Upanishads* by S Radhakrishnan (OUP, 1953) and from the *Man-Eaters of Kumaon* by Jim Corbett (OUP, 1944).

The Anvil Press and Alan Marshfield for Poem 705 by Rufinus and the Anvil Press for Poem 807 by Paulos from *The Greek Anthology* (Penguin Classics, 1973).

The Hindu: Excerpt from *The Hindu Century* (Kasturi & Sons, 1976).

Little, Brown and Company: Excerpt from *Raj* by Lawrence James (Little, Brown and Company, 1997).

The Sri Aurobindo Ashram Trust for an excerpt by Aurobindo Ghosh published in the volume, *Sri Aurobindo Karmayogin*.

The Navajivan Trust for an excerpt from *The Collected Works of Mahatma Gandhi*, Vol.76 by M.K Gandhi.

While every effort has been made to trace copyright holders and obtain permission, this has not been possible in all cases; any omissions brought to our attention will be remedied in future editions.

*

I'm indebted to my wife Rachna, first and last, for without her constant support, patience and good advice this novel wouldn't have been written. I am also entirely grateful to Vikram Seth for spurring me on to complete the manuscript. Having acted as a catalyst, he then read and commented on the manuscript, acts of generosity not easily forgotten.

I delight in my agents and principal publishers, they are the best any writer could hope to have. David Godwin and Katie Levell in London; Nicole Aragi who placed the book in New York; Cathy Hemming, Terry Karten, Lisa Miller, and Andrew Proctor at HarperCollins in the US; and Maggie Mckernan, Geoff Duffield, Katie White and Alice Chasey at Orion in the UK whose enthusiasm and support breathed life into the manuscript as well as shepherded it through the publication process — to all of you my heartfelt gratitude.

My brilliant colleagues at Penguin India – in order of their appearance in the book's life, Rajesh Sharma, Aparajita Pant, Ravi Singh, V.K. Karthika, Hemali Sodhi, Bena Sareen, Philip Koshy, Sayoni Basu and P.M. Sukumar — ensured the book was published exceptionally well in its place of birth. Thank you all very much indeed.

Grateful thanks too to David Wan, Peter Field and Aveek Sarkar who were supportive of me every step of the way.

Others I am indebted to for contributing their time and effort to the book's cause are my father Eddie Davidar (whose knowledge of the tea industry is unrivalled); my uncle Reggie Davidar, for sharing a couple of stories; Kamazh and Kenaz Solomon who guided me through the intricacies of caste and tradition (as did M.S.S. Pandian); Dr Paul Thottam who vetted the chapters on siddha; Drs Raj Kubba and N.P.S. Chawla who explained the mysteries of pigmentation and diabetes respectively; S. Krishnan who read and commented on portions of the manuscript; Vivek Menon who pointed out that 'nightjars drift and do not whir'; John Ashworth who suggested the names of England's dreariest towns; and most importantly, Raman Mahadevan who patiently and assiduously worked his way through the manuscript pointing out inaccuracies and errors.

Friends and family who were generous in their support include Dee Aldrich, Rupayan Bhattacharya, Urvashi Butalia, Vikram Chandra, Harry Davidar, Ruth Davidar, Nirmala Lakshman, Vijit & Divya Malik, Suketu Mehta, 'Mooma', Bipin Nayak, Aggie Perilli, Monisha Shah, KD Singh & Nini Singh, Pia & Mallika Singh and Pavan Varma.

*

I am grateful to Prabuddha Das Gupta for taking the author photograph, Dinesh Khanna for shooting pictures of mango trees, Tanthoni for his photographs of blue mangoes and Sunita Kohli for ferreting out the owners of whitewashed bungalows in Delhi. The wonderful map of Kilanad district and Pulimed at the front of the book is the creation of Uma Bhattacharya, P.Arun and Benu Joshi. Thank you very much.

I would like to thank Nasir and Parul Prakash for their hospitality in Peermade, my aunt Shakuntala and Erik Carlquist for giving us the run of the house in Puthalam, Aradhana Bisht for drawing my attention to the poem from which the epigraph is extracted, and Gillian Wright for insisting the rosy pastors return to the wild guava tree.

Finally, it is my deepest regret that my mother Sushila is not alive to celebrate the publication of the book. She was the best writer in the family and her stories and insights have filled my head for as long as I can remember. I can only hope *The House of Blue Mangoes* does justice to her memory.

ABOUT THE AUTHOR

David Davidar started out in journalism and now works in publishing. He is married and lives in New Delhi. *The House of Blue Mangoes* is his first novel.